BODY FARM Z

DEBORAH SHELDON

SEVERED PRESS
HOBART TASMANIA

BODY FARM Z

ISBN: 978-1-925840-97-1

For Allen and Harry

1

The drive from the Melbourne City Police Complex to the body farm in Wooriyanda was about four hours northeast along the Hume Highway. Four bloody hours trapped in a car with Lawrence Garcia. And then, once their business was done, the long trip back again. *Shit.* They had been travelling all morning, and Garcia was still yapping and messing with his mobile phone. A grown man acting like a kid. And when he wasn't on his phone, he was checking his hair; a combed-back pompadour filled with so much styling product that it could withstand a hurricane, no doubt. Men shouldn't use hair-styling products. Not real men, at any rate. Detective Senior Sergeant Rick Evans tightened his grip on the steering wheel and recommenced mindful breathing to keep his temper in check.

In through the nose. Hold. Out through the mouth.

At first light this morning, as Rick had been buttoning his shirt, his wife had said, "Remember, don't let Garcia get to you. Think of your blood pressure. Just concentrate on the scenery. It'll be a lovely drive into the countryside with lots of trees, lots of birds. Darling, you have to learn how to ignore him."

Ignore him? When at every possible second, Garcia was flapping his gums?

"Hey, get this," Garcia was saying, eyes glued to his phone. "Wooriyanda has a population of just one hundred and ten, and its post office closed in 1962."

"Yeah? Well, so what?"

"So, it's not officially a town. Only places with a post office are considered towns."

Rick grimaced. "Fascinating. What a font of knowledge you are."

"Or is it places with a pub? Hang on, I'll check."

"No, don't bother. Who cares? We're not even stopping at Wooriyanda. The body farm's off the road and into the bush a fair way." Rick hunched his shoulders and shifted in his seat, agitated. "Whether or not the place is a town or a township is a moot point that doesn't concern our investigation or this experiment. All right?"

Garcia went back to messing with his phone. Without glancing over, Rick already knew that Garcia would be googling post offices and pubs and towns. It did his head in. Why the Detective Inspector had plucked this arrogant, smarmy dolt from Missing Persons to replace old Phil, Rick could not fathom. But some of the other blokes on the squad seemed to like Garcia. *He's funny to have around*, said Jake whenever Rick complained. *Good for a laugh*, Robert would add. But working in Homicide was no laughing matter. And besides, how much work did Garcia actually get done? Oh, he was talented at *looking* busy, that's for sure. Talented at fooling people who weren't paying enough attention.

"Hey, guess what?" Garcia said. "Turns out I was wrong on both counts. The definition of a town actually depends on its population, not the—"

"And another thing," Rick interrupted. "This is important. Listen up. When we get there and I introduce you to everybody, don't call the place a 'body farm'."

"Why not? You do."

"Yeah, but not to the people who work there. It's disrespectful."

Garcia swiped at his phone. "Then what am I meant to call it?" Reading from the screen, he added, "The Victorian Taphonomic Experimental Research Institute?" He snorted out a laugh. "I mean, come on. What a mouthful. Nobody can remember that."

"Use the acronym."

"VITERI. Huh. Sounds like a brand of vitamin water."

Rick squeezed the steering wheel. "Okay, call it 'the facility'. Can you do that?"

"Sure, why not." Garcia laughed again. "Or a brand of olive oil."

"What?"

"VITERI. Sounds like a brand of olive oil." Garcia slapped his thigh. "Oh shit, you know what? It's actually a Spanish surname."

"I don't much care, mate."

"Oh, I remember now. When I was a kid, my old man had a friend called Viteri but he was from the Basque region. Didn't consider himself a Spaniard. Some coincidence. Weird, huh?"

Maybe Garcia was winding him up on purpose. Rick's three daughters did it all the time; he ought to be an expert at deflecting shit-stirring by now. Fine, he would take his wife's advice and concentrate on the scenery. Not much to see. The odd house. Smatterings of eucalyptus trees. Flat, empty paddocks of dry, yellowed grass and hard-packed dirt. It was October—supposedly the middle of Spring—but the frequent rain showers had been a no-show this year. Rick leaned over the steering wheel to glance up at the sky. Bright blue with nary a cloud. So much for the supercell storm that was coming later today. A "rain bomb", the weather bureau was calling it.

"Make yourself useful," Rick said. "Look up the forecast."

"Okay, boss." A few seconds passed. "Right, it says here, 'The east coast of Australia will be hit with a torrential downpour stretching from Melbourne to Brisbane.' Um, blah, blah, stuff about New South Wales... Oh, here we go: 'Melbourne is set to receive almost a month's worth of rain over the next thirty-six hours.' Huh. I guess we'll see. Meteorologists are so fucking useless. Hey, want to know tomorrow's temperature?"

"Nah, I'm good."

"Twenty degrees with an overnight low of nine."

Rick sighed. *In through the nose. Hold. Out through the mouth.* At least the traffic was light. He checked the dashboard display. They were making good time, and should reach the body farm before midday. Hopefully the office manager, Stella Vasilakis, will have provided some lunch for them. She had done so at Rick's last visit back around Christmas. Gourmet pies and sausage rolls. At the thought, Rick's stomach grumbled. His wife had given him nothing but a bowl of porridge and a banana for breakfast. Apparently, he was on another diet. Middle-age spread came with middle age, in his opinion, but the missus worried about his blood pressure.

"The Victorian Taphonomic Experimental Research Institute," Garcia mused, thumbing at his phone. "I wonder what 'taphonomic' means."

"Never mind what it means. It's irrelevant."

"According to Wikipedia, taphonomy is the study of how organisms decay and become fossilised."

"Now listen," Rick said, "when we get to the body farm—the *facility*—let me do the talking."

"Hey, whatever you reckon."

"I've worked with these people before and know how to treat them."

Garcia pulled a face. "Huh? *I* know how to treat people too."

"Bear with me, all right? It's a new place, only about a year old. It hasn't got that many bodies on it yet. Every homicide copper in the country is fighting to get an experiment done to help out with a cold case."

Garcia smoothed a palm up and over his pompadour. "Well, duh."

"We can't afford to ruffle any feathers at the body farm. Because if we do, next time we want them to re-create a crime scene for us, we'll find ourselves at the bottom of the pecking order. Got me?"

"Yeah, sure, I got you."

Rick nodded. "As long as we're clear."

Garcia fell silent and started looking at his phone again. Rick could tell the little bastard was pissed off and getting sulky. *Ha, gotcha; the shoe's on the other foot.*

"Are we clear?" Rick said.

"Yep, no worries," Garcia muttered. "You're doing the talking. I don't care. Whatever."

"Good." Rick smiled and relaxed. "Just follow my lead. Everything will be hunky-dory."

Saying *hunky-dory* always made his daughters roll their eyes. Happily, it had the same effect on Garcia.

***

When they reached the outskirts of Wooriyanda, Rick used the touch-screen on the GPS and brought up the coordinates to the body farm.

"Latitude and longitude?" Garcia said. "So, no street address?"

"Of course not. They don't want every Tom, Dick and Harry dropping in for a gawk."

"Fair enough." Garcia fiddled with his phone. "Hey, what do you know, the body farm in Sydney's Blue Mountains doesn't have a street address either."

"Well, duh," Rick said, grinning.

Garcia tightened his mouth and looked out the side window. Rick chuckled. This long trip with Garcia was a blessing in disguise; it was giving Rick the chance to figure out how to handle and shut down the smarmy little shit. Garcia was about thirty years old but acted like he was fifteen. Okay, well and good. Rick had experience with teenagers in *spades*.

He slowed the car and paid closer attention to the GPS.

Paddocks and the occasional farmhouse lined the road, with a backdrop of blue-green and hilly eucalyptus forest on both sides.

"In two hundred metres," the GPS intoned in her clipped British accent, "turn left."

"Do me a favour," Rick said. "Put your phone away if you can manage it, and keep your eyes peeled. We're looking for not much more than a goat track."

Sighing, Garcia slipped his phone into his jacket pocket and made a big show of sitting forward in his seat. Just like Rick's youngest at the dinner table whenever they told her to stop slouching. Rick chuckled again. Some four hours of one-on-one time with Garcia had tipped the scales to Rick's favour. He couldn't wait to tell the missus tonight.

"Turn left now," the GPS said.

Rick braked and steered the unmarked BMW off the road and onto the gravel. The track was only wide enough for one car. Gum trees pressed in close. Another six kilometres and a few more turns, and they would reach the body farm. The dashboard clock read 11.48 a.m. Right on time. Rick's stomach grumbled. Please, let Stella Vasilakis have bought those Tandoori chicken pies again. If he remembered correctly, Stella lived in Mount Beauty, a town some forty minutes further out from the body farm, and by God they must have a killer bakery there. He would be sure to snaffle the Tandoori pies first and leave Garcia with the spinach and feta.

"You got the file?" he said.

"Right here," Garcia replied, and picked up the bound manila folder from the footwell.

"Check over it."

"I already have."

"Then do it again," Rick said.

Garcia huffed, opened to the front page and bent his head. How the bastard didn't get car-sick while reading, Rick had no idea. His oldest daughter, even now, had to sit where she had an unobstructed view of the windscreen. Otherwise, she would spew. Had done so since the first day they had put her in a booster seat. She was eighteen now, in her final year of high school, on her L-plates and shooting for her license by the new year. Driving didn't upset her stomach, thank God. His baby somehow eighteen... Time flies, Rick thought. And the older you get, the faster it goes.

The GPS broke into his thoughts. "In fifty metres, turn right... Now turn left... Now turn right... You have reached your destination. Your destination is on the left."

"Whoa," Garcia said. "It's a prison."

The VITERI compound had a high cyclone fence topped with razor wire, and double gates with a no-man's land of some three metres between them. CCTV cameras loomed from both gates. A placard stated RESTRICTED AREA AUTHORISED PERSONNEL ONLY with no other sign-posting. The buildings were obscured by trees. To Rick, it looked like the property of a doomsday prepper.

He braked. "Are you ready?"

Garcia seemed almost cowed. "Yeah, sure. Let's do this."

Rick coasted the BMW towards the gate, braked again at the intercom post, and cracked his window. The intercom fizzed into life.

"A very good morning to you, Detective Senior Sergeant Evans," said a female voice. "Oh, sorry, I mean good afternoon. Wait, is it morning or afternoon?"

Yep, sounded like Stella. He glanced at the dashboard display. "It's one minute to twelve."

Her smoker's laugh wheezed through the speaker. "Oh, morning or afternoon, you know what I mean. Hello! Just hang on, I'm buzzing you in."

The first gate rolled back on hidden mechanisms. Rick nosed the car into the no-man's land and stopped. The gate closed behind them.

"Are you right?" Stella's voice sounded from a second speaker.

"Yes, go ahead."

"Whoa, this is *exactly* like a prison," Garcia whispered, as if scared of being overheard.

"They have to keep out the riff-raff somehow," Rick said, and shut his window.

The second gate rolled back. Rick eased the car along the track towards the parking area some ten metres distant. Behind them, the second gate screeched as it closed. Garcia swivelled his head this way and that. Rick smiled. *Greenhorn.*

The carport was large enough to hold a dozen cars. Most of the spots were taken with a wide cross-section of vehicles. Two parking bays had VISITOR stencilled on the concrete floor. Rick steered the BMW under the carport roof and into one of the visitor bays.

He killed the engine. "Don't forget," he said, wagging a finger. "Let me do the talking."

"Yeah, sure." Garcia went to get out of the car.

"Wait," Rick said. "Don't forget the file."

"What?"

"The file on the Wilson murder. Don't forget to bring it. And the beach towel."

Garcia reached into the footwell for the manila folder as Rick got out of the car and buttoned up his suit jacket. Dear God. The stink of the place was so thick—as thick as woodsmoke—that it literally reached into your mouth and scrabbled at your throat. Your first reflex was to hold your breath. Your second was to cough. Third to spew. But Rick had known what to expect. Garcia got out of the car, white-faced, nose crinkling.

"Aw, fucking hell," he said. "What's that *stench*?"

Rick opened his arms and gestured around him. "Death."

"Fuck." Garcia held the beach towel up to his nose and mouth. "Fucking *fuck*."

Poor kid. Rick almost felt sorry for him. The two cases Garcia had helped investigate in his few weeks on the squad had involved (a) bones, decades old, lying in a shallow dirt grave and (b) a corpse about three hours deceased, with signs of marbled lividity but no decay. Too old and too fresh; neither crime scene had smelled. However, rotting skin, organs and tissue presented another ball game altogether. Even if sniffed only once, death had a particular odour that you would never forget for as long as you lived: a hellish and powerful combination of pond scum, sulphurous farts, shit, and rancid meat. The kind of combination that can instantly evert your stomach contents. But after some fourteen years in Homicide, Rick could hold it down. In fact, he was considered a "cadaver dog" in the squad: if there was a putrefying corpse or body part anywhere in the vicinity, Rick Evans would smell it first.

"Garcia," he said. "You're not going to spew, are you?"

"Nah. I'm fine."

Rick approached, touching Garcia lightly on the elbow. This was only the second time he'd made physical contact: the first being a handshake when Garcia had strutted into Homicide Squad. But now Rick felt benevolent, almost fatherly. It had something to do with Garcia's ashen face, the way he was trying to mask his nausea. Oh no, maybe *I'm* the arsehole here, Rick thought in alarm, and it's not Garcia after all.

"You right, mate?" he said gently.

"Fuck, just leave it," Garcia said, wrenching his arm away. "Where do we go?"

Rick pointed at a flat-roofed building some twenty metres distant. Garcia slung the beach towel over his shoulder, clutched the case file to his chest, and strode towards the building without looking back. Rick felt a pang of regret.

Shit. He'd done it again.

When would he ever learn to give a little ground?

At home, his wife enjoyed smooth and friendly relations with their girls. Oh, but not Rick. No, almost every night at dinner he would somehow get caught up in a stupid, pointless, unwinnable argument without even trying—socialism doesn't work, vegetarianism is an eating disorder, all rap music including mumble, trap and grime is woeful—and his daughters would leave the kitchen table in a snit, leaving the missus to glare daggers at him.

"You coming or not?" Garcia called.

Rick locked the car and jogged after Garcia, his soft belly jouncing.

Waiting for them on the veranda was Stella, the old gal looking exactly as he remembered her: as if she had dressed in the dark. Purple jacket, orange striped t-shirt, green trousers, wedge heels, blue-framed spectacles, dyed ginger hair scraped into a top-knot with a chequered scrunchie. He smiled with genuine warmth. Bouncing a little on her toes, she waved both hands at him, bangles and charm bracelets rattling on her wrists. She must be pushing sixty, but had somehow retained the ditzy gusto of youth.

"Hello, hello!" she said. "Detective Senior Sergeant Evans, it's lovely to see you again."

"Same here, and please call me Rick."

"Okay, Rick." She turned to look up at Garcia. "And who's this fine young man you've brought with you today?"

Rick clapped Garcia's shoulder, and said, "Detective Senior Constable Lawrence Garcia. He's new to the squad, and I've got him on my crew. Garcia, this is Stella, office manager."

"Ooh, he's a nice young man, isn't he?" she said to Rick.

"Pleased to meet you," Garcia said. "Could we go inside now?"

Stella play-slapped her forehead. "How stupid I am. For goodness sakes, yes, it's a bit whiffy out here, isn't it? I hardly notice it myself anymore. Come this way."

They followed her into the building with the placard MAIN OFFICE: PLEASE REPORT TO RECEPTION. Once the door closed, the air conditioning kept out the smell. Rick recalled the simple layout—most of the offices, kitchen and toilets at one end, morgue at the other—and Stella was leading them right to the kitchen. Lunch! God, he was ravenous. A man of his stockiness couldn't be expected to subsist on a breakfast of porridge and banana.

In the kitchen, however, was the VITERI Director, a tall handsome woman in her mid-forties, Professor Joan Kendall. Next to her was a young Asian girl Rick didn't recognise. The girl wore green scrubs like a hospital worker.

Professor Kendall stood up from the table with great effort, and lumbered over to them. Her peculiar gait was stiff-legged, rocking her from side to side like an elephant. Must be a permanent affliction, Rick thought. Bloody shame. The last time he had seen her, some eleven months ago, she had walked the same way.

"How are you, Rick?" Kendall said. "Hello, Lawrence. Do you mind if I call you that?"

"Yeah it's okay," Garcia said, and gestured at her legs. "What happened?"

Rick froze. *Shit.* In lieu of face-palming, he kept a blank expression.

Kendall smiled. "I'm sorry?"

"Your limp," Garcia said. "Did you hurt yourself?"

"Look, I'm sorry about—" Rick began, but Kendall's breezy laugh cut him off.

"No, it's quite all right," she said. "Arthritis. In both hips." She turned to the girl. "I'd like to introduce Cheryl Zhao. She's one of our graduate students in forensic entomology. Cheryl will be overseeing the experiment."

"I'm glad to be working with you," Cheryl said. "Let's hope we can get a breakthrough on the Wilson case."

"Thanks for your time and expertise," Rick said as they shook hands. "It's a pleasure to meet you."

"A pleasure that's all mine," Garcia added, taking the girl's hand and holding it too long.

She gave him a slow, knowing smile. Garcia ran a palm up and over his pompadour. Shit, Rick thought. Here we go. *Lothario Larry.* That's what the blokes in the squad called him behind his back. Any compassion that Rick had felt for Garcia evaporated instantly, replaced by outrage. In the car on the way back to Melbourne, they would have *words.*

"Shall we eat lunch before we get started?" Stella said. "I bought a range of pastries."

"Any Tandoori chicken pies?" Rick said.

Stella winked. "You bet. I got two for you especially. Lawrence, are you okay with spinach and feta?"

**

The VITERI compound sprawled across some one-hundred-and-fifty acres; about the size of a large golf course. They travelled to the experiment site on postie bikes—the small and gutless Honda CT110—with Cheryl on one bike, Rick on the other with Garcia riding pillion. They passed corpses in various states of decomposition, both human and pig, since pigs were a reasonable substitute for humans and their carcasses easier to come by. The landscape was sparsely vegetated. Gum trees, a few shrubs here and there, very little grass. Not many birds apart from crows and ravens.

But shit, so many *flies*.

For the quarter-hour Rick had puttered the bike after Cheryl, about one thousand houseflies and blowies had bounced off his face. The air was crowded with the droning of a million wings. For Christ's sake, the flies triggered his spew reflex more than the stink of rot.

Then the car came into view.

Amazing.

They had got the same make and model: a 2011 Lexus IS250 automatic Prestige. A different colour, of course, but virtually the same car.

The hair stood up on Rick's neck.

The scene came back to him. Popping the boot some seven years ago, knowing that it would be bad, *smelling* that it would be bad. The naked woman curled up inside. Head wounds. Throat wounds. She must have been dumped in the boot while still bleeding, still alive, because of the amount of blood soaked into the carpet. She had been in the foetal position with both hands balled up beneath her chin, the tip of one thumb in her mouth. The sight had brought tears to his eyes and the memory still did now. Alexandra Wilson, twenty-three, college student completing her last year of a Bachelor degree, majoring in philosophy and Australian literature. Alexandra lived at home with her parents, cared for a tank of freshwater tropical fish, and had a boyfriend. They had met while working part-time at the same KFC during their final years of high school. The boyfriend had collapsed when Rick had broken the news of Alexandra's death. Seven years since her murder, and no arrests. Seven years and *nothing*.

Cheryl parked her bike next to the Lexus and hopped off. Rick and Garcia did likewise.

"Here we are," she said, and popped the boot. She opened her voluminous leather satchel and handed out latex gloves. "Ready? Here comes Magnus."

"Who's Magnus?" Rick said.

"The caretaker. He's bringing our donor."

Rick looked around. Through the trees, he saw movement. The monotonous drone of a motor came to him next. A man was coming straight for them, a large and bald man on a quad bike. Rick didn't know him. The caretaker he'd met last time had been Charlie, a sullen pisspot.

Magnus pulled up. Hitched to the back of his bike was a long trailer. On the trailer was a black zipped-up body bag. And inside the bag, the remains of the person who had gifted their body to science. What a selfless sacrifice. No final resting place, no grave. Rick's heart fluttered. Tears pricked his eyes and he blinked them back.

Magnus dismounted from the bike. He wore boots, navy trousers and an orange high-vis shirt. One at a time, he stared at them all with his ice-blue eyes and then nodded, once. No handshakes offered by this giant. The bastard must be about six and a half feet tall.

"Are we ready to start?" Magnus said, lightly accented. Rick guessed Finnish. Norwegian? No, definitely Finnish by the way he swallowed his vowels.

"Thanks, yes," Cheryl said, and waved her little hand towards the car boot. "Could we put the donor in there, please? Curled up like a baby." She looked at Rick. "Is that correct?"

"Yes," he said. "That's correct. Laying on her left side. And wrapped in a beach towel. We brought one with us that's identical in size and material." He reached for the towel folded over Garcia's arm but Garcia, hushed for once, didn't seem to notice.

Everyone put on gloves. Magnus undid the zip. The body bag exhumed an odour of disinfectant and refrigerated air.

2

Professor of Forensic Entomology, Walter Boyce, stood up and took a pack of cigarettes from his desk drawer. He encountered Stella in the hallway.

"Would you like to join me?" he said, holding up the pack.

She tapped her upper arm. "Not today, sweetie, I'm wearing a nicotine patch."

"Ah. Quitting again?"

"You never know," she said, breezing past, "I might just do it this time."

"Well, my dear, I wish you the best of luck."

She laughed. "Yeah, and I'll need it too. Isn't that a bugger?"

Before heading to the back patio, Walter visited Kieran Pocock's office. Kieran looked up from his monitor, took out both earbuds and raised his eyebrows in a silent question.

"I received a message about a Java update on my computer," Walter said.

"That's fine. Completely legit. Go ahead and install it."

"I tried, but when I clicked the *click here* area, as instructed, the entire box disappeared."

"Okay, Professor Boyce," Kieran said. "Give me a minute."

"Thank you very much. No rush. Whenever you're ready."

Walter went back down the hallway.

The back patio was about two square metres of decking enclosed with horizontal wooden palings. No exit stairs. It brought to mind the stern of a boat. At one end of the decking sat a dusty, leaf-strewn outdoor setting: a plastic table with four chairs. Walter usually had the deck to himself—apart from the times when Stella took up the fags again—because who else but a smoker would choose to be out here? The smell was quite unpleasant. The staff liked to call this area the poop deck; pun intended.

He lit a cigarette and scanned the nearby trees.

"Cookie," he said in a calm and even tone. "Can you hear me? Cookie?"

The whoosh of wingbeats turned his head. The cream and brown kookaburra swooped over and landed delicately on the top railing within reach of Walter's arm. The patches on the bird's wings looked almost iridescent. Oh, what a handsome bird. Those flecks of blue that continued throughout the plumage of the back and tail suggested Cookie was male. On the nights when Walter stayed in the bunkhouse, Cookie's laughter bade him goodnight at sunset and woke him at sunrise, and in those first few confused seconds of stunned and dopey wakefulness, it seemed the bird was calling and chortling just for him, only for him.

Walter smiled. "Good boy. Who's my good little boy? You are, Cookie. You are."

Cookie inclined its head and gazed at him. Walter patted the pocket of his lab coat. Inside was a zip-lock bag of raw beef stir-fry strips. A relatively expensive cut, yes, but one cannot feed mince to a kookaburra. The gummy consistency sticks the meat inside the beak.

"It's lunchtime, Cookie. Would you like something to eat?"

Dangling the cigarette from his lips, Walter took out a beef strip. Slowly, casually, quietly, he leaned his elbow on the railing and wiggled the strip between forefinger and thumb. The meat would seem alive like a snake. Cookie appeared to consider, looking first with one bright eye and then the other. Oh, how Walter longed to run his hands over its plumage.

"Come on, little chap," Walter murmured. "Come on."

The kookaburra hopped closer. Stared intently at the treat. Began to murmur its hoarse little chuckle of excitement. At last, delicately, it extended its neck and nipped the very end of the beef strip in its beak, pulling the strip from Walter's grasp.

"Good boy," he whispered.

Cookie proceeded to "kill" the strip, whacking it repeatedly against the railing as if to break vertebrae. Habits die hard. In that respect, birds were no different to people. Walter leaned on the railing and smoked for a while, watching Cookie consume the treat. Then he brought out another treat, not extending his arm as far this time, tempting the bird to hop closer.

In the top pocket of his lab coat, Walter kept a doll-sized straw hat. With enough trust-building exercises, one day he would place that hat on Cookie's head. It had taken the best part of four months to get this far. The hat might take another four months, perhaps longer. Walter could wait. He was nothing if not patient. Why he wanted to put a hat on a kookaburra's head, he couldn't exactly figure. Yet something about the endeavour both amused and intrigued him. When it happened, he would take a photograph for posterity.

"Is that tasty?" he said, as Cookie wolfed down the second strip. "Do you like beef more than chicken? More than pork?"

The back door opened. At the noise, Cookie tensed, opened its wings and headed for the trees. Walter frowned at Kieran standing in the doorway. The young man's smile was rueful.

"Sorry," Kieran said. "Didn't mean to interrupt you with your pet bird."

"No, no, that's quite all right."

"Why don't you just leave the food out for him on the table?"

Walter scowled. "That would lure crows, ravens, butcher birds, magpies, currawongs—"

"Okay. I've installed your Java update. You shouldn't get any more notifications."

"Ah, yes." Walter nodded. "Brilliant. Much appreciated."

"No worries." Kieran closed the door.

Kieran was a nice enough young man, the newest addition to VITERI after the last IT manager went on maternity leave, although Walter didn't much care for Kieran's sartorial tastes. Skinny jeans, tight shirts, boots with absurdly long and pointed toes and, for Pete's sake, mutton-chop sideburns. Kieran looked as if the sixties had rolled back around again in all their ridiculous glory.

Walter turned to the bush. "Cookie. Cookie?" He took out and waved another beef strip. It felt a little warm. "Cookie? Where have you gone?"

No good. The kookaburra was spooked. Or perhaps full—after all, it had gobbled two strips of meat, each as long as a man's finger.

Walter pushed the cigarette butt into the windproof metal ashtray and went inside the building. He had to finish this week's lecture notes for his first-year students: *The use of insect succession to estimate time of death in an individual deceased for one month or more: part 2—beetle infestations.* He would need to put extra effort into this lecture. For some reason, most of his students were more interested in the activities of flies.

In the kitchen, he returned the zip-lock bag to the refrigerator. On the bag he had written in black marker STRICTLY FOR USE BY WALTER BOYCE ONLY. From habit, he lay the bag face up to display the warning. Pointless, really. Everyone knew he was handfeeding a kookaburra. None of them knew why. And Walter had no desire to enlighten them. No doubt if he told them, they would think him a foolish—or even senile—old man.

When he got to his computer, he found that Kieran had minimised his lecture notes. He opened up the Word document again. His gaze fell upon a couple of random lines, the brief recap of his previous lecture. "The bright colourations of the *Calliphora* thorax gave rise to the colloquial and generic term 'bluebottle fly'. Other common-use Australian terms include 'blowfly' or 'blowie'..."

He thought of Cheryl Zhao. His best graduate student, out there with two homicide detectives. The *Calliphora vicini*, or European bluebottle, was Cheryl's favourite exotic fly. Perhaps Walter should have joined them in setting up the experiment. At the very least, he should have met with the detectives, made a pretence at social niceties. For a moment, he felt anxious, panicked. Oh Christ, never mind. This lecture was more pressing. And Cheryl could handle the experiment herself, couldn't she? Yes, she had his full confidence.

Full confidence.

Walter scrolled to the end of the Word document and tried to pick up from his last typed sentence. His mind drifted again to Cheryl. A gem. If only he could persuade her to consider teaching Forensic Entomology at Fraser University. At nearly seventy, Walter needed someone capable to follow in his footsteps.

Someone as devoted, as single-minded and passionate, as Cheryl Zhao.

There were only about one thousand forensic scientists in the country and not many vacancies. He could put in a good word for her. Unquestionably, his recommendation would be her golden ticket; Walter happened to be one of only five forensic entomologists in Australia called upon by police to help investigate and solve crimes. He averaged ten or twelve cases a year. In bad years—usually those with long, hot summers in his anecdotal experience—there might be twenty or more cases. And he was frequently asked to testify in court for the prosecution.

Contrary to most people's expectations, the cases weren't always homicides, and weren't always high-profile. Only a few weeks ago, in fact, he had taken the stand in a case of criminal negligence against a nursing home. One of the patients in their care had been found with various insect infestations, including lice and maggots, on her skin and within her numerous bed sores. Walter's expertise had been required to help the police and prosecution estimate how long the woman's purgatory in that god-forsaken place had been going on.

He was thorough in his investigations and articulate on the stand. Police and prosecutors "loved" him. Outwardly, he feigned nonchalance but their praise and admiration felt as vital as oxygen.

Only Cheryl Zhao could be his successor.

While all of his students applied themselves, Cheryl had what most of the others did not: poise under pressure. From her very first semester in his class, he had recognised this quality in her. Crime scenes could be chaotic and noisy, crammed with uniformed police, detectives, forensic technicians and perhaps other emergency responders such as firefighters. Often there were witnesses, reporters, members of the public ghoulishly hoping for a glimpse of the dead. Most of Walter's students could barely speak in front of their class mates, and faced with the pandemonium of an active crime scene, would surely crumble. Ah, but not Cheryl.

She would be Walter's perfect replacement.

Yet she wanted to go to the Top End, the northern-most part of the Northern Territory, and set up Australia's third taphonomic facility somewhere there. It made perfect sense—the decomposition of bodies depends entirely on the environment, and God knows Australian forensic scientists needed research in the tropical regions to expand upon their current database—but, peevishly, Walter didn't want Cheryl to go. He wanted her to take over his VITERI office, his position at Fraser University, his two lab rooms. Wanted her to place her notes on the same lectern, address students in the same lecture hall, tread the same boards.

Pathetic, really.

It came from having no children, he supposed.

The desire for someone to "take over the family business"—wasn't that the root of his unreasonable desire for Cheryl to become his heir apparent?

Walter scratched at his thinning goatee, ran his finger and thumb over his moustache. Happened to notice the time on his monitor's task bar and sat up, shaken from his reverie.

Pay attention. Concentrate on the lecture notes.

Only the recap and introduction written so far. He gazed at his chapter headings. *Early-arrival beetles such as* Histeridae *and* Staphylinidae *that feed on fly larvae. Later-arrival beetles such as* Cleridae *and* Dermestidae *that feed on tough and dry connective tissue. Varied-diet beetles such as* Silphidae *and* Scarabaeini...

The cursor on the screen blinked at him.

Who would take over from him when he left the University?

No, when he was *forced* to leave.

Lately there were noises in upper management about his retirement. No one had ever before given this possibility a moment's thought; Walter had always been considered one of the fixtures at Fraser University. And then Deputy Vice-

Chancellor Professor Gail Herman had barrelled into the place at the start of the school year, sticking her nose into everyone's business, whispering into the Vice-Chancellor's ear. Redundancy packages, reshufflings, allowing contracts to lapse, out with the old and in with the new, that was Herman's philosophy. But Walter Boyce was not just a fixture at Fraser, he was an *asset*. One of only five forensic entomologists in Australia called upon by police! One of only *five*! The Vice-Chancellor would be mad to let Walter go. But Herman liked to talk about insurance risks, Work Care investigations, punitive fines for an unsafe workplace. Herman's favourite theoretical example: an elderly lecturer falling down stairs and breaking a hip. For "elderly lecturer", read Walter.

And if he were forced into retirement?

Many decades had enshrined his routine. Two days at VITERI, two days at Fraser University, two days working from home, appearances at crime scenes or court when required, and Sundays devoted to housework, laundry, grocery shopping, errands. If he retired, how would he fill each week? He didn't care for hobbies. Oh, he fiddled about with a cryptic crossword every now and then. Had tried playing golf once and hated the tedium of it. And the thought of joining a PROBUS group made him grimace.

What then?

He had his theories. The most central being: he would simply die. From boredom, probably. And then his remains would be returned to VITERI, reuniting him with his flies, beetles, mites and moths in the most intimate way imaginable. Perhaps Cheryl would study his decomposition processes. Unless, of course, she had succeeded by then in establishing a taphonomic research facility in the Top End.

"Knock, knock."

He glanced at the doorway and smiled, relaxing back into his chair. "Stella, my dear. You're just in time to save me from having to deal with the dreaded writer's block."

"I've already told you the answer to that one: booze."

"*Pshaw.*" But he chuckled anyway at the familiar joke. She always looked so pleased with herself when she said it.

"If boozing was good enough for Ernest Hemingway, it's good enough for you." She breezed into his office with a clatter of bracelets and bangles, and perched herself on the edge of his desk. "Oh God, you smell good."

"You're not trying to seduce me, I hope."

"No, silly billy, I mean the cigarette smoke." She sniffed elaborately. "Not even twenty-four hours and I swear I'm climbing the walls."

"What about your nicotine patch?"

"Useless. Maybe I need to chew on it."

They both laughed. Walter made an elaborate show of picking up his cigarette pack and stowing it inside a drawer.

Stella said, "You should have met the detectives going out with Cheryl. Rick Evans brought some new kid with him. Lord, the hairdo on this kid. Unreal. Must have had a bucket of grease in it."

"Hmm, perhaps I'll pop out and say hello when they come back," Walter said, but knew he wouldn't. Somehow, seeing Cheryl with detectives made him feel overly protective of her, much like a father watching his daughter going out on a date. Or so he imagined. The two scenarios probably had no parallels whatsoever.

"This kid's hair, though," Stella continued. "No way I'd let him in my swimming pool. He'd leave an oil slick a mile wide. Gosh, I shouldn't say such nasty things, should I? Do you think I'm awful?"

"Of course, my dear, but in the most wonderful way." He hesitated, took the plunge. "What are your retirement plans, if you don't mind me asking?"

"Oh, that's easy." She started counting on her fingers. "One: hubby and I taking the caravan around Australia. Two: going back to school to learn Greek until I'm bloody fluent this time. Three: off to Greece with hubby to visit rellies. Four: back home and it'll be grandma duties, I reckon. Melanie should have had her brood by then. She and Greg are planning on four kids, but we'll see. The first one comes as a bloody shock, I can tell you."

"Hmm," he said, and scratched at his beard.

Stella regarded him for a time. "Good grief, you're not worrying about that battle-axe bitch Herman, are you?"

He sighed and shrugged.

"The Vice-Chancellor won't listen to her, trust me."

He shrugged again.

Stella play-slapped his shoulder. "Oh, stop. No one's getting rid of you. What would the forensics department be without Walter Boyce?"

"Modernised."

"Ugh, come off it. Now look, have you had any lunch?"

"Not yet."

"But I bet you've taken the time to feed your little kookaburra friend, haven't you?" She hopped off the desk. "There's pies in the kitchen, bought fresh this morning. Have something to eat, Walter, you'll feel better. Your blood sugars are low, that's all. Chop, chop."

Possibly she was right. He got up and followed her into the hallway. His joints ached and he was stooping, as if his nigh-on seventy years were catching up with him all at once.

***

The donor was female, Caucasian, aged in her early fifties or thereabouts. Honey-brown hair, dyed, with grey roots. Eyes serenely closed, mimicking sleep. No autopsy incisions; she must have died from a known and nonsuspicious cause, Rick surmised, such as a stroke or heart attack. The skin on the back of her neck was deep purple. It was the discolouration of stilled and coagulated blood, first visible about ten to twelve hours after death. Unmistakeable. Rick had seen this scores of times. If you were to push a finger into that skin, it wouldn't blanch.

How might her family have reacted to her decision to donate her remains to the body farm? Badly, no doubt, considering most people baulked just at the idea of organ donation. This woman must have argued hard to get her way. Once the VITERI scientists had gleaned everything they could from her decomposition, her skeleton would be dismantled and the bones added to the Forensic Skeletal Collection. Archived in cardboard boxes. Kept in perpetuity as a data set for researchers and anthropologists.

Jesus, it must be tough on the family.

Not only losing someone you love, but knowing they were being placed by scientists out in the open somewhere, perhaps half-buried in leaves or hidden under a mattress or weighed down in a creek bed, and deliberately left to rot in the sun and wind and rain. Left to be eaten by bugs and worms. The horrors of death dialled the whole way up to eleven. An expensive mahogany coffin and a fancy wreath helped the bereaved to skate over the grisly bits in their minds. The body farm shoved the grisly bits right in their faces.

Could Rick donate himself?

Probably not.

Decaying in the open didn't bother him that much. Everyone becomes worm shit no matter their final resting place, whether a coffin or hollow log. But the idea of these scientists—these people he *knew*—seeing him naked felt too embarrassing to contemplate. Immature? Yes, but a man can't help the way he feels.

And if his wife decided to donate her body or, God forbid, if one of his daughters wanted to do it, how would Rick react? He had heard of one crime scene re-creation that had required a donated body to be burned inside a forty-four-gallon drum. Jesus. He gave an involuntary shudder. He looked down at the donor.

You've got bigger balls than me, he thought.

Out of nowhere, he choked up. Shit. That's what comes from playing hypotheticals, he scolded himself. *Stop imagining your own family in a situation like this.* He focused on the details of the donor's face. Her dark eyelashes. The little beauty spot next to her mouth. A scar on her cheek, perhaps from a childhood accident like falling off her bike.

Thank you, he thought, for trying to help me get justice for Alexandra Wilson. If he'd been wearing a hat, Rick would have doffed it. As it was, all he could do was surreptitiously hold one hand over his heart.

Cheryl said, "Detectives, I'd like you to meet Violet."

"You know her name?" Rick said. "I thought donor information was confidential."

"It is. We like to name our donors rather than call them by case numbers."

Rick nodded and pressed his palm harder against his chest. "Hello, Violet," he said.

"Yeah, hi," Garcia mumbled.

Everybody gazed down at her. Rick again felt the warm prickle of tears.

Magnus was the one who decided when the moment of respect was over. "Okay," he said with a curt nod, then grabbed the woman under the arms. He stopped to stare at Garcia.

"The legs," he said. "Come on, young man. The legs."

Garcia rushed forward, squatted down, reached out his gloved hands and hesitated, just for a fraction of a second, just long enough for Rick to feel a wave of pity. Then Garcia held the ankles. Cheryl supported the woman's head.

"On my mark, okay," Magnus said. "One, two, three, *mark*."

They lifted her out of the body bag. Rick wrapped the beach towel around her torso and held it there. She felt icy cold. The four of them shuffled her across to the car's open boot. The coldness radiated in waves from her white, goose-fleshed skin. Who would have thought goose flesh could occur in the dead? But the little muscle at the root of each hair follicle goes into *rigor mortis* like any other skeletal muscle and pulls the body hair erect. So strange. The first time Rick had seen this on a dead body, he had assumed the victim was simply unconscious and hypothermic. *Madam*, he recalled saying as he had patted her face, trying to wake her up. *Madam, can you hear me?* Back then, some thirty years ago, he had been in uniform, a gangly lad, used to handling traffic violations and burglary reports.

"Which way round for Violet?" Magnus said.

"Lying on her left side," Rick said, holding tight to the towel so it wouldn't fall. "That's right. Now, legs tucked up. A little more, Garcia. Thanks, I can take it from here."

He knew the arrangement of Alexandra Wilson's body by heart. Gently, he moved the donor's head towards her chest, folded her arms so that her knuckles were at her chin. And then, with great care, took one thumb and worked it between the bloodless lips. He studied her for a few seconds. Pulled up the towel. Tucked the fold of it beneath her stomach.

"Have we got it?" Magnus said.

Yes, Rick thought.

"Any more adjustments?" Cheryl said.

No, none. Instead, he replied, "Let me check. Garcia, give me the file."

Garcia complied. Rick flipped through the pages to the crime scene photographs. Alexandra Wilson had had blonde hair bobbed to her shoulders, like his middle daughter, except Alexandra Wilson had sported a fringe. He made a show of comparing Violet's posture to one of the photographs, then shut the manila folder and gave it back to Garcia.

"That's it. A perfect re-creation."

Everyone took off their gloves. Cheryl collected them inside a large zip-lock bag, and put the bag inside the leather satchel.

She turned to Magnus, and said, "Thanks so much."

The giant was already securing the folded body bag on the trailer with an occy strap. "Okay," he said, and threw one long leg over the seat of the quad bike.

"I appreciate your help," Rick said.

"Yeah, cheers, good on you, mate," Garcia added.

Magnus started the motor and, without looking at any of them or saying a word, turned the bike and rode back in the direction he had come. Garcia's low whistle got Cheryl's attention.

"Chatty old bastard, isn't he?" he said and winked. Now that the body was in the boot, and the caretaker gone, it seemed Garcia had regained some of his cocky composure.

"He's not one for small talk, but we love Magnus. He's so much better than the last caretaker."

"Charlie the pisspot?" Rick said.

"Oh, you noticed?"

"Hard not to when his breath reeked of grog."

"Listen, Cheryl," Garcia said, one hand on his hip, puffing out his chest. "This whole insect-thing that you're into. Life cycles, bugs, eggs. What's all that about? I'm intrigued, I really am. I mean, what's the attraction? You know, maybe you could tell me about it some time. Over a coffee. Or a drink maybe."

"Watch your step, Garcia," Rick said.

"No, it's okay," she said. "I don't mind telling him."

"Great. Over coffee or—?" Garcia began.

"My interest in forensic entomology came about from a lecture by Professor Walter Boyce that I attended in my first year. He talked about this one time, early in his career before he specialised in forensic science, when he met a woman whose gums were packed with fly larvae."

Garcia gave an uncomfortable laugh. "He 'met' a woman? So, she wasn't dead?"

"Technically, no. Still breathing and walking around but in terrible shape from a lengthy heroin addiction. It was the worst case of dental neglect that Professor Boyce had ever seen. This woman was so out of it, she didn't realise she had a mouthful of squirming maggots until he told her. She took the news quite well. She said, 'That explains why I keep tasting cashews.' Larvae have a nutty flavour, you see."

Cheryl's smile was pointedly sweet and bright. Garcia, looking confused, gave a half-hearted chuckle. Crikey, what a girl, thought Rick in admiration. How to shut down a sleazebag in ten seconds or less. Hopefully, his daughters would develop such a skill, if they hadn't already.

3

Cheryl went to her leather satchel and took out a mallet and a wooden stake.

"Hey, so you're off vampire hunting?" Garcia said, his lame attempt at a joke falling flat.

"She's marking the spot," Rick said. "What else would she be doing?"

"That's right. See this little plaque?" She showed them the stake. Affixed to it with a screw was a metal plate that read *D-H-13*. "The 'D' refers to the zone. We've got the grounds split up into ten zones of about fifteen acres each. 'H' means human. The '13' is Violet's ID number." She knelt down and hammered the stake into the ground by the car's rear tyre.

"Does that mean you've got thirteen bodies in Zone D?" Rick said.

"Yes. Only four of them human. The rest are pig carcasses." She returned the mallet to her satchel. "Now I'm going to make my initial report. I'll come back three times a week to note the insect activity during the decomposition changes. To be clear, I'll be following her through the fresh, bloat, active decay, advanced decay, and dry stages. Rick, for the Wilson case, you specifically want data from the active decay stage, right?"

"Right."

"Okay. Just so you know, we're following Violet's decomp all the way to skeletonised or mummified, whichever way she turns out. After that, the forensic anthropologists will take over the experiment. You want me to keep you in the loop to the very end?"

Rick nodded. "Thanks, if you wouldn't mind."

"Not a problem. I'll add you to all the email lists for Violet." She took out a camera and a clipboard. "You guys don't have to hang around. Go ahead and take one of the bikes. It's easy enough to follow the signposts back to the main building."

"Okay. Don't forget to close the boot when you're done," Rick said.

"Sure, will do."

"Well, it was nice to meet you. Oi, Garcia, you ready to go? Garcia?"

But the dickhead had wandered off a short way and had his back to them, looking up at something in the trees.

"Garcia!" Rick shot an apologetic glance at Cheryl. "Sorry," he said. "He's new."

"Yeah, I figured."

"What *is* that?" Garcia said, pointing vaguely into the air.

"I don't know," Rick said. "A koala? Come on, let's go."

"No, but what *is* that? Can't you see it?"

Dumb-arse. He was about to tell Garcia off, but as soon as Rick opened his mouth, he shut it again, stupefied. Drifting down, swirling and eddying, luminous in the beams of sunlight glinting through the canopy, was a shower of a substance he'd never seen before in his life; what looked like fluorescent dandelion seeds but without the stems. The tiny white tufts floated in the breeze over Garcia, towards Rick and Cheryl. Fairy lights, Rick thought in wonder. But that was a hangover from when his girls were young. Fairy lights didn't exist in the real world.

"It must be pollen of some kind," Cheryl said.

Rick closed his hand and trapped some of the strange seeds. When he peeked into his fist, the seeds were gone. Funny. He was positive that he'd caught a few.

"This is so fucking weird," Garcia said, holding out an arm, the other clamping the Wilson file to his side. He scrutinised his jacket sleeve. "As soon as the specks touch something, they disappear. Like they've melted or evaporated or something."

Rick held out both arms. Garcia was right. As the glowing tufts floated down, they were clearly visible against the dark grey of Rick's suit. But when they landed on his sleeves, *pop*, they winked out of existence. The sight confused him, made his heart race.

"How is it vanishing?" Cheryl said, staring intently into her cupped hands.

"Fucked if I know," Garcia said.

"I can't even feel the stuff against my skin," she continued. "Maybe body heat disintegrates it. If this is pollen, it's unfamiliar to me."

"Are the specks absorbing into our clothes?" Garcia said, brushing at the shoulder of his jacket and inspecting his fingers.

"If so, they must be absorbing into our skin as well," she said.

The shower of seeds—or whatever the hell they were—had spread out. Rick turned in a slow circle. The glowing tufts were falling everywhere now, like rain. He squatted down to inspect the dirt and leaf litter. Same deal. The tufts hit a surface and dematerialised. He stood, gazed around. Where the hell was this shit coming from? He looked up.

The sight of the cloud made him gasp.

It was small, compact, low to the ground, comprised of dozens of hanging sacs that reminded him, perversely, of breasts. And the colour was wrong. Instead of the regular white, grey or dark blue, this udder-like cloud was a vivid orange, as if it were sunset instead of early afternoon. Further, pearlescent veins of green and brown zigzagged through each sac. The seeds streamed from this bizarre cloud like salt from a shaker. They were landing on Rick's upturned face—Jesus, even landing in his *eyes*, he could actually *see* the tufts approaching—but he couldn't feel a thing. Not a single thing. He blinked and blinked. His eyes felt normal. And there were no other clouds in the sky. Absolutely none.

He found his voice. "You two ever seen anything like *that* before?"

They looked where he was pointing, straight up.

Garcia flinched and dropped the manila folder. "What the *fuck*?"

"Pick up the file," Rick said.

"Let's get out of here," Cheryl said.

The explanation occurred to Rick in a sudden rush of relief. This must be a cloud that scientists had chemically treated to provoke rainfall. Hadn't this

Spring been dry? It made sense. He had never seen a treated cloud, but knew silver iodide was used to help form ice crystals. Perhaps they were being pelted with silver iodide. Did shit like that cause cancer?

"It's okay," he said. "I think I know what's going on."

Scraping, scratching, scrabbling noises drew his attention. Coming from behind.

Coming from the car.

From the *boot* of the car.

Garcia and Cheryl both paled as they looked past him, their mouths dropping open. A queasy sensation moved through Rick. He didn't want to turn around but couldn't stop himself. So, he braced himself and turned.

Shit. His heart slammed in his chest. What he was seeing was impossible—

Don't think about that. Let your training and experience kick in. Assess the situation.

The first detail he noticed was the hue of the fingernail beds. A bruised mauve. The second detail was the stiff, jerky motion of the fingers as they spasmodically tried to hold onto the lip of the boot. The hand soon found purchase. A chill crept up the back of Rick's thighs, shrivelled his scrotum, put a lead weight in his belly. The corpse was getting up.

A crown of honey-brown hair.

Next, Violet's forehead appearing over the boot.

Then hazel-coloured eyes, wide and startled.

Now her full face visible. Confusion in the furrow of her brow. She looked at each of them in turn. Gazed about at the shower of seeds.

Both Garcia and Cheryl were panting, panicking. Rick had to take control of the situation. Take charge. He was good at taking charge. He held out a hand, palm down, in a placating gesture. Violet stared at his hand as if it were a snake.

"Madam," he said, voice trembling, "everything is all right."

The doctors had made an error. Simple as that. Coma, not death. *Coma.* Being out of the morgue's cold storage and warming up to air temperature had allowed Violet to awaken. This kind of mistake happened often in the Middle Ages. Coffins even had a bell rope so the prematurely buried could ring the gravediggers for help. *Saved by the bell.* Violet had been saved by the bell. Okay, then.

Okay.

Rick was calm. Yes, he was very calm. He'd seen a lot of shit in his time—a whole *lot* of shit—and he was completely, utterly, professionally and profoundly calm. *In through the nose. Hold. Out through the mouth.*

"Madam," he said, "can you hear me?"

Violet struggled into a sitting position and pushed the hair out of her eyes.

Oh, no. Wait a minute. Her skin colouration. If Violet wasn't dead, she wouldn't *have* this kind of lividity. Only *dead* people had this kind of lividity. The realisation choked his breath.

"Madam?" he whispered. "Madam?"

She fixed her gaze on him and bared her teeth.

***

At the reception desk, Stella pressed the button that operated VITERI's interior gate and watched on the CCTV monitor as the gate closed. She followed the progress of the refrigerated van from one monitor to the next. The van braked at the morgue's exterior door.

She clicked on the intercom and said, "Boys, we'll be right with you. Hang fire."

"No worries."

Professor Joan Kendall's office was right across the hall from Stella—they could see each other from where they were both sitting—but Joan didn't like it when Stella "hollered" at her. Instead, Stella had to get up, walk three metres, and knock on the open door. Ridiculous, but oh well, people had their quirks, didn't they? The world would be a boring place if everyone was the same. Stella went over and tapped her knuckles against the door jamb.

"Joan," she said. "Sorry to disturb you. The van's here."

The director's face lit up with delight and she clapped her hands together a couple of times, like a kid being offered a slice of chocolate cake. "That's wonderful, thank you."

Tactfully, Stella left the room so that Joan could haul herself out of the chair in privacy. Poor thing. Too young to be suffering from osteoarthritis in the hips, that's for sure. Why she didn't use mobility aids was a mystery. Perhaps a matter of pride? Why she hadn't opted for hip-replacement surgery was a mystery too, and would always remain so. Joan had never *ever* shared any personal information at work. Perhaps the idea of an operation scared her.

Stella returned to the reception desk as Joan lumbered down the hallway to the morgue. To the casual observer, the morgue door appeared to be of the ordinary hollow-core variety, but it was actually insulated—like the walls, floor and ceiling—to keep the refrigerated room at a constant four degrees Celsius. Joan went into the morgue and closed the door behind her. The familiar smell of disinfectant and something else, something decidedly *sweet*, wafted out for a moment, then was gone.

Stella wasn't squeamish anymore about the odours. When she had first started working here, she'd tried to mask the smell with perfume. It hadn't worked. And she ended up *hating* that perfume and never being able to wear it again. The power of association, she supposed. Too bad. Chanel No.5 had been her favourite. Just the thought of it now made her feel sick.

On the CCTV monitor, the two orderlies from the university transferred the body bag onto the gurney that Joan had wheeled outside. The orderlies pushed the gurney up the loading ramp. Joan stood by the open roller-door, supervising, even though the orderlies knew what they were doing.

Stella consulted her desk diary and put a big tick next to the entry that read: *Between 1 p.m. and 3 p.m.—delivery of donor.* Once Joan had completed the paperwork, Stella would scan the documents and email them as attachments to young and old. Good grief. She had worked in plenty of admin positions before, but VITERI had them beat when it came to the mountains of paperwork required every day.

She tipped back in her chair and called out, "Yoohoo! Walter!"

"Yes, my dear?" he called back from the other end of the building.

"The donor's arrived."

A few seconds passed and Walter trotted out of his office. He smiled and gave a jaunty salute on his way past her desk. "I'm off to say hello," he said.

And he meant it too. Walter liked to talk to each donor, to introduce himself and thank them personally. Weird. But, then again, basing an entire life around the study of the creepy-crawlies that eat dead people seemed weird too. Oh well, takes all kinds.

The intercom buzzer went off. On the CCTV monitor, the refrigerated van idled at the gates. Stella clicked on the intercom's microphone. "Gee, boys, that was quick."

"No flies on us."

"Ha, good one." She pressed another button and the interior gate opened. "Drive safely."

"Thanks, will do."

She closed the first gate behind the van and opened the second one. The van trundled out of the facility. She closed the second gate. *Lockdown.* In the year or so she'd been working here, not once—not *once*—had an uninvited stranger turned up. And who would want to anyway? What kind of person, apart from a forensic scientist, would be interested in gawping at decaying cadavers? Even so, the place was kept as secure as Fort Knox.

Oh, *cadavers*, that reminded her…tomorrow morning, a training session for cadaver detection dogs. The human and canine officers were turning up at 10 a.m. and would need the grounds to themselves for a maximum of five hours. She had to send another reminder email to the doctors and graduate students. Then again, no matter how many reminders she sent, there was always that one person who forgot and turned up. Some people would forget their own heads if they weren't screwed on.

The day after, fire detection dogs. They had become regulars, dropping in every few days, the officers trying to establish how long it took the dogs to stop detecting accelerants.

Then again, a huge rainstorm was predicted for later today. If that happened, both squads would have to rebook. Dogs can't smell anything when it's raining, apparently.

And now Stella had to attend to the requests for crime scene re-creations. So many from police officers all over the country. She had a pile on her desk to sort. Lately, Joan trusted her to triage them. That usually took Stella a long, long time. She hated to put any request at the bottom of the pile. At the heart of every single one was a crew of frustrated detectives, a grieving family desperate for an arrest and to find out why… Busy, busy, busy. *What do you do all day when there's nothing but dead bodies to worry about?* her husband Con liked to say. He was joking, but still. Cheeky sod. She worked her *arse* off at this joint.

"Hey, Stella."

She looked up. Kieran, scrolling on his mobile, was heading for the front door.

"Going home early?" she said.

"Nah, we've run out of skim milk. I'm off to raid the bunkhouse."

"Ooh, while you're there, snaffle some Tim Tams."

"We're out of them too?" He winked theatrically. "Gee, I wonder why."

Stella made a face and he laughed. Then she said, "Before I forget, my computer wants me to do an update."

"Let me guess. Java?"

"I don't know, mate. Wouldn't have a clue. Sorry. Could you do it for me?"

"Yep. Soon as I come back."

"Thanks, Kieran, you're a lifesaver." As he reached the door, she added, "Don't you want to put on some dust socks?"

He smiled and shook his head. "When are you going to stop ragging me about my shoes?"

"I'm not ragging you, mate, I'm serious. They'll get dirty. What are these ones made of anyway, crocodile skin?"

He shook his head again and pushed open the door.

Stella stood up. "No, it's a serious question, I swear. Crocodile skin? Snake skin?"

He stepped off the porch and strolled towards the bunkhouse. The door shut on its pneumatic closer. Stella sat down and watched his progress on one of the CCTV monitors. Kieran had his shoes handmade to order. Amazing. IT wages must be astronomical. The most she'd ever spent on a pair of shoes was $180.00 at a chain store, and Con had gone nuts—

What the frick was that?

She leaned closer and squinted at the CCTV monitor. Bright white flakes of some kind were floating down. Flakes? Maybe feathers? The down from a bird caught by a kestrel or falcon? No, the spots glimmered as if giving out their own internal illumination. Perhaps that was a trick of the light, a reflection on the camera lens. She got up and went to the nearest window. No, the flakes still shone, intensely, like the tips of soldering irons.

Together, Joan and Walter exited the morgue, chatting excitedly. Stella glanced around. Both of them looked thrilled to bits. Walter was even rubbing his hands.

"Guys, you should take a squiz at this—" Stella began.

"My word, the donor is simply *terrific*," Walter said. "The largest we've ever had."

"The tallest too, I believe," Joan said.

"Must have been a weightlifter or a bodybuilder," he continued. "A protein and lipids differential decomposition experiment, I suggest, would be the best option. We could bury him alongside smaller donors, at least a metre down or so, and see if he's more likely than the others to preserve rather than skeletonise."

Joan nodded enthusiastically. "It would back up the data from the pigs."

"Or disprove it entirely," he countered.

"Yes, that's very true," Joan said. "Won't Helen be elated? She's at the bunkhouse right now, isn't she? I'll give her a call. Oh wait, I'll call Bradley Shaw too, remember him? The archaeologist who investigates mass graves for the UN?"

"Good Lord, that's a splendid idea."

"Shaw and his team will be *ecstatic*," Joan said. "We're scheduled to receive two more donors before week's end. I should think a total of three would be sufficient for the experiment, don't you?"

"Indeed." Eyes wide and bright, Walter leaned on Stella's desk and said, "My dear, we need a name for our newest donor. What do you suggest? He's a big lad. Goodness, he's a *tremendously* big lad. Must be a hundred kilos."

"And the rest," Joan scoffed. "Didn't you see the paperwork? Logged at one-thirty-two."

"What about something macho," he said, "something rough and tumble, to go with his shaved head, beard and tattoos? What about, let's see... What about 'Butch'?"

"Oh, God no, we need to give him a *proper* name," Joan said. "A *real* name."

"Stella, you're the expert at this. Any suggestions?" Walter paused. "Stella? Stella?"

"Look out the window," she said.

A few seconds passed.

"Oh, cripes, that's very odd," Joan said. "What do you think it could be?"

"Hmm," Walter said.

They walked around Stella's desk and stood next to her at the windows.

Outside, the spots shifted and twirled about separately as they floated down, reminding Stella of swooping flocks of budgerigars or starlings that make giant, morphing patterns in the air. Each individual careful not to bump into another. Therefore intelligent. Sentient.

Absently, she bit at a nail.

Walter muttered, "It appears to be snowing."

"In October?" Joan said. "Besides, it never snows around here. The elevation's too low. I want a better look."

She went out on the veranda.

Before the pneumatic closer could shut the front door, a puff of flakes entered the building and wafted across the floor. Stella hurried over, leaned down and scrutinised the linoleum. Inexplicably, the flakes weren't there. She lifted her glasses and rubbed her eyes.

Joan came back inside. Another puff of flakes came in with her. Again, the flakes disappeared. Stella felt baffled, uneasy.

"I've never seen anything like this in all my born days," Joan said, hands on hips.

"Well, what is it?" Walter said.

"No idea. I'm completely dumbfounded."

She went over to the window next to Walter. Stella followed. They continued to watch the eerie spectacle. A few moments later, the drifts stopped.

Abruptly. Like a hose turning off, Stella thought uncomfortably. The others must have felt disquieted too, since they didn't move away from the window and didn't speak.

Finally, Stella said, "Shouldn't the ground be white? Where's all the stuff gone?"

Walter took his phone from his pocket. "I'm checking the weather bureau."

"You reckon they'll have a clue?" Stella said.

He thumbed his mobile and frowned. "Well, no mention of snowfall or sleet in the area, and nothing on the radar. You know, I think it's best if I give them a call."

***

Alisha Singh had elegance and poise. Even while picking fried egg out of her teeth.

Helen went for redheads as a rule but there was something about Alisha's long, straight and shining fall of jet-black hair that got to Helen's nervous system, triggering a jolt like a shivering buzz somewhere deep in her solar plexus. She wanted to run a comb through that beautiful hair, run her fingers through it, trail it over her own lips and breasts.

And Alisha's *skin*. So smooth, the colour of latte. Unblemished. (Unlike Helen's face, covered in fucking freckles from widow's peak to chin.) Eyes so dark you couldn't distinguish the pupil from the iris. Black lashes and brows. No mascara or pencil required.

Helen Macauley picked up the glass of orange juice and, as she sipped, wondered for the umpteenth time what Alisha might taste like. It pained her to think she would never find out.

Alisha was *straight*.

Straight as the proverbial arrow. Twenty-eight years old, devoted to the same man for three years and engaged to be married, no less.

Helen looked away, tried to focus her attention on the pool table. Just a crush, she thought. A silly infatuation. Except...except at odd times like these—whenever she watched Alisha doing something gross, such as picking food out of her molars—the flitter in Helen's stomach insisted that she wasn't infatuated but *in love*. When the object of your desire stops acting perfectly, and you adore them anyway, isn't that the very definition of love?

"Thanks for breakfast," Alisha said. "Or brunch? Lunch?" She checked her watch. "Crap, it's after one already. We ought to get going."

Their experiments were side by side in Area E.

Alisha's pig: dressed in a t-shirt and shorts, left to rot above ground to determine how clothing retards decomposition rate. Helen's human donor: naked and above ground to determine whether Melbourne's climate mummifies corpses—similar to the data collected by the taphonomic facility in Sydney's Blue Mountains—or skeletonises them as at the Texan facility. (Helen's money was on mummification, hands down.)

Alisha and Helen, side by side.

For a fortnight, they had spent three days a week side by side at VITERI.

Last night, staying over as usual at the bunkhouse, they had intended to turn in early. Well, that didn't happen. Helen had cooked a stir-fry. They had talked for a while, easy and friendly, then played pool, talked some more, started into Helen's slab of beer, listened to music, danced a little, kept on the beer until the early hours. Shared secrets like best friends, like sisters. Like lovers. At various times, Helen had considered making a move. Now or never. *Now or never.*

But she couldn't muster the nerve.

And the ideal opportunity had failed to present itself.

In fact, Alisha didn't seem to realise that Helen was gay. Why would she? There were no obvious signs. Helen eschewed conforming to stereotype. The fad of identity politics bored her shitless. Generally, she wore t-shirts, jeans, her curly shoulder-length brown hair worn loose or sometimes tamed into a ponytail. That said, even if she'd sported a buzzcut and a man's watch, she doubted Alisha would pick up on the cues. Alisha was the most naïve and non-judgemental person Helen had ever known. That kind of extreme innocence both annoyed and aroused Helen in equal measure.

Because...

Because they would make the perfect couple. A yin-yang of two opposing but complimentary personalities: Alisha's optimism grounded by Helen's cynical realism; Helen's propensity towards gruffness tempered by Alisha's sweet nature. And, most importantly, they shared a common passion: forensic science. Alisha's fiancé, *Marty* (what a babyish and gutless name, more suited to a prepubescent boy), was an *accountant*. With a *weak stomach*. The sight of blood made him faint. *Literally* faint. Jesus. What the fuck did they talk about? Movies and books, probably. TV shows. What colour towel sets to buy for the bathroom—

"Look at you," Alisha said. "A million miles away."

"Huh?"

"Staring at me but thinking about something else. Should we do the dishes before we go?"

Helen winked. "Nah, I'll wash them later. No worries."

They pulled on shoes, stepped into their white hazmat suits, sprayed each other with insect repellent (how personal), grabbed their petite knapsacks containing notebooks, thermometers, measuring tapes, cameras, gloves, dust socks, and left the bunkhouse. No need to lock the front door. The fenced perimeter with razor wire took care of security.

The two postie motorbikes sat under the eaves on the veranda. It was customary—and polite—to take only one, leaving the other for use by somebody else if required. As usual, Alisha would steer while Helen rode pillion.

Alisha started the ignition. Helen put her arms about Alisha's waist. The smell of death out here in the open wasn't enough to swamp the scent of Alisha's hair. Chamomile and passionflower. Late last night—or early this morning—Helen had offered to shampoo Alisha's hair. *I'm too tired*, Alisha had slurred. *Maybe tomorrow.* In the sober light of day, however, such an intimate suggestion had felt too much for Helen to risk mentioning again.

4

The ground was flat, hard-packed, covered in dry leaf litter from the surrounding eucalyptus and paper bark trees. Area E was about ten minutes away. The little motorbike didn't have any grunt. Alisha rode slowly. Helen pretended that it was intentional; that Alisha wanted to make her hug last as long as possible.

"What do you reckon Marty's up to right now?" Helen said.

"Probably working on more tax returns."

"Wow. Numbers, numbers, numbers. Boring. It'd put me to sleep."

Alisha said, "We deal in numbers too, you know."

"But not like accountants. Their numbers represent money. Kind of meaningless from a philosophical perspective, right? If you take the long view, I mean."

"Standard of living is crucial to happiness," Alisha said. "Marty actually helps people."

"Huh, I suppose, but if you consider—whoa! *Stop!*"

Alisha hit the brakes.

Helen jumped off the bike, squinted and blinked.

Up ahead was the cage for Alisha's pig. The cage, a simple structure of wooden struts covered in chicken-wire, was built by the caretaker, Magnus, to discourage scavengers. Such cages could be found all over the grounds. This particular cage was shaking, bucking, rising.

"Why have we stopped?" Alisha said.

"I thought your pig was through the bloat stage."

"That's right. Why?"

A chill gripped Helen's kidneys. "Your pig is rolling onto its back."

"Impossible." Alisha engaged the kickstand, slipped off the bike and fumbled for her spectacles. "The abdominal cavity has already ruptured. There's no internal gases to cause movement."

The pig, clad in a blue t-shirt and footy shorts, was wriggling about with its shrivelled and blackened trotters in the air, flailing.

Alisha whispered, "There must be a creature inside the body. A fox. Or a feral cat."

Helen didn't answer. She was fixated on the nearby site of her own experiment, the ground where the cadaver, a male that Stella had dubbed Bartholomew, should be resting face-down. Bartholomew was gone.

***

This can't be real, Rick thought.

With her back turned, Violet grabbed the lip of the car boot and hoisted over a leg as if preparing to descend a ladder. Her toes splayed and groped for the ground. She was climbing out. The corpse was climbing out. No, she was *alive*, she had to be. Nothing else made sense. Somehow, Violet was alive.

"Oh Jesus," Cheryl gasped. "Oh shit. Oh God."

"Fuck! Fucking *fuck*," Garcia wailed.

Both their voices sounded distant and tinny, funnelled down a pipe. Rick knew what it meant: his system was overloaded with adrenaline. That also explained the tingling in his extremities, the shaking hands, loss of peripheral vision, his laser-like focus on Violet.

Another side effect of adrenaline was overthinking.

Pointless overthinking.

Circular reflections incapable of problem-solving. Reflections that can get a police officer killed. *What's happening? I don't understand. How should I respond? I'm scared. What should I do?... What's happening? I don't understand. How should I respond? I'm scared...*

If he didn't shake off his confusion, panic would continue to paralyse him.

He had to *act*.

First, he put his hand on his gun, a Smith & Wesson M&P40, nestled in his shoulder-holster. Then he sucked in a breath of fetid air and took a couple of steps to force his legs out of their jellied state.

"Madam," he said, voice loud, stern and commanding. "My name is Detective Senior Sergeant Rick Evans. I'm from the Victorian Homicide Squad. Please stay where you are. Stay inside the boot. We need to talk. I need you to stay inside the boot while we talk. Understand?"

"Shit, oh *shit*," Cheryl moaned.

"That donor is dead," Garcia said. "Boss, she's *dead*. What the fuck?"

"Madam, stay where you are."

Violet continued to struggle backwards out of the car. Her shoulder blades, buttocks, calves and heels were fish-belly pale, the rest of her a bright and livid purple. Hypostasis. Post-mortem lividity. After death, capillaries are unable to fill with blood when under pressure. Violet must have laid supine on a hard surface, such as a floor or mattress, while her blood circulation came to a standstill and coagulated.

No, it couldn't be... *It just couldn't.*

Sweat ran from Rick's hairline. His vision pinned.

Both her feet touched ground. The blanched toes, wrinkled as if soaked in water for a long time, grasped and found purchase in the dirt. She turned. Took a hesitant, faltering step.

"Stay where you are or I'll shoot," Rick said.

He had discharged his weapon in the line of duty only once before. To defend against a man wielding a machete. A man running and slashing at people in the city. Rick had sprinted towards him and, at approximately seven metres— the minimum safe distance—aimed at the man's chest and squeezed the trigger. *Blam*. The man had survived the ambulance ride but expired in hospital. An internal investigation had absolved Rick after a gruelling pass through the wringer. But the nightmares Rick had endured, the flashbacks, the second-guessing...

Stop thinking. Stop thinking and do *something.*

Violet edged closer, slowly and with effort, shuffling her stiff legs. Dark green veins showed in her face. This whole time she hadn't blinked. Rick was sure of it.

"Stay where you are!" he shouted, and the cracking of his voice frightened him.

He stared at her in disbelief, noticing every little detail. Her breasts were long and empty as if she had recently lost a considerable amount of weight. Below her navel, a baggy roll of skin hung like an apron and obscured her bush. Perhaps she had a scar beneath that apron. Perhaps a surgical scar from a hysterectomy had contracted, pulled the skin tight as a purse-string and bisected her belly. Rick's wife had the same problem but from an emergency C-section, their third daughter, a breech birth...

What's happening? I don't understand. How should I respond? I'm scared. What should I do?... What's happening? I don't understand...

"My fucking God!" Cheryl shrieked.

The terror in that shriek jolted Rick like a slap. He unclipped his holster with trembling fingers and took out the gun, pointing it at Violet. The sight of her threatened to loosen his bladder. Maybe even his bowels.

"Stay where you are," he said. "Stay."

Like talking to a dog, he thought. That neighbour's dog when he was twelve, the pit bull—

"For Christ's sake, she's a zombie!" Cheryl cried. "Shoot her!"

A *zombie*? But how on earth—

"Come on!" Garcia yelled. "Boss, shoot the fucking zombie! Do it now!"

Absolutely nothing was preventing Garcia from using his own gun. The dumb bastard must have forgotten that he was armed too. The exact same standard-issue M&P40 in a shoulder-holster. Dumb bastard. *I ought to tell him.*

What's happening? I don't understand...

Violet shuffled closer.

A cloud of buzzing flies hovered and landed on her face. The flies ran, exploring, over her hair, cheeks and forehead. She didn't react. They ran into her mouth, disappeared inside her nostrils and ears, crawled over the surface of her open eyes. Still, she didn't react. The bile rose in Rick's throat. His finger tightened on the trigger.

BANG.

The report of gunfire echoed in shock waves. His ears rang.

The bullet had entered the middle of Violet's chest at the sternum. Bullseye. No blood. Just a clean and circular hole in the pasty flesh. So how come she was still shuffling forward? *Because she was already dead, fuckwit.* How do you kill someone that's already dead? Terror rose like a tide to overwhelm him.

"Shoot her in the head!" Cheryl yelled. "In the head!"

Garcia ran for a postie bike and threw his leg over the seat. Great idea. But even from this distance, Rick could see that Garcia's fingers were shaking too hard to twist the key in the ignition. Too much adrenaline messed with fine motor control. Rick would have to help him. But wait. Behind Garcia, through the trees: movement. Or else, scared out of his wits, Rick was imagining things. No. Was that movement? Yes. A shape, recognisably human.

"There's another one," Rick shouted. "Coming this way. Garcia. On your six."

"Fuck that. I'm getting out of here."

"Draw your gun. Draw your bloody gun."

Cheryl lunged at Rick and clawed at him, desperate, as if drowning and about to sink.

"Blow her fucking brains out!" she shrieked.

Violet.

Dear God, Violet was almost upon them. Rick aimed blindly and pulled the trigger.

The bullet rocked Violet's head back. Teetering, she held out her arms to keep balance and, for a blessed moment, he thought she would drop. But no. She straightened up. The bullet had taken off an ear. The remaining cartilage hung from a gristly thread, swinging. Flies hopped over the exposed flesh, droning and wriggling, feasting.

He fired again.

The bullet entered Violet's throat and exited the other side, smacking into the trunk of a eucalyptus tree. She paused to gulp convulsively a couple of times, then tottered forward. Rick stumbled back. Cheryl, clinging to his arm, stumbled back too.

"Help me," Garcia said. "I can't start this fucking bike."

The second zombie was now within a few metres of Garcia. Man or woman, too decayed to tell. Large, fleshy, turning black. Mouth opening and closing. Long teeth bared.

Rick fired.

Garcia ducked. "Fuck! Boss, what the fuck are you *doing*?"

"Use your gun. Behind you. Another one's behind you."

Garcia sat bolt upright and froze. Made no attempt to turn, to look at the approaching threat, to reach for his weapon. Rick knew exactly what was going through the dumb bastard's mind— *What's happening? I don't understand. How should I respond? I'm scared. What should I do?*—and staggered over, gun held at arm's length, lining up the second zombie down the barrel.

A weight lifted: Cheryl.

She'd been holding onto him, getting dragged along. She'd let go.

Rick was too busy protecting Garcia to glance back, pulling the trigger over and over, firing straight into the zombie's forehead.

The top of the skull came off in pieces, white and shiny, a broken dinnerplate. The zombie shivered and fell straight down in a messy heap. Rick exhaled in a rush. Garcia, gripping the bike's ignition key, still didn't move. Terror had fixed his expression into a rictus grin.

"You're okay," Rick said. "It's okay."

Looking past him, Garcia pointed a wavering finger. Rick's stomach dropped.

Oh no. Violet.

And Cheryl.

Where was Cheryl?

He spun around. The girl was on the ground, legs thrashing, Violet on top of her, gnawing at the girl's throat. Rick wobbled over on rubber legs and shot at the back of Violet's head. Did he miss? Perhaps he'd missed. He couldn't tell. Violet looked up at him.

He'd missed.

Shit.

Blood covered Violet's chin. She ran a forearm over her lips. Chewing, chewing, chewing—she must have taken a sizeable chunk out of Cheryl—but the meat dribbled from her mouth. Was she consuming any of it? No. The zombie was chomping her jaws in a kind of reflex action, but didn't appear to be eating.

In his peripheral vision lay Cheryl, unmoving.

Right now, he couldn't afford to look at her.

His heart banged and slammed around inside his ribcage. It occurred to him that he might be having a heart attack. At some point, his bladder had voided. The warm, damp material of his trousers stuck to his legs. Despite everything, despite this surreal fucking nightmare, he felt embarrassed. He tried to catch his breath. How much time had elapsed since he'd first heard Violet scrabbling and scratching around inside the car boot? He couldn't tell.

"Garcia," he whispered. "Garcia, are you there?"

No answer. Rick couldn't chance looking back. Violet licked her lips, bent her head towards Cheryl's prone body, and bared her teeth. There was a huge and jagged hole in the side of Cheryl's neck. An enormous puddle of blood soaked the dirt, more blood than it seemed possible for a human body to contain. Cheryl was either dead or dying, he didn't know which, but he had to help her. At least *try.*

And yet...

The gun's magazine held ten rounds. How many rounds were left? He tried to remember the sequence of events and tally his shots, but failed. Now, he was too afraid to pull the trigger again in case nothing happened. There were additional magazines and a couple of shotguns in the squad vehicle back near the main building, parked a million miles away from here, a million billion miles away.

He dropped awkwardly to one knee. Steadied his gun with both hands. Cheryl may have already died, but he didn't want to hit her by mistake. He aimed behind Violet's ruined ear, at the mastoid bone, for a guaranteed fatal shot to the brainstem. And pulled the trigger.

Dry fired.

Shit.

He pulled the trigger again and again and again, just in case, because you never know, you never know your luck in the big city. *Click, click, click.* He overcame the irrational urge to hurl the firearm to the ground. Instead, he re-holstered it. No other weapons on his person. Not even cuffs. The batons and tasers were in the squad car along with the shotguns.

"Garcia!" he yelled. "I'm out! Shoot!"

Violet was chewing on Cheryl's forearm, holding it delicately at the elbow and wrist, gnawing along in a straight line as if the limb were a corncob. Rick's stomach lurched. Cheryl's eyes were open and sightless. Good God, Cheryl Zhao was *dead*. And Rick had let it happen thanks to his indecision, his panic. And thanks to his useless greenhorn of an offsider.

"Garcia," he yelled, staggering to his feet. "Get over here. Garcia!"

No answer.

He spun around. Garcia, still sitting on the bike, was gaping open-mouthed in all directions, pointing a shaking finger—*there and there and there*—as if counting.

"Wake up, you stupid bastard," Rick said. "I need your gun."

"Boss, what are those?"

He looked where Garcia was pointing.

In half a dozen places, the leaf litter stirred, moved. Flapped. Rick groaned. What fresh hell was *this*? Were the goddamned *leaves* coming back from the dead now? Too much, he thought, feeling a maddening desire to laugh and scream at the same time.

"Boss...? Boss...? What *are* those?"

A blackened clump of leaves peeled itself from the ground and stood up on shaky, dark grey legs. No, not a clump of leaves. A raven. Dried out and flattened on one side, missing an eye, the empty socket crawling with ants. Lopsided, the dislocated beak opening and closing.

A raven.

A *dead* raven.

"No way," Rick breathed.

It cocked its ruined head to regard him with one remaining eye.

Crying out, he hurried over and stamped on it with great fury, over and over, crushing it into the dirt, cracking its skull beneath his shoe, snapping the bones in its wings, until the raven stopped moving. And then a few more stamps for good measure.

He stared around, gasping.

Some of the birds—he could recognise a few species, a magpie here, a crow over there—were too decayed to do anything more than feebly wave a tattered wing. Others were coming to life. Behind him, the sounds of Violet chewing and slurping at Cheryl's corpse brought the taste of vomit to the back of his mouth.

Charging over to Garcia, hand out, he demanded, *"Give me your fucking gun!"*

Wild-eyed in terror, Garcia fell from the bike, stumbled, straightened up, began to run into the bush, pinwheeling his arms to keep balance.

"Stop!" Rick called. "It's only me! Stop! That's an order!"

Garcia ran in the direction they had come: back towards the main building.

Rick jumped onto the postie bike and twisted the ignition key. The little motor puttered lamely into life. He was afraid the noise would draw Violet's attention. Violet, however, was preoccupied. Cheryl's ulna and radius shone through the tattered bite marks in her forearm.

"This isn't over," Rick said to Violet, who took no heed. "I'm going to kill you."

He booted the kickstand, swung the handlebars around and took off. Broken wings waved at him. He zigged and zagged, running over as many damned birds as he could, while still keeping an eye on Garcia's retreating form.

Bloody hell, that boy could *sprint*.

It occurred to him, with dismay, that he'd left behind Alexandra Wilson's file, abandoned in the dirt where Garcia had dropped it. But he couldn't go back. Wouldn't dare go back.

***

"For the record, young man," Walter said, "and since I know you're taping this conversation for 'training' purposes, I've found your customer service to be woefully inadequate and unsatisfactory. Good day." He hung up.

"Well?" Stella said. "What did the weather bureau reckon?"

"Pollen," he said, pocketing his phone.

She screwed up her nose. "Pull the other one. From what kind of plant?"

"Exactly."

Joan sighed and checked her watch. "So, that's the end of that. I've got paperwork to fill out." She began to lurch back to her office, rocking on her ruined hips.

"Will you call Helen Macauley about Butch?" Walter said to her.

Joan spun around to arch her brows. "Professor Boyce, I thought we'd already decided and agreed that 'Butch' is a disrespectful name for our donor."

"Ah yes, of course," he conceded. "Sorry. I was using a shorthand reference."

Joan pulled her face into a tight smile and shut the office door behind her.

"Oops," Stella whispered, and giggled. "Mum's a bit pissed off."

Walter rubbed his goatee. "My dear, chalk me up for another case of foot-in-mouth."

"Aw, you know what? I think 'Butch' is fine." She patted his arm. "But I'll come up with a name that passes muster for Joan, don't worry. And something that sounds like 'Butch' too. Ooh, how about 'Bruce'?"

"I'll leave it to your discretion. Now, excuse me, I have to stare down that blank page for my lecture."

"Nah, you'll be right. Give it hell."

He nodded and walked from the reception desk towards his office. Beetles, beetles, beetles. Why did his students prefer flies? How could he hook their interest? He sat at his desk and moved the computer mouse. The screensaver retreated. In its stead, the Word document with its chapter headings appeared. *Early-arrival beetles such as* Histeridae *and* Staphylinidae *that feed on fly larvae. Later-arrival beetles such as* Cleridae *and* Dermestidae *that feed on tough and dry connective tissue. Varied-diet beetles such as* Silphidae *and* Scarabaeini...

The cursor winked. The blank spaces beneath each chapter heading fatigued him.

Perhaps he ought to retire.

For a while he tapped his fingers on the desk in a repetitive, familiar beat: *shave and haircut, two bits...* Finally, he opened a drawer and took out the pack of cigarettes.

On his way to the back patio, he went into the kitchen and put the zip-lock bag of raw beef strips into his coat pocket.

Despite the smell, it was pleasant to be outside. The day was turning out to be warm. The blue sky didn't hold a single cloud. Walter lit a cigarette. The first inhalation made him cough. After some fifty years of using tobacco, he had reached that uncomfortable point where his need for nicotine outstripped his physical capacity for smoke inhalation. Hence, the cravings never entirely went away. But what to do about it? He took a deep breath and listened to the crackle of his phlegmy lungs, coughed again. Quitting seemed ridiculous at his age. After all, he had to die of something, didn't he? May as well be respiratory cancer.

Movement caught his eye.

Cookie.

Precious Cookie, swooping over for another treat. Walter's heart lightened. Dear little Cookie. One day, his kookaburra would wear a doll's straw hat and, after that, Walter wouldn't care anymore about forced retirement or even death. A hat on top of a kookaburra's head was one of the few notions that gave him joy these days. Joy was harder to come by as one got older, in his experience.

The bird landed on the banister and folded its wings with a dry rustle.

"Hello, Cookie." Walter reached into his pocket for the bag of beef. "Hungry already?"

No, wait. Walter's hand, halfway into his pocket, froze. Cookie was as still as a statue. Something was wrong. Was that *blood?*

Yes, blood. Open wounds. Exposure of underlying soft tissue.

Walter's cry of dismay came with a rise of tears. Cookie had been *attacked.* By the size and shape of the wounds: *pecked.* Other birds—those vile butcher birds, how Walter longed to wring each one of their blasted necks—must have been fighting for territory. And Cookie had lost. Oh, the poor, wretched thing.

"What have they done to you?" he whispered.

It was Walter's fault. Trying to domesticate a wild bird? Encouraging it to lose its native instincts? Its natural reticence? Insanity. And to what end? For the bird to wear a hat? Folly, such dreadful folly. Walter blinked. Hot tears coursed down his cheeks. Oh, if he'd known in advance, if he'd had even an *inkling* that this would be the outcome of his foolish errand, he would have never, not ever—

Cookie flew up and landed closer. Close enough to touch.

Walter held his breath. Dropped his cigarette.

Cookie needed comfort. That was obvious. Comfort from a trusted friend.

"Oh, Cookie," he said, chin trembling, and reached out both hands.

Slowly, gently, so as not to startle the kookaburra.

But Cookie must know his hands by now. Be familiar with their look, their smell. There was no need for Walter to be timid. The plan? Nothing fully formed as yet. Except he would take Cookie inside the building, care for the bird, maybe put it in a large plastic tub with water and food until it recovered. Did kookaburras sleep in nests? Walter had no idea. But he could find out. The information was only a google-search away.

"Cookie," he breathed. "My dearest friend. My only friend."

The placid kookaburra sat very still. Before Walter's hands could close around its body, its head slammed with the force of a hammer. Sharp pain made Walter yelp and pull away.

His hand. His left hand.

The webbing between his forefinger and thumb was gone.

Blood gushed. He closed his fist and pressed his other hand over it, squeezing both hands to his stomach. Betrayal. Oh, the betrayal hurt more than the injury. But wasn't life merely a series of betrayals? He thought of kookaburras eating snakes headfirst. They were birds designed to eat meat. Walter had never thought of himself as "meat" before. Until now.

Cookie's beak snapped a couple of times—*thock thock*— and allowed the flesh to drop.

The pale pink webbing of Walter's left hand landed on the banister in a smear of blood.

He expected Cookie to gobble it up. Instead, Cookie tipped its head and stared at Walter's ears. Nose. Cheeks. *He wants to eat me*, Walter realised. Stunned, he took a step back. Towards the door. Towards safety. His injured hand throbbed terribly.

Then he noticed something.

None of the deep peck-wounds on Cookie's body were bleeding. Why not?

Cookie lowered its head and arched its wings. A bird of prey ready to take flight. Could Walter get to the door before Cookie reached his face? Letting go of his injured hand, he reached into his pocket, into the zip-lock bag of raw beef, and threw a couple of worm-like strips as far as he could. The raw strips landed wetly on the decking.

"There," he said. "Some food for you. Scarf that instead."

Cookie glanced at the strips, then back at Walter.

"I'm going inside."

They stared at each other. Heart racing, Walter clutched his bleeding hand. Cookie unfurled and delicately extended its wings. Walter hadn't really noticed before the cruel sharpness of the beak, the size of the skull, the musculature of the thick neck, the reality that this bird—his pleasant little Cookie—was a carnivorous killing machine which struck terror into the hearts of reptiles.

He groped for the door handle.

"Goodbye for now. I'll see you later. Goodbye."

He flung open the door and tripped on the step.

Cookie dropped from the banister and swooped in a straight line. The beak yawned. For a split second, Walter saw inside it. Beyond the orange and delicately-veined tissue of the beak's lining glistened a red, gaping, wet gullet.

5

Walter slammed the door shut.

Cookie's beak clunked and bounced off the glass. The bird tumbled across the decking, dropping feathers. Then it got up on its preposterously small feet and, head lowered, gazed through the glass door with its red and beady eyes.

Gazed directly—malevolently—at Walter.

With a gasp, Walter tightened his grip on the door handle. Cookie, at a wing-fluttering run, smacked and banged and bashed itself against the glass. Over and over. In a frenzy. The door had a simple lock, the kind with a latch. Walter turned it.

Sweating and panting, he realised that he was shaking. And bleeding. Goodness gracious, he was bleeding one hell of a lot. At the very least, he would need the first aid kit.

Dazed, clasping his injured hand to his chest, Walter staggered towards the kitchen. Grabbed the first aid kit from the pantry. A quick glance down the hallway. Stella was at her desk, preoccupied. Joan's office door was still closed.

He ducked into the men's room. Put the first aid kit next to the basin. Caught his reflection in the mirror and flinched at his ashen face. Good Lord, he had aged ten years. Blood drizzled from his injured hand. He held it over the sink. *Drip, drip, drip.* Awkwardly, using his good hand, he unzipped the kit and scanned the card that listed the contents...

Plasters in various sizes. Sterile gauzes in various sizes. Bandages. Triangle bandages. Crepe rolled bandages. Elastic bandages. Dressing pads. Non-stick dressing pads.

So many choices.

Too many choices...

With a sob, he collapsed against the basin. Considered asking Stella for help. But no, no, what would bubble-headed old Stella actually *do* except become hysterical? And how would he explain the injury? Pecked by his own "pet bird" as everyone in the office so patronisingly referred to Cookie? Oh God. Oh Cookie. The attack came back to him, fresh, and Walter sobbed again. This is what happens when you pin what little joy you have in life onto a single thing. The Universe comes along, grinning wickedly, and *fucks* you with it.

Shocked at himself, Walter stood up, stopped crying, wiped his running nose.

Enough crass and childish nonsense.

He ran the tap and put his injured hand under the water. The water ran crimson. The wound gaped in a wide V-shape. Stitches were required. Damn. For now, he would patch himself up and worry about medical treatment later. He had an important lecture to write.

Using multiple paper towels, he dried his hand.

And then...

Then opened a bottle of distilled water and sprayed it into the wound. Squirted antiseptic cream. Covered the wound with a couple of non-stick dressing pads. Secured the dressing pads with plasters. Wrapped a bandage around his webbing and wrist, not too tight. Secured the bandage with adhesive tape. Contemplated the result. Good enough. Gathered the packaging and, using a paper towel, wrapped it all up and buried it at the bottom of the waste basket. He didn't want anyone to see it. Something to do with embarrassment, he assumed. With humiliation. He held his breath against the urgency of a blossoming anxiety attack. If he kept up the levels of carbon dioxide in his circulatory system, the palpitations and panic would not manifest.

He waited a while, eyes closed, steadying himself.

Now, he had to return the first aid kit to the kitchen, unseen. He zipped the kit closed. Quietly cracked the men's room door. Peered out. The coast was clear.

Thankful for his crepe-soled shoes, he sneaked into the kitchen and put the kit in the pantry. Ducked into his office. Closed the door. Dropped the zip-lock bag of beef onto his desk. Took the doll-sized straw hat out of his top pocket and threw it into a drawer. Shrugged off his blood-soaked lab coat. Stuffed it into the wastepaper bin. On the back of the door hung another coat, which he donned. Buttoning it was difficult with only one hand but he managed.

Relief, relief. He closed his eyes and exhaled. Now, he would pretend nothing had happened. His window faced the back patio. Cookie might be out there. Without looking, Walter closed the venetian blind. Switched on the overhead light and the desk lamp. Shook the computer mouse. The screensaver disappeared, replaced by his Word document. *Early-arrival beetles such as* Histeridae *and* Staphylinidae *that feed on fly larvae. Later-arrival beetles such as* Cleridae *and* Dermestidae *that feed on tough and dry connective tissue. Varied-diet beetles such as* Silphidae *and* Scarabaeini...

Walter's hand continued to throb.

But then, after a while, it didn't seem to hurt so much.

He began to type, slowly at first, pecking at the keyboard with both forefingers. Then quicker and even quicker again. Writing his lecture with ease. With *zest*. The sentences weren't particularly coherent but he'd fix that in the second draft, wouldn't he? Better something than nothing. The words poured out of him in a release, a purge, erupting like pus and corruption from a lanced boil.

***

Magnus Vestergaard sat at his tiny kitchen table, writing a list of items to purchase on his next trip into town. Toilet paper. Light bulbs. Garbage bags. Bullets. Wood glue. Treated pine plinth boards. Galvanised roofing screws. Phillips-head galvanised screws. Mesh wire. He wrote slowly and carefully, in capital letters, using a pencil on a sheet of lined paper. Magnus occupied the lone seat at the table; a canvas outdoor chair. He wore his full uniform except for his boots, which he had arranged side by side on the veranda.

The caretaker's cabin was situated at the far northern end of the VITERI site, away from other buildings for the sake of privacy. It had three rooms, which had been offered unfurnished at the time of his hiring. What little furniture there was in the cabin belonged to Magnus.

Room one: the living area and kitchenette with table and chair, stove and oven, microwave, bar-fridge, portable television, armchair. Two: a bedroom containing a king-sized bed (any smaller and his feet would hang off the mattress), freestanding wardrobe, side table with both digital and wind-up alarm clocks. Three: a bathroom with shower, compost toilet, basin, washing machine. Out the back: a two-string clothesline. There were no photographs, knick-knacks, books or magazines.

Next door to his cabin, under the same corrugated iron roof, was the work shed. It contained the equipment a caretaker would need in this environment including a range of loppers and pruners, saws, hammers, drills. Next door to the shed was a small carport that housed his quad bike and trailer.

Magnus had lived here for almost seven months.

Moving in after the previous caretaker, a drunkard named Charlie, had required much cleaning and elbow-grease. For instance, Charlie had left dried-out vomit in hidden places: crusted under the hinges of the toilet seat, around the bolts anchoring the toilet to the floor, along the tracks of the rear sliding door. And black mould had been everywhere: the shower, the windows, on the backside of the window blinds. For his first day of employment, Magnus had done nothing else but clean the cabin from top to bottom.

Cleanliness and order. Two non-negotiable dictums.

Pinned with thumbtacks to the wall behind the kitchen table were his checklists. Magnus had separate checklists for duties that he must perform daily, every second day, weekly, fortnightly, monthly, and "as required". He also had his priorities.

Number one: maintain the integrity of the fence and double-gates.

Two: maintain the solar panels that powered VITERI.

Three: perform simple grunt work such as removing fallen branches, mopping the floors of the office and bunkhouse, making minor repairs.

Every now and then, he was required to build a hutch to protect a new donor body from rodents and carrion birds. A carpenter by trade, he could turn his hand to just about anything. Plumbing, mechanics, electrics, you name it. If a job was beyond him, he was authorised to find, hire and liaise with specialist tradesmen.

Total autonomy.

He lived rent-free, had the use of a 4WD Toyota ute and a quad bike, got paid a stipend, and was generally left to his own devices. The stink of decay didn't bother him like it seemed to bother other people. The corpses didn't bother him either. He was, and always had been, a pragmatic man. Death happened, and along with it, came decay. Such is life.

Magnus worked diligently six days per week—even though he was paid for only five—and lived simply. Breakfast was bacon and eggs. Lunch four rounds of cold-meat sandwiches. Dinner a pan-fried steak or chicken breast with microwaved vegetables. For reasons he didn't understand, a few staff members and students often gifted him food. Pastries. Donuts. Chocolate bars. He would thank them and consume the treats while watching TV in the evenings. His preference was documentaries, and reality shows about buying or renovating houses. At a pinch, infomercial channels. After 8 p.m., he drank two IPA stubbies. At 10 p.m., he went to bed and set both alarm clocks for 5 a.m.

The routine suited him. It wasn't for everyone. He understood that.

He was alone and he understood that too.

He didn't have friends and preferred it that way. Most people were too needy, weak and grasping. They irritated him with their endless whining and self-pity. *Get on with things* was his philosophy. His only social contact was his elderly mother. On Sundays, he visited her at the hospice. She was thin and frail, often confused, and didn't seem to know him anymore. Lately, she called him Yngvar, his dead father's name. Magnus never corrected her. If believing herself to be chatting with Yngvar gave comfort, so be it.

Sometimes, he would even pretend to be Yngvar and reminisce with her about "their" son, Magnus. To her, Magnus was forever six years old. She enjoyed talking about Christmas. How Magnus liked the rutabaga casserole the best out of all the dishes she prepared on Christmas Eve. How Magnus behaved himself so beautifully when they visited the cemetery to pay their respects to deceased loved ones. How Magnus took his Advent Calendar seriously, and never opened one of the cardboard flaps before its due date.

Yes, yes, the fifty-three-year old Magnus would agree, stroking his mother's bony hand. *And this year, Leena,* he would say, *we must teach our little Magnus how to make the Christmas ornament, the* himmeli. An intricate decoration, a mobile, made by twisting and tying lengths of straw into geometric shapes, named after the Swedish word for *sky* or *heaven*. As a child, a teenager, Magnus used to make them by the dozen to hang over his mother's dining table. But Leena no longer remembered. *Yes*, she would say. *Yngvar, this year we will show little Magnus how to make the* himmeli. And she would nod and smile, her eyes shining. The long drive back to VITERI always helped Magnus shake off the hollow feeling of loss in the pit of his stomach.

Slowly, carefully, he continued writing his shopping list. Dust masks. 10mm rope. Baton screws. Pausing, he gazed at the ceiling and tried to remember the item that Dr Joan Kendall had requested earlier that day. Magnus closed his eyes. Aluminium foil? Washing detergent? No. It was on the tip of his tongue. Dr Kendall had even cautioned him to not forget. Garbage bags? No, he already had them on his list. He glanced out the window and saw a red kangaroo. Reds were the largest kind of roo. The most aggressive kind.

A male. It stared back at him.

The kangaroo's upright posture, high on its tiptoes and balancing with its tail, was a clear threat display. It was a big buck, nearly six feet tall and probably weighing close to two hundred pounds. Kangaroos, especially reds, were an occasional problem. The males could jump very high.

In fact, only this morning during his routine inspection of the fence, Magnus had encountered a male red caught in the razor wire. It must have been caught since the night before. For such a strong animal, its struggles were relatively feeble. Saliva ran in thick ropes from its mouth with every hoarse cry. Magnus had turned his quad bike around and headed to his cabin. From his work shed, he retrieved the .22 rifle, and went back to the kangaroo. Its flailing and thrashing made a clean head-shot unlikely. He shot it in the chest. He had intended to take a ladder this afternoon and throw the animal's body over the fence.

He stood up from the kitchen table. Planned to go next door and fetch the rifle.

The red approached. The short fur revealed bulging pectoral muscles.

And a bullet hole.

This didn't make sense to Magnus. He put down the pencil and opened the front door for a better look. No, he was not mistaken. This was the same roo. It not only had the single wound to the chest—the kill-shot that Magnus had delivered himself—but the cuts over the back legs from its entanglement in the razor wire.

"*Perkele*," he muttered.

The roo puffed out its huge chest. Stepped closer. Claws outstretched.

Magnus nodded. Okay. The dead roo was now alive? He would have to kill it again. And this time, he would do it properly.

***

Garcia stopped running at last.

The bush was all around them. Rick eased off on the throttle, coasting the postie bike to a stop within a few metres of his senior constable. He had to be careful. Psychotic episodes could happen to anyone, including police officers. Every once in a while, a crime scene was so overwhelming, so *fucked up*, that a first responder freaked out. And anyone freaking out was a potential threat. Once, some dozen years ago, Rick had witnessed, in real time, the complete mental disintegration of an ambulance officer at a particularly nasty scene involving children. The ambo had attacked everyone on site, requiring the concerted efforts of detectives, firemen and the ambo's partner to subdue him. Even so, the bloke had bitten through his own tongue.

Sanity could be a delicate thing, easily unbalanced. After so long on the job, Rick knew this very well. It came down to exposure. The more shit you saw, the greater your tolerance to seeing more shit. Every new crime scene was a booster shot against PTSD. But you had to start a rookie off *slow*. Don't swamp them with too much, too soon. They have to learn how to bend, and that means learning how to bend in their *own* way, since you can't teach someone to be psychologically resilient. And if a rookie can't figure out how to bend, they will break.

And this situation—whatever the hell *this* situation was—looked like it had broken Garcia.

Rick kept the bike's motor running just in case. Garcia still had a loaded gun. Anything was possible. The thought of riding on past and leaving Garcia to his own devices crossed Rick's mind but only for a second.

Sweat ran into his eyes. He wiped it away. Scanned the bush around him, scoping for movement. Situational awareness. He couldn't afford to let one of those dead things come within striking distance. *Shit*. Dead things somehow reanimated. *Zombies*, according to Cheryl. Unbelievable. He wasn't a religious man, but this sure ticked the boxes for the End Times or the Final Apocalypse, whatever it was called. Judgement Day. Cultist whack-jobs had finally got it right. He glanced at the sky, half expecting to see angels with flaming swords or black phantoms on horseback, but there was only the deep fathomless blue. Wait a second, where had the orange cloud gone? The cloud that had dropped those seeds—

He had to push aside these speculative thoughts. For now, he and Garcia must retreat to the main building. Plenty of time for hypothesising when they were safe behind locked doors.

"Garcia," he said, in a calm and even voice. "It's Rick Evans. Can you hear me?"

But Garcia didn't turn around.

"Hey," Rick continued. "Hey! I need you to answer me. All right? That's an order."

Slowly, stiffly, Garcia looked back.

Oh shit, his face was whiter than chalk, his eyes bugged, lips drooling. The sight gave Rick the willies, made him scared. He got angry instead.

"Pull yourself together," he snapped. "You're a detective in the Victorian Homicide Squad, remember? The best of the best. Get a bloody grip."

Garcia began shaking his head. Gently at first. Then faster. Harder. Then frantically, violently, as if he were trying to scramble his brains.

"Stop it!" Rick shouted.

Garcia obeyed. For a moment, he stood motionless. Then he pointed and stammered, "Boss, what's going on over there?"

Oh no, *no*, Rick thought. Not this again. Not the grisly reveal ushered in by the greenhorn. Screw that. Rick didn't know and he didn't want to know.

"Listen to me," he said. "Forget it. I don't care. Hop on the bike."

"Please take a look."

"For the love of Christ, Garcia, get on the bike."

"Boss, please look. Just *look*."

And so, he did. And immediately wished that he hadn't.

Bums up and heads down were three pigs and two people arranged in a tight circle. Five in all, and all were dead. Clearly dead. Blackened, blistered, oozing with greenish fluids. Fly-blown. Maggots in the ears, around the nostrils and eyes. Rick felt a sideways drift of his consciousness, a kind of swoon. He clenched his fist. The pain of fingernails spearing his palm cleared his head.

The dead pigs and people. What were they doing face down? With such concentration?

Sounds came to him next. Munching. Biting. Slurping.

They were eating. But what?

Pulling back his focus, he took in the scene, tried to assess it like the seasoned pro that he was, tried to view it dispassionately, as if it were a crime scene. *Observe the details*. Torn clothes, the remains of denim jeans and a shirt. Pair of fancy shoes, pointy toed and gore-spattered. A sheared scalp of short blonde-tipped hair discarded like a dropped sock. The pile of internal organs glistening a deep russet. Bones glowing white in contrast against the bright red of blood.

Skull, picked clean.

Rib bones wet and raw.

Twin bows of the exposed pelvis.

Long bones still holding meat, still holding the attention of the three dead pigs and two dead people, the quintet chowing down with long teeth and vacant eyes, chewing, chewing, chewing, slopping the meat inside their mouths. The only other sound was the drone of blowflies.

"Am I seeing things?" Garcia whispered. "Fuck, am I hallucinating?"

"No, mate. I can see it too."

One of the corpses, an old man, had a rotted throat hanging open. The meat he swallowed fell straight out and onto the ground, only to be snaffled up again by his greedy jaws. Again, and again. *Lather, rinse, repeat*. The woozy feeling seesawed through Rick once more. He compressed his lips. Scooted with both feet to bring the bike alongside Garcia.

"Stay very still," he said. "I'm about to reach into your jacket. Okay?"

Garcia didn't reply.

Rick took the Smith & Wesson from the holster.

In his periphery, a flurry of motion drew his eye. A dusty, crumpled raven was flying erratically towards him, beak open wide. *Fuck*. Using the side of the gun, he swatted the bird out of the air. It tumbled and skidded along in the dirt. When it came to a stop, it tried to lift off but one wing had snapped clean away. Earthbound, the bird twirled in pointless circles, scuffing at the dust with its claws, running over its own severed wing while fluttering the other, spinning around and around and around.

Mindless, Rick thought in revulsion. These…*zombies*…were completely mindless.

Sighting down his extended arm, Rick swung the gun towards the group of pigs and humans. Head shots. That's what Cheryl Zhao had advised. And it had worked on that one zombie, the blackened monstrosity that had crept up behind Garcia at the car boot as Violet had slaughtered Cheryl.

Now to identify—and eliminate—the most urgent threats.

Theoretically, the more intact the body, the more active the zombie. Rick had no hard proof of this but it seemed logical. Biology must play a significant role. A skeletonised corpse wouldn't have the soft tissue necessary to rise again, correct? Yes, that made sense. A zombie would need functional ligaments, tendons and muscles in order to move, correct? Yes, of course. Therefore, Rick would shoot the most intact zombies first in case the noise of gunfire stirred them all to attack *en masse*. Those that were physically compromised by advanced decay, like the raven, could be picked off at leisure.

The gun held ten bullets. If he aimed carefully, took his time, he could dispatch this hellish coven of five monsters in five clean shots.

In through the nose. Hold. Out through the mouth.

His finger tightened on the trigger.

And released.

Why waste ammunition?

These zombies didn't even know that Rick and Garcia existed. Why not simply ride past them? There may be greater threats lying in wait between here and the main building. Threats that might need every single one of those precious ten bullets.

Rick shoved the gun inside his belt. Tugged at Garcia's jacket sleeve. Garcia gazed about with the classic thousand-yard stare that Rick had seen time and time again with rookies that broke instead of bending. Poor dumb bastard, he thought. You should have stayed in the Missing Persons squad where you belonged. Ego got the best of you.

"Come on, mate," Rick said gently. "Get on the bike."

"Boss?"

"Yeah, it's me. Come on."

"Fuckin' hell," Garcia croaked. "Hey, this whole thing is strange. Really fucked up."

"I know. I know it is. Listen to me. Get on the bike."

Garcia's chin wobbled. "I want my mum."

"Yeah, no problem. Get on the bike, mate, and I'll take you to her."

"Promise?"

Rick glanced around, checking for the advance of any more zombies. These shitheads were so *quiet*. It came from not breathing, he realised. No lung function, no vocalisations.

"Yeah, I promise," he said. "Now, *get on the bloody bike*."

***

Frozen, dumbfounded, Helen watched the pig wriggle its bulk and shake its blackened trotters. After a while, the pig managed to roll onto its other side. With great effort—heave, heave, *heave*—the pig at last got its trotters beneath itself and stood up. Back legs first, then front legs. It wore a t-shirt and shorts, both wet with putrescence. Tossing its greenish-grey head, the pig threw off the chicken-wire cage. The small deep-set eyes fixed in the direction of Helen and Alisha.

Helen's flash of a long distant memory lasted but a split-second.

Those eyes.

Pride of place in Nana's vintage doll collection: the Pierrot clown that sat on the top shelf of the display cabinet. Its eyes were too far apart, painted on opposite sides of its face and disproportionately tiny. Just a couple of dark and fathomless dots. As a little girl, Helen had feared those eyes. Pits into another world. A scary world full of pain and danger and fear. She didn't like being near that doll. But every Saturday when Helen visited, Nana always insisted on having lunch in the front room. So, Helen always insisted on sitting where she could see the Pierrot doll. Whenever she had her back to it, her skin goose-pimpled as she imagined terrible things crawling out of those pits for eyes, miniature sets of teeth and claws and stingers, the doll clambering down from the shelf to run over and climb up Helen's clothes to press its white, shiny, painted face against hers and disgorge all of its nightmares.

After Nana died, the will specifically requested that Helen be gifted the Pierrot clown. In Nana's words, the doll had "fascinated my granddaughter who never tired of looking at it". What a joke. What a sick joke.

She declined the doll.

Her parents made her accept it.

Helen first stowed the doll under her bed. No good. At night, she could hear it clawing up the valance. The torture of waiting for the feel of cold porcelain against her skin kept her awake. Next, she put it in her wardrobe, buried and weighted by a tennis racquet covered in shoes. No good either. In the dark, she heard the wardrobe door opening, whispering over the carpet, even though the door seemed closed if she peeked over the blankets. When she couldn't stand it anymore, she hid the doll in the garage but, listening in bed, could discern the little porcelain feet clicking across the kitchen tiles, coming nearer, coming for her.

At last, she stuffed the doll into the wheelie bin, smothering it under a bag of rubbish. The next morning, a garbage truck had emptied that bin into its maw, crushing the doll inside its compacting mechanism. Helen had heard the carnage and shed tears of relief. In the interim, somehow, her parents must have forgotten about the doll since they never asked for its whereabouts. And Helen had never expected to see those eyes again.

Those eyes.

Dark and fathomless dots.

Pits into another world. A scary world full of pain and danger and fear.

This undead pig had eyes. Just. Like. That.

6

"What in Christ's name is going on?" Alisha cried.

Helen shook her head. Weak at the knees, she sat back down on the bike. Alisha stepped closer and gripped Helen's shoulder, digging her fingers into the flesh. For a time, without moving or speaking, they both watched the laborious exertions of the dead pig. It was ploughing its snout through the dirt, sniffing or licking, hard to tell which. Helen thought of pigs searching for truffles. How strange. How funny. She felt lost inside a soft and blurry dream.

Was that a noise?

Helen jolted. Her ears became super-acute. All at once, she could hear *everything*. The droning of each insect. The rattle of thousands of eucalyptus leaves stirring in the breeze. Alisha's hard, rasping breaths. And beneath those sounds, hushed and barely audible, a regular tread—*step, step, step*—which was either the blood pounding in Helen's head or the footfalls of some horror as yet unseen. In the pit of her guts, she knew what it was. Oh no, she knew, could *feel* it, as her skin crept and shrivelled.

"Bartholomew's gone," Helen said. "And now he's coming back."

"Huh?"

"Bartholomew. My human donor. He's gone."

Alisha's grip tightened painfully. Helen winced.

"Gone?" Alisha said, her voice high-pitched. "Gone *where*?"

Oh fuck, the pig took a step.

Its body shivered. A pattering of maggots fell from its nostrils. It took a couple more tentative steps towards them, buckling a little. Both trotters on the left side, having rested against the ground, were more decayed than those on the right side. A dead body walking was quite a sight, Helen mused in a disassociated kind of calm shock. Quite an education.

For instance—

A dead body doesn't respirate.

No expansion and contraction of the rib cage. No breathing noises. Interesting.

A dead body doesn't walk the same way as a live body.

Because a live body has an intact musculoskeletal system. That system, in the dead, is not intact. For example, any sac that contains liquid bursts, which affects the joint capsules. Soft tissue, including muscle, liquefies.

And a dead body does not evenly decompose from head to toe. Some places decompose quicker. *Aha*, Helen thought, as her consciousness retreated further and further away down a long and narrow tunnel. The asymmetric rate of decay explained why the pig was limping. For starters, decay depends on a wide range of factors including the size of the corpse, its fat-to-muscle ratio, the ambient temperature, moisture, aeration, climate, soil type and pH, the presence of inhibitory factors such as the positioning of the corpse, tannins, the C:N ratio—

What was that noise coming from the pig's body?

Though in a swoon, she identified it: crepitation. The crackling, snapping and creaking noises which emanate from a corpse's internal organs as they simultaneously dry out and bloat with gas. The kind of noise you might hear when pumping air into an old and tattered football that's splitting at the seams. *Crepitation.* Oh, she was used to this disquieting phenomenon with *dead* dead bodies, but not like this. Not with *animated* dead bodies. Dear Christ, not ever in a million years like *this.*

The pig staggered towards them, picking up speed.

Helen felt the bracing sting of a sharp, adrenaline-fuelled clarity.

"Let's go," she said.

Alisha's grip on her shoulder ripped away, hard enough to upset Helen's balance on the bike. She almost toppled but grabbed for the handles. Straightened up. Beside her, kicking in the dirt and leaf litter, were Alisha's sneakered feet. Helen didn't understand. Had Alisha fallen over? Helen turned her head.

And gasped.

Dry-retched.

The last time she had seen her young male donor, Bartholomew, was two days ago. He had been prone in the dirt and swollen with decomposition gases, discoloured, skin rippling with insect activity. And now…

Now he had Alisha on the ground.

Helen screamed in raw, heedless, abject terror. Bartholomew gnawed frantically at Alisha's face and throat. Alisha thrashed for a few moments and stopped. Helen screamed again. Vomit rose and she gagged, swallowing it down. She let out heaving sobs, animal sounds she didn't recognise. Dizzy, reeling, she fell off the bike.

Her first instinct was to run. She ignored that. Crawling out from beneath the bike, she shucked her knapsack, grabbed the nearest fallen bough and got to her feet. She swung the bough over and over at Bartholomew, swatting him, trying to knock him away. Those efforts didn't work. Next, she lifted the bough high in both hands and rammed it straight down onto his head. The wet, slimy flesh of his scalp parted cleanly, revealing his skull, but the injury—if it were even possible to injure a corpse—didn't interrupt his chewing. Defeated, Helen threw aside the bough, panting, quivering, shrieking.

—now what, now what, now what, now what, now what, now what, now what, now what—

"Stop it!" she yelled, and began to kick at his ribs. "Stop it! Stop it!"

Each kick rocked Bartholomew into the air but did not distract him.

"Stop it!"

Blood. So much blood.

Dear God, Alisha.

Alisha.

Helen kicked and kicked and kicked, to no end. No end. To no fucking end at all. She buckled, wanting to weep, to throw up—

Oh Christ.

The pig was closer, shambling in a lopsided gait, hindered by its blackened and decayed trotters. Its cracked lips opened to reveal long, yellow canines and incisors.

Helen backed away as it approached.

Pigs are eating machines. Offer a treat and watch a pig do anything—literally *anything*—to have it. Their teeth are strong enough to crack bone. Wild boars are known killers. But regular domestic pigs, like this one, attack humans too. Sometimes cooperatively. In an awful case she remembered, a British farmer was knocked over by one pig so the others in the pen could eat him. Starve a domestic pig for a few days and it would eat the entirety of a human being without pause, without care, no matter the previous relationship. Your placid, friendly pig—even a beloved pet, treated like a member of the family—would happily eat you alive given the right circumstances.

If there were no limits to the omnivorous appetites of a living pig, what might a dead pig do? Helen contemplated this, in the giddy and swirly slow-motion world she now inhabited.

The pig lowered its head.

Fixed her with its tiny deep-set eyes.

Charged.

Helen came to her senses. The bike lay on the ground, motor still running. Wrenching at the handles, she pulled the bike upright and managed to put it between herself and those long, yellow teeth. The jaws came together anyway, bit on some part of the bike, making a sharp grating sound like metal on metal. The pig stopped and pulled back. A handful of loose teeth stirred around inside its working mouth and dropped to the dirt.

She had injured it. The dead/alive pig had been injured.

Hope gave her ferocity and strength. Could she run over the pig with this bike? Kill it?

Fuck no, of course not. This lightweight, pissy little bike? What was she thinking? The pig must be a hundred kilos. The bike would just bounce off. Jesus, the eerie creaking and popping sounds of the pig's internal organs made Helen's hair stand on end. Her every breath made a loud *ugh, ugh, ugh* sound. She had to stop that, had to be quiet, in case she attracted more monsters hiding in the bush.

Other sounds came back to her.

The ruffle of leaves.

The buzzing of flies.

The sloppy slurping and chewing of Bartholomew nearby—

Oh my God. In the same instant, the pig appeared to notice Alisha's prone body too. Limping over, it bit into Alisha's ankle with a solid *crunch*. Terror ran up Helen's entire being from heels to head, an electric and freezing sensation. She couldn't move, couldn't breathe. Alisha's face was no longer there. Only tattered red meat and skull bones remained. Even her eyes were gone, replaced by deep pools of dark and wet gore.

Black and fathomless dots.

Pits into another world. A scary world full of pain and danger and fear.

In turn, as if in concert with each other, Bartholomew and the pig ripped and chewed at Alisha's body, tugging it this way and that. Behind Bartholomew limped a surreal handful of magpies, staggering along the ground towards them, each bird mangled, each bird dead.

Drawn by the kill, Helen realised.

Like blow flies. Attracted by the scent of warm blood.

A loud rustle of leaves and breaking twigs spun her around. Something was falling out of a nearby gum tree. Whatever it was hit the ground and bounced. A grey and furry mass. As it tried to stand up, she recognised it: a possum. Not the cute, petite and doe-eyed ringtail, a timid species, but its opposite: the brushtail. Large as a cat. Prone to aggression. When they ran over rooftiles, it sounded like full-grown men wearing hobnail boots. They made sounds in the night like devils, hissing and screeching during vicious fights over mates, over territory. Some mornings at home, Helen's back veranda would be strewn with ripped clumps of their ashy fur.

And brushtail possums ate meat.

Stirring in the leaf litter, the possum staggered upright. Most of its fur had sloughed off. It stared at her with giant, vacant eyes. Nearby ran smaller creatures, perhaps mice or rats. Dead as well. Helen had somehow left the known world and segued into another; into the underworld. Holy Christ. The gates of hell had opened up.

The flutter of nearby wings shook her from her stupor.

Birds, birds, birds. Dead birds, beaks yawning and snapping. Fuck, fuck, *fuck*.

She remembered the postie bike. Could she ride it? She'd had a riding lesson, months ago, like everyone else who worked at VITERI. But she had chosen to ride pillion ever since. As a child, she had never mastered a pushbike, couldn't seem to get a feel for its centre of balance. Oh shit, could she ride this fucking postie bike or not? Revving the throttle, she jumped on and took off, wobbling. Each tree, each shrub, was a threat. Nightmarish monsters hid behind them all, waiting to pounce. Her breath came and went in dry, puking gasps.

Alisha.

Oh my God. Alisha.

What the fuck is happening here?

For a few moments, her mind emptied by intense fear, Helen had no idea where she was going. Then reality came flooding back.

The closest point of refuge was the caretaker's cabin.

Please God, let Magnus be there.

Magnus, tall and heavily built, stoic, *emotionless*, would know exactly what to do, would know how to handle this situation without panic, without fear or hesitation.

And if he wasn't at his cabin, she would break into his shed and arm herself with whatever tools she could fucking well find. Please God, a chainsaw. There must be a chainsaw.

***

Sweating, chilled, Walter leaned back in his chair and contemplated the ceiling. There were dead bugs inside the light fixture. He would have to tell Magnus. The bugs must have crawled inside the fixture, attracted by its illumination and then, trapped, starved to death. The poor chaps. Poor bugs. Dead bugs. Desiccated and dead bugs.

What kind? Could he tell from their silhouettes?

He squinted. Perhaps alderflies. Lacewings. Mosquitoes.

Arthropoda. Making up sixty-five per cent of known species on Earth. Able to thrive in every conceivable type of habitat whether land, sea or air. Vital to the food chain, each individual ecosystem utterly dependent. Without the phylum of *Arthropoda*—insects, crustaceans, myriapods, spiders—life on this planet would cease. The sudden, overwhelming rush of love and gratitude for these remarkable creatures brought tears to his eyes.

Arthropoda. The backbone of his existence. The one through-line from his childhood to old age, and which would no doubt continue well into his feeble dotage. Sixty years, so far, of devotion. Unfailing, unfaltering and loyal devotion. And if dear Aunt Flora had not bought the young Walter Boyce that ant farm for his tenth birthday, what would have become of him? He wiped away a tear. Felt a moment of warm nostalgia.

He had been disappointed with the mysterious contraption at first, not realising what it was. A flat, glass box. How dreary. *You love creepy critters so much, I thought you might like to raise your own colony of ants*, Aunt Flora had said. *My own colony?* he had replied. And even now, all these years later, he could recall the rapturous swell of fascination and curiosity that had filled his breast at the idea. His very own colony...

And how he had loved that ant farm. Watching the industrious little souls toiling away within the dirt and digging their tunnels, creating an intricate maze, interacting with each other, cooperating with each other...

After that, he had got a worm farm. A stick-insect kit. Butterfly nets and boxes...

Walter passed a trembling hand across his eyes.

The lecture. He must stop reminiscing and procrastinating and attend to his lecture.

Sitting up, he focused on the bright, glaring white screen of his computer monitor. Focused on his notes. The black letters seemed to move and crawl, bug-like. He rubbed at his watering eyes, leaned in and read the most recent paragraph:

> Generally speaking, beetles share a similar life cycle to flies. Beetles are just as interesting as flies. Anyone who thinks otherwise is not a true entomologist at heart. All beetles have egg, larval, pupal and adult stages, although the range of instars for larval beetles can span from two to sixteen, unlike flies. To reiterate, the beetle larval stage is complex and intricate, which is the complete biological opposite of the typical fly larval stage. Why do you like flies more than beetles? Beetles are unappreciated. Old people are unappreciated. Retire, retire, retire. Life cycle of a career: growth, exploration, establishment, maintenance, decline.

Professor Walter Boyce is in decline. Deputy Vice-Chancellor Professor Gail Herman knows he is in decline. She will force him out. I will force him out. Walter, I am forcing you out.

Flinching, shocked, Walter pushed back from the desk with both feet. The casters of his chair squeaked over the linoleum. The chair hit the wall. He put a hand over his face, realised that he was shaking. How had those vile words got onto the page?

There was only one explanation.

Gail Herman had hijacked his lecture notes.

No, impossible. Perhaps he was mistaken. Perhaps he had misread the paragraph. Cautiously, he reached out, gripped the desk, pulled his chair closer. Stared at the monitor. At the awful words.

Walter, I am forcing you out.

He had the wildest idea that she was watching his reaction through the miniature camera atop the monitor. With a cry of alarm, he jumped from his chair and out of view.

At least Gail Herman couldn't see him now.

Clearly, this was some kind of remote interference. But via what sort of mechanism? His mind raced. Herman, at her office in Fraser University, must have found some way to hack into his hard drive. The university computers shared a mainframe, didn't they? Or a central hub? Whatever it was called... For goodness sakes, he didn't know the terminology of this blasted new-fangled stuff, didn't know how it worked, but Fraser University and VITERI had a shared network, didn't they? Yes, yes. And if Herman had the requisite computer skills—like Kieran Pocock—she could inveigle herself down the wires, creep along the silk of this shared web, insert her venom onto Walter's page and poison him.

"You bitch," he said, eyes filling with fresh tears. "You utter, irredeemable bitch."

He had an intense desire to smash the monitor. But no, no... Be calm, he told himself. Kieran would help him. Kieran would know how to block Gail Herman.

Walter flung open his door and hastened to Kieran's office. Pulled up, shocked, in the doorway. Empty. The office was empty. For a moment, he didn't know what to do.

"Walter?" Stella called out. "Everything okay, mate?"

He turned. She was at her desk, surrounded by CCTV monitors, about a dozen of them. Every day, she sat there and spied on the VITERI complex. She stood up, bangles clashing and jangling, and the noise scraped on his nerves.

"Walter?"

He had no choice but to reply. Otherwise, she would hound him. "I'm looking for Kieran."

"At the bunkhouse pinching low-fat milk." She glanced at her watch. "Actually, he's been gone a while. Is there anything I can do for you?"

A nosy parker. Stella Vasilakis was the absolute living embodiment of a nosy parker. Forever talking, gossiping, questioning—

"Good God!" she cried, raising both palms to her cheeks in that flamboyant, ridiculous way of hers, how she loved to over-react to every little thing. "What happened to your hand?"

"Oh? I'm not sure what you... Sorry, to my...?"

"*Hand.* Walter, you've got bandages all over it. What the frick happened?"

Confused, he lifted both arms and gazed at them. His left hand was indeed bandaged. Stella loomed at his side. He jumped. How had she sneaked up on him like that? So quietly, so quickly? He narrowed his eyes and stepped back.

"Walter, jeez, you don't look right."

"I'm fine."

"Sweetie, have you got a fever?" she said, and reached for his forehead.

Ducking away, he said, "I told you, I'm *fine*."

She blinked at him, owlishly, her eyes magnified by those ridiculous blue-framed glasses, her mouth open and downturned and working *oh-oh-oh* as if aghast. Well, well, so he had hurt her feelings. But if Stella chose to wear her heart on her sleeve, then she must expect that her feelings would get hurt from time to time. She *allowed* them to get hurt. Perhaps she was feigning hurt in order to manipulate him. Women did that all the time, didn't they? Lied to men. Lied and wheedled to get their own way.

"What happened to your hand?" she said.

For a moment, he couldn't remember. Images flickered at the edges of his mind. Brown wings. A flurry of brown wings. Oh no, it came back in a crushing tide. *Cookie.* His dearest friend, Cookie. The attack. The betrayal. His throat ached with the sudden need to sob.

"Oh, Walter," she murmured, and touched him on the arm.

He flinched and steeled himself. "Piffle. I cut myself."

"Cut yourself how?"

"With scissors. You see?" He took the large pair of scissors from his pocket and held them up. The sight surprised him. Odd. He couldn't remember taking any scissors out of a desk drawer. When had he put them in his pocket? While typing his lecture?

Oh, heck, *his lecture.*

"I have to get back to work," he said, and turning on his heel, marched down the hallway.

"Are you sure you're not sick?"

He reached his office. "Good day, Stella."

"Walter, are you feeling—?"

"Good day!"

He closed his office door and leaned against it. Caught his breath. Edged towards his chair. Sat down. Rolled the chair closer to the desk but offside, so that Gail Herman couldn't get a good look at him. He hung both forefingers over the keyboard, preparing to type. Couldn't recall his writerly train of thought. As a prompt, he read over the last paragraph:

Professor Walter Boyce is in decline. Deputy Vice-Chancellor Professor Gail Herman knows he is in decline. She will force him out. I will force him out. Walter, I am forcing you out. Pack up your shit, old man, I'm booting your arse through the fucking door and don't you ever come back or I will do everything in my considerable power to fuck your shit up—

Yelping, Walter leapt to his feet.

"Knock knock."

Oh no. Stella was on the other side of the door, wanting in. Clamouring at him, suffocating him. The spikes of an impending anxiety attack jabbed into his chest, closing his throat as if he were trying to respirate underwater. For a moment, he felt light-headed.

"I'm busy," he shouted, choking on the words.

"Walter? Mate, I'm worried about you."

He pinched at the bridge of his nose. These thoughts, these crazy thoughts...he had to get a hold of himself. If he didn't... With determination, he held his breath to ramp up the carbon dioxide in his blood and stop the anxiety attack from blooming. Stella, his close friend Stella. She had never done anything bad to him. Then why the animosity? Why feel this way, act this way? He didn't know and it frightened him.

"Stella, please," he croaked. "Please come in."

The door cracked. Stella looked around, brought her hand to her mouth with a startled gasp, and hurried over to him. He fought the urge to weep as she helped him into his chair.

"What's wrong?" she said, patting at his head as if he were a child. "What's up?"

In response, he pointed at the monitor, touching his forefinger against it, pulling away quickly as if the surface burned.

"Please read that paragraph aloud," he said.

She blinked at him, confused. "Read the paragraph?"

"Aloud. If you wouldn't mind."

She nodded, put a hand on his shoulder. "Generally speaking," she recited, "beetles share a similar life cycle to flies. All beetles have egg, larval, pupal and adult stages, although the range of instars for larval beetles can span from two to sixteen, unlike flies. To reiterate, the beetle larval stage is complex and intricate, which is the complete biological opposite of the typical fly larval stage." Then she stopped.

He gestured impatiently. "And the rest."

"But sweetie, that's the whole paragraph."

Spooked, he opened his eyes, leaned towards the monitor and scanned the words. A cold shiver moved through him.

"I don't understand," he stammered. "It was there just a moment ago..."

"*What* was there?"

He opened his mouth to answer, shut it again, and shook his head. "Nothing, nothing."

"Are you having another migraine?"

Migraine… Yes, that must be the explanation. They happened occasionally. Painless, usually presenting with the loss of his central vision and an inability to articulate thoughts into words. He gripped Stella's wrist, sobbed once, nodded.

"I'll get you some painkillers," she said. "Don't worry, I'll be just a minute."

She fled from the room, her jacket flowing, her bangles clattering and ringing. He put his head in his hands. Peeked through his fingers. At the lecture notes. Which should be benign and normal. Hadn't Stella proved them to be benign and normal?

> Pack up your shit, old man, I'm booting your arse through the fucking door and don't you ever come back or I will do everything in my considerable power to fuck your shit up six ways from Sunday, you doddering senile over-the-hill bastard—

With a moan, he clamped his palms tight over his face. Dear God, what was happening to him? What was going on?

Stella raced back into his office.

"Give me your hand," she said. "The one that isn't hurt."

She pressed four capsules into his grip.

He said, "The usual dosage is two."

"I know but this is an emergency."

Tearing up, he put the capsules on his tongue. They tasted different from usual. Bitter, astringent. The smooth texture provoked his gag reflex. She gave him the glass of water. He took a sip, baulked, held onto the whole lot inside his mouth. The first instinct that struck him was to spit. Poison, he thought. *Gasoline.* Saliva flooded his mouth. His stomach cramped. Any second now, he would vomit.

"Walter, take the pills," she urged. "Hurry up."

He obeyed and swallowed. The water scorched like acid. The capsules scraped down his gullet, four alien and foreign objects, contaminating him. He winced and grimaced.

"Maybe you ought to lie down," she said, hand on his forehead. "You're burning up. Come on, let me walk you to the bunkhouse. You need to relax, be in a dark room for a while. A nap would do you good."

He shook his head. "My lecture," he whispered. "I have to finish my lecture."

The problem being he couldn't quite remember what the lecture was about anymore. Something pertaining to an ant farm. To the act of burrowing. Working in tandem. Dirt.

"You know what?" Stella said. "I ought to call an ambulance. This could be a stroke."

He forced out a chuckle. "Oh, it's nothing as serious as that. Let's give it twenty minutes or so before we hit panic stations. The painkillers will do the trick by then. Now, if you wouldn't mind…" He gestured vaguely at the door. "Work calls."

"Really?" she said, looking doubtful. "Are you sure?"

"Completely."

"Well…I'm keeping your door open. No arguments."

"Of course."

"So that I can see you from my desk."

"I understand entirely."

She hesitated at the doorway. "I should tell Joan."

"Pshaw. I've a bad headache, nothing more. And besides, Joan is filling out the paperwork for Butch. There's so much of it. She's not to be disturbed. In fact, she *hates* to be disturbed."

Stella bit at her lip. "Okay, I guess. Give us a hoi if you need anything."

He managed a salute. The smile she gave in return was fake.

Irritation tightened his jaw. *Damn you.* Leave me alone, he thought. For once in your stupid moronic life, woman, mind your own business.

7

Magnus put his hands on his hips and regarded the kangaroo.

"Friend, what does this mean?" he said. "I put you out of your misery this morning."

The kangaroo worked its jaws, as if chewing on something. Took a couple of hops closer.

Magnus tensed. Red kangaroos are dangerous. They have claws, a killer instinct, and two lethal manoeuvres: either grasping you in a chokehold with the front paws, or leaning back on the tail and kicking the hind legs to disembowel you.

"Which will you try with me?" Magnus said, first in English, next in Finnish.

The roo kept staring and chewing. The bullet hole in its chest wasn't bleeding. Its ribcage wasn't rising or falling. Magnus knew he should feel afraid, but instead, he felt determined. His pulse was steady, mind clear. He must kill this animal for a second time. Like it or not.

Adjacent to his cabin and beneath the same roof was the work shed. And locked inside the shed, a .22 rifle. He had the key to the shed in his pocket. Just standing here was achieving nothing. On the other hand, a red kangaroo could leap far. When travelling at speed, a single bound could cover seven metres. If the roo meant to attack, Magnus might not have time to reach the work shed before the animal was upon him.

What then?

Retreat indoors and hide like a child? No. Therefore, if he couldn't reach the shed in time, he would battle the roo with his bare hands.

Never in his life had he been in a physical fight. His height and build intimidated others, and had done so all the way back to his school days. For example, on the rare occasion when a fellow pupil had given him stick, Magnus had simply to take off his wristwatch. And without fail, by the time he pocketed his watch and rolled up his shirtsleeves, the aggressive pupil, cowed, had stood down. Perhaps this kangaroo would also be cowed.

Magnus hoped this would be so.

He took off his watch and put it in his pocket. Rolled up his sleeves. Stood to his full and considerable height. Broadened his shoulders. The roo, staggering as if dizzy, adjusted its stance. Good, Magnus thought. It's having second thoughts.

But then it recovered. Lifted the ribcage and flexed, popping the muscles in its wide chest. Magnus pondered the bullet hole in its breast and decided to make sense of that on another day. The roo scratched at its stomach. Magnus nodded at the threat display.

"I killed you once," he said. "And I'm prepared to kill you again."

Should he try putting on his boots first? No. He would have to kneel to lace them up, and didn't want to put himself in a vulnerable position. Shoeless, in his socks, Magnus left his doorway and began to tread the veranda. He didn't reach the shed. The roo jumped and landed right next to him.

"*Vittuperkele!*" Magnus shouted.

Dust filmed its blank eyes. Blowflies twitched and buzzed in and out of its ears. Ants roamed over its nose. These sights took Magnus aback. Shiny claws slashed near his face. He ducked. His next instinct was to punch. In his youth, Magnus had boxed. Not for sport, but for the purposes of physical fitness; working the speed ball or the heavy bag, punching into his trainer's gloves. His trainer had urged him to compete. Magnus had had no desire. He abhorred violence and didn't wish to inflict it onto another living soul.

Except, this kangaroo was no longer living.

The roo had its jaw jutted. Magnus swung a right-hook and rapped the chin with a solid *thump*. The roo's head snapped sideways at the impact. Magnus's knuckles rang.

The animal rallied. Lashed out.

Magnus ducked again, lifted both arms, fists clenched. He put one foot behind the other, weight on his front leg. *Protect your face*, his trainer had insisted at every lesson. *Left hand at your left cheek in defence*. Automatically, Magnus obeyed these decade's old instructions, even as the dead kangaroo lunged at him. And he punched. Again, and again.

Jab. Cross. Hook. Uppercut. Even overhand once the roo tumbled off the veranda.

Magnus followed up with a kick to knock the animal off balance. It floundered in the dirt, a scramble of ungainly limbs and thrashing tail.

He had time to reach and unlock the shed door, swing it outwards and get one foot over the threshold before the roo bounded in one stride and struck out with both hind legs. The impact slammed the door shut against Magnus's back, knocking him forward. He fell over the wheelbarrow. His knee and elbow struck the concrete floor. The pain was sharp and intense. For a moment, he thought he may have broken both joints.

The roo battered at the door. However, since the door opened outwards, the roo could not gain access. Unless it could kick its way through, which Magnus doubted.

With a grunt, he got to his feet and righted the wheelbarrow. Carefully, he flexed his arm, bent and straightened his leg. Nothing seemed to be broken.

The small window at the rear of the shed never permitted much light. As was his habit, Magnus clicked the light switch. A bank of three fluorescent tubes blinked on overhead.

He kept the rifle in a freestanding metal locker secured with a stainless-steel combination padlock. The four-digit combination was 1404—14th of April, his mother's birthday. The wooden stock of the gun felt smooth and warm in his palm. He crossed to the workbench. The roo's hammering blows on the door continued unabated. He kept the loaded magazines on a particular shelf, the highest one. He had to stand on tiptoes and reach up. Anyone shorter than

Magnus—and he stood just shy of 6 foot 7—would require a stepladder to even see the magazines, let alone reach them.

He selected a magazine. Pulled back on the .22's bolt to open the breech. Slid the magazine in place. Closed the breech. Through his hands, he felt the firm *snick* of the bolt as it stripped a round from the magazine. The rifle was ready to fire.

Now, he had to figure a way to exit the shed.

The roo's feet smashed at the door in regular intervals, roughly every four seconds. He could picture the animal in his mind: leaning back on its tail and thrusting its hind legs forward, BANG, regaining its footing to try again. He glanced at the only window in the work shed. Too small to fit through. Even for a normal-sized person.

What would be the best course of action?

He could wait until the roo gave up and went away. No, he decided. Other staff members were on the VITERI grounds. And if one of them happened to encounter this dangerous roo? It was unlikely—the grounds sprawled over one-hundred-and-fifty acres—but no one else was armed. They would get hurt, perhaps killed. His *duty* was to kill this animal.

Shooting through the door was a possibility. However, it was solid core. The bullet may deflect and ricochet instead of penetrate. He didn't know enough about guns to know for sure. Besides, until he had figured out why the roo had come back to life, he didn't want to waste ammunition. How many bullets would it take to kill an animal that was already dead?

At that thought, he reached up to the shelf again and pocketed the last loaded magazine. The rest were empty. Bullets were on his shopping list, which was sitting abandoned at his kitchen table. He had planned to go shopping today. He would have bought a fifty-pack box of bullets. That much ammunition would have come in handy. Bad luck.

So, he had two magazines and that was it. No point dwelling on a factor he couldn't change. Back to the immediate problem: exiting the work shed. The easiest option would be to behave like an enraged male red roo, and issue a direct challenge.

He kicked the door.

Careful to use his heel, since he wore socks without boots. And gently, since the door was unlatched. He had no desire to admit the roo into the close confines of the work shed.

The roo's assault stopped.

Magnus kicked the door again. It juddered open, creaking on its hinges. He waited. Nothing. The roo did not kick in return. Perhaps it had moved back from the doorway, cautious now, expectant. Magnus listened carefully. Could hear nothing. Had no idea where the roo might be. This was a clear disadvantage. Nonetheless, he would shoulder the rifle, remove the safety, put his finger on the trigger, exit the shed and fire on the kangaroo.

Yes. It was a good plan.

Only if he managed to hit the animal. If he missed, he would need to reload, which would take a few seconds. And the roo could disembowel him by then if it were so inclined. No, he couldn't afford to miss. But how many times had he shot this rifle? A dozen times? Not enough. He was an amateur. The question remained: how many bullets to kill an animal that was already dead?

With a sniff, he pushed the question aside. What was its purpose if he didn't know the answer and could therefore not predict the outcome? He frowned. Alert but not afraid. Grateful for the stalwart constitution he had inherited from Yngvar and Leena.

He approached the door, hesitated for an instant.

A fleeting memory came back.

As a young man, hiking and camping through a wood in his home town of Kajaani, he had once stumbled across a brown bear. They were a few feet away from each other. The bear looked surprised too. Magnus hadn't worn bear bells—the animal should have been hibernating by that time of year—and had moments to decide what to do. Run? Bawl and roar? Retreat while bawling and roaring? Instead, a strange thing happened to Magnus. A focused sensation of calm drained the tension in his body, allowed the breath to sigh out in a slow and steady stream from his open mouth. He spoke to the bear in low, even tones: *I'm pleased to meet you. Friend, I'm taking a walk and mean you no harm.* The bear had grunted, wrinkled its nose, and loped away.

Ever since that day, after learning that it wasn't in his constitution to panic, Magnus had felt...blessed. Secure in his ability to face life's challenges head on without blinking first.

He put the stock of the .22 to his shoulder. Relaxed and exhaled. His pulse beat calm and steady. All he needed to do was kick open the door, sight the roo, and fire.

On my mark, he thought. *One, two—*

The puttering whine of a little motor came to his attention and froze him. One of the VITERI motorbikes. At full throttle. Someone from the facility was heading towards his cabin. Heading towards the dead and vicious kangaroo. No, no, *no—*

"Magnus!" a female voice yelled. "Help me! Magnus!"

He didn't recognise the voice.

"Oh, fuck!" the voice screamed in an even higher pitch, the motorbike's brakes squealing. "What the *fuck* is *that*? What the fuck *is* that?"

She must have seen the roo. Even now, it was most likely turning on her, ready to attack.

Magnus kicked open the door.

In an instant, he took in the scene. The graduate student, a girl called Helen Macauley, dressed in the full hazmat suit and astride the motorbike, her mouth issuing a shrill and full-throated scream. The dead roo watching her, flexing its tail on the ground, elbows out as it scratched its belly furiously, preparing to attack.

Magnus pulled the trigger.

The report of the .22 hurt his eardrums. A concentrated circle of red fur between the roo's shoulder blades tufted out momentarily with the impact of the direct hit. The roo faltered. Magnus expected the roo to drop. Hoped it would drop. But no. The roo straightened up. *How many bullets would it take to kill an animal that was already dead?*

Helen motored towards the cabin.

"Get back," Magnus said, swinging an arm. "Get out of my line of fire."

"Shoot its brains out," Helen yelled, starting to steer the bike in a clumsy arc.

"I'm shooting it already," he explained.

He reloaded, shot again. The bullet thumped into the roo's side. The roo faced him.

Helen dropped the bike and scrambled onto the veranda. "In the head! Shoot the fucking thing in the *head*!"

He pulled the trigger just as the roo darted away, as if startled. His bullet went wide and missed. *Pahuksen.* The roo vanished into the bush with a few long leaps, obscured within seconds by trees and shrubs. He had to follow it. He had to follow it and kill it—

But Helen clutched desperately at his arm.

"Thank Christ you're here. Oh, thank Christ," she whimpered.

Red stains smeared her hazmat suit. Great swathes of it.

"Are you hurt?" he said. "The blood—"

"Not mine."

Horrified, Magnus pointed behind her into the scrub. "What have you brought with you?"

Her eyes widened. She moved her eyes first and then, very slowly, her head.

The devil's menagerie. Crows, magpies, ravens, possums, rats—and was that a wombat?— hobbled along the ground, so many broken tiny creatures, all of them making a beeline for the cabin. Tattered birds dropped from the trees. Some dropped like rocks. Others fluttered a short way and fell.

The breeze lifted. Brought the concentrated scent of death. Next came the sound of droning flies. A cloud of them buzzed over the approaching mass of fiendish creatures.

"What in God's name does this mean?" he murmured.

"Alisha's dead. My cadaver killed Alisha. Bartholomew killed her right in front of me."

"Your cadaver—?"

"Bartholomew. Don't you remember him?"

Magnus's heart tripped over itself. Yes, he remembered Bartholomew. Remembered building the young man's chicken-wire cage. Remembered helping to lay him out on the ground next to a pig that wore a pair of shorts and a t-shirt. Remembered Alisha too; an Indian girl with long hair. On occasion, she used to bring him a kind of slice made of milk and nuts. Unsure of how to eat it and not wishing to ask in case his ignorance caused offence, he would heat the dessert in the microwave and top it with prune jam. Pleasant enough for a pudding, yes, but with a strange texture. Alisha was a nice girl. But now she was dead? Astonishing. Murdered by a *donor*?

The expired menagerie came closer.

With shock, he understood the imminent danger. He grabbed Helen's arm.

"Quick," he said, and dragged her into the shed.

He closed the door. Helen swiped off the hazmat hood, revealing her sweat-soaked hair. She put both hands to her head, leaned over, screamed through her teeth, straightened up, and began to pace. Stopped. Repeated the ritual from the top. Then again. Over and over.

At last, she stood still and said, "We've got to destroy these motherfuckers."

"Yes. Agreed. First, explain what's going on."

"The dead are coming back to life."

"But how?"

She barked out a single laugh. "I don't fucking *know*. Because they're zombies."

"Zombies?"

"Yeah, like in the movies."

He considered for a moment, and shook his head.

She dropped her arms, rubbed her forehead. "Oh, for God's sake..."

Magnus put the rifle on the work bench and sat on the stool, trying to calm himself. Outside, the shuffling and scratching of the menagerie sounded on the wooden boards of the veranda. *Things* knocked at the door. Helen gaped at the door in terror.

"It opens outwards," Magnus said. "They can't get in."

"So, we're safe?"

"For the time being."

"Okay, wow. Shit. Holy fucking shit. We need help. Have you got a phone?"

He sighed. "Next door in my cabin."

"Is there a way into your cabin from here?"

"No. Only from the outside. Along the veranda."

"Fuck. My phone's in my knapsack. I lost it when Bartholomew...when Alisha... Oh *Christ*, when Alisha..."

Helen seemed close to tears. Tears wouldn't help.

Magnus didn't know this graduate student very well. They had interacted two, maybe three times. She had seemed efficient, matter-of-fact, the owner of a strong stomach. No doubt she would return to this state once she had processed the initial shock of Alisha's death. He could only hope. The last thing he needed was a distraught liability when everyone on the VITERI staff could be in imminent peril, needing assistance. If Helen couldn't take control of herself, he would leave her here, lock her inside the work shed. He made up his mind to do just that if she didn't pull herself together within the next five minutes.

"Stop," Magnus ordered. "Tell me. Is every dead thing in VITERI coming to life?"

"I don't know. How the hell should I know?"

"Because you are a forensic scientist. You study death."

"Yeah, but this is...fuck, this is...I don't know *what* this is, some sort of..."

Helen let out a see-sawing, hysterical kind of laugh. Magnus got up and offered her the stool. She didn't sit down. Instead, she began pacing again.

"Please," he said gently. "Keep still. Tell me. What's going on?"

She was staring at the door. Listening to the hellish scratching and scraping. Magnus frowned. She wouldn't think like a scientist again until she was away from those sounds. He steered her by the arm to the rear of the work shed and pushed her against the window.

Blanching, she squawked, quailed.

Damn, I've frightened her, Magnus thought in resignation. He let go. Stepped back.

The weak October sun beat through the pane. The clothesline stood beyond the glass. His jocks, socks and t-shirts hung in rows. Beyond the clothesline grew a stand of wattle trees. The window, like an ordinary snapshot, showed a commonplace world.

Tears spilled down Helen's cheeks and off her chin. *Drip, drip, drip*. She ignored the tears as if unaware. Such disassociation was troubling.

Reminded him of his mother.

At the nursing home, at this hour, Leena would be eating lime-green jelly for afternoon tea. Spooned into her mouth by an untrained, underpaid, uncaring staff member. He had threatened all the staff members one day. That time he had found bruises on his mother's face and wrist. He had flexed on the staff and bellowed, *Treat my mother right or deal with me*. The manager had declined to call the police. Decided instead to cool Magnus down with reassuring words, by showing him the many CCTV cameras throughout the facility, the nursing log-books, the security. Had Magnus's show of bravado helped? Or hindered? Magnus didn't know. One couldn't tell. Hindsight was everything. When it was too late, hindsight revealed the truth of how you had won or lost. At life's crossroads, you unwittingly took the right or wrong path without any way of telling which was which.

"Helen," he said. "An educated guess. Why are the dead coming back to life?"

"For fuck's sake," she whispered. "I'm not a horror fan, okay? I prefer action films."

"A fan? How does that—"

"You watch movies, right?"

"No."

"What about books? You read books? Novels?" When he didn't answer, she crossed her arms and said, "You know what a zombie is, right?"

"Yes." After a moment, he added, "Zombie is a type of marijuana. You believe the dead have been exposed to it? A bad batch?"

"Oh Jesus, I'm not talking about *grass*."

"Then what are you talking about?"

Helen stalked in circles. Magnus waited, perplexed. He should lock her inside the shed.

Finally, she faced him and said, "Zombies are fictitious monsters like werewolves or vampires. You know, like Count Dracula? Please tell me you've heard of Dracula."

"Yes, but I don't understand. Fictitious? You mean pretend?"

"Yeah. Pretend. Zombies are the dead reanimated, caused by who-the-fuck knows what. Take your pick. A virus, an infection, a type of plague. A man-made pathogen. Something from outer space. Or something supernatural. The gates of Hell opening up, I don't know, it could be anything. Fuck, sometimes there *is* no reason."

Magnus shook his head. "The dead coming back for no reason? That doesn't make sense."

"That's right. It doesn't. And yet, here we are."

"Yes. Here we are." He studied his hands. Large, callused, strong. "How does one kill a zombie?"

"By destroying its brain."

"Yet the brain is already destroyed. From lack of oxygen. And after that, from rot."

"Hey, I didn't make the fucking *rules*," she said. "For all I know, this shit is something else, but it seems like the fucking zombie apocalypse to me, okay? I'll operate on that assumption until proven otherwise. Are you satisfied? Have I answered your question?"

He waited quietly. She went back to pacing. The dead animals scraped at the door.

"How many cadavers are there on the property?" he said.

Helen's voice sounded flat and exhausted. "I don't know the exact number."

"An estimate."

She ran a hand over her sweating face. "There's ten zones of about fifteen acres each."

"Go on."

"In each zone about four humans, give or take, and eight or nine pigs."

"If that's so," Magnus said, "and if every cadaver has come to life, then VITERI has at least forty human and eighty pig zombies. For a total of one-hundred-and-twenty. Does that sound correct?"

"Oh, Jesus…"

"Does that sound correct to you?"

"Yeah. And the wild animals that happened to die inside the fence-line...?" She scrubbed at her forehead and laughed wildly. "Oh shit, it's the Rapture gone wrong. Don't you reckon? The dead getting up but nobody rising to heaven."

Vaguely, Magnus knew about the Rapture. It had something to do with Christianity.

Helen, trembling, looked like she was ready to fall down. Magnus rolled the stool across the floor and helped her to sit down. He watched as she panted, scrubbed her fingertips over her forehead and eyes, made choked, whimpering sounds.

He assessed her. Help or hindrance?

Definitely hindrance.

He put a hand on her shoulder. "I'm leaving," he said. "To assist the others at the office. They don't have weapons. No way to fight. If they get hurt, it'll be on my conscience."

She ran the back of hand beneath her sniffling nose and looked up. "Okay, I'm in."

"What?"

"I'm coming with you."

He shook his head. "I'll get you when this is over. You're in no state—"

She stood up, wet eyes flashing. "I'm in the absolute *best* fucking state."

"You need to be calm—"

"I need to be angry! Those fuckers killed my *friend*! Right in front of me! You think I'm going to *sit* here and *hide* while more people die? They're my colleagues! My lecturers, for Christ's sake!" She struggled with the zipper on her hazmat suit. "Shit, I've got to take this fucking thing off first. I'm sweating like a bitch."

"The suit might offer protection—"

"Nope. My cadaver and the pig bit straight through Alisha's suit."

Helen shucked the plastic hazmat and threw it aside. She wore a long-sleeved t-shirt and jeans soaked in sweat. Face pale and clammy. Eyes crazed.

"No," he said. "Stay here."

"Fuck that," she said, and gripped his forearm with great strength in her small fingers, hard enough to hurt. "How many bullets have you got for that rifle?"

"Not enough."

"We'll conserve them. Be creative instead. You got a chainsaw?"

He shook his head. "Broken. In the shop."

"Fuck. What about a whipper-snipper? You know, a weed-whacker?" She stamped her foot and pointed. "What do you call that thing over there?"

Magnus glanced towards the corner of the shed. The hand-held line trimmer had a long plastic filament instead of a blade. When activated, the filament span at great speed, designed to instantly chop weeds and grass into mulch.

"We'll kill the little bastards on your veranda with the whipper-snipper," Helen said.

Yes, that filament would slice through birds and rats. Helen's ingenuity, her *ferocity*, lifted Magnus's spirits. He smiled in delight. Such a dainty woman, with her heart-shaped face covered with childish freckles, her curling and bouncy hair...there was no clue of the lioness within. Then again, looks could be deceiving. His fellow students at school had thought Magnus to be a beast and they had been wrong. Leena had called him a puppy. The nickname she had given him: *Pentu*.

"What are you waiting for?" Helen said. "Come on."

Magnus hurried to the line-trimmer, knowing the reservoir was full of fuel because that is how he always left it. He turned. Helen was already next to him. No tears now. No tears.

Magnus smiled. "We'll put up a good fight, you and me."

"Fucking oath," she said, and snatched the line-trimmer from him. "Now, what else have you got? We need hammers. Maybe shovels. Anything that can cause either blunt force or penetrating trauma. What about tool belts? We have to find a way to carry all this shit. Oh, and by the way—and look, this is really,

really important to remember—if you get bitten by a zombie, you turn into one."

He jolted. "Wait. *What?*"

8

Stella had been trying her best lately to stop biting her fingernails. Instead, she gnawed on her hangnails and cuticles. Something wasn't right. She could feel it in her guts. How on earth did Walter manage to hurt himself badly enough to need so much gauze? An accidental snip with scissors, yep, she could understand that; a cut needing a sticking plaster or two. But he'd wrapped his whole fricking hand and wrist in bandages! And his behaviour was a definite worry. Could he be having a stroke? Poor Walter was pretty old. Maybe she ought to call an ambulance to be on the safe side.

She should tell Joan. Joan would know what to do.

But the director's door was shut. That meant KEEP OUT unless the building was literally on fire. Joan's words, not Stella's. The last time Stella had knocked on that closed door, Joan had flipped her shit and actually given Stella a written warning. *A written warning.* Get enough of those, and it can mean instant dismissal. Stella needed this job. Con brought in good money from the factory, sure, but they had that bad investment to pay off, and Melanie's husband was too busy retraining at uni to bring in sufficient money to always meet the repayments on the mortgage, and Stella couldn't let her daughter default on the loan...

No, bugger it. Stella was on edge enough without a dressing down from the boss. Those funny flakes of snow—*funny-weird* not *funny-haha*—that had swirled through the front door and somehow disappeared against the linoleum. Kieran having gone AWOL.

And at the end of the hallway, Walter's door being shut. Now *that* was out of character. He always had his door open and they always called out to each other. At first, Joan had loathed the "hollering" and asked them a number of times to use the phone system instead, but that had turned the hollering into a shared joke between Stella and Walter. They even had a call-and-response where one would yell COO and other would reply WEE. How this had originated, Stella couldn't remember. It didn't mean anything but it made them laugh. After a few months of exasperation, Joan had mellowed and now seemed to tolerate their shenanigans...

Oh shit, *what was happening to Walter?*

Stella took her fingers from her mouth and drummed them on the desk. Checked work emails. Nothing. Stared at the silent landline. Checked her mobile phone. A text from her husband: *Car service booked for Nov 8 ill get chops for tea xoxo*. She texted back: *Yum thanks Con xoxo*. She put the phone back in her bag and bit at her cuticles again.

Oh, something wasn't right. Lots of things weren't right.

She grabbed her mobile and texted Con: *Has it snowed at the factory? Serious question xoxo.* Stowing her phone, she went back to her cuticles.

Where the frick was Kieran? For a quick nip to the bunkhouse to fetch a carton of low-fat milk, he'd been gone a bloody long time. She bit past the cuticle and into the skin. Not far enough to draw blood. Just enough to satisfy her urge to chew.

God, it was *quiet* in the building. The two closed doors only tightened the knot in her stomach. She snatched up her mobile. No answer yet from Con. *Snow or pollen?* she texted. *Feathers?* Pressed "send". Leaned back in her chair. Checked the CCTV monitors for any sign of Kieran. The cameras focused on the gate, the exterior morgue door, the building's front door, and the perimeter of the fence. That's it. Not an overview of the entire grounds. The bunkhouse was perhaps a brisk two-minute walk away. Whoever had designed the layout of VITERI had decided to place the bunkhouse some distance from the main building, probably so that you didn't feel "at work" while staying overnight. Fair enough.

Two minutes there, a minute to raid the fridge, two minutes back...

Maybe Kieran was taking a dump. If so, he must be severely constipated and trying to birth the world's hardest crap. Nope, she didn't buy it. Something was wrong. Something had happened to him.

Grabbing the landline's handset, she pushed the speed-dial for Kieran's mobile. After four rings, the call went to voicemail.

You've reached Kieran Pocock. Please leave a message.

"Where are you, mate?" she said. "It's Stella. You've been gone for yonks. Call me back."

She hung up.

Tapped her fingers on the desk. Fiddled with her bangles. Started to worry about Cheryl Zhao and the two coppers. Picked up the handset again and dialled Cheryl's mobile.

Hi, this is Cheryl Zhao. I can't come to the phone right now, but please leave your name and number and I'll call you back as soon as I can. Thanks.

"Cheryl," Stella hissed. "It's me. Hey, maybe I'm being silly but...jeez, just call me back, would ya? Soon as you can."

She hung up. Chewed on her bottom lip. Reached a decision and rang Helen's mobile.

You've called Helen Macauley. Please leave a message and I'll get back to you.

Stella hung up, gasping now. Next, dialled Alisha's mobile.

Alisha Singh. I'll return your call as soon as I'm able. Bye.

"Frick," Stella said through her teeth. She disconnected, pressed another number. Waited with her breath held, fingers drumming fast, faster, frantically on the desk.

Magnus Vestergaard. Leave your message.

With a cry, Stella dropped the handset onto the cradle and jumped from her chair, panting, heart racing. She started towards Joan's closed office door. Even reached for the handle before stopping herself. Oh, forget it, she could hear the lecture already: "Stella, there's no need for your Mother Hen routine. People aren't answering their mobiles because they're busy. Now please leave me to my paperwork, and attend to your assigned duties."

Turning her head, she gazed down the corridor at Walter's closed door.

Well, it would be a good excuse to check on him.

She stopped outside his office and called her usual greeting: "Knock, knock." No answer. She tapped with her knuckles. "Walter? Can you hear me? Are you all right, mate?"

The door flung open. Walter stood there, glaring. Pale and haggard, dark circles under his eyes, two blotches of high colour on his cheeks as if he were raging with fever. Shocked, her mouth worked but no words came out.

"Yes? Yes?" he snapped. "What is it? What do you want?"

She didn't know how to reply. Without thinking, she said, "A cigarette."

Yes, that was true. To hell with nicotine patches. She needed a bloody smoke.

His attitude softened. Like the Walter of old, he opened the door wide and ushered her inside with a slight bow and a stately sweep of his arm.

"Are you sure you're feeling okay?" she said, entering the room.

He croaked out a laugh, shut the door, dusted off his visitor chair and helped her into it. "I'm perfectly fine. Fit as a fiddle. A cigarette, you say? Why, of course. And I'll join you."

"Walter, I'm worried. I can't get a hold of anybody. Nobody's answering their mobile."

"Ah," he said, taking a pack of cigarettes from his desk drawer.

The veins on his hands stood out, deep pink, as fat as worms. Shouldn't veins be bluish-green? He proffered the open pack. Gratefully, she took a cigarette and stood up to leave.

"Oh no, my dear," he said. "No need for us to go out on the poop deck."

"You mean smoke in here? Inside the building? It's not allowed."

He shrugged, smiled, held out his lighter and fumbled with it.

"Allow me," she said, and took the lighter. The chill of his fingers startled her.

God, if they got sprung, Joan would write them up for sure... After a moment of indecision, she lit Walter's cigarette and then hers. The tobacco crackled. The first inhalation of smoke tasted oh-my-god *fantastic*. She actually moaned as she exhaled. One day off the darts and she'd cracked already. What hope did she have? Con would be so disappointed. Right now, however, she didn't care. She took one greedy drag after another. What Con didn't know wouldn't hurt him. And it was only one cigarette. Only *one*. No big deal.

"We'd better open a window," she said. "If Joan catches us, she'll have kittens."

Walter didn't reply. Instead, he groped for the chair and lowered himself stiffly, awkwardly, as if his back were hurting.

Stella crossed the room and wound open the window. "It's like being back in high school and hiding in the dunnies from the teachers," she said, exhaling through the flyscreen. "How often do you smoke in here, you cheeky so-and-so?"

"Never."

She straightened. "Never? This is the first time?"

He nodded.

Oh, she didn't like that. Too out of the ordinary. Everything was out of the ordinary today.

"Did you hear what I told you before?" she said. "I can't get a hold of anybody. I've called Cheryl, Helen, Alisha, Magnus. Straight to voicemail. Oh, shit, and Kieran too! Voicemail again. He nipped out to the bunkhouse for milk. To the bunkhouse! He should have been back by now. I'd tell Joan, but God, you know what she's like. She'd only bitch about me wasting her time, and maybe write me up. But I'm worried, mate. I really am."

Walter nodded sagely.

"It's linked to that weird snowfall," she continued. "Don't you reckon? Hey? Don't you reckon, mate? Pollen, my arse."

He didn't reply. Kept nodding.

She watched him for a time. He was smoking differently. Instead of drawing back, he just smacked at the filter with his lips like a beginner, puffing the smoke in great clouds about his head. Fresh anxiety beaded her top lip with sweat. All of a sudden, she didn't like being alone in this office with him.

"Why aren't you inhaling?" she said. "Can't you breathe properly?"

He opened another desk drawer and took out a plastic bag of raw meat strips. This was the meat he fed to his kookaburra. He dropped the bag onto the desk.

"That ought to be in the fridge," she said. "It'll spoil at room temperature."

"You're a good cook."

She waited, but he didn't say anything else. After a while, she replied, "Well, I guess I am. Con and Melanie don't complain. And I've never given anyone food poisoning."

"How do you make raw meat warm without cooking it?"

"I'm sorry?"

Walter scratched at his goatee. His fingernail beds were blue. "Let's assume, for argument's sake, that I wanted to eat raw meat but I wanted it to be warm." He coughed, a small choking sound. "However, any technique that heats meat also cooks it, correct?"

"What the hell are you talking about, mate?"

"The technique of roasting is out. Along with poaching. Frying. The microwave too. Any method of warming raw meat cooks it, as far as I can fathom. Your thoughts?"

She stared at him. Took in the grey and wrinkled skin of his ears, the bloodshot whites of his eyes, the waxy yellowing about his lips. The bandage on his hand showed a patch of liquid. Something dark, almost black.

"Why do you want to eat raw meat?" she whispered.

"There must be some way to eat it warm. But there's only one way I can think of. And I'm not entirely sure if that would be appropriate."

He kept puckering his lips around the filter. The cigarette had burned out but he hadn't noticed. Stella's gaze darted around the room. Wadded up in the wastepaper basket was what appeared to be a lab coat covered in bright red blood.

Stella crushed out the cigarette on the windowsill and stepped towards the door.

"What happened to your hand?" she said. "Tell me. No bullshit this time."

Puzzled, he looked down at one hand—his uninjured hand first, as it happened—and then the other. He seemed genuinely surprised at the bandaging.

"Why, goodness gracious, I'm damned if I know," he said, and made that strange choking sound in his throat again. He looked at her and smiled. "An excellent job at first aid. This looks like your expert handiwork, Steffy."

A chill prickled up the nape of her neck. "It's Stella."

He raised his eyebrows. "Hmm?"

"My name is Stella."

"Oh," he laughed. "Of course. Forgive an old man his occasional lapse of memory."

She grabbed for the door handle.

***

Garcia resembled a hopeless drunkard, albeit one in a thousand-dollar suit. Leaning forward from the hips. Arms hanging down loose. Jaw dropped open. Dribbling. Swaying on his feet. Blank-eyed, he stared at the murder scene. Which comprised a dismembered body—guts, flaps of skin and scalp; pelvis, spine and long bones stripped of meat; torn clothes and fancy shoes—and the killers. Three dead pigs and two dead people. Zombies. Clustered together like starving dogs around a bowl of Pal, slurping in desperation at the remains.

Soon they would run out of soft tissue. And then what?

"Garcia," Rick said again, feeling every one of his forty-nine years. "Get on the bike."

Around them, dead animals shuffled in the dirt. Birds and possums and Christ-knows-what falling out of the surrounding trees.

"Garcia!" he ordered. "Do as I say!"

Shit. The greenhorn may as well be deaf. Rick kicked the stand and got off the postie bike. He would have to retrieve Garcia himself. The dead monsters, the *zombies*, were unaware of them as yet, too fixated on their meal—whoever that had been. The poor bastard. Rick put one hand on the gun in his waistband.

"Garcia. Can you hear me? It's Rick. Detective Senior Sergeant Rick Evans."

The chewing sounds turned Rick's stomach. But the crunching noises indicated that the dead were starting on the bones. They had run out of soft tissue. He grabbed Garcia by the arm to spin him around. Garcia made eye contact, let out a high-pitched screech, and ran.

"Come back here!" Rick called. "Come back!"

Movement from the monsters. The two used-to-be humans. They lifted their heads from the dismembered corpse and looked in Rick's direction. He jolted in alarm. Could they even *see* him? One of the zombies had nothing left in its sockets but slime and bugs. The other still had eyeballs, but blackened and seemingly blind ones. Perhaps they'd heard him. Smelled him? Christ, who *knew* what senses they had left.

While the pigs kept noshing, the two human zombies, in concert, pushed up with their grey, tattered arms and began to get their legs underneath them. Heart dropping and pounding, Rick pulled out the gun and fired—BANG BANG—first into one forehead and then the other.

Bullseye and bullseye.

The zombies collapsed, motionless.

"Get fucked!" he cried, close to tears. "Fuck you!"

Something touched his foot. With a yelp, he stepped back. It was a wallaby, most of its fur sloughed off, dragging itself paw over paw, tiny mouth opening and closing. He put a bullet in its skull before it occurred to him that doing so was a waste of ammunition. He tucked the gun back into his waistband. Jumped onto the bike. Looked around.

Oh shit, shit, *shit*…

"Garcia!" he shouted at the top of his lungs. "Garcia! Where are you?"

Rick's breath and heartbeat were loud. Like being underwater. Snorkelling. Off the coast of Lombok with his wife on their last Bali holiday, face down and lolling seasick in the waves, trying to breathe through a fucking tube and panicking. His breath and heartbeat in his ears. He worked the bike's throttle and took off.

"Garcia!"

There, *there*, far off in the scrub. Blue suit.

Rick motored after him.

Back-up. They needed back-up. All around him, the leaf litter was rising, turning into crumpled birds, flattened rats, mice. He reached into his jacket pocket and took out his phone. Up ahead, the blue suit kept flailing. Garcia had lost his fucking mind. Thank God Rick had taken the gun off him. *Thank fucking God.*

Steering one-handed, Rick thumbed at his mobile phone for his Detective Inspector.

"Yeah, g'day Rick, how's it—"

"Phil!" Rick shouted, a sob in his throat. "We're in big trouble."

"At the body farm?"

"Yeah, yeah, at the body farm. We need reinforcements."

"*Armed* reinforcements?" Phil said. "What the dickens for?"

Rick inhaled, about to blurt out the truth. Stopped himself. No, he would have to think about his answer for a split-second. Sounding crazy wouldn't work. Saying crazy things wouldn't work. If he told Phil Austin that the dead had come back to life and were attacking them, no, that wouldn't work.

"Are you still there?" Phil said. "Hello?"

"Terrorists," Rick said.

"Terrorists? Good Lord, what kind?"

"Not sure. The kind with semi-automatics. Send the SOGgies. The army."

"The *army*? Mate, what the fuck is going on?" Phil Austin was panting, huffing down the line. "Are you shitting me?"

"No sir. We have deaths, multiple deaths. Send reinforcements. Send everything to VITERI in Wooriyanda. You've got the longitude and latitude. Hurry. Or we'll die."

"Wait, hold your horses. I need more intel. How many terrorists?"

"Twenty. No, thirty. Maybe more."

"What do they want?"

"Not sure, sir."

"A wild guess. Hostages in exchange for something? Or are they on a massacre?"

"I don't know their reasons. Don't know their affiliations. Could be political. Could be environmental. Don't know."

Phil said, "But why the bejesus would terrorists want to storm a fucking *body farm*?"

Through the trees, the dead were heading towards him. People. Pigs. Moving slowly but surely in his direction. He had to keep quiet. He had to stop making so much bloody noise.

"I've got to go," he whispered. "Terrorists nearby."

"Holy Mary and Joseph. Look, I'll send everything I can get. Hang tight. You hear me? Hang tight."

Rick hung up. The cavalry would be coming. The intensity of relief churned his stomach. He eased off the throttle. The bike stuttered to a stop. He leaned over and heaved up his lunch. Tandoori chicken pie. Shit. He spat, sniffed and hawked. The sour taste of bile made him want to vomit again. He kept spitting. Looked around. Through the trees were about a dozen human and pig zombies, shambling on unsteady feet, closing in.

Now...

Where the hell was Garcia?

Plan B: if he couldn't find him soon, Rick would abandon the search, follow the signposts and return to the safety of the main building. Forget motoring around this hellhole, trying to find Garcia's cowardly arse.

Wait. The blue suit.

There, on his left, about fifty metres away.

Rick opened up the throttle. He would reach Garcia within a minute. Get him to sit pillion. Deliver him to the main building where everyone could hole up and wait for help to arrive. Rick smiled through a shimmer of unshed tears. He had arranged a way out of this nightmare. Nearly over now. It would be okay. He ought to ring office manager, Stella, tell her to put VITERI into lockdown, tell her to contact everyone on site and instruct them to seek shelter behind closed doors. And he would ring Stella once he got Garcia onto the back of the bike.

Garcia was standing with his legs spread, hands clasped at his temples and elbows together, looking like he was having a full-blown mental breakdown.

Just as long as he didn't take off running again.

The bike motored along. Rick steered the front wheel over every little zombie; the fluttering birds, the slowly moving rats dragging their limbs. Tiny skeletons crunched.

Almost there. Garcia lowered his arms.

Which, to be honest, worried Rick. Garcia was so *still*. All of a sudden. Rick felt scared by that, but didn't know exactly why. He slowed the bike, trundling it between trees. Garcia remained motionless. Rick stopped a few metres distant.

"You okay?" he said.

"I'm okay, boss."

Was he? Almost without thinking, one of Rick's hands reached to the loaded gun in his waistband. The thought of having Garcia riding pillion, pressed up against the back of him, gave him the willies. But there was no reason to be afraid. Mostly, he'd had Garcia in sight ever since Violet had climbed out of the car boot and killed Cheryl Zhao. Nothing had happened to Garcia. The greenhorn was unharmed. Unbitten. You change into a zombie if you get bitten by one, right? Everybody knew that.

"Come on," he said. "Come on, Garcia. I'll take you to safety."

"Safety? Meaning what?"

Rick wiped sweat from his hairline. "The main building. I've already called the Detective Inspector. Back-up's coming."

Garcia brightened. "Really?"

"Really. Including SOGgies."

"How long before they get here?"

"I don't know," Rick said. "Not long. Would you please get on the bike?"

"Boss, it's four hours from the Melbourne City Police Complex to here. *Four hours*. You truly believe we're going to last four hours?"

Now that was a sobering question. One that Rick didn't want to entertain. "Look, they might travel here by helicopter," he said. "Now shut up and get on the bike." The greenhorn didn't move. Rick twisted the throttle. The pissy motor of the postie bike revved. He trundled closer. "Let's get going," he said.

"What for? You know we're not getting out of here alive."

Rick swallowed. "Don't be ridiculous."

"There's too many of them."

"No, we're faster, smarter. And we've got guns. In our car, remember? Shotguns."

Garcia shook his head. "There's too many of them. Weapons don't count for shit when there's too many of them."

"So, what do you want to do?" Rick snapped. "Give up? Is that it?"

"There's too many of them."

"Get on the fucking bike and that's an order."

"There's too many of them." Garcia gestured in a wide arc and laughed. "See?"

Rick glanced about. The human and pig zombies were nearer than he expected. Shit. Motion flashed in the corner of Rick's eye. He turned. A large animal was leaping between the trees and shrubs. A red animal. The speed of it frightened him.

"Look out!" Rick said, and pulled the gun.

The animal was a kangaroo. Rick hadn't seen a kangaroo in the flesh since he'd taken his daughters, back when they were in primary school, to the Healesville Sanctuary where the kangaroos had been around people for so long you were able to feed them by hand. He remembered the feel of a warm, snuffling muzzle in his palm, the way a kangaroo (or was it a wallaby?) tended to hold delicately to your wrist, as if it were balancing a plate at a cocktail party and snacking on canapes... But *this* kangaroo was a huge bastard, and looked like it had been hit by a bus. Were those *bullet holes* in its torso? Rick shot at the animal. To no avail. The zombie kangaroo stopped in front of Garcia, flicked its ears, scratched its stomach.

"Garcia," Rick said. "Get out of the way."

Instead, Garcia gaped at the kangaroo with his mouth open as if mesmerised. Rick aimed and pulled the trigger. The bullet snapped the kangaroo's head to one side and took off its lower jaw. Unfazed, the animal approached Garcia, leaned back on its muscular tail and flung out its hind legs. The claws punched into Garcia's belly, knocking him backwards. He staggered but kept his footing. At first, there was only a line of blood, a red stain flowering across his torn shirt. Next, Garcia's abdomen opened up.

Under pressure, his intestines ejected in a wet and slippery run of grey guts, shimmying out line after line onto the ground as Garcia dropped to his knees.

Rick, screaming, jumped from the bike and ran at the kangaroo, shooting over and over—BANG, BANG, BANG—until the top of its skull blew off. The kangaroo fell and stayed down. The pulse beat in Rick's ears. His breath came and went in high-pitched wheezes. He tasted vomit.

Garcia gazed in wonder at his own spilled guts. Prodded them experimentally.

The kangaroo must have cut an artery. There was so much blood. Jesus fucking Christ, there was *so much blood*. Spurting in jets.

Garcia swayed. Stared back at Rick in bewilderment. In the next second, the life snuffed out of his eyes. He toppled over and lay still.

The crunching of leaf litter made Rick look up. The zombies were trotting now, zeroing in from all directions, no doubt drawn by the smell of blood, their mouths working.

His heart leapt into his mouth when he saw the pale, naked woman. Oh God. *Was that Violet?* Yes. Walking briskly, with great determination, her heavy breasts and stomach lathered in blood: Cheryl Zhao's blood. And Violet was staring right at him.

Rick scrambled onto the bike and took off.

9

The old woman named Steffy ran from his office. Her heels clicked on the linoleum. Walter realised that he held a burnt-out cigarette butt. He put the butt in the wastepaper basket. From the zip-lock bag sitting on his desk, he took out a piece of meat. It didn't feel fridge-cold anymore. He put the meat on his tongue. No. The meat was not succulent. It tasted dead. He did not want to chew and swallow dead meat. Just the *thought* of dead meat festering inside his body was *repellent*. He spat it into the wastepaper bin.

He noticed the computer monitor. There were words on it. He leaned in closer. Something about beetles. Interesting. He liked beetles. And further along, a private message from Vice-Chancellor Gail Herman:

> Pack up your shit, old man, I'm booting your arse through the fucking door and don't you ever come back or I will do everything in my considerable power to fuck your shit up six ways from Sunday, you doddering senile bastard. I can see you. I can see you right now through your computer. I can hear you via the phone lines. The CCTV cameras. You can't hide from me.

Walter grabbed the mouse, closed the document, turned off the computer. If he'd needed proof, there it was. Clearly, Gail Herman had been typing while he'd been preoccupied with Steffy. No...Stella? Yes, he meant Stella. Those last few sentences, about Herman's surveillance of him, had not been there before. He was sure of it.

So, he pulled the electrical plug from the wall.

Might that be sufficient? Or could Herman access his computer anyway? Perhaps via Wi-Fi or the Cloud, or other sorts of invisible technology that kept tabs on everyone nowadays?

A noise at his door. Must be Stella.

"I told you, I'm busy," he shouted, his throat feeling clogged and dry, withered. "Don't make me tell you again. Be off with you. Be off!"

He waited for half a minute. No response. She must have walked away again, on tiptoes this time, soundlessly. She must be back at her desk, scanning and scrutinising the CCTV monitors. For all he knew, there was a secret monitor that showed the goings-on inside this very office. He scanned the walls, the ceiling. The camera must be *somewhere*. Telecommunications were so advanced these days. A camera lens could be as slender as a fibre optic cable. He might not even see it. Where? Where could it be? He spotted the light fixture full of bugs and realised the truth.

Ah ha. Not bugs as in *insects* but bugs as in *recording devices*.

The perfect deception.

Nodding, he scratched at his beard. He had outwitted his foes. The realisation calmed him. Whistling through cracked lips, he stood up on his desk, tore off the ceiling light fixture, and hurled it into the corner of the room where it broke in two. The husks of dead bugs fluttered about. *Bug confetti.* Next, he dragged the chair into the opposite corner of the room where the cameras in his monitor couldn't see him, and sat, steepling his fingers.

Why hadn't he realised the truth before?

Stella was a lackey for Gail Herman. Together, they were gathering evidence against him, building the case for his dismissal. Only this week, Stella had ribbed him about his zip-lock bag of beef strips with its hand-written message STRICTLY FOR USE BY WALTER BOYCE ONLY that he always kept in the staff refrigerator. Laughing, she had said *Who'd want to steal that shit anyway?* Ah ha. Disdain. Disrespect. The signs were there. Had been there all along. She probably took photographs of each weekly zip-lock bag on her mobile and sent them to Herman. Blinkered, fooled by her cosy familiarity, he had assumed Stella to be one of his closest friends, but oh, how he was *mistaken.*

It made sense. Throughout history, the best spies have always been the people most trusted, most beloved. Wasn't that true?

Good gracious. First Cookie. Now Stella. Was there no safe refuge? He wanted to weep.

No.

No time for self-indulgence. He had to protect himself.

He unplugged every cord to his computer, unplugged his landline phone, took the scissors from his lab coat pocket, and cut, cut, *cut*. Now he was safe from Gail Herman. Relief took the strength from his legs. He sat, dropped his chin to his chest, puffed until his breath came back. His eyes closed. A great weariness washed over him. If he slumped right down in this chair, he might be able to take a nap. It was comfortable enough. High-backed, ergonomic, well-padded. And he was so very tired.

His mobile phone buzzed.

Startled, he sat up and took the mobile from his pocket.

A text from Stella, in CAPS no less: PLEASE TELL ME YOUR OK I'M WORRIED.

He tut-tutted. Such atrocious spelling. And then a larger concern struck him. Stella could access him via his mobile. Therefore, Herman could access him too. This mobile was a conduit which allowed his enemies to *get* to him and wreak their havoc.

Safety. He had to prioritise his safety.

He put his mobile on the desk and, using the orange handles of the scissors, hit and hit and hit the screen again and again and again until the device was in pieces. Picking up the wastepaper basket, he swept the pieces into the bin. Noticed white cloth. What was that? Reached in and pulled it out a little way. A bloodied lab coat. What?

After a second, he remembered.

Cookie, that beautiful bird, the chuckling little kookaburra, had pecked a huge chunk out of his hand. And his hand had bled over the coat. So, he had stuffed the coat into this bin. His reasons for doing that escaped him. Why not call for help? Go to a hospital? He needed stitches in the torn webbing between his thumb and forefinger. Good God, why hadn't he sought medical attention?

His injured hand was bandaged. But who had bandaged it? He scratched at his beard and lost his train of thought.

Tired.

Oh, that's right, he was tired.

He would slump down in this chair and try to doze for a while—

His mobile buzzed. Impossible. Wasn't it broken? He retrieved the pieces from the bin. Another text from Stella. YOU CAN TRUST ME, DODDERING OLD FOOL.

Of course. Gwen Herman had contacted Steffy, telling her that the surveillance in Walter's office was down. Walter would have to take *steps*.

I'M PERFECTLY FINE he texted back in facetious CAPS, mashing his fingers against the shattered fragments of screen, piercing his fingertips with splinters of glass. THANK YOU VERY MUCH.

He left his office. Steffy was at her desk. She half-rose. He waved at her then went into Kieran's office and shut the door. He pulled out every plug on every device, and used the scissors to cut every cord. Good. Walter was feeling better already. However, there was more work to be done here. He opened the drawers in Keith's desk, rummaging, not knowing what he was looking for, but sure he would recognise it when he saw it.

Ah ha. Thumb drives. Portable spy machines.

First, he tried to break them in half by hand. Then cut them with scissors. Crush them underfoot. Nothing worked. They were too small, too tough. Finally, he stuffed the thumb drives into his mouth and swallowed them. They cut on the way down but didn't hurt.

Far off in the distance, at the very edge of his hearing, came Gwen Herman's voice. *Blast you, Walter, you're thwarting my plans to control you.* Insufferable bitch, he thought, you can't beat me. And he knew that she had heard him because she wailed back in anguish.

He ducked into the other empty offices. Cut every cord.

Now…now the reception desk. But how to lure Steffy away?

Walter shuffled down the hallway. Oh my, his rheumatism was acting up. The tendons of his quadriceps felt extraordinarily tight. He could hardly bend his knees. Steffy gawped at him with wide eyes, both fists pressed to her mouth. Well, well, if that didn't speak of guilt, he didn't know what would. As he neared her desk—slowly, slowly, God, his knees were locking up—she pushed back in her chair and began to tremble. Ah ha. Guilty as sin. Body language doesn't lie. Traitors can't disguise their treacherous body language.

"My dear," he said. "Would you please make me a drink?"

She kept trembling.

"Please, a drink?" he continued.

"Coffee?" she whispered.

He nodded. She scurried from behind the desk and almost ran to the kitchen, those infernal bangles of hers jingling and jangling.

Out with his scissors. Unplug, unplug, unplug. Cut, cut, cut. The computer disabled, the phone line down. He thought he'd destroyed the CCTV connections, but the images still showed on the various screens. With stiffening fingers, he laboriously followed the severed cord back to its source and realised that he had cut the power supply to the printer. Damn. On the desk sat Steffy's handbag. An internal pocket held her mobile. He took out the phone and smashed it against the side of the desk until the blasted device folded in half. *There*, he thought victoriously. Take *that*, Vice-Principal Gwen Harding. Put *that* in your pipe and smoke it.

"What are you doing?"

He glanced up. Steffy was on the other side of the desk, eyes as big as peeled eggs, her shaking hand slopping coffee from the cup.

"You can't fool me." Walter tapped the side of his nose. "I know what's going on."

"I don't," she whispered.

"This conspiracy."

"Conspiracy?"

"Hah. Don't pretend. Don't insult my intelligence."

The director's office door opened. The woman with the shonky hips, what's-her-name, Jody Something-Or-Another, limped out. In one hand, she held two bright blue nametags, one for the wrist and one for the ankle. Jody didn't even glance in their direction.

"I'm labelling our donor," she said, stumping her way along the hall.

A tug of memory ribboned through his brain, vague as a dream upon waking. The new donor. The biggest they'd ever had. Tall and heavy, bearded, with tattoos. *Butch*. This woman was talking about Butch.

"I've decided to call him Herakles," the director added, talking over her shoulder. "The Greek name for Hercules. Seems appropriate considering his size."

"Joan, wait," Steffy said, sounding close to tears. Crocodile tears, no doubt. And who the hell was Joan, by the way? The director's name was Jody, wasn't it? Or Jamie.

"I'll be a moment, Stella."

"But something's very wrong—"

"Yes, and as I *told* you, I will *deal* with it in a *moment*," Jody or Jamie Director said, and opened the door to the morgue and went inside. The door hissed shut on its pneumatic closer.

Walter took the opportunity to dart into Jamie's office. Unplugging and cutting. Unplugging and cutting. Searching and finding her mobile, smashing it. Go to hell, Vice-President Gwen Herring. Bitch, you'll never spy on me again. Never ever again.

"Walter, stop it. You're *scaring* me."

He looked up. An old woman with ginger hair and glasses was in the doorway, gaping at him, wringing her hands and crying.

"Who are you?" he demanded. "How did you get in here? What do you want?"

"Oh God, oh shit. Oh Walter, *please*. Please, it's *me*."

"Walter?" He grimaced, looked around the empty room. "Who the devil is Walter?"

***

Outside, the scratching and scraping noises continued against the door of Magnus's work shed. The sounds raised the hairs on the back of Helen's neck. She clenched her fists. Focused on the details of their hastily constructed plan.

"To reiterate," she said. "Number one, we kit up with weapons. Two, we open the door, and use the whipper-snipper to kill every single zombie animal on your veranda—"

"Then leave the whipper-snipper behind."

"What? No. Are you serious?"

"The machine is heavy and must be operated with two hands. The filament line can't lop off a human head. Certainly not a pig's head. It's designed for trimming grass."

"Shit, fair enough." She shook off the bad news. "So, we kill whatever little monsters are on the veranda, dump the whipper-snipper, go next door into your cabin—"

"First I get my boots. They're on the veranda."

"Yeah, yeah, all right, you grab your boots and we run into your cabin. Ring Stella on your mobile, tell her what's happening, assuming she doesn't know already. Ring the police."

He rubbed at his chin. "We can't tell them zombies. They'll think us cranks."

"Goddamn it." Helen bit her lower lip. "Okay, we'll say there's a shooter on site."

"Yes, yes, much better. A shooter."

"Then we jump on the quad bike and head to the main building. We avoid zombies whenever we can. But run over the little ones if doing so doesn't take us out of our way. We take a *straight* fucking line to the office. But if necessary, if we're engaged, we kill any big zombies. By destroying their brains, remember?"

Magnus nodded. "Yes. Their brains. And we try not to get bitten."

"Once we reach the main building, we grab everybody, jump in our cars, and get the fuck out of here. Making sure to close the gate behind us so none of these fuckers get out."

"Except for the birds."

"What?"

He frowned. "Zombie birds could fly over the fence. Peck and infect other animals. Spread the infection."

She hadn't thought of that, but hey, if the whole world was under attack from zombies, it was a moot point anyway. "Look, we'll worry about that bridge when we come to it. The most important thing is to get everyone out of VITERI in one piece. So, what else? What have I forgotten?"

He said, "Conserve bullets where possible."

"Yep. Well, I think that's everything—"

"And on the quad bike, we hold an umbrella overhead."

"An umbrella?"

"Yes. Because zombie birds and possums are dropping out of trees. I've got an umbrella in my cabin."

"All right. Great. Are we sweet?"

"Yes. Very sweet."

She went towards the shadow board of tools and halted, stricken, as thoughts of Alisha came back to her in a rush. Oh God. *Alisha*. That long fall of hair. The black eyes. Dimples. Alisha liked old-fashioned films. Disliked modern films on principle, *despised* the superhero franchises to the point where she refused to watch them. (And who could blame her, honestly?) Had never eaten McDonald's. *Ever*. Not even a single French fry. Amazing. The only person Helen had ever known to have shunned Macca's. Probably the only person in Australia, for that matter. *Alisha*. Somehow, she was dead. *Dead*. The memory of her flayed skull and empty sockets, the noshing sounds of Bartholomew's teeth, her bones cracking in the zombie pig's mouth—

Stop it. *Stop*. Helen squeezed her eyes shut.

Remembered, instead, the first time she saw Alisha.

At the start of the semester during Professor Dillon's lecture on bog people.

The lecture hall had been tiny. Nothing more than a room off a hallway in one of the biology buildings at Fraser University. Carpeted. Smelling like all-purpose cleaner. A blank white-board on the wall behind the lectern. About twenty students at plastic tables with their tablets, recording devices, jotter-pads, pens. Some students had tattoos and gauge earrings, under-buzz cuts; others wore collared shirts like they worked in a bank. An odd mix. Oil and water. Helen didn't know yet in which camp she belonged and didn't particularly care. She picked a seat near the door and took out her phone to record the lecture.

Professor Dillon was a neat old woman, her white hair worn in an unruly, fluffy halo about her head, her thin lips accentuated with a slash of violent red lipstick.

"Good afternoon. I'm Professor Dillon and I prefer to be addressed as such. Now. Mummification. Not of the supernatural bandaged kind, obviously. Not the Hollywood 'Boris Karloff' kind, if any of you happen to be cognisant of that reference."

An awkward chuckle murmured around the room. Dillon smiled. Her lips disappeared.

"In short," Dillon continued, "mummification occurs when the environment, either natural or artificial, prevents the liquidising of putrefied soft tissues. The most obvious example: the hot sands of Egypt, where interred corpses—"

The door clattered opened. Everyone looked around at the dark-haired girl. She was flustered, breathing hard. God, what flawless skin. Helen's heart gave a hectic flippity-flop.

Professor Dillon adjusted her glasses. "Excuse me?"

"I'm so sorry," the dark-haired girl said, books clasped to her chest, scurrying into the nearest seat which happened to be next to Helen. "A car ran out of petrol and blocked the tram. I had to run the rest of the way to the bus stop, and by the time I—"

"You ran?" Dillon said. "To a bus stop?"

"Yes, ma'am."

"What's your name?"

"Alisha," the dark-haired girl said. Perspiration ringed her hair-line. "Alisha Singh."

Professor Dillon lifted her glasses to peruse a sheet of paper. Presumably, she was long-sighted. She put her glasses back on her nose and offered a chilly smile. "Thank you, Miss Singh. You've made a bad first impression. Now, for your sake only, I have to begin my lecture again. That's not fair on the students who made the effort to attend on time."

"But it wasn't my fault. I was on the tram, you see, and the car in front—"

"No, tardiness is not fair, Miss Singh. If you prefer, watch my lectures online. There's no reason to be here in person. Unlike high school, attendance doesn't influence your marks."

"Wow. Okay, look, it was a tram that couldn't—"

"I hope you won't be late again."

"Ugh, no worries," Alisha said, sitting back. "If the circumstances are under my control."

"I'll take that as an apology." Dillon consulted her notes. "As I was saying: mummification. In the hot sands of Egypt, buried corpses are generally preserved with a life-like appearance due to various factors—"

Alisha leaned towards Helen and whispered, "Is she always such a fucken bitch?"

Helen grinned back and, by accident, unexpectedly, got lost in those black eyes. Helen breathed in. She could smell her. Alisha's sweat exuded odours of cinnamon and honey. Perhaps these were the fragrances of Alisha's shampoo. She wore a simple peppermint-green t-shirt. White skirt. Sandals. No nail-polish. A plain silver chain about her neck. No visible makeup. Except for mascara? Eyeliner? No. Forget the makeup, her showstopping eyes were natural.

"Are you going to faint?" Magnus said.

Startled, Helen looked around the work shed. Magnus was standing next to her.

"You're very pale," he said.

Helen scrubbed at her face with both hands. If she didn't get it together, she would die too. Die horribly. Just like Alisha.

"I'm all right," she said.

"You can stay here if you want."

She shook her head.

"I'll lock you in," he continued. "You'll be safe."

Lock her in? As if she were useless? A delicate little flower who needed smelling salts?

She went over to the shadow board of tools. "Blunt force and penetrating weapons. That's what we're after. To get through the skull and into the brain." She picked up the hard rubber mallet, waved it around. "Pow. This is good."

He plucked the claw hammer from the board. "So is this."

"And this," she said, taking the long screwdriver. "Ooh, I like this one best of all," she said, removing a hatchet and hefting it, feeling its weight.

"This could be also good," he said of the ball peen hammer.

They kept perusing the shadow board. Spanners, pliers… No other tools appeared suitable.

She turned to scan the rest of the shed. "Have you got anything else?"

"What about these?" Magnus said, lifting a garden fork in one hand and a spade in the other. "To attack zombies at arm's length."

"Perfect. What else?"

They both looked around. Planks of wood. Chicken wire. Nuts and screws…

"It doesn't matter," he said. "We have enough to carry."

"How are we gonna carry everything? On tool belts?"

"I have only one. Too big for you."

"Shit," Helen said, gazing about, hoping for inspiration.

Magnus took a coiled rope from a shelf, measured out a length, and cut it. "Here, tie this through the belt loops of your jeans. You can hang weapons off it."

"Good thinking." She grinned at him as she began threading the rope. "You know what? No kidding. You're great to have around in a crisis."

"It's always best not to panic."

"I'll keep that in mind."

Magnus put on his tool belt. They loaded their impromptu weapons. In a strange way, it reminded her of going fishing with Dad. *A place for everything and everything in its place.* Dad had always kept his tackle box organised. Always cleaned and maintained the equipment. After she turned six, her permanent job was to clean the reels. She remembered the routine even now, many years after his death: tighten the slack of line; sponge the reel with soapy water; rinse; dry with a cloth; if necessary, remove the spool and douse under running water from the tap; spray lube on a cloth and polish the reel. Dad had a system when they were packing for a fishing trip. The system never varied. Kitting up with Magnus felt like that. Methodical. Decisive. Thorough. Dad, she thought, wherever you are, please help us out if you can. *We're in deep shit.*

They divvied up the weapons. Helen had the mallet, hatchet, ball peen hammer and screwdriver. Magnus had the claw hammer, spade, garden fork, and the .22 rifle slung by its strap over one shoulder.

It didn't seem enough. Not by a long shot.

Magnus picked up the whipper-snipper and put his ear to the door. The scraping and scratching noises gave her goose bumps.

"I can't hear anything large moving outside," he said. "On my mark, you push open the door and step back. Okay?"

"Okay." The pulse began to thrum in her ears.

He turned the choke, pumped the button to prime the carburettor, and pulled the zip cord. The whipper-snipper started first try. The smell of exhaust fumes in the enclosed space made her feel sick. Then again, maybe she felt sick because she was scared. Scared shitless. Magnus turned down the choke, dropping the revs, and looked at her with his eyebrows lifted as if to say *Ready?* She blew out a hard breath and nodded.

He faced the door. Lowered the whipper-snipper's head to the floor. Cricked his neck, rolled his shoulders. Maybe he was scared too. Just better at hiding it.

"One," he said, his voice flat and even, and she wanted to blurt out *No, wait, I'm not ready*, but then he continued and said, "Two. Three. *Mark.*"

Dry mouthed, she shoved open the door.

The drenching sunshine dazzled her vision. She caught a glimpse of magpies, currajongs, rats, other creatures, dozens of them, huddling together in a frenzied, pressing mass. They surged forward. The whipper-snipper's motor screamed as Magnus pulled the trigger and spun the line. Swinging left, swinging right, sweep, sweep, back and forth, cutting into the mob, the animals breaking apart and flying in tattered bits, body parts cartwheeling, spraying.

No squeaks of pain. Made sense. Awful, terrible, terrifying sense. Dead animals don't breathe. There can't be vocalisations without breath. The only sounds were the whipper-snipper motor and the chunking, glopping slap of organic tissue as it tore apart.

The animals didn't fall back. Senseless, they kept pushing forward. Helen's revulsion tasted sour. These zombies smelled live meat and didn't care about anything else. Not even a whirring machine dicing them to pieces. Magnus stepped over the threshold onto the veranda. How many more animals could there be? As he walked, a bizarre Catherine Wheel of fur, feathers, muscle, organs and bone continued to spin and churn at the whipper-snipper head.

Hatchet in hand, she followed him outside.

The dismembered animals squished beneath her shoes. Magnus wore only socks. They were bloodied and gory right up to the ankles. Yuck. Christ only knew how disgusting it must feel to step on those meaty pieces—

A horrifying thought occurred.

What if a sharp piece of bone stabbed into his foot? Would that be enough to infect him?

Would that be enough to turn Magnus into a zombie?

The idea of this giant turning into a flesh-eating zombie made her want to piss her pants in fear. He would be unstoppable. Unassailable. For a second, she felt woozy.

But wait.

Zombies weren't *real*. These reanimated dead creatures only *reminded* her of zombies. The zombie "rules" might not apply. Most likely *didn't* apply. Because zombies were fictitious. She was a scientist and should damn well remember to think like one. Shit, for all she knew, you could get bitten by one of these little undead animals and suffer nothing more than a wound that might require stitches. Perhaps there was no "infection" to pass on. Because, again— and she couldn't stress this enough—*zombies were fictitious.*

And yet...

And *fucking* yet...

If it looks like a duck, swims like a duck, quacks like a duck—

"Don't step on them!" she screamed over the roar of the whipper-snipper. "Magnus!"

He didn't react. Hadn't heard. Kept sweeping like the grim reaper wielding a scythe.

10

No answer. Again. Rick hung up, put the mobile in his pocket. Saw the main building up ahead through the eucalypts and paperbarks. Thank God. For a minute there, he had suspected he was lost, feared he had taken the wrong direction at the last signpost. Fresh perspiration broke out across his body, swamping his armpits. Some kind of bird—a zombie one—dropped from a branch and fluttered towards him in an ungainly spiral of feathers. He swatted it with an arm. The bird tumbled across the ground, flapping.

In the postie bike's rear-view mirrors, undead people and pigs shuffled in his wake. Scores of them. Shit, he was actually *leading* these monsters straight to the VITERI staff. But what else could he do? He had to get to the cache of weapons in his car boot, didn't he? And to protect the VITERI staff, he had to go inside the main building, didn't he?

He veered left, winding through trees. Next to the main building was the generator room, then the water tanks, the carport. He could just make out the unmarked squad car through the scrub. The thought of holding one of the Remington 870P 12-gauge shotguns actually made his mouth water. The smooth feel of the synthetic stock. The clean action. Oh, *yes*. The only way to quell this rise of panic would be to load that beautiful gun, four and one, and blast the ever-loving crapola out of these bastards. He'd only ever used the shotgun on the firing range. The recoil pad was nothing to write home about, sure, but that only bothered your shoulder if you were shooting a hundred rounds or more. The other drawback was the lifter mechanism. If you weren't careful, you could pinch your thumb while loading a round.

Apart from those small gripes, anything you shoot with a 12-gauge *stays shot*. One direct hit and the threat is exterminated. And with the gun's wide spread, if Rick got close enough, he could destroy four or five zombies with a single shell. Which is what he might have to do... How much ammo was in the boot? No idea. No bloody idea...

Ha. That one time he had taken Garcia to the shooting range for shotgun practice, the dumb-arse had pinched his thumb in the lifter mechanism. Not once, but dozens of times. Dozens! By the end of the day, the tip of his thumb was a fat, bruised and weeping blister. *Stop jamming your whole bloody thumb in there*, Rick had advised. *I'm not*, Garcia had protested, but it was as plain as the nose on your face that he was using an incorrect technique and wouldn't admit it. Not even the instructor could get through to him. *There's something wrong with the shotgun*, Garcia had argued. *No, mate, there's something wrong with your common sense*, Rick had snapped. *You've got bugger-all.*

Tears rose. Garcia was single with no kids; a small mercy. But both his parents were still alive and he had a number of siblings. How many exactly? Rick couldn't remember. Whenever Garcia had run off at the mouth, Rick had tuned out. Now, he tried to imagine what it might be like to inform the family members of Garcia's death. How they might react. Oh, how on earth could Rick explain the circumstances? That a fucking *zombie kangaroo* had disembowelled him? No, no, it sounded crazy. It *was* crazy.

He checked the rear-view mirrors. Felt his butthole clench when he caught sight of Violet. She was using the trees as cover. While the others blundered onwards, she was sly. Maybe a zombie's degree of brain function depended on its rate of decay. And Violet had looked fresh—that is, if you ignored the marbled, purple lividity of the stilled blood in her veins.

Rick slowed the bike for a recce of the main building.

No sign of life. Whether that was good or bad, he couldn't tell.

He rode on towards the carport, and began to fret.

Why hadn't Stella answered his phone calls? Straight to voicemail both times. He didn't know her well enough to ascertain if her failure to call back was out of character or not.

He ought to call his wife. She'd be at the swimming centre by now, doing laps of the pool. Since turning forty, the kilos had started to creep on, despite her vigorous attempts at weight loss: portion control, eliminating sweets, cutting down carbs, slashing her wine intake. She was trying to keep middle-age spread at bay, and while Rick admired her efforts, he also knew she couldn't fight biology. Hormone imbalance was a bitch that wouldn't quit. She had started on the road to menopause and all roads led to a fat belly. Not that he minded! But he couldn't make her understand that he loved her no matter what. Found her desirable no matter what, even though their love-life in the last ten years or so had tapered off, no, dropped off, into not much more than ABC sex: anniversaries, birthdays, Christmas. *I'm losing my market value*, she kept saying, and sometimes she said it while her bottom lip trembled. *But you're not on the market*, he always replied. *You're already taken. And you're beautiful. Can't you see how beautiful you are? How beautiful you are to me?*

No, the missus would be in the pool, her mobile stashed in a locker.

Perhaps he should leave a message anyway.

Just in case…in case—

What would he say? Well, that he loved her. Even though she knew that already…

He ought to call his daughters too. But mobile phones weren't allowed in the classrooms. Again, the point would be to leave a farewell message. Just in case…in case—

He'd argued with his daughters last night over dinner. Over something dumb, something trivial. *Dad, why don't you buy a digital subscription for the newspaper? Because I prefer to have the thing I'm paying for in its physical form, not in some virtual form that doesn't actually exist. Okay, um, but you throw the "real world" newspaper in the bin; think of the environment. Yeah, Dad, what difference does it make if you're not keeping the newspapers anyway?* And on it went. The girls leaving the table in a huff, the missus rolling her eyes at him, as per usual. *Why can't you let things go?* she had said while clearing the dishes. *Why do you have to be so stubborn?*

God, I don't know, I don't *know*, he thought desperately. You may as well ask me why my eyes are hazel. The innate qualities that made him a good homicide detective—tenacity, attention to detail, a no-bullshit attitude—happened to make him a pretty shit father, in his opinion. Whenever he caught one of his daughters uttering a ridiculous comment, such as *You only use ten per cent of your brain*, he couldn't ignore it. No, he had to correct her. *Pick your battles*, his missus would say. *Don't get your knickers in a twist over things that don't matter*. And he tried. But for whatever reason, biting his tongue was just too damned difficult.

The door of the generator room was open. Uh-oh. That couldn't be right. He squinted into the shadows, fearful of an ambush. No zombies appeared. He motored past the generator room and the water tanks. There was his car. Relief made him laugh out loud.

In the boot would be two shotguns. Boxes of shotgun shells. Boxes of bullets for the Smith & Wesson semi-automatic pistols. Collapsible batons. Capsicum spray. Tasers. Even a couple of cricket bats, courtesy of Robert, the Detective Senior Sergeant of crew eight. *You never know when a bat might come in handy*, he always insisted, and Rick would never disagree with Robert on that point ever again.

He was almost at the unmarked BMW. Groping in his pocket for the keys—

Zombies.

Yelping, he jammed on the brakes.

Zombies in the carport. Converging on the building from the other side.

He grabbed the Smith & Wesson from his belt and, mindful of being low on ammunition, took careful aim. Right between the eyes of the leading zombie, a grey and suppurating monster, something that resembled a tall and thin man. Hopefully, the sound of the shot might scare off the others. There were six or seven humans and three pigs shuffling and bumping about with no purpose. It was as if they had been drawn to the vicinity of the main building but, once there, hadn't any idea what to do next.

He pulled the trigger—*click*—and dry-fired. *Shit*.

The zombies stopped their pointless meandering.

Turned.

Spotted him.

Began to head in his direction.

Gasping, he hauled on the handlebars to wrench the bike around. He had to get back to the main building. Oh shit, the small army that had followed him through the grounds was almost upon him. Violet broke into a lolloping run, her arms dangling loose by her sides.

He opened the throttle. Looked from the front door to Violet. She was closing in fast. Christ, was he going to make it? Front door, Violet, front door, Violet—

Oh no, oh *shit*, he wasn't going to make it—

With a yell, he leapt from the bike and slung it at her. She tripped over it, face-planting without the smarts, or perhaps the physical ability, to put out her hands to break her fall. He sprinted, arms pumping, took the steps in a single bound. Shoved his way into the main building. The pneumatic closer wanted to take its sweet time and kiss the door back into the jamb, but he used his shoulder and forced the door shut. Was there a lock? Yes, a latch set into the handle. He turned the latch. Could zombies open doors? No fucking idea, but he didn't want to find out.

He leaned his sweaty forehead against the door, trying to get his breath while his heart punched into his throat.

"Rick?"

He glanced about. *Stella*. Her face streaked with mascara and tears. And next to her, gormless, an old man in a lab coat with a bandaged arm. Rick grappled for his holstered gun, remembering at the same instant that it was empty, and then pointed a finger at the old man.

"What's wrong with him?" he demanded.

Stella wrung her hands and shook her head. "A stroke? I don't know."

"Get away from him, *now*," Rick said.

Nodding, she took a few unsteady paces, reached her reception desk and leaned over it. Palm over palm, she worked her way around the desk and fell into the chair, gasping. The old man had watched her this whole time, unblinking, giving Rick the creeps.

"Rick, what happened?" she croaked. "What happened out there? Where's your partner?"

"He's dead."

"Huh? *Dead?* Oh jeez. Are you serious?" She gazed about with glassy eyes. "Oh no. Oh dear. Where's Cheryl? Why isn't she with you? For Pete's sake, what's—?"

"Shut up!" He scraped both hands through his sweating hair. "Shut up for a minute. Tell me. How many people are on site?"

"Huh? How many people—?"

"Are on site! Christ, woman, how many staff members are here today at VITERI?"

Her face gurned, mouth opening and closing soundlessly, and the uncanny reminder of zombies and their gnashing jaws made his flesh squirm. And this deathly pale old man. What the fuck was the story with this old man? What the actual *fuck*?

"Get back," Rick boomed in his most authoritative voice. "Get back right now."

The old man obeyed, tottering backwards, taking stiff-legged steps along the corridor, the soles of his shoes rubbing and squeaking on the linoleum. When he was about ten metres away, he came to a standstill and smiled pleasantly. Okay, maybe the codger wasn't a zombie after all, but experiencing some kind of medical emergency. Rick would deal with that emergency later. One crisis at a time, he reminded himself, addressed from most to least important. *Triage*. The best and only way to deal with any shit-fight.

He would have this situation under control soon enough, by Christ.

Meanwhile, Stella had sifted through the papers on her desk. Her breath came and went quickly as if she were about to cry. "Eight staff members are on site today," she said. "Director Joan Kendall, Professor Walter Boyce, IT specialist Kieran Pocock, student Helen Macauley, student Alisha Singh, student Cheryl Zhao, caretaker Magnus Vestergaard, and me. Ten people on site including you and your constable." She crinkled the pages of the notebook compulsively in her shaking hands, and looked up at Rick with wide eyes magnified by her spectacles. "Are you hurt? Is that your blood?"

Mystified, Rick looked about before glancing down at his shirt and tie. His clothes were spattered. The blood could belong to Cheryl or Garcia. Maybe both.

"No, it's not mine," he said. "How many staff members are accounted for? As of this moment?"

"Only three. Me. Professor Walter Boyce over there. And Director Joan Kendall."

"Where's Joan's location?"

Stella pointed at a nearby closed door.

He said, "That's her office?"

"No. It's the morgue."

His guts tightened. "What's Joan doing in the morgue?"

"Putting identification labels on our new donor. One on the wrist, one on the ankle. You know, like in a maternity hospital? So that you don't mix up the babies."

"You mean there's a dead body in there?"

Stella nodded.

A chill moved through him. "Just one?"

She nodded again.

Rick's knees began to shake. Breathe, he reminded himself. *In through the nose. Hold. Out through the mouth.* He squeezed his eyes shut and pinched at the bridge of his nose. "Fuck. One of them in the building with us."

"One of *what* in the building with us?" Stella said.

"Can you lock the morgue from this side?"

"Lock it? Why would we need to lock it?"

The morgue door opened. Rick put his weight on his back foot and lifted his arms, trying to remember any details at all from his training on unarmed combat: strikes, take-downs, throws. The pear-shaped woman with the shonky hips lumbered out of the room, saw him and Stella and the old man, and stopped in her tracks, both eyebrows climbing her forehead.

Relief drained the strength from Rick's limbs and he dropped his arms. It was only Joan Kendall. The door whispered shut behind her. A sweet smell of chilled disinfectant and death wafted over Rick for a split-second and was gone.

"Madam," he said. "Joan. Can you lock that particular door?"

Joan put both fists on her hips. "Hell's bells." She looked at each of them, alarmed now but feigning anger, her nostrils flaring. "I turn my back for *five* minutes... Somebody, please explain this situation to me."

"First, I need you to lock the morgue door. That's extremely important."

She lifted her chin and glared at him as if he were an idiot. "There's no need for locks inside this building. Haven't you noticed the fence? The razor wire?

Our security systems? Officer, you've got blood on your shirt. Would you mind telling me why?"

Something heavy slammed against the front door. Rick jumped, turned. The front door rattled in its frame to the pounding of fists, dozens of fists. The zombies. Oh shit, the zombies were at the front door.

"What's happening?" Stella wailed.

"We're under attack," Rick said. "Are there any other doors in or out of this building?"

Frightened, white-faced, Joan said, "Only the back door onto the patio."

"Go and lock it. Now. *Now.*"

She ran on her ruined hips, a stilted side-to-side lope that reminded him, again, of the zombies. The old man—Walter—didn't flinch. Didn't react.

"You!" Rick yelled at him. "Get inside your office and stay there."

The bastard remained frozen in place. Rick was about to man-handle him into a room when he heard a sharp gasp. He looked around.

Stella, seated at her desk, was waving a shaking finger at one of the monitors. "Look at this. Look."

He scrabbled around to her side of the desk. There were about a dozen CCTV monitors. The black and white images showed zombies. Scores of them. Zombie humans. Zombie pigs. Everywhere. Shuffling around the building, with more coming out of the trees.

"Which monitors show the area directly outside?" he said.

"These two," Stella said. "Front door. Morgue exterior door and ramp." She whimpered and stared at him. "What *are* those things?"

"Your cadavers."

She blinked her glazed eyes very slowly. "Our…cadavers?"

"Brought back to life."

"I don't understand…"

"Neither do I. But I've got a theory."

Something in his periphery made him glance up. *Shit.* The old man, Walter, was standing right there in front of the desk. He had somehow snuck up on them without Rick noticing.

"This is the end," Walter said, his voice hoarse and dry.

"The end of what?" Rick said. "And I thought I told you to get inside your goddamned office. Don't make me tell you again."

Walter dropped his head and stepped back.

"How could our donors have come back to life?" Stella said. "It's impossible."

Limping footsteps sounded. Joan Kendall hurried around the corner, her face grey, her brunette hair flying. "The patio door is locked."

She reached the desk, panting. Stella gestured at her frantically, *come here, come here.* Joan moved around the desk and gazed at the CCTV cameras in silence. The pounding on the front door went on and on.

"Is this some kind of…protest?" Joan said. "A bunch of…activists?"

"No," Rick said. "Listen to me. Both of you. This sounds crazy, but I swear on my daughters' lives what I'm about to tell you is true. We put the donor,

Violet, in the boot of the car. A fucking weird cloud dropped some kind of seed—"

"We saw it, we saw it!" Stella yelped, bouncing up and down in her seat. "Like a snowfall. Joan went outside to have a better look and some of it swept into the building."

"And disappeared?" Rick said.

She nodded. "Right into the lino."

"Listen. Here's the crazy part. Violet came back to life." Against their cries and protests, he put up his palm. "Wait. There's more. It's bad news. Very bad. Brace yourselves. You prepared? Okay, here it is. Violet killed Cheryl Zhao."

The women gasped.

"Attacked her like some kind of wild dog," he continued. "Bit out her throat."

Stella blanched. "Bit out her *throat*? Oh my God…"

"What? This is absolutely insane," Joan said, her voice seesawing in a high register.

"Zombies," Stella murmured.

Joan turned and promptly slapped Stella across the face. Rick grabbed Joan's wrist before she could have another shot. Stella, however, seemed hardly to notice. Dazed, she shook off the slap and pointed at the monitors.

"Zombies," she said. "The living dead. Somehow, it's come true. Hell must be full. Isn't that the cause? When there's no vacancies left in Hell—"

"Good grief, Haitian voodoo?" Joan cried. "Witchcraft and mind control? Are you mad?"

"No, no," Stella insisted. "Not that kind."

"Joan, look at the CCTV," Rick said. "You put on all of their tags, correct? All of their I.D. tags. You know what they look like. So, do you recognise any of them? Do you?"

She seemed to hold her breath as she leaned on the desk. A dazed expression came over her face. "Why, that's Indigo. And Fabian. Andreas. Uyen." She put a hand to her mouth and retched a little. "Oh God, that's *Violet*. And our cadaver pigs… How can this be?"

"Listen to me," Rick said.

"Oh," Joan said, bringing both fists to her temples. "Oh no, no, no—"

"Stop. *Stop it*. Don't freak out," he said. "Stop! We can't afford to freak out. We'll freak out later when all this is over. Right now, we have to keep our wits. Are you listening? As far as I can tell, the VITERI compound is full of zombies. Human and pig, but other animals too. Wild animals that have died on site. Birds. Possums." He swallowed. "Kangaroos."

Stella's mouth gaped open and closed. "Kangaroos?"

"That's how Garcia died. I haven't seen any zombie snakes, lizards or insects, so I guess that means only warm-blooded animals are affected."

Joan put her palms over her ears. "Impossible. Ridiculous. This doesn't make any sense."

"No, it doesn't," he said, "and yet it's true. Listen. I've already called the authorities. Okay? Can you hear me? Can you both hear me? I've got trained officers with lots of guns coming here to help us. But you have to call every VITERI staff member on site. Immediately. Tell them to take shelter."

"Do it, Stella," Joan gasped. "Hurry."

"I can't." Clasping hands to her breast, Stella turned her head to look at— Walter.

Everyone looked at Walter.

His smile was a mechanical tic which tugged at both sides of his mouth.

Stella continued, "He destroyed our communications equipment."

Joan stood up straight, as if remembering her authority. "Walter? Is this true?"

The old man nodded.

"He smashed our mobiles as well," Stella said.

"My word," Joan said, hands back on her hips. "Explain yourself, Professor Boyce."

The old man kept grinning. The zombies outside kept thumping and knocking and tapping. Thank *fuck* Rick had locked the door. Thank *fuck* that both external doors were locked. If Rick had a bullet in his gun, he'd put it straight into the forehead of Walter Boyce. The seeping of dark sludge on his bandaged hand gave it away: *zombie bite*. That's how the infection was passed, right? Like rabies. Yeah, Rick had seen some of those particular horror movies. His eldest daughter was a fan.

"I had to do it," Walter said, and his voice was choked, phlegmy.

"Why?" Joan said. When he didn't answer, she added, "I'm the director of this facility. I demand that you tell us. Why did you vandalise company property?"

He seemed to laugh but no sound came out. He lifted a finger and dipped his head as if to say, *Give me a minute*. They waited. Finally, he said, "To stop Ice-Prepper Gin Haddock."

His answer didn't make sense to Rick. Apparently, it didn't make sense to the ladies either. A moment of stunned silence passed.

"He's gone crazy," Joan said. "A history of panic attacks. It was only a matter of time."

"No, he's having a stroke," Stella said. "He complained of a bad headache earlier. Tell them, Walter. Tell them. I gave him tablets. I gave him four pain tablets. I wanted to call an ambulance but I didn't. Tell them, Walter. Please. Oh frick, we should call an ambulance."

The zombies beat at the door. Rick's heart slammed in his chest. Walter gazed at the floor for just a second, then slid his feet across the linoleum as if he were ice-skating, gliding, sailing nearer to the reception desk—

"Halt!" Rick barked, lifting both arms as if he knew Kung Fu. "Stay where you are!"

Walter stopped. A change came over his face and he stared at them each in turn, mournfully, his pale cheese-yellow lips turned down as if readying to sob.

"Gin Haddock." He worked his jaws, grunted, but no other words came out. He coughed once, twice. Seemed to struggle. Then he smiled again. A death's head smile. "Zombie. I'm a zombie."

"Please," Stella said. "Please, Joan. Rick? What's the matter with him?"

Walter lifted his bandaged arm and gazed at it with great joy, his mouth wide open in a smile that showed a blackened tongue. Stella shrieked, put her hands to her face.

"Zombie," Walter said, his voice thick and clogged in the back of his throat. He patted his chest with his bandaged hand and nodded. "Zombie. Yes."

"No," Stella said. "It's a stroke. Only dead people turn into zombies."

"And anyone alive who gets bitten," Rick said. "They die and then they change."

"How do you know all of this?" Joan said.

Rick, feeling stupid, replied, "From the movies."

"From the *movies?*"

"But he's been inside the building this whole time," Stella wailed. "This whole time."

Walter flicked his gaze to the ceiling as if exasperated. Then an idea must have dawned on him, signalled by a broad grin and a raised finger which together seemed to say *A ha, I'll prove it*. He took a large pair of scissors from the pocket of his lab coat. Opened the blades. Snipped them a couple of times in the air. The joint was oiled, soundless.

Rick would tackle him to the floor. Take out the threat with a forearm under the chin. No one would get stabbed. Rick would not allow a stabbing. No one else would die. No one else.

Walter stuck out his black tongue. Opened the blades. Thrust them into his gaping mouth.

Rick froze. The women screamed.

When operating the scissors with one hand didn't provide enough grunt, Walter used both hands. He hacked and sliced and cut under and through the meat of his tongue, angling the blades of the scissors towards the tonsils. He made ack-ack-ack sounds as he cut-cut-cut. Blood—not real blood, not *alive*-person blood, since it was the colour and viscosity of golden syrup—slid in lazy snail-trails down his beard. *He's really putting his back into it*, Rick thought in stunned amazement. *This is a man on a mission.*

The scissor handles went deep into Walter's mouth, his lips splitting to accommodate both fists. Rick thought the old man might continue, and ram his hands—and arms too, why the hell not—all the way down his own oesophagus. Anything seemed possible at this point.

But then Walter took out the scissors, closed the blades, and stowed the scissors in his lab pocket. A steady drip-drip of dark, congealing blood ran off the point of his goatee. With his bandaged hand, he reached up and took hold of his tongue. It reeled out. Longer and longer. Past his chin. Reaching almost to his chest.

Rick lost the ability to breathe.

A final tug. With a wet tearing sound, the tongue came away in Walter's fist. He raised and waggled it; his facial expression triumphant as if to say *You see? I told you.*

After inspecting the organ for a few seconds, he dropped his arm and let go. The tongue fell at his feet. Somehow, Walter had managed to remove his own tongue by the root. It looked like an ox tongue that you might see doubled up and wrapped under clear cellophane in a butcher's shop, except this tongue was human-sized and black. Walter smiled. A fresh gout of thick, dark blood oozed over his lips.

Well, I'll be damned…Rick thought, pondering the severed organ in shock. Well, I'll be…

Joan fell sideways. When she hit the ground, Rick understood that she had fainted.

11

Magnus swung the line-trimmer from side to side, blitzing the little animals. Too bad he had forgotten to put on safety glasses. The idea of getting blood or flesh particles in his eyes was repugnant. And too bad he wasn't wearing boots. Walking in socks along the carpet of gore which littered his veranda felt disgusting, like treading through mud and the slime of decomposing leaves. Never mind. He was almost at the door of his cabin. The girl, Helen Macauley, should be following close behind him.

His boots, side by side on the veranda, got sprayed with muck. No, he wouldn't be wearing those boots ever again. Good thing he had another pair in his wardrobe.

And now, every last zombie rat, mouse and bird was pulverised. The carnage had taken perhaps a minute. He took his finger off the trigger. The line-trimmer's motor dropped to an idle and he turned it off. Opening the door, he turned to check that Helen was there and saw a disquieting sight. In what he considered his "front yard"—a cleared patch of land about ten metres out from his cabin and work shed—came a dozen or so zombie pigs.

Some of them wore clothes. Others did not. They varied in their states of decay. A few were more or less intact but discoloured with black, brown and white patches of blistered skin, their misshapen bodies wrinkled and puckered. Most had the soft tissues of their snouts missing. One pig in particular stood out. Decomposition gases had blown its stomach. As it lumbered unsteadily across the ground, its blackened trotters kept stumbling over the tattered remnants of its own belly flesh.

But there were no skeletal pigs. Just as there had been no skeletal rats, mice, birds. Interesting. He would mull this over in a moment.

"Get inside," he said, and crossed the threshold.

Helen hurried after him and he closed the door. He put the line-trimmer in the corner, took off the rifle and tool belt and laid them across the armchair. Then he took off his socks. His work trousers were spattered in bloody remains.

"You see those pigs coming for us?" she said.

He nodded. "I'll get changed. Then we can worry about the pigs."

"Did you cut your feet?"

"With the line-trimmer? Of course not."

"No, on bone fragments," she said, and took hold of his arm. "Let me see your feet."

"I'll wash them first." He indicated the kitchenette. "Please. Make yourself at home. There is coffee. Teabags. Beer if you want it. Cold chicken in the fridge."

She stared at him, open-mouthed, as if she couldn't fathom drinking or eating at a time like this. But Yngvar always used to say *You can't solve problems on an empty stomach*. It was one of the adages that Magnus lived by, and found to be both true and helpful. He went into the bathroom, stripped to his underwear, bundled his fouled clothes and stashed them under the basin. Quickly soaped and rinsed his feet, hands and forearms under the running shower. Dried off.

Cracking the door, he said, "Excuse me. I'm not dressed. Please look the other way."

But she was at the front window anyway, beer in hand. Her weapons were lined up on the kitchen bench. She still wore the rope belt. "Now, this is a peculiar development," she said.

He went to his bedroom. "What is?"

"The pigs seem lost, confused. They're wandering in circles out there, not approaching the veranda. You know what? I think it's noise. The small zombie animals followed me because they could hear the bike. The pigs came here because they could hear the whipper-snipper."

"Does that mean the ear takes longer to rot than the eye?"

"Well, the inner ear is protected by the skull, for one thing."

He put on clean trousers and a work shirt. He was about to put on socks when he remembered Helen wanted to check his feet. However, there was no pain. He was not injured.

"The fact is," she continued, "I've got no idea what we're dealing with. I mean, yes, they look like zombies, but since zombies aren't real, can I assume anything about their origin or behaviour?"

"There are no skeleton zombies."

She turned to face him. "Very true," she said. "Okay. So, they need soft tissue." She gazed out the window. "Yep. The more decayed the pig, the slower they move. When they don't have any soft tissue, they can't move at all. You'd make a good scientist, Magnus."

He shrugged. "Science is just logic."

"True again." She walked over, placing her beer on the table. "Sit and show me your feet."

It felt strange, holding out his leg to this young woman, as she knelt before him and took his heel in her hands. He felt himself blush. As he was fair-skinned and almost bald, his embarrassment would show. But she didn't look up. Head bent, she scrupulously examined the sole and toes of first one foot and then the other. It tickled despite her firm grip. He clenched his jaw to stop himself from kicking. Then her reasoning became clear to him and his heart gave a lurch.

"You believe if I cut myself on zombie bones that I'll become a zombie?"

"Well, your guess is as good as mine."

"You believe it can spread like an infection?"

"Could do."

He sat quietly for a time, imagining what turning into a zombie might feel like. The idea made him uncomfortable. "And?" he said at last, anxious. "Am I cut on the feet?"

"Not that I can tell." She smiled, but it was strained and wan. Standing up, she added, "Let's get your phone and call Stella."

Rolling on a sock, he said, "If I turn into a zombie, you have to kill me."

She slapped him on the shoulder and tried to laugh. "Oh, come on, you're a pretty big fella, Magnus. I'll try my best, all right?"

"I mean it. Take the rifle and shoot me."

She stopped laughing. "How am I going to get the rifle off you if you're a zombie?"

"It must be a process. The change must take time."

"Good point."

He rolled on the other sock. "If I begin to feel strange, I'll give you my rifle."

"And then what? I shoot you in the head?"

"Correct. You shoot me in the head."

It seemed she would laugh again. Instead, her shoulders sagged and she rubbed both hands over her face. "Oh God. Oh fuck," she began to mumble.

"Promise me."

"Oh God, what the *fuck* is going on here? How can any of this—?"

"*Helen.*"

She dropped her hands from her blanched face. "All right. I promise."

"Do you know how to shoot a rifle?"

"Yeah. Now call Stella."

His mobile sat in its usual place when he wasn't working the grounds: on top of the microwave and plugged into the charger. While he made the call, Helen took another beer from the fridge, opened it, and gave it to him. It seemed odd to be drinking so early.

"Is it ringing?" she said.

He nodded. The call picked up. For a second, he felt a lifting of spirits.

G'day, this is Stella Vasilakis. I can't wait to call you back. Please leave your name and message. Ooroo and have a great day.

He hung up. "Answering machine."

"You mean voicemail?"

"Same thing."

"Try the office number."

He scrolled through his contacts list, found VITERI. Dialled. Waited. Helen stood by his elbow, her eyes wide and pleading, fixed on him. He could hear her breathing.

The call picked up.

Thank you for calling The Victorian Taphonomic Experimental Research Institute. Our office hours are Monday to Friday, 9 a.m. to 5 p.m. For more information about us, and to find out how to contact our facility via email, you can visit our website—VITERI-dot-Fraser-dot-Vic-dot-Edu-dot-Au. Alternatively, please leave a message with your contact details and we'll get back to you as soon as possible. Thank you.

He hung up.

"Try the other staff members," Helen urged. "Professor Kendall, Professor Boyce, Kieran Pocock. You've got their numbers, haven't you?"

"Yes. Drink your beer. I'll call them."

She wandered over to the window, sipping from the bottle, watching the pigs. He reached voicemail over and over.

"It's no use," he said.

She bit at her lips. "You think they're dead?'

"I don't know."

They fell silent for a time.

She took a deep breath. "Let's move on. The pigs are still out there. Maybe they can smell us, but are confused because they can't see or hear us. Or they know we're in here but don't have the brain power to figure out what to do next without an external stimulus." She turned from the window to face him. "Call the police."

"Yes. As we decided, I'll tell them we have a shooter on site."

"Make it more than one."

"How many more?"

Briefly, she put a palm to her forehead. "Oh, fuck it, um…how about six?"

"Six?"

"We want them to come prepared, don't we? No, wait, it should definitely be more."

"Agreed," he said. "Ten shooters?"

She hugged her arms about herself. "Yep. Ten. Sounds good. Let's go with that."

He dialled triple zero. It rang out. He lowered the mobile.

"Voicemail?" she whispered.

"No answer," he said, sliding the mobile into the top pocket of his shirt.

"What do you think that means?"

"I don't know. That the emergency operators are busy."

She leaned against a wall. "Maybe this—*plague*—isn't confined to VITERI. Maybe it's happening everywhere."

"Now you're guessing."

"True." She rubbed her temple. "Fine, we stick to our original plan: ride the quad bike to the VITERI main building. Kill zombies on the way if necessary. Chuck everyone in our cars and get the fuck out of here." She took a sip of beer. "Assuming there's anybody left."

"There will be. And that's a good plan."

"But with one significant problem." She smiled grimly with one side of her mouth. "How do we get to the quad bike with those zombie pigs out there?"

He went and stood next to her at the window. The herd of swine was exactly as she had described: aimless, staggering in circles. Yet not dispersing.

"They're pretty slow," she said. "Could we run along the veranda, jump on the quad bike and ride off before they catch us?"

He took a drink and thought about the logistics. Watched the pigs and how they moved. Considered the eight metres of veranda, slippery and covered in gore. Finally, he said, "No. You see the ones in better condition? Those with the dark patches on their skin?"

"They'd cover the distance and cut us off." She sighed. "Okay. We have to thin the herd. Without wasting bullets. You know what I think? Kill them by hand."

He considered this for a moment. "Okay."

"But we divide and conquer."

"You mean split them into two groups?" he said, surprised. "Have one group each?"

"I reckon that's our best bet."

He didn't like the sound of that idea: Helen was short and slightly built. "No, too dangerous for you," he said. "We should fight back to back."

"Forget it. Back to back, they'll close in on us. From all sides. We won't have any room to manoeuvre. We're swinging hammers and tools, remember? But if we fight separately, one group each, we can stay nimble. Keep moving. Pick off a single pig at a time."

Magnus turned over the plan in his imagination. Then he said, "Yes. I see."

She began to guzzle her beer in fast swallows. Getting ready to leave. To do battle.

"Helen," he said, taking the mobile from his pocket and offering it. "Do you wish to call anybody?"

Her smile was wry. "Oh, I get it. Last goodbyes. You reckon we're gonna die?"

"We might."

Her smile faded. She put down the beer on the windowsill. Hesitantly, she went to reach for the mobile. Stopped. Made a fist and dropped her arm.

"You have no one to call?" he said.

"No one who would care. What about you?"

His mother's face came to mind. Poor Leena, with her neatly combed hair and mischievous, dancing eyes. At first glance, she always seemed well. Like herself. The mother he had always known. Sometimes she looked at him politely, as if he were a stranger, as if he were a nurse on his first day. Occasionally, she frowned and said *Mag-nus* very slowly and tentatively, as if the syllables felt strange in her mouth. Other times, she fooled him. He would approach her in the sunroom and she would beam and hold out her hands for him to clasp. As if she recognised him. *Yngvar*, she would say. *You're home at last. How was your shift at the bakery?*

"Magnus?"

He glanced down. Helen was staring at him. He put the mobile back into his pocket.

"You don't have anyone to call either?" she whispered.

"No one who would remember me."

To his astonishment, Helen suddenly hugged his waist, pressing her cheek against his chest. Awkwardly, out of practice, he put his arms about her in return. When was the last time he had embraced someone? He couldn't recall. It felt nice. Perhaps he should have lived his life somewhat differently. Perhaps he should have tried harder to make friends. To find love. To connect with others before it was too late.

But now it was too late.

Helen let go and turned her back on him. Trying to hide her tears, she was brushing them away even as she hung the ball peen hammer and screwdriver from her rope belt. Magnus wanted to offer words of comfort but couldn't think of any.

With the mallet in one hand and the hatchet in the other, she said, "Okay. Let's do it."

"Give me a minute."

He went to his bedroom. From his wardrobe, he took out the box containing new work boots. The cushiony inner soles were in the old pair on the veranda, no doubt covered in gore from the little zombie animals. He didn't have a spare set of inner soles. These new boots would hurt his feet. So be it. He pulled on the boots and stepped into the kitchen. Propped in the corner was an umbrella. He picked it up. When they rode to the main building, Helen, riding pillion, would have to hold the open umbrella over both their heads to protect against zombie birds or possums dropping from the trees.

"Are you scared?" she said.

He buckled on the tool belt, added the umbrella, slung the rifle over his shoulder. "Of course."

"Me too."

"We'll be all right."

"Or not," she said, and smiled.

He nodded. "Yes. Or not."

The keys were sitting on top of the microwave next to the charger cord for the mobile. He slipped the keys into his pocket. Grabbed the spade. Hanging off his tool belt was the metre-long garden fork. He lifted it and said, "You want this?"

"It might be too heavy."

"No. It isn't heavy. Try it."

She put the mallet and hatchet on the table. He handed her the fork. Experimentally, she hefted it, first in both hands and then in one, swinging it, lunging it through the air.

"Well?" he said. "You like the fork?"

She crinkled her nose. "I feel kind of clumsy with it."

"The mallet and hatchet are close range."

"Yeah, but I can swing them faster."

"You don't want it?" he said.

"Nah."

"It would be safer to use the fork. Not so close."

She held out the garden fork. He shrugged, took it and hung it off his tool belt. She picked up the mallet and hatchet from the table, rolling her wrists as if to loosen and warm the joints.

"If you change your mind," he said, "tell me."

"If I've got time. Sure. I will."

They approached the door of the cabin.

***

Incredulous, revolted, terrified, Stella watched as Walter ripped out his tongue. He dropped it to the floor. It landed with a wet squelch. Her vision pinned and she was looking through a long tunnel. Her hearing muffled as if wads of cotton stuffed both ears.

And then Joan Kendall hit the floor in a dead faint.

At least, Stella *hoped* it was just a faint and nothing to do with being dead. Or was Joan turning into a zombie too? She'd gone out in that weird snowfall, could have got herself infected that way. Bloody hell, if Walter had transformed—somehow, despite being safe inside the building this whole time—then *anybody* could be at risk, including Stella herself. Sounds came back to her. The efforts of countless zombies trying to get inside. Their relentless scraping and thumping at the front door gave her the willies.

She threw off her shock, her panic, and tried to figure out what to do.

First things first—

"Get Walter out of here!" she shouted at policeman Rick Evans. "Shut him in an office!"

With his bloodied mouth, Walter smiled. He opened his ruined lips, as if trying to speak, but no words came out and he shook his head, dropping his chest in defeat.

God, he was a zombie. He *had* to be. What kind of sicko cuts out their own tongue? And the stain on that bandage wrapped around his hand? Certainly not blood. The stain was dark and thick, almost chunky, reminding her of kalamata tapenade. She dry-heaved. Walter had been telling the truth; he *was* a fricking zombie. What other explanation could there be?

"No, wait," she gasped. "Don't put him in an office. Shoot him, Rick. Before he bites us."

"I don't have any bullets."

"Oh, jeez, get *rid* of him. We have to help Joan. Move him away from here!"

Rick took a couple of steps, but she could tell by his shaking hands that he was all bluster. Shit. Back in her day, coppers were mean bastards, tough enough to crack skulls. Crims used to be scared of them. But, oh my word, thanks to the PC brigade and sensitivity training, coppers these days were so bloody *weak*—

Pointing at what happened to be the open door of Kieran's office, Rick shouted, "Inside that room and close the fucking door, old man! Quick smart! Get a move on!"

Walter lifted his bandaged arm, stiffly, and gave a mimicry of his familiar salute. Tears sprang to Stella's eyes. Was this grief? Was she mourning her poor friend? Yes, because he was dead, wasn't he? Or was terror making her want to cry... It occurred to her, in a sickening and swooping rush, that she was in grave danger. In fact, she might die today. Would very likely die. She had to get in contact with Con. But how? She didn't have her mobile. The computer and landline were out—

"Go on, get!" Rick yelled, as if to a dog. "Scram!"

Unsteadily, arms out for balance, Walter turned on his heel and headed down the hallway towards his own office. His gait was like nothing Stella had ever seen him do before, including that one time he'd walked funny after spraining his ankle. His knees didn't bend. It was as if the joints were frozen. He kept his legs spread and *slid* his feet across the floor. It didn't look natural. The crepe-soled shoes whisked against the linoleum in a steady rhythm.

Whisk. Whisk. Whisk.

Hand at her throat, Stella watched him. If he stopped and came back, well, she might just lose her mind. He was almost at his office now. She imagined him turning around and running back, arms outstretched, mouth open. What would she do? Scream. Puke. Get bitten. Die. She glanced at Rick. He was staring at Walter's retreating form too.

Walter opened the door of his office. Went inside. Looked back. Saluted again.

"And stay in there!" Rick yelled.

Walter shut the door.

Stella exhaled and sagged in her chair for a moment. Then she clambered around from behind her desk and dropped to one knee by Joan's side. *Déjà vu.* The old and ghastly memory came back in a flash. Her daughter Melanie. A pool party at Stella's brother's house over Christmas. Plenty of kids. Plenty of adults. An inground pool and a cabana. Kids squealing, jumping in the pool, running around the pebbled deck. Melanie, six years old, hair in pigtails, arms in yellow plastic floaties. One minute, Melanie is swimming with her cousin Nick, happy as can be. Stella looks away, picks up her plastic wine-glass, pours and chugs some cask Riesling.

Next minute, kids shrieking. Adults screaming.

A limp body is dragged from the pool. The pigtail bobbles, the cherry-striped swimsuit with frills. Melanie.

It's Melanie.

The world cracks in two. On one side, Melanie is dead. On the other, Melanie is alive. This is the moment upon which Stella's entire life will hinge.

Stella bolts over to her child, is performing mouth-to-mouth before she even realises what is happening. Melanie coughs and bawls. Stella hugs her, too shaken to cry. Con rushes over. Poor Con, who had been retrieving another case of beer from the kitchen, and had missed the commotion, missed his daughter's near death. Could only, as the years pass, mention it occasionally to Stella when he was drunk, usually at Christmas or New Year. *If it wasn't for you, Koukla, we wouldn't have our girl.* Don't say it, Stella would reply. Don't jinx us. The Universe will hear and finish what it started.

"Is she okay?"

Stella blinked, confused. Looked around.

"Is she okay?" Rick said again. "Is Dr Kendall okay?"

Stella put one hand beneath Joan's head, cradling it. With the other, she stroked and patted at Joan's face. *White as a sheet.* How strange that a cliché expression could be literally true.

"Wake up," she murmured. "Joan? Come on, wake up."

"Has she got a pulse?" Rick said.

Why don't you kneel down here with me and check for yourself? Instead, Stella said, "I can see it beating in her throat. And besides, she's breathing."

Joan's eyelids fluttered and opened. The poor woman looked dazed, drugged. "Why am I on the floor?" she mumbled.

"You fainted," Stella said. "But you're okay now. Let me help you up."

Joan struggled to a sitting position. Stella grabbed one arm and Rick grabbed the other. With effort, they managed to get her to her feet.

"That's Walter's tongue," Joan said, matter-of-factly, yet she swayed as if readying to faint again.

Rick kicked the severed organ underneath the desk. A congealing splotch of black blood remained on the linoleum. The ripe, pungent smell of still and stagnant water, of green algae, wafted up from it.

"Are you all right?" Stella said.

Joan nodded.

"You won't pass out if we let you go?"

Joan shook her head.

Cautiously, they released her arms. She remained standing. For a couple of seconds, they all looked at each other with frightened eyes.

"What's turning them into zombies?" Joan said.

"The stuff that came from that weird-looking cloud," Rick said. "At first I thought it was chemical seeding to make rain. Now I reckon it must be a biological experiment. Scientists put some kind of chemical agent into that cloud and released it over the VITERI grounds. To see if it would work. To see if their chemical agent could bring the dead back to life."

"Why here? Why not over a cemetery?" Stella said.

"I guess the chemical can't penetrate six feet of soil, let alone coffin lids. Even if it could, how does a rotting body have the strength to get out of a sealed coffin? Not even a living person in their prime could do that."

"Jeez," Stella said. "Do you really reckon that funny cloud was meant for us?"

"Put it this way: there weren't any other clouds like it."

"Oh, this is *nonsense*," Joan said. "What scientific organisation would do such a thing?"

"An evil one," Stella suggested.

"Sweet holy Mary." Joan rubbed at the back of her neck, wincing, as if she had cricked it during her fall. "So, we have a zombie horde outside. What do we do?"

"Sit tight," Rick said. "Armed specialist police forces are on the way."

"How long 'til they turn up?" Stella said.

His face took on a guarded, reluctant expression. "Soon."

"How soon?" Stella said. "Rick? Tell us. Come on, mate, just tell us."

"A few hours."

"A few *hours?*" Joan exclaimed.

"By road. But they might get here by helicopter."

"Mother of *God*. What if the zombies break in?"

"Look, take it easy, I'll call my boss, see if I can get an ETA—"

"You have a mobile?" Joan said. "Excellent. Stella, we can ring the other staff members. We can warn them after all."

"Good idea," he said, handing over his phone.

Stella went behind her desk and took out her contacts book. Unlike Melanie, who put her entire trust in digital devices, Stella was old-school and always had back-ups written down on paper. Her hands trembled as she leafed through the pages. Who should she call first? Kieran. He might have some idea of how to fix the computers. Oh, why hadn't he come back from the bunkhouse? Perhaps he was hiding inside.

"Rick," she said. "On your way past the bunkhouse, did you see anybody? A young bloke?"

He blew out a breath. "I saw the remains of a person eaten down to the bone."

"How could you tell it was a person?" Joan said.

"How could I *tell*? I'm a homicide detective, lady. I see that kind of shit every damned day. It's literally my job."

Joan flushed, insulted, nostrils flaring.

"Was it a man or a woman?" Stella said. "Could you see any clothing?"

"It was definitely a man. The clothing was bloody and torn, but there were these fancy men's lace-ups."

Feeling a wave of nausea, Stella closed her eyes. "Like the leather was made from crocodile or snake skin?"

"Yeah. Who was he?"

"Kieran Pocock. Our IT guy."

"Oh, my Lord," Joan murmured.

"I'm sorry for your loss," Rick said. "But at least he won't come back as a zombie."

"How do you know?" Joan said.

"Because as far as I can tell, zombies need muscles and tendons and ligaments to move."

"I see." Primly, Joan pursed her lips. "I think I might need to vomit."

"While you're doing that," he said, and turned to Stella, "you call the other VITERI staff."

Stella consulted her contacts book. Alisha Singh. Helen Macauley. Magnus Vestergaard.

"Should I ring Magnus first?" she said. "He's our caretaker. He's got loads of tools in his shed that we could use as weapons if the…"

She trailed off. What was that noise? The tap-tap-tapping. Where was that noise coming from? The others heard it too. They cocked their heads, looking about. Insistent knocking and scraping noises. Not coming from the zombies at the front door.

Coming from inside the building.

Simultaneously, they all looked at the morgue door.

"Christ," Rick said through his teeth. "I bloody well *knew* it."

"This can't be," Joan said. "That donor hasn't been exposed."

Stella said, "No, I reckon he has. You stood outside to look at the chemical snow. When you went into the morgue, you must have had flakes on your clothes."

Joan blanched. "I didn't know… How could I have known?"

Stella thought of Butch. *The largest we've ever had*, Walter had proclaimed. *Must have been a weightlifter or a bodybuilder…shaved head, beard and tattoos…*

"Oh jeez," she muttered. "I'm sorry, guys, but I think we're screwed."

"Calm down," Rick said. "Zombies can't open doors."

The morgue's door handle rattled.

12

They stood by the cabin door. Helen held the mallet and hatchet. The ball peen hammer and screwdriver hung from her improvised rope belt. Magnus held the spade. In his tool belt were the claw hammer, garden fork and umbrella. He had the .22 rifle slung by its strap over his shoulder. Would their arsenal be enough? She didn't think so.

Magnus reached for the door handle. A sudden panic thumped the blood in her eardrums.

"Let me check the window first," she said.

The pigs, walking in circles, had slowed their pace. As if bored or tired. It gave her the idea that, given enough time, the zombie pigs would run out of motivation and simply lie down in the dirt. Become harmless again. Dead again.

"See that?" she said to Magnus, who had moved next to her at the window.

"Yes. They're winding down like clocks."

"Why not wait for them to stop?"

He rubbed at his chin. The short whiskers made a rasping sound. For a split-second, her father's early morning stubble came to mind. He used to hug her before breakfast and tickle his stubble against her cheeks while she screamed with laughter and struggled to get away. It was a game they had played every morning until she hit puberty, when her mother had put a stop to the game. For what reason, Helen had never fathomed. Dad had improvised by rubbing at his whiskers and winking at her. But it wasn't the same. At the time, Helen had suspected her mother of jealousy.

"There's no point in waiting," Magnus said.

"You sure? They look like they're ready to give up."

"No. The pigs are already dead. Waiting a few minutes won't make them more so. As soon as we go outside, whether now or later, they'll get excited and try to kill us."

Helen sighed. "Why didn't you ever become a scientist?"

"Because I became a caretaker."

"Is that what you've done your whole life?"

"Yes."

Helen considered. "You never regretted that career choice?"

"No." He stepped towards the door. "Let's get started."

"Okay, hear me out first," she said, heart racing. "Here's my plan. As soon as we get outside, we jump off the veranda. You run to the right, heading towards the quad bike. I'll run to the left. That way, we'll split the herd and you'll be ready to start the bike as soon as we're done slaughtering the pigs."

"Yes. Agreed." He narrowed his eyes and faced the door. "On my mark," he began.

Her mind flew. My God, she thought, I've never felt so *present*. It must be the adrenaline, norepinephrine and cortisol. Every nerve ending awake. Every corpuscle and cell zinging. No, wait, this was more than a simple biochemical reaction, more than a mere fight-or-flight response. For the first time in her life, she was facing certain death and a part of her marvelled at the singularity of the experience. She had occasionally wondered, abstractly, what facing death might feel like. She wondered about it whenever she read a news article about a plane crash, say, or a blog post by someone with a terminal illness.

And now she knew.

Facing death felt as if your whole being had transformed into a collection of microscopic crystalline shards; billions of intense, sharp-edged, bright, vibrating and painful points upon which to cut yourself. An out-of-body experience, in fact. Was she dissociating?

"One," Magnus said.

She should have called her mother when Magnus had offered his phone. But what would she have said? *Hi Mum. I just wanted to let you know that I'm about to die.* How might Mum have reacted? The news may have shattered her hostile carapace, softened her, reminded her of how she had once cared about Helen. For some time after the estrangement, Helen used to call on Mother's Day. In case Mum had changed her mind. The conversation always went the same way:

Hi Mum, it's me. Don't hang up.

Are you still a dyke?

Yeah.

No thanks. Followed by the click of the line disconnecting.

A few years ago, Helen had stopped calling home. Now she spent every Mother's Day deep-cleaning her flat: removing the flywire screens and venetian blinds and hosing them on the balcony; shampooing the lounge suite; emptying out and scrubbing the pantry, refrigerator, kitchen cupboards and drawers; polishing the wooden furniture. At the end of the long day, aching, she would shower and fall into bed, out cold in an instant.

No, Helen was right not to call. What would be the use? Did she really want her last minutes on earth to be poisoned by her mother's disgust and contempt? No, fuck that. Helen brought to mind her friends, colleagues, old flames. Her research. Tried to hang on to something. Anything good. But it all felt so *slippery*. Out of reach. Yes, she was dissociating.

"Two," Magnus said.

Oh, she'd miss a lot of things. Big things, sure, but small things seemed to hold the most poignancy right now. Chicken curry laksa from her local Malaysian takeaway. IPA lager. Turning over the pillow at night and laying her head on the cool side. The warble of magpies in the morning. She was in the middle of reading a trilogy of novels and now she would never find out how the story ended.

Thousands of little tragedies. Thousands of little losses.

Did everyone feel this way upon facing death?

"Three," Magnus said.

Goodbye, she thought in a hectic and blind sort of panic. Goodbye to me forever.

Had she liked herself? Enough, she supposed. If only she'd liked herself more. Why fret, for *years*, about the thickness of her thighs? About her freckled skin? After Mum turned her away, Helen had even fretted, for *years*, about being gay. How stupid. What a stupid waste of time and energy. Live and let live, the old saying went, and now she understood the full import of its meaning. Too late. Oh, terrific: another little tragedy. And those times she had, melodramatically as it turned out, wished to be dead? What an idiot. Now, at the age of twenty-six, she was actually about to die. *Fuck.*

Was Magnus feeling the same way? Grappling with the same turmoil of thoughts?

He was staring at the door.

"*Mark.*"

He reached for the handle. Helen's fists tightened on the mallet and hatchet. The door opened, hard, banging against the wall. The sunlight glared. The carpet of gore on the veranda looked black. The pigs, as one, stopped and looked over. Those that still had ears pricked them. The herd charged.

Magnus ran over the threshold and leapt from the veranda. Helen followed. He veered right. She veered left.

The pigs, momentarily confused, didn't seem to know what to do.

Helen checked behind. No zombies approaching through the trees. She should have reminded Magnus to keep checking his surroundings but he was already so far away. Near the carport where the quad bike was housed.

The herd split, unevenly.

A few trotted towards Magnus. The rest, about seven or eight, shambled towards her.

She had only ever killed trout and rabbit. The fonder memories: trout fishing with Dad. Once the fish landed, her job was to hit them over the head with a club. As a child, this practice had seemed cruel until Dad had pointed out the alternative: suffocation.

But she wouldn't be *killing* these pigs. They were already dead.

She ran alongside the clearing for a few metres, keeping the trees at her back, to separate the fast pigs from the slow. The breeze picked up, carrying the unmistakable scent of decay. The scent made up of some five hundred organic compounds, if she recalled correctly. According to the mass spectrometer, the difference between the smell of a rotting human and a rotting pig was only five esters. Was she dissociating again? Yes. Yes, she was.

She shook herself as if coming awake.

Stop rambling and act.

A pig, in a floral sundress stained with putrefaction juices, galloped in a stiff limp, leading the pack. Blowflies crowded its festering snout. A new cadaver. By the looks of it, only a few days old. Whose experiment could it be? Helen didn't know every student in the forensic courses at Fraser University. But the sundress... This could be Dan's experiment. Dan with the waxed moustache and gauge earrings. He had asked her out once. The point of his research was to establish how different environmental conditions affected clothing. Very similar, in fact, to Alisha's experiment. Alisha... *Don't think about her*. Instead,

Helen recalled one of Dan's conversational snippets: clothing buried by itself is quickly eaten down to the hemline by soil bacteria, while the decomposition fluids and melting lipids of a dead body help to preserve material. He was experimenting with different fabrics: leather, denim, polyester, cotton, cotton-blends. The sundress. Yes, this must be one of Dan's pigs. Dan with the hand tattoos. She couldn't abide hand tattoos. They always looked dirty.

She shook herself again. *Focus.*

The pig's teeth were long and yellow.

Blackened gums crawling with maggots.

Cloudy eyes.

No sounds, no breath.

Helen raised the hatchet. Shrieked as the pig came within striking distance. How dense was a pig's skull? Could she break through the bones? She brought down the hatchet. The shock of the blow travelled up her arm, ringing, as if she had struck concrete. The pig ducked and reared. Oh shit, the blade was *stuck*. She remembered the mallet and hit at the animal over and over like a drum, ferociously, desperately, while tugging to free the hatchet.

Other pigs converged. So *quiet*. Only the sounds of trotters dragging through the leaf litter, the buzzing of flies taking off and landing.

The hatchet came loose.

With a cry, Helen spun the handle and brought down the backside of the blade, again and again and again. The skull of the sundress pig cracked open. Helen chopped at the exposed brain. Clots of tissue flew. The pig collapsed. The cloud of blowflies boiling about its face dove into its open cranium.

She stumbled backwards. The herd changed course to keep her in sight.

Another set of teeth, a pair of small and milky eyes. She used the hammer this time. The first few blows seemed to bounce. She remembered the pterion. The cranial suture located just behind the temple where the four main bones of the skull— frontal, parietal, temporal, and sphenoid—come together. At least in humans. Did pigs share this particular anatomy? Worth a try. Gasping with effort, she rained down hammer blows on the pterion. She could feel the bones splintering, the break and crumble telegraphing through the handle. It sounded, incongruously, like the popping of bubble wrap. The hammer-head broke through the skull. When she wrenched it out, a smattering of pulverised brain came with it. The pig's jaw fell open. Then it lost its footing and crashed onto the dirt.

Two down. Six to go.

Sidestepping, she moved in a wide circle. Checked her surroundings for other zombies. Clear. The herd continuously shifted to keep her lined up. Like magnetised needles always facing north. She risked a glance over at Magnus. He was in mid-swing of the spade. The blade took off half a pig's head in one gory swipe. Damn. She should have accepted the large garden fork as he had suggested. She ran around behind the herd. Picked the slowest pig. Its ribs shone through a laceration in the leathery, mummifying skin. She smashed the hammer into the temple. There was little resistance. The skull shattered.

Five to go.

Hey, she was *good* at this.

Her confidence began to skyrocket. Maybe she wouldn't die after all. These zombies were so fucking slow and dumb. They had watched her pick off the weakest member of their ungodly herd, and none of them was changing behaviour to counterpoint her next attack, which was to use the *exact same manoeuvre*.

No ability to think. To predict. Adapt.

She picked her next victim. With a lunging sweep, like a cricketer intent on slogging the ball to the boundary, she used the hatchet to slice through the orbital bones. The cranium came off clean and in one piece, reminding her of the top of a boiled egg.

Four left.

No, these zombies weren't *predators*. This didn't feel like, say, coming up against a pack of dogs. No, these zombies were more akin to…a natural disaster. A flood. Bushfire. A terrible hailstorm. Some mindless event without sentience or consciousness or malice. An event that could be managed with intelligence and forethought. I'm going to live, she thought with surprise. The giddy excitement of it sent a fresh surge of power through her limbs.

She darted, circled, selected her next target. Little more than a piglet. Dressed in a t-shirt and denim jeans. Hatchet or hammer? Tricky to decide. Why not both?

The skull crumpled under the double assault.

Only three left.

Goddamn, what a liberating release for pent-up anxiety! This is how it must have felt way back when humans were hunter-gatherers, living in caves and pitted against sabre-toothed tigers. Modern humans kill themselves ruminating and choking on stress from office politics, traffic jams and shitty relationships, using pills and booze to ease the pressure of so many formless hassles that no one can flee or bare-knuckle fight. But this? Oh, this physical brutality was *primal*. This felt *invigorating*.

More than that. This was *fun*, and the realisation shocked her.

A game of Whack-A-Mole with higher stakes.

"Come on, you fuckers!" she yelled, and found herself laughing. "Come get some!"

She wished for a set of golf clubs. A forged iron with a swing-weight of D6. *Fore!* Now that would be entertaining. Wow, I'm a monster, she thought as she hacked at another pig. I'm the shit, a bad-arse killing machine—

And then she heard footsteps.

Coming up swiftly behind her. Heavy. *Bipedal*. A wash of terror rinsed through her. Blinkered by bloodlust, she had forgotten to check her surroundings. She froze. Remembered Alisha's flayed and gory visage. Collapsed eyeballs filling the sockets with choroid and vitreous humor; a curdled, greyish slop. The frantic chewing sounds as Bartholomew gnawed on Alisha's face and slurped at the tattered remnants of tissue as if sucking up spaghetti.

Running behind her, right now, was Bartholomew. She knew it. Felt it.

The adrenaline bomb went off in her chest, boomed her heart, and flashed down the median nerve in both arms like a double lightning strike. Bartholomew was almost upon her. Anger replaced terror. She would avenge Alisha. She would take off the motherfucker's head and crush it between her bare hands. With a fierce yell, she turned and simultaneously raised the hatchet and hammer.

Magnus skidded to a halt and flinched away. "It's me!" he cried.

As he fell to one knee, Helen dropped her arms and stumbled, nearly losing her balance too. Fucking hell, she had almost killed Magnus...

Fucking HELL.

She had almost killed Magnus.

"Look out!" he bellowed.

A giant pig, a sow that must have weighed in excess of one hundred kilos, was barrelling at her, its head down, jaws agape. Weeping cheeks writhing with maggots. Blackened eye sockets abuzz with gnats. Sockets tiny and deep. Like pinholes. Black and fathomless dots. Like the eyes of Nana's clown doll, pits into another world. A scary world full of pain and danger and fear. The doll under the bed climbing up the valance to bite off Helen's fingers as she slept. Oh fuck, Helen thought, reeling, lost in those holes that once had been eyes. *I almost killed Magnus—*

A glint of wood and metal, a whoosh of displaced air right in front of her, a sudden *thud*.

What happened? Helen shook herself.

The sow toppled, missing half its skull. Magnus lifted the spade, darted forward, and dispatched the last pig of the herd by chopping the blade straight down into its head. Dazed, Helen looked about. Carnage. Absolute and utter carnage. Felled pigs everywhere. Brain parts scattered in the leaf litter.

"Are you all right?" Magnus panted. "Helen?"

"Huh?"

He grabbed her arm and said, "Are you all right?"

"Yeah, yeah, I'm fine. Shit, Magnus. What the fuck? You scared the crap out of me."

"I'm sorry."

"I thought you were a fucking zombie."

"Understood."

"You were supposed to be getting the quad bike, remember?"

He nodded. "Yes. But I came over to help."

"And nearly got your noggin stoved in."

"Next time, I'll call out first."

"Please do." Shivering, she began to giggle. "Fucking hell. Holy fucking *hell*, Magnus—"

"We should go."

"Hang on. Let me catch my breath."

"No time."

She roamed her gaze. The little zombies were coming. Drawn by her vocalisations? Her "battle cries"? Wave after wave after wave. Birds tottering, their dusty and broken wings held out, beaks snapping. Large birds like magpies and currajongs, but sparrows too. Fairy wrens. A few could take flight for brief periods, rising and tumbling, rising and tumbling, resembling the disorganised movements of butterflies. And there were rodents, missing clumps of fur. Cat-sized and furry beasts that she couldn't identify. Possums? Wallabies? All converging on the clearing. All in various states of decay.

Christ almighty, how many animals had died across VITERI's sprawling grounds? More specifically, how many dead animals that still had enough soft tissue to permit locomotion? It seemed a ridiculously high number.

Maybe this…*cataclysm*…was re-fleshing the skeletal remains of the long-dead.

A faint glimmer from childhood surfaced, flashing through her mind in a split-second. Nana had been some kind of fundamentalist Christian. Exactly what sort, Mum had never divulged. On Nana's shelf, a hardback book. Thick, creamy pages with large text, every second page featuring a detailed and full-colour painting or line drawing. So lifelike. Helen had always loved to peruse that book for the artwork. One plate showed rays of soft yellow sunshine pouring from the sky, each ray lifting people from the ground as if along a pneumatic tube. People with their faces upturned, smiling. The ground covered in opened graves. And those believers who didn't have a whole body after death—those who had been cremated, lost at sea, or butchered and dismembered by murderers—would be put back together by the love of God according to Nana…

The Rapture…

But no, no, *look around*. These pigs were not re-fleshed. Bartholomew had not been re-fleshed. This was clearly *not* the Rapture of ancient biblical texts but the zombie apocalypse of modern literature. Okay, hold on, that was ridiculous. The Rapture made more sense as a workable hypothesis because it had the weight of history behind it. The zombie apocalypse? Not so much. Modern zombies had existed in literature for, what…fifty years? From a movie, if Helen's memory served correctly. Was that even possible? The end of the world predicted by a fucking *movie*? A concept plucked from a writer's imagination? Unless the writer had been some kind of angel or apostle. Hey, wasn't that the explanation for the Bible? A long time ago, some blessed blokes thought up some interesting shit and happened to write it down… Oh, she didn't know what to think. She *didn't know*.

Magnus pulled at her arm. "We have to go," he said.

Before she could reply, he took off, dragging her behind him. She staggered and pitched, but kept her footing. Her breath came in whooping gasps. Some of the little zombies had reached them. Magnus kicked and stomped with his boots. Helen only had the strength to run in his wake. She tripped over something large and round and heavy, perhaps a zombie wombat, and would have fallen if not for Magnus's vise-like grip on her elbow.

Shit.

Palpitations, tremors, dizziness. Classic side effects of adrenaline overload. She must have low blood pressure. If she didn't conquer this physical reaction, she would fuck up and die. Her legs felt rubbery, the knee joints fluid and slack.

Toughen up, she thought. Get a grip.

They hurried past the cabin, past the work shed. And there was the quad bike sitting beneath the flat tin roof of the carport.

The last time Helen had seen the bike was when it had hauled a body bag on a long trailer. Inside the bag had been the donor she had dubbed Bartholomew. At Area E—dry and flat, with minimal vegetation—Magnus had stopped the bike. Unhitched the trailer. Slid the body bag off the rear of the trailer. Unzipped the bag and gently tipped out Bartholomew. Assisted her to arrange Bartholomew's naked body on the ground: face up, legs straight, arms at the sides. *Wait here*, Magnus had said, and took off on the bike.

She had stared down at Bartholomew. A young man, perhaps in his twenties. Clean-shaven. A healed and neat hole in his bottom lip, denoting where a piercing had been. A similar hole in his eyebrow. Perhaps his family kept both of his facial rings in a jewellery box on the mantle. A smoky tattoo of a cat on his chest; for remembrance of a beloved pet? His body as pale and puckered as chicken skin. Appendicectomy scar. Flush of dark pubic hair. Scrunched up clutch of genitals. Long, thin toes. A slightly open mouth that showed a missing lateral incisor on the upper right-hand side of his jaw. These small and ordinary things had brought tears to Helen's eyes. What to do?

Well, Professor Walter Boyce liked to thank the donors.

"Thank you," Helen had said. "Thank you for helping me to help the living."

Magnus had returned some ten minutes later with a custom-built cage made from wood and chicken-wire to protect the donor from scavengers. The cause of Bartholomew's death? No idea. Helen's university lecturers always had the same advice to their students: do not dwell. Your donors are no longer people, with truncated aspirations and grieving loved ones, but puzzles that will allow you to solve mysteries.

And yet, despite her agnosticism, Helen had prayed for Bartholomew. Albeit in her own fashion. Wherever you are, she had thought as she had gazed at his cold and waxy face, I hope you see the good you're doing. I hope you see how much I appreciate your generosity—

Helen tripped on the edge of the carport's concrete slab.

Magnus, still holding her elbow, didn't let her fall.

In the trees behind the carport were two human zombies shuffling closer.

"Hurry," she whispered.

"I see them."

Magnus swung his leg over the seat of the quad bike and started the ignition. The vehicle looked like a regular motorbike except for its four wheels. The trailer was not attached. Tipped forward and resting on its hitch, the trailer was tucked against the exterior wall of the work shed.

"Hold the umbrella over us," he said, handing it to her.

Helen stowed the hammer and hatchet in her rope belt, took the umbrella and opened it. Black panels alternating with black-and-white chequerboard panels; the words *Australian Formula 1 Grand Prix Adelaide* stencilled on the sides. A keepsake from when Magnus had been a young man. It nearly broke her heart. *Don't crack.* The strain of stress chemicals must be making her sappy. Sitting astride the storage rack behind Magnus, she put her free arm about his waist and lifted the umbrella high over their heads.

"Okay, let's get the fuck out of here," she said.

He took off with a jolt. His back was so high and broad that she couldn't see ahead. The bumps and divots in the ground kept taking her by surprise. She held on to him tighter than she would have liked. The physical contact seemed too intimate. Then again, what could be more intimate than slaughtering a herd of zombie pigs together? She tried to chuckle but her throat was too dry.

For a moment, trembling and exhausted, she closed her eyes and rested her forehead against him. His shirt smelled of laundry detergent and fresh sweat. At least he had not turned into a zombie. So, he mustn't have cut his feet. Or, if he had, blood-to-blood exposure wasn't a form of transmission. If transmission were even possible. On the other hand, perhaps turning a live person into a zombie took more time.

The terrain continued to meander by. Jesus, was he going to speed up or not?

"Come on," she urged. "Faster. Pull your finger out."

"I ride at ten kilometres an hour and no more."

"What the fuck?"

"Too fast and we tip."

"Magnus," she said. "This is a fucking *emergency.*"

"Too *fast* and we *tip.*"

The quad bike began to weave. Bones crunched beneath the tyres. He was running over little zombie animals. She turned her head to glance back. Emerging from the bushland behind Magnus's cabin were dozens of pigs, at least five humans, all of them homing in.

She put her forehead to his back again and squeezed her eyes shut.

Even if this zombie infestation *was* like a natural disaster, without sentience or malice, that didn't make it any better. People still died in floods, bushfires, storms. No matter how smart you might be, non-sentient elements can overwhelm you. The VITERI grounds had about eighty dead pigs and forty human cadavers. Their sheer weight of numbers was not just a tidal wave but a goddamned tsunami—

She looked up and saw Bartholomew.

"Stop the bike!" she yelled, hurling aside the umbrella.

"No, we should—"

"Stop the fucking bike *now*. Right *now*. I'm *killing* that son of a bitch."

13

The door handle to the morgue twisted and rattled. Stella and Joan shrieked. Rick felt his scrotum constrict as his balls tried to retreat inside his body. Without thinking, by reflex, he leapt to the door and grabbed the handle.

"Does it open inwards or outwards?" he said.

"What?" Stella yelped.

"The door, the bloody *door*. Does it open inwards or outwards?"

"Inwards, inwards, inwards."

Gripping the handle tight enough to pop his knuckles, he leaned back to pull the door hard against the jamb. Even if the zombie on the other side could turn the handle, it wouldn't have the strength to counteract Rick's considerable body weight. Shit, he could feel the resistance on the handle. Feel the dead bastard on the other side working and worrying at it. The thought that he was connected to the zombie via this polished chrome fitting made the bile rise in his throat.

"Why don't you have any bloody locks in this building?"

"There's never been a need," Joan whispered.

"Is there another way out of the morgue?" he said.

Stella nodded. "The delivery entrance: a roller-door to the outside."

"How does it open?"

"Manually. You rotate a knob. But there's a latch-bolt."

"Which means no zombies can get inside?"

"I wouldn't think so."

The handle jiggled. Rick squeezed tighter. Beads of sweat popped along his hairline.

If he got out of this predicament, he would take the missus to Italy.

In fact, he would book the airline tickets the minute he arrived home.

She had travelled throughout Italy as a young woman fresh out of college. Loved the bridges and art museums of Florence, the *trattorie* and ancient ruins of Rome, the hectic and chaotic bustle of Naples. Over the course of a year, she had visited a dozen European countries and Italy remained her favourite. Rick had never been overseas. Well, technically speaking, yes, he'd been to Bali, but that didn't count since the island was full of Aussies anyway. When we retire, he'd say to the missus whenever she reminisced about Italy, I'll take you there. Dickhead. Why wait? He shouldn't have waited. You can't expect to live until you're ninety. Life can be snatched away at any age. Seize the day. His oldest daughter liked to hector him on this point. *Carpe diem*—until now, nothing but a catch-phrase from a mediocre film. His older daughter would often taunt, "How can a *homicide* detective not *get* this?"

Because death had nothing to do with him.

Death was a factor in his job. Something he investigated. It was never personal. Once it gets personal, you can't do your job. He'd seen it many times. A young bloke, swaggering into Homicide, proud of himself for cracking the most elite squad, soon crumbling under the weight of grief, of the families left behind and shattered. Crying in the men's room after processing a scene with a dead child. Taking time off. Losing weight. Losing sleep. Drinking.

Grimly, Rick held the door handle, determined to stop it from moving.

He would take the missus to Florence, Rome and Naples. With a side trip to Sicily, birthplace of the mafia. Apparently, they had shrines to murdered Dons and he wanted to see them. Also, he wanted to sample genuine Sicilian cannoli. Surely, the missus wouldn't expect him to stick to his diet on an overseas holiday—

"Are you right?" Stella said. "Can you hold the door?"

"No worries."

"Okay. I'm calling Magnus. Rick, what's your phone's passcode?"

"One, nine, seven, three." 1973. The year his wife was born.

Stella thumbed the touch screen. "It's ringing," she said, and held it to her ear. Then her shoulders dropped. "Bugger. Voicemail."

"Leave a message anyway," Joan said.

Stella nodded. "Hi Magnus, it's Stella. Look, I guess you know what's going on. This phone belongs to Rick Evans, one of the detectives. His partner is dead. Cheryl Zhao is dead. Kieran's dead. Walter Boyce is…infected." Her voice broke. She wiped at her lips and continued. "Here in the main building, it's me, Joan and Rick. I can't reach Alisha Singh or Helen Macauley. Please call me back on this number. There are police on the way. It might take a few hours for them to get here. Could you bring over some of your tools for weapons? Oh no, wait, on the other hand…look, I don't know, mate. We've got zombies around the building. Maybe it's best if you just sit tight, wherever you are." She stopped, gazed at Joan and Rick. "Anything else you want me to add?"

"I don't think so," Rick said.

Joan shook her head.

"All right, mate," Stella continued. "I hope you get this message. Call me back. Bye." She hung up. Wiped tears from the corners of her eyes, jingling her bangles. "If you don't mind, I'd like to call my husband."

"Sure," Rick said. "Go ahead."

She dialled. Put the phone to her ear. Waited. Jumped in her seat and cried, "Voicemail!"

"He's probably at lunch," Joan said, too quickly.

"Or dead," Stella wailed. "Infected. The whole country is overrun with—"

"No!" Rick yelled, lifting his forefinger for emphasis. "There was *one* cloud. One single solitary cloud. In a blue sky. It's happening nowhere else but here. Nowhere else."

"But why isn't Con answering his phone?"

"Because he's busy eating lunch," Joan said.

"Oh my gosh, do you reckon? Really?"

"Of course, I do."

He caught Joan's eye. A moment passed between them. Joan thinks Con is dead, he realised. She thinks this is Armageddon. What had Walter Boyce said before cutting out his own tongue? *This is the end.* Of everything? Rick thought of his daughters. His heart gave a hiccup. Yesterday morning for breakfast, they had requested waffles.

The waffle iron, along with the barbecue, was Rick's responsibility. The missus did the rest of the cooking. Usually, Rick made waffles on Sunday morning while his wife made the accompaniment of caramelised bananas. Occasionally, they had this breakfast during the week but only if Rick had time to whip up the batter. Yesterday morning, he hadn't had the time. Okay, truth be told, he hadn't *felt* like he'd had the time.

He'd been too preoccupied with his cold case of Alexandra Wilson, twenty-three-year old student in her last year of a Bachelor's degree. Majoring in philosophy and Australian literature. Lived at home with both parents. Tropical fish for pets. Worked part-time at KFC with her boyfriend. Dead and naked, save for a towel, in the boot of a 2011 Lexus IS250 automatic Prestige with her thumb in her mouth. For seven years, Rick had searched for the offender. Seven *years...*

A lot to think about.

When his daughters had requested waffles for breakfast yesterday, he had snapped at them. Typical. Did he have any patience for the people he loved? Apparently not. While there had been plenty of time to make waffles—the whole process took twenty minutes, tops—there hadn't been enough *mental space* for him to stop thinking about Alexandra Wilson and start thinking about batter instead. The next day, he would be rising before dawn, getting dressed in the dark, picking up Lawrence Garcia in the squad car, and driving to the Victorian Taphonomic Experimental Research Institute in Wooriyanda to replicate Alexandra's murder scene with a donor cadaver in the hope of gleaning some kind of lead...

What do I look like to you, a short-order cook? I've got work. Make some toast.

They had grumbled. Eye-rolled together. His wife had stared at him and sighed.

And if he died today, that is how his daughters would remember him: a grouch. This morning, he had risen early. The missus had risen too. His daughters had remained in bed. Buttoning his shirt, the missus had said, *Remember, don't let Garcia get to you. Think of your blood pressure. Just concentrate on the scenery. It'll be a lovely drive into the countryside with lots of trees, lots of birds. Darling, you have to learn how to ignore him.*

This morning felt like a hundred years ago.

"My phone," Rick said, wriggling the fingers of his free hand.

Stella ducked around her desk and held out the mobile. He took it and thumbed for the speed-dial. Hesitated. Felt the sweat gather in his armpits. His breath cutting short.

What if his wife didn't answer?

Maybe it was best not to know. He always thought about that, about the bliss of ignorance, every single time he stood at a front door and raised his knuckles ready to knock, ready to deliver the bad news to parents, spouses, children, who assumed the knock on the door would be something innocuous like a parcel delivery, a Jehovah's Witness, a neighbour. Once he introduced himself, showed his badge, without fail there came the same look on their faces of confusion, fear, and then a terrible understanding—

"Rick, are you okay?" Stella said.

"Yeah." He put the phone in his pocket.

The door handle twisted. He gripped it harder.

Now what? Do nothing but hold this handle until the cavalry arrived?

The door at the end of the hallway opened. Stella gasped. Walter, that creepy tongue-less bastard, stuck out his head, his goatee black with congealed blood.

"Get back inside!" Rick bellowed, pointing at him. "Get the fuck back inside your office!"

Walter hesitated as if considering whether or not to comply. Oh Christ, Rick thought in alarm, don't come over here. *Do not come over here.*

Because I don't have a plan, he suddenly realised.

Unbelievable but true. Detective Senior Sergeant Rick Evans, the leader of his crew, a man that every officer in the Homicide Squad looked up to—more than that, *deferred* to—always had a plan. No matter how chaotic the crime scene. Regardless of hysterical family members or distraught bystanders. Despite the monstrous obscenity of a slaughtered victim. When Rick was called out, he took charge and never overlooked a single detail, including the minute or obscure. He could identify potential hazards, determine the focal point of a crime scene, estimate how much of the surrounding area would need to be cordoned off to contain the physical evidence, propose a plausible theory to help direct the initial investigation. Always controlled access to prevent contamination. Always coordinated the forensic teams perfectly. Always knew what to do. How to move forward. Choose the next step.

Until now.

The absurdity of this nightmare had turned him into a stunned mullet. Enough. He had years of experience, didn't he? Now was the time to draw upon them. Assume command.

Walter scratched his beard and shuffled his feet. Oh, shit. *Do not come over here.*

"Get back inside!"

Nodding, Walter gave a feeble salute, retreated, and shut the door.

"Jeez," Stella muttered. "I almost had a fricking heart attack."

"You and me both," Joan said.

A window broke. One of the windows by the front door. The weight of enough dead bodies had finally shattered it. Arms groped. Rick thought he might shit himself. And then he saw the reception furniture where visitors were invited to wait: a round wooden table covered in magazines, four armchairs, a water cooler—

He pointed, yelling, "Push that stuff against the window! Hurry!"

Fear gave Stella and Joan the strength of ten men. The furniture was heavy, Rick could see that, yet the women slung the pieces without care of torn muscles or cricked spines. Within a minute, they had built an effective barricade. They stood back, panting. The zombies waved their arms through the spaces but couldn't get inside.

Yet.

Rick glanced along the corridor. Assessed the building's many windows.

Oh, we're rooted.

It was a matter of time. Just a matter of time before the masses broke another window and managed to clamber inside. Sitting tight was no longer an option. They had to flee. No option now but to flee. The morgue's door handle continued to work and twist against his grip. He tightened his fingers, his forearm muscles aching and burning.

"In my car," he said, "I've got shotguns, ammunition, batons, pepper spray, tasers. Cricket bats too."

"So what?" Stella jabbed her thumb at the CCTV monitors. "These pricks are *everywhere*. You can't reach your car, can you? It may as well be on the moon."

"We need to arm ourselves," Joan said. "There are knives in the kitchen."

Stella brightened. "And a fire extinguisher. We can spray them in the face and then bash them with the canister."

"Good," Rick said. "What else?"

"I don't know," Stella said. "Can you stab people with pens? I've seen it done in movies."

He remembered something he'd seen in one of those horror films his girls liked so much, and said, "Have either of you got an aluminium water bottle?"

"Yeah, me," Stella said.

One-handed, he unbuckled his belt and pulled it from his trousers. "Fill the bottle with water. Put my belt through the key ring. We can bash zombies from a distance."

"Like a medieval flail," Joan said, hollow-eyed, and clapped as if delighted.

***

Magnus braked. Helen jumped off before the quad bike came to a stop.

"Give me the goddamned fork," she panted, gesturing frantically with both hands. "Now, now, now, right *now*."

He took it from his tool belt and held it out. "This is a bad idea—"

"I don't care."

"Listen, we must get out of here—"

"I don't *care*," she said, and her smile was a terrible grimace.

She snatched the fork and turned.

Magnus remembered Bartholomew because of the chest tattoo of a cat. It had seemed very sad. About two weeks ago, Magnus had assisted Helen in arranging Bartholomew on the ground, and had kept looking at the tattoo. The everlasting love of a child for a pet. A universal pain. Bartholomew must have grown up with a cat that had subsequently died, perhaps of old age.

Magnus had had a rabbit.

Inka had liked to sleep on Magnus's bed. He had taught her to shit in a litter tray. She enjoyed fresh raspberries but only as a treat, since the fruit is quite acidic. He would put his nose to hers so that she could tickle him with her wriggling little nostrils. And whenever he was lying on the floor in front of the TV, Inka would hop over and nudge her head beneath one of his hands so that he would pat her. She craved his attention. He never minded. The softest parts were her ears. When Inka had died, Magnus's nine-year old body had not been big enough to contain the grief. Crying, crying, crying. Until Yngvar had slapped him, hard on both cheeks—*crack crack*—and ordered him to be a man. Leena, sitting in her customary armchair, had watched but not commented.

And now Bartholomew, he of the sad cat tattoo, was staggering towards Helen.

The cadaver's eyes were milky glass marbles, flesh a mottled greenish-purple, belly pregnant with bloat, mouth and genitals swarming and squirming with insects. The tattoo was intact. Magnus supposed that it would last as long as the skin remained.

Helen ran at Bartholomew with the metre-long garden fork raised in both hands, parallel to the ground like a pole vaulter approaching the bar, screaming through her teeth.

Bartholomew held out his arms. Did he recognise the threat? Or recognise Helen?

For a moment, it occurred to Magnus that he ought to help her.

But she didn't need any help.

With great fury, she thrust the tines of the fork into Bartholomew's throat. The contact made a *chunk* sound. Her impetus threw Bartholomew backwards, easily and lightly, as if he were made of balsa wood, his desiccating corpse too lean and stringy to hold any weight.

Helen pinned him under the garden fork, leaning on the stock, a woman possessed. She grabbed the hatchet in her other hand and buried the blade over and over in Bartholomew's face, her arm making swooping arcs. If Magnus were to close his eyes and transport himself away from this place, he might assume the noises to be the chopping of wood. Yngvar liked to chop wood. Their house back in Finland had featured an open fireplace. Magnus had known how to use an axe from the age of five. *Good form is everything*, Yngvar had instructed, manipulating Magnus's arms.

Bartholomew resisted at first. Limbs thrashing. But as facial skin and skull bones started to fly, his actions became less organised, more lethargic. Helen kept screaming through her teeth. Kept slamming the hatchet. Got covered in gore but didn't seem to notice.

Alisha Singh must have been her best friend to evoke such passion.

Momentarily, Magnus wondered what having a best friend might feel like. Like this, he thought as he watched Helen in surprise, in awe. Best friendship must be very powerful to provoke such a no-holds-barred vengeance. He could only imagine how it must feel to be overcome with that degree of vehemence.

And now?

Now, Bartholomew's head resembled a dropped lasagne. Magnus laughed. No, wait, that wasn't funny. Clearly, the surreal situation was beginning to wear on him. He must sit on his emotions, stop any memories from bleeding into the present, and concentrate only on *action*, on doing the next thing. *Be a man.* Magnus looked about. Zombies emerged from the trees all around. No doubt drawn by Helen's screams and the drone of the quad bike's idling engine.

"We must leave!" he shouted. "Come on!"

She slammed the hatchet over and over. Bartholomew lay motionless, dead for the second time in his young life. Her furious actions severed what remained of the head from his neck. And yet she persisted. The spattered tissue across the ground started to resemble the consistency of spilled mushroom soup.

"Helen! Please!"

Her screams had turned into sobs. Hysterical sobs.

"Fuck you," she was saying through tears, in time with each blow of the hatchet. "Fuck you, fuck you, fuck you, fuck you—"

The zombies pressed closer. He recognised a few of them. The man in the stained three-piece suit: Bradley. The naked, fat old man with his belly drooping over his genitals: Simon. The donor that Magnus had recently helped arrange in a shallow dam and weigh down with stones: Vanessa, her sodden skin peeling in long sheets and ribbons, hanging from her, revealing the fat and muscle beneath. And the pigs trotting beside the cadavers. Bizarrely, the scene reminded Magnus of a dog-walking park he had once lived alongside. Every weekend he could look out of his bedroom window and watch the hordes of middle-aged men and women in the neighbourhood diligently exercising their leashed pets around and around the perimeter in an orderly circuit.

Something fell onto his shoulder, startling him, and tumbled to the ground.

A magpie, bereft of most of its feathers. A zombie magpie. Threshing in the leaf litter, trying to stand upright, its beak snapping.

"Helen!" he cried again.

When she didn't answer, too intent on her chopping, he leapt from the bike and hurried over. He grabbed her wrist and tore the hatchet from her grasp. Used the same arm to pick her up at the waist. With his free hand, he wrenched the garden fork out of the ground.

"What are you doing?" she wept, struggling. "Let me go, let me go."

He shook her violently and she stopped fighting him.

With his mouth at her ear, he whispered, "The zombies are coming for us. Look."

She swivelled her head and gasped.

"Bartholomew is dead," he continued. "You've avenged Alisha Singh. Let's go."

She nodded.

He carried her to the quad bike. When he released his grip, she staggered but stayed upright. He tucked the garden fork and hatchet into his tool belt, and swung his leg over the bike.

"Get the umbrella," he said.

It had rolled away some distance. Helen kicked at a zombie magpie, sending the bird sprawling, and picked up the umbrella. Then she raced to jump on the bike.

He opened the throttle. The engine roared. He accelerated.

But they had left their run too late.

Escape would be like threading a needle. The ring of zombies had corralled them. Were the zombies coordinating their efforts? Communicating with each other somehow? Their strategy—of closing the circle—seemed too perfect to be a coincidence. He wondered if Helen, in her upset state, could also recognise that the zombies appeared to be working together in an organised manner.

He slowed the bike, came to a stop.

"What's the matter?" Helen said.

"There's no gap we can ride through."

He could feel her body trembling against his back. The zombies advanced. The stench was terrible, the air thick with flies. Perhaps he could wield the spade, use it like a jousting stick, push his way past this blockade—

"For Christ's sake," Helen said. "Just *shoot* the motherfuckers."

Perkele. In the heat of the moment, he had forgotten the .22. Unslinging the rifle, he lifted it and sighted down its barrel.

Head shot. An old woman with grey hair dropped.

Head shot. Down went a naked man.

Head shot. A pig crumpled onto its stomach.

Head shot—no, a miss. The bullet whacked into the pig's chest. Unfazed, the zombie animal kept walking. So, it was confirmed: the brain must be destroyed.

But missing the pig didn't matter because Magnus had created a wide enough gap.

He slung the rifle, revved the throttle and took off at speed. Helen clutched at him. He swerved around gum trees and bottlebrushes, happened to run over another bird, and zoomed through the space he had made in the zombie ring, which was about three metres wide.

And then they were clear.

Helen's grip was so tight it impeded his breathing.

"Don't worry," he said, patting her hand. "We're safe."

"You got us out?"

"Yes."

Her grip relaxed. It felt as if she put her forehead against his back. Was she still crying? He never knew what to do when faced with tears. Leena had never cried. At least, not in front of Magnus. Her stoicism had dried up his own tears as a child, out of embarrassment. He couldn't recall the last time he had wept. Perhaps when Inka the rabbit had died. He had found her in the hutch one morning with her eyes closed. At first, he had thought Inka asleep.

Consoling people was not his forte. Could he feel tears soaking his shirt? Poor Helen.

"Alisha Singh was your best friend?" he offered.

"More than that. Actually, I loved her."

He nodded. "You're lucky to have had such a friendship."

But Helen didn't reply.

The signpost indicated that the main VITERI building was to the right. Magnus adjusted their course and sped up. And for the first time, with a shiver of dread, wondered what they might find when they arrived.

***

Lost, perplexed, Walter sat at the desk. The desk had papers on it. He moved the papers around. After a while, he picked up a sheaf. There was printing on it but he couldn't make out the words. The man out there had yelled at him. Walter didn't know why. The man was a stranger. *Get back inside! Get the fuck back inside your office! Get back inside!*

So much fatigue. Heavy as a woollen blanket.

Walter dozed.

Upon coming awake, he glanced at the desk and noticed a zip-lock bag. It appeared to contain strips of meat. Saliva filled his mouth. He groped for the bag. His fingers were stiff. It took some time to open the bag. The meat resembled fat worms. He plucked a fat worm from the bag and put it in his mouth. Chewed.

Spat it out.

Dead. Dead. Dead.

His mouth felt strange. Empty. He opened his mouth to poke out his tongue but nothing happened. His fingers groped, searching inside his mouth. There was so much room in there. Ragged, unfamiliar textures. He gave up and dropped his hand. Stared at the desk. Stared at the papers.

Dozed.

In his dreams, he saw blood and teeth. Felt cold and warmth. A squirming sensation pulsing through the muscles of his arms and legs. Bright lights. Such bright and clear lights shining on the black of his closed eyelids, paining him, lancing him through like knives.

Hunger woke him.

The sensation wasn't limited to his stomach. The hunger prowled around his body, clawing at temples, seizing joints, cramping muscles, twisting bowels. It raged, insistent and maddening. If he didn't have warm and raw meat, he would go crazy.

Crazy. Crazy. Crazy.

He wanted to lick his dry lips but nothing happened. Groping about his person, at his clothes, he found a pair of scissors. This seemed significant. He couldn't remember why. He put the scissors on the desk. Stared at the blades. The blades were clotted dark red.

People were outside his door.

He could hear them. Voices. Human voices. He began to salivate. A phrase started up and ticked inside his head with the regularity of a metronome.

Warm raw meat.

Warm raw meat.

Warm raw meat.

The phrase got louder, hammering at his skull, making it hurt. He felt chilled. With his bandaged hand, he touched the back of his other wrist. His wrist felt icy, delicately boned, like fried chicken ribs from the fridge. Ribs. Meat on ribs. He fussed in the chair. Hungry. He was so hungry. Deranged with hunger, insane with it, agitated and distraught.

The voices outside the room called out and mewled to him. Softly. Seductively.

Saliva ran from his mouth and pooled onto the desk.

His head pounded.

WARM. RAW. MEAT.

14

Stella surveyed the arsenal on her desk. Pathetic. What a fricking disappointment. Two carving knives, a steak knife, the 4.5kg dry-powder fire extinguisher, and a shitty flail made from her water bottle and Rick's belt. Hardly the weapons you'd want in a zombie apocalypse. Joan and Rick looked as downcast as she felt.

"Chin up, it's better than nothing," Joan said briskly.

"Is it?" Stella said.

"Look, I just need some way to get to my car," Rick said, still holding the door handle to the morgue. "I'm after a shotgun. It's a bloody good long-range weapon. You can aim at someone forty metres distant and still hit them, if not kill them outright. At close range, I could kill five or six zombies per shell. No bull, I'd clear the whole lot out there with maybe half a dozen shots. Then I'll drive us away in my car."

"Yeah, but how are you going to get to the weapons in the first place?" Stella said. "Jeez, we need an actual *plan*, not this fricking pie-in-the-sky stuff."

"How about a distraction?" Joan said. "To get them away from the front door?"

"They're attracted to noise," Rick said. "I don't suppose you've got any fire crackers?"

Joan put her hands on her hips and sneered.

"A portable radio?"

"Nope," Stella said. "We're not allowed to listen to music."

"That's because you're paid to *work*, not to pretend you're at a *disco*."

"Anything else that would make a continuous loud noise?" Rick said. "Anything at all?"

They pondered on this for a few moments.

"If we had a spare phone," Joan said, "we could play songs out on the back decking."

Stella huffed. "But we've only got *Rick's* phone. Jeez, come on, we've really got to forget about pie-in-the-sky stuff. 'Oh, if only we had a Sherman tank.' I mean, *honestly*."

The sound, hovering at the very edge of her hearing, became louder. Blowflies? From the zombie crowd outside? The sound grew. As she recognised it, a flare of excitement and relief shot through her body.

"Magnus!" she cried, heading to the nearest window. "You hear that? It's his quad bike."

"Good Lord, I think you're right," Joan said, scrambling behind the desk and wrenching aside the blinds. "Where is he? I can't see him."

"It's getting closer," Rick said. "He must be heading for this building."

Tears pricked Stella's eyes. Good old Magnus. If anyone could survive a zombie apocalypse, it would be that tough old bugger. Look up "frosty" in the dictionary and you'd find his picture. Had she ever seen him smile? Mr Chilly, she called him—right to his face—and he never seemed to mind. Then again, if he minded, how could you tell? His expression always remained the same: cool and stern. Whenever she made baklava, karythopita or loukomadies, she would save a few pieces for him. Something about his remoteness seemed to throw out a kind of challenge. *I'll thaw out that bloody Finn one of these days*, she would remark to Con while she baked. Apparently, Magnus had the same effect on others. At Easter, Stella had discovered that at least three other people from Fraser University regularly brought him snack foods, including Alisha Singh. When Stella had told Con, he had guffawed and said, *He's scamming you all.* And yes, she had to admit, it was as if Magnus had figured out how to tug at their heartstrings.

"There he is!" Joan cried. "Hang on a minute. What's that over his head?"

"An umbrella?"

"Why on earth would he have an umbrella over his head?"

"Because zombie animals are dropping out of the trees," Rick said. "Haven't you been paying attention? Wild animals are turning into zombies too. Birds and whatnot. Possums."

"Oh hey, wait a second, he's got someone with him," Stella whispered, straining her eyes, pressing her face to the glass. "I can see their legs… Oh, it's Helen Macauley! Holy frick, it's Magnus and Helen!"

"Warn them away," Rick said, holding out his phone. "There's too many zombies."

Stella fumbled with the mobile and called Magnus's number. The call went to voicemail. "Bugger, he's not picking up."

"Of course, he isn't," Joan said. "He's too busy steering the bike."

"Magnus," Stella shouted into the phone, "don't come any closer. We've got zombies at the front door—"

"Forget it," Rick said. "He won't get the message until he finds cover. *If* he finds cover."

Stella hung up, pulse thrumming.

"He's going to ride straight into this mess," Joan muttered.

The quad bike got louder. The frantic scraping and knocking at the front door eased off. The arms at the broken window withdrew. Oh, shit. *They can hear the bike too.* Stella shot a glance at the CCTV monitors. Gasped and put both hands over her mouth. Yes, the horde at the door was turning around, noses up and faces twitching as if sniffing the air. Magnus rode out of the trees and into the clearing. Oh, this was torture. Watching a friend put themselves in danger and not being able to do a damn thing about it was pure torture—

Hang on. Magnus had stopped the bike.

"Don't come any closer, mate," Stella whispered. "Please don't come any closer."

"What's he doing?" Rick said, unable to see from his position at the morgue door.

"Braking," Joan said.

Magnus had a variety of tools hanging from a belt, including a spade and garden fork. And, thank God, a rifle over his shoulder. Was Helen all right? She seemed lifeless, unmoving, one arm about his waist. No, she must be okay or at least *conscious*—she was holding up the umbrella in her other hand. Shit. There was blood streaked along her forearms. And on her clothes. Oh shit, there was blood on Magnus too.

"I reckon they're hurt," Stella said, her voice trembling.

Magnus turned his head towards the windows. Galvanised, Stella began to jump up and down and wave.

"Look out!" she yelled. "Look out!"

"He can't hear you," Joan said.

"If he hasn't seen the zombies by now, he's never going to," Rick said. "What's he doing?"

"Turning the bike around," Joan said.

"In the direction of the bunkhouse," Stella added.

"And what are the zombies doing?" Rick said.

Stella checked the CCTV monitors. "Some are following. The rest are staying put."

"Okay, good, that's good," Rick said. "We can work this to our advantage if we can coordinate with Magnus. I've got a plan."

***

Helen felt the bike move and veer left. But wasn't the main building on their right? She opened her eyes. Yes, there was the main building: a fibro one-storey with a flat tin roof, so basic in design it always reminded her of a shipping container. Magnus was steering away and she didn't know why. Until she spotted the zombies at the front door.

She twisted her head to keep them in sight. "We've got a few coming after us," she said.

"Yes, I see them in my mirrors."

"What are we gonna do?"

"For now, head to the bunkhouse."

She gazed about. Small creatures were emerging from the leaf litter, brought back to life by the sound of the quad bike. *Fuckers*. The sight exhausted her. How could this hellish army ever be defeated? There were so goddamned many of them. The tyres crunched over a bump. She smiled weakly. *Suck on that, you little zombie bastard.*

Considering the width of Magnus's back, there was no way to look ahead so she didn't even try. Closing her eyes, she leaned her forehead against him and rested. After a minute or so of riding, the bike slowed, weaved slightly, came to a stop. The engine cut out. She looked about. No zombies. They must have outridden the fuckers. At least zombies were slow.

"We're here," Magnus said.

Stiffly, Helen got off the bike. She collapsed the umbrella, furled it and secured the strap. Her whole body pained her. The muscles of her arms, legs and lower back trembled with lactic acid build-up. From slaughtering Bartholomew, she realised. No, from *liquefying* his skull with the hatchet. Christ. She had never felt such rage. She had glowed with it, felt incandescent with it. Otherworldly. Almost godlike. The memory of his ruined face came back and queasily stirred the contents of her stomach. She looked down at her hands. They were covered in flesh, clotted brain matter, bone shards. Soap and water seemed more urgent than oxygen.

Magnus got off the bike. She laid the umbrella on the seat. He went up the steps to the veranda and opened the front door. With a nod, he urged her to go inside first. She obeyed. He followed her and locked the door.

The normalcy of the place took the wind out of her.

She leaned against the wall. Here was the first lounge room, with its modular furniture and wall-mounted TV. She preferred the second lounge room located on the other side of the kitchen; the sofas had springs and firmer cushions which offered better lumbar support. And the LCD TV had a non-reflective screen. Added bonus.

How trite. How meaningless and trite it all seemed now.

Magnus walked through the first lounge into the kitchen. Weary, she trailed after him.

"I have two messages on my phone," he was saying, as he propped against the bench. "Perhaps from Stella. I saw her at the window."

"At least we know she's okay."

"There could be other survivors. I thought someone was next to her but I can't be sure."

Survivors? Really? So, this was their new reality?

Helen gazed about the kitchen. In the sink were the dishes from breakfast. Alisha had called it brunch. After a night of steady drinking and a bit of inebriated dancing, Helen had made them fried eggs and mushrooms on toast. Coffee and orange juice.

It felt so long ago.

The frying pan glistened with coagulated butter. The toaster still smelled of bread. Their plates and cutlery were stacked on the draining board where Helen had left them. On Alisha's plate were drag marks; she had run her forefinger to pick up specks of sautéed mushroom.

Alisha had said, *Look at you. A million miles away.*

Huh?

Staring at me but thinking about something else. Should we do the dishes before we go?

Nah, I'll wash them later. No worries.

Helen touched the handle of the frying pan. Held her breath against the memory of Alisha's ruptured eyeballs and flayed cheeks. Began to shake, the regurgitate rising in her throat.

"Can you hear me?" Magnus was saying.

"I'm sorry, what?"

"This message from Stella. Listen."

He held up his phone. *Hi Magnus, it's Stella. Look, I guess you know what's going on. This phone belongs to Rick Evans, one of the detectives. His partner is dead. Cheryl Zhao is dead. Kieran's dead. Walter Boyce is…infected. Here in the main building, it's me, Joan and Rick. I can't reach Alisha Singh or Helen Macauley. Please call me back on this number. There are police on the way. It might take a few hours for them to get here. Could you bring over some of your tools for weapons? Oh no, wait, on the other hand…look, I don't know, mate. We've got zombies around the building. Maybe it's best if you just sit tight, wherever you are… Anything else you want me to add?*

I don't think so, said an unfamiliar male voice.

"That would be the police officer," Magnus suggested.

Stella again: *All right, mate, I hope you get this message. Call me back. Bye.*

"Professor Boyce is infected?" Helen felt herself blanch. "What the fuck does that mean?"

He thumbed at the phone. "Here is the second message."

Stella's voice: *Magnus, don't come any closer. We've got zombies at the front door—*

"That's it?" Helen said after a few seconds.

He nodded.

"Why does it cut off?"

"I don't know," he said.

"You think they're in trouble?"

"I don't know. Maybe not. I saw Stella at the window. She waved at me."

"That doesn't mean she's okay." Helen let out a long, hard breath. "Professor Boyce is *infected*? Jesus Christ. So, he's become a zombie? Stuck inside the building with them?"

Magnus rubbed at the thin stubble on his scalp. "Perhaps, yes."

"Oh, fuck. Whatever." She raised her gory hands. "Look, I need to clean myself up."

"Yes. I'll ring Stella."

"Go for it."

Helen shuffled out of the kitchen, through the second lounge with its superior sofas and non-reflective LCD TV, and into the games room.

Not much of a games room, to be honest.

A billiard table. A chess board: game left in progress. A table-soccer game, the kind with steel rods that skewer miniature plastic figurines. Very retro. Some of the students played these games ironically, yet still enjoyed them— which negates the "ironically" part, doesn't it?

On the other side of the games room was the hallway.

The single-storey bunkhouse was huge, designed to sleep sixteen people at full capacity. After the bulge of common areas, it opened into a narrow and long hallway—about twice as long as the typical suburban bungalow—with four fully-equipped bathrooms, two separate toilets just in case, two laundries, and eight bedrooms that each contained a bunkbed. At the end of the hallway was the back door which led to the bins.

Helen kept her eyes down, watching her sneakers as they squeaked on the linoleum. Too many memories. She hesitated at the bedroom that Alisha had occupied last night. Despite herself, Helen looked. On the top bunk was Alisha's hard-shell suitcase. Purple: Alisha's favourite colour. On the bedside table a water glass half-full, a novel with a bookmark, a pair of spongy ear-plugs. The bottom bunk held a crumpled sleeping bag, a pillow with a pink slip. The pillow would smell of Alisha's shampoo: chamomile and passionflower.

Hey, how about I wash your hair?

I'm too tired, Alisha had slurred. *Maybe tomorrow.*

That beautiful fall of hair. Thick and straight. Glossy. Alisha had never used dye and it showed. *Virginal*, as a hairdresser would say. Helen had touched that hair once. During a lunchtime in one of the coffee shops at Fraser University. A crowd of them had ordered and been served burgers. While laughing at Taylor's joke, Alisha's long hair had slipped over her shoulder. *Careful*, Helen had said, gathering up the fall in her hand, *watch out for your food*. Alisha's smile had shot a thunderbolt straight through Helen's chest.

And now Alisha was dead.

No, *worse* than dead.

Murdered. Desecrated. Mutilated... *Eaten alive.*

Holy Christ...

Wretched, sniffing back tears, Helen continued down the hallway. She had a favourite bathroom. While the four bathrooms shared the same design and fittings, the accent tilings differed. Blue, red, green, yellow. Her preferred bathroom featured blue accent tiles with seahorses. The red bathroom had fish; the green had dolphins; the yellow had whales. As it turned out, Alisha's favourite was also the one with seahorses. Another sign that they had belonged together.

It was cool inside the bathroom. From the common area end of the bunkhouse, she could just make out the murmur of Magnus's voice. He must have reached Stella on the phone. Good for him. Her heart gave a spasm of gratitude. If Helen could pick anyone to be with in a crisis, it would be Magnus—

She saw the mirror and baulked.

Her own blood-spattered face. Wild and staring eyes. The visage of a ghoul.

She hyperventilated.

If she didn't contain this mounting hysteria now, right now, she would start screaming and never stop. Steeling herself, she began to mentally recite the NATO phonetic alphabet in time with her breath, a trick she often used to overcome insomnia. *Alpha, Bravo, Charlie, Delta, Echo...* By the time she reached 'Victor', her terror had subsided to a low simmer.

She opened her eyes and approached the sink. There was a scatter of bobby pins by the liquid soap dispenser. Alisha's bobby pins. One of them held strands of dark, shiny hair.

Fuck.

Was she going to be sick? She felt like being sick. She heaved but brought up nothing.

Helen ran the taps. Put her trembling hands under the steady flow. The blood and gore resisted the water for a few seconds. Once soaked, the hardened clots began to slough away and swirl down the drain. Helen pumped the dispenser and lathered her hands, then her arms. Vigorously. Desperately. Clawing at her skin. Fresh tears filled her eyes. Sobs choked her throat. She crumpled over the sink and wept.

Then stopped. *Forced* herself to stop. She could cry all she liked once this crisis was over.

She soaped her face. Rinsed. Goddamn, the water felt *good*. She groped for a towel and dried off. Appraised herself in the mirror. Better. Although her t-shirt was soaked in blood. Jeans too. Her duffel bag was in a nearby bedroom. She could change outfits. Perhaps even shower first. Feeling clean was a great psychological boost. She would suggest that Magnus have a shower too. It would help them confront whatever nightmare might be coming next—

Oh shit. Her hair...?

Squinting, she leaned into the mirror.

Jesus Christ, her *hair*. Matted with blood. And with...? She reached up, plucked at a white chip and examined it. Skull fragment. From Bartholomew? She dropped it. Wanted to retch.

Quickly, she rinsed her fingertips. Forget the hair. Forget the shower. Their priority was to save themselves, Stella, Professor Kendall and the police officer. And Professor Boyce...? Oh, God. What would they do about Professor Boyce? She remembered him behind the lectern, so mild, softly spoken. And now? What would he be like now that he was infected?

Get a move on, she scolded herself.

About to exit the bathroom, Helen paused and regarded the toilet.

On impulse, she laid her weapons on the sink, untied the rope belt, dropped her jeans, and sat down. Oh, *yes*. Urinating felt like a blessing. She hadn't realised the fullness of her bladder. Next, a grumbling stomach came to her attention. Okay, there was food in the bunkhouse fridge. And she was suddenly so *thirsty*. How incredible that adrenaline and cortisol had masked her body's every need.

She stood up, zipped, flushed, passed her hands under the taps again. Stared at the rope belt which was stained with dark fluids. Knotted it back around her hips. One by one, hung the weapons from it. Now her hands were dirty again. What was the point in washing them?

Leaving the bathroom, she was about to call to Magnus when she felt a breeze on her neck. *A breeze?* She pulled up. Every muscle tensed. Fear ran down her body in drenching sheets. The hallway, usually so dim, was well-lit.

Why hadn't she noticed this before?

Rigid, she turned. The back door, situated at the end of the hallway, was open. She could see the concrete slab through the doorway, the garbage and recycle bins. The breeze lifted again, wafting over her face, bringing VITERI's familiar outdoorsy smell of dirt and decay.

Before they had left the bunkhouse to check on their experiments, Alisha had volunteered to put their empty beer stubbies in the recycling bin. She must have left the door ajar. Which meant that the bunkhouse had been open all afternoon.

All afternoon.

Helen must close the back door. But there were six rooms between her and that door: three rooms on each side of the hallway. Any one of them might contain a zombie. Could she yell for Magnus? No. What if there were zombies already in the bunkhouse? Yelling would draw them out. Could she flee straight to the kitchen? No. Don't be a coward. The threshold separating the hallway from the common areas didn't have a door. She *had* to secure the common areas of the bunkhouse against zombies.

She took the mallet from her rope belt. Began to edge along the hallway. Eucalypts ringed the clearing. Pigs milled amongst the trees, staggering in circles, waiting to be animated by a sound from the living. Helen's knees felt weak. She stopped. Looked into the room on her left, on her right. Both bedrooms were gloomy, curtains drawn, bunks empty.

Edging, she took a few more steps.

Peeked into the next set of rooms. Deserted.

Fuck, she couldn't take this suspense anymore. On flat feet, noiselessly, she hurried towards the back door. Backlit with sunshine, the concrete slab shone bright, the silvery bark of the trees vivid and saturated with colour, the meandering zombie pigs hyper-real. She pulled the door shut. The latch made a loud *click* as it engaged. She winced. The lock was a simple dial inside the knob. She turned it and spun around.

The common areas of the bunkhouse were so far away. Separated by sixteen rooms: eight on each side of the hallway. On rubber legs, holding the mallet aloft, she began to walk the gauntlet. Her breath came fast and hard. At each doorway, she halted, mallet overhead. But each room was vacant, vacant, vacant—

And then a room wasn't vacant.

Helen froze. The curtains were open. Perhaps the light had been an attractant. The zombie was short and squat, naked, greenish-black and covered in suppurating ulcers. Insects crawled, writhed and dug within each sore, wriggling beneath the skin. The bald pate and hair stubble suggested the male sex. The zombie stood facing the high window, its belly pressed against the wall, marching in place. Dear God, the...*unnaturalness* of its futile locomotion shot goose pimples across Helen's body.

How long had the zombie, stuck, been trying to walk forward?

A forgotten memory flashed. A toy robot, wind-up, made of tin. Something that her father had kept from his own childhood. You twisted the key in its back, set the toy on a flat surface. With a whirring sound, sparks shooting from its rectangular slot of a mouth, the robot's metal legs would stamp doggedly onwards until its key ran down. Helen used to put obstacles in its way to see what the toy robot would do. Sometimes it would walk over them. Other times it would fall over. But whenever she faced it into a wall, the internal mechanism would run out its clockwork while the legs kept fruitlessly pacing. She used to say to Dad, *Why doesn't he turn around?* And Dad would reply, *Because he's mindless, honey.*

Mindless.

All she had to do was close the door. The zombie wouldn't figure out how to open it.

The room smelled putrid, dank and sweet, like rubbish left in the sun. The room was tiny, containing only a bunkbed and a bedside table. The zombie was a couple of metres away, perhaps less. The soles of its feet made squelching sounds with every step.

"Helen?" Magnus called from the other end of the bunkhouse. "Where are you? Helen?"

Oh, shit.

The zombie stopped marching. Lifted its head. Darted its face from side to side.

Shut up, Magnus. Shut the fuck up. Leaning over, shaking, she reached out for the handle.

"Helen? We've got a plan."

The zombie turned and looked at her. Its jaw hung open. Twitching bugs filled its mouth.

Helen gripped the handle.

The zombie pushed off from the wall and raced over. Helen tried to slam the door. The zombie got there first, wedging an arm between the door and the jamb. The dead fingers groped for her but she couldn't afford to let go of the handle. The zombie found and gripped her forearm, its touch cold, wet and oily.

Adrenaline fired through her body. With a cry, she dragged on the door with every ounce of strength, putting one foot against the wall. She trapped the zombie arm against the jamb. The pressure began to cut through the putrefying flesh. The popping sound of tissue as it separated made her gag. The shrivelled, blackened fingers raked at her, pinching with skeletonised fingertips. Gnats flew up in a cloud around her face. Beetles scrabbled over her knuckles, seeking out fresh food, mandibles nipping.

"Magnus!" she shrieked.

His heavy footsteps pounded. The doorways in the common areas lined up, so she saw him running from the kitchen. Empty-handed, the tools jouncing from his belt, in too much of a hurry to stop and equip himself with a weapon.

It occurred to her, fleetingly, that the only person on earth who would ever matter to her ever again for as long as she lived would be Magnus Vestergaard.

And then the second zombie emerged from another bedroom.

15

The second zombie, staggering as if dazed, exited one of the bedrooms that lay between Magnus and Helen. Magnus, running full tilt, could not possibly stop in time. Dear God, Helen thought, was he going to plough straight into that monster? There wasn't enough space in the hallway for anything other than a collision.

Magnus raised his elbow and connected with the zombie's head. The force of the blow slammed the head into the door frame. The skull split with a loud *crack*. The zombie fell, toppling full-length like a felled tree, back into the bedroom from which it had emerged. Magnus hadn't even broken stride.

She couldn't let go of the door handle. Skeleton fingers squeezed, pinched and groped at her forearm.

"It's got me," Helen gasped.

At her side in the next instant, Magnus grabbed the spade from his belt and brought it down with force through the zombie's limb, severing it at the elbow. With the obstacle removed, the door slammed shut.

Helen let go of the handle and stumbled. Relief made her dizzy.

But the amputated limb had *life*. Aghast, she looked down. The hand still gripped her, its fingers digging spasmodically into her skin. She opened her mouth to scream. With a cry of disgust, Magnus wrenched the thing away and flung it to the ground. It crawled like a spider across the linoleum. Magnus chopped it to pieces with the spade and kept chopping until the tattered fragments had no more life left in them.

Then he rested the spade on the floor and leaned on the handle.

For a time, they both stared at the remains, panting. From the other side of the door came soft knocking and tapping sounds. Goose flesh popped on Helen's skin. The zombie, no doubt, was marching in place against the door. The realisation made her shiver.

"Jesus," she whispered at last. "Jesus Christ almighty."

"Yes. I agree."

"The arm was still alive because we didn't destroy the brain."

"Very true."

He was puffing, breath ragged. For the first time, she remembered that Magnus was middle-aged, in his fifties at least. How was his cardiovascular health? Blood pressure? Could the stress of this nightmare give him a heart attack? Impulsively, she put her arms about him. Oh fuck, he was trembling. *Trembling*. Now she felt more afraid of this situation than ever before.

"Come and sit down with me," he said. "I have good news."

Reluctantly, she let go and followed him along the hallway. Once in the games room, she veered towards the nearest armchair and collapsed into it.

"You want to talk in here?" he said.

"If I try to stand up, I'll fall down."

"Okay. I'll get my phone. It's on the kitchen table."

"While you're there," she said, "grab a couple of beers from the fridge."

He smiled, his face pale and strained. "Yes. A beer would be nice."

She watched him walk through the common areas. Magnus was the absolute physical antithesis of her father—who had been petite and slender with a full head of salt-and-pepper hair—and yet the two men were remarkably similar in personality. So very matter of fact. Not prone to emotional displays. Practical. Capable. You could present Dad with any kind of DIY problem—burst waterpipe, broken down car, blown-over tree—and he could fix it or figure out a way to make it work until the professionals came along, just like Magnus. Dad never read books. She supposed that Magnus wouldn't care for reading either. And hadn't Alisha given Magnus desserts from time to time? The gesture had seemed ridiculous but now Helen understood. Dad had liked desserts too. Apple crumble, rhubarb pie, self-saucing puddings…

No, wait.

It wouldn't do either of them any good if she started treating Magnus like some kind of reincarnation. *Get a grip.* Damn, was she so psychologically needy that she would attach herself to anybody who seemed to care? Thanks Mum, she thought. Thanks for nothing.

Now Magnus was returning with a beer in each hand. Helen couldn't help but smile. For a moment, she imagined their shared future: he would visit every Sunday for dinner, and she would cook Finnish meals like his mother used to make. Hold up, what did Finns eat, anyway? Venison? Reindeer? Cabbage? Pickled herring? She had no idea. Fuck, was she relying on northern European stereotypes? Maybe he didn't limit himself to traditional foods. Maybe he enjoyed modern Australian favourites like barbecues and salads, chicken parmigiana, barramundi... He might even have wider ranging tastes. Why, he could love plenty of cuisines from Chinese to Italian to British. To Thai to Moroccan to French to Vietnamese. Caribbean, Mexican, Greek, Japanese, Turkish, Spanish, Estonian, Nepalese—

Stop.

Calm yourself, she thought, heart racing. Don't let anxiety get the better of you. Breathe with your diaphragm. *Alpha, Bravo, Charlie, Delta—*

"Here," Magnus said.

She took the proffered stubby. "Thank you."

The beer was cold, crisp and bubbly. Perfect. She drank again. Her forearm was scratched and criss-crossed with angry red welts. Could she be infected? Who knew? And if she *was* infected, would changing into a zombie hurt? Would she know if it were happening? Oh, for fuck's sake, she had to stop this endless *fretting*. She put the bottle to her lips and tipped it upright, glugging down most of the beer in a few quick swallows.

"I'm ready for another," she said.

"Please don't. You can't afford to get drunk."

"Drunk on two stubbies?"

"Don't forget the beer we had at my cabin."

She laughed without mirth. "You sound like my father."

"I've spoken with Stella and the policeman, Rick Evans."

She raised her eyebrows. "And?"

"He called his superiors. Special armed police are on the way."

"That's fantastic! Oh my God—!"

Magnus held up his hand. "Except these officers are in Melbourne city. It'll take them hours to get here. Rick, Stella and Joan Kendall had intended to stay inside the main building and wait for rescue, but zombies are breaking through the windows."

"Oh, fuck," she gasped. "They're getting *in*?"

"Not quite yet. The broken windows are barricaded with furniture. But Rick thinks it's too dangerous to stay. Professor Boyce is also a threat since he is infected. And a donor is trying to get out of the morgue."

"They've got a zombie in the morgue too?" Helen felt ill. "Oh, this keeps getting better."

"It's okay. We'll all escape in Rick's car, which is full of guns, and go into town and wait there for the police. However, there are zombies outside the main building and in the carport. So, you and I will lure the zombies away while Rick gets his car."

"Lure them away? Any thoughts on how?"

"I told him we would ride the quad bike in circles around the building until the zombies follow us."

The plan made her feel light-headed. "Fair enough," she said. "When?"

"As soon as I call Rick and let him know we're coming." Magnus sipped at his beer and regarded her, frowning.

"What?" she said.

"You can stay here if you want. I can do it myself."

"Are you shitting me? No way. We're in this together."

"But you look…"

"Like crap?"

He considered then nodded. "Yes. Like crap."

"Right back at you, mate. Let's finish our beers and get out of here."

Magnus smiled. She raised her stubby. He mimicked the salute and they drank. With a twinge of unease, she studied his pale and sweating face. Was he feeling all right?

Tapping sounded nearby. Helen blew out an exasperated breath. Fucking zombies. They must have reached the front door. "Can you hear those gormless dickheads trying to get in?" she said. "I swear to God—"

Magnus was looking over her shoulder. At the hallway. As his eyes bugged in alarm, Helen's stomach dropped in a sudden, awful realisation.

She hadn't cleared every room.

***

He came awake. He was sitting in a chair at a desk. The desk had papers on it. He touched the papers. The papers felt dry. The markings on the papers didn't make sense. The desk had drawers. He took a doll's hat from a drawer. The hat was straw with black ribbon. The hat made him happy but he didn't know why. He took a pack of cigarettes from another desk drawer. The colours on the pack made him happy but he didn't know why. His jacket had many pockets. He took out a cigarette and put it in his pocket. He put the hat in his pocket.

He stood up. His legs hurt. He went outside the room.

He walked down a corridor. He passed open doors and empty rooms. He found a glass door that led outside. He touched the handle and wasn't sure what to do. His fingers turned a latch. The door opened. The air outside was cool and smelly.

Poop deck.

He stood on the poop deck. A table and chairs. Trees and shrubs out there. He looked at the cigarette in his hand. *Desire.* He put the cigarette in his mouth and chewed it. No. He spat it out. He was hungry. He wanted to eat raw meat. The raw meat had to be warm. He gazed at the trees. The trees were blurry. He couldn't hear through his ears but could hear voices in his mind. The voices were saying the word *friends*.

A bird flew from the trees. It landed on the railing.

Dark plumage and large beak.

COOKIE. COOKIE. COOKIE.

He approached Cookie. The bird looked at him. He reached out. Cookie did not flinch. He patted the bird. Its feathers were soft. He opened his lips to say *Cookie*. No sound came out of his throat. He kept patting the bird. The bird rubbed its face into his palm. He mouthed the word *Cookie*. The bird heard him. It clacked its beak together. He heard the word *friend*.

In his other hand was a doll's hat. He put the hat on Cookie's head. The hat did not fall off. He liked seeing the hat on the bird's head. The bird stayed still so the hat did not fall off. The bird liked the hat. Cookie was happy.

He heard voices in his mind. He could hear the word *friends*.

Cookie clacked its beak. The bird was hungry. The bird wanted raw meat. The raw meat had to be warm. He did not know where to find raw and warm meat. He was sad.

He could hear the word *friends* getting louder.

He saw pigs. Some of them wore clothes. The pigs were walking out of the trees towards the building. He saw people. Some of them wore clothes. The people were walking out of the trees towards the building. He saw one young woman. The young woman was Cheryl.

CHERYL. CHERYL. CHERYL.

He opened his lips to say *Cheryl*. No sound came out of his throat. He mouthed the word *Cheryl*. She heard him. She opened her lips. No sound came out of her throat. She mouthed the words *Professor Boyce*. He heard her.

He must be *Professor Boyce*.

Cheryl walked to the railing and put up her hand. He walked over and took hold of her hand. She climbed the railings. She stood next to him on the poop deck. He was happy. She was happy. He went to Cookie. She followed. He patted the bird and mouthed the word *Cookie*. Cheryl patted the bird and mouthed the word *Cookie*. She pointed at the hat. She mouthed the word *hat*. Yes. He mouthed the word *hat*.

Cookie clacked its beak. The bird was hungry. The bird wanted raw meat. The raw meat had to be warm. He was hungry too. Cheryl was hungry too. They all wanted raw meat. The raw meat had to be warm. He did not know where to find raw and warm meat. He was sad.

Why was he out here? He did not hold a cigarette. He only came out here to hold a cigarette. No cigarette. Time to go back inside the building.

He picked up Cookie and put the bird on his shoulder. The bird sat on his shoulder. The hat did not fall off. Cheryl mouthed the word *pirate*. Yes. He mouthed the word *pirate*. Long John... He couldn't finish the thought. It didn't matter. He was happy. He held Cheryl's hand. He walked her to the door. Cookie stayed on his shoulder. He opened the door. They went inside. They walked past the room where he had got the cigarettes and the hat. They turned a corner.

There were screams. The screams came from sacks of *raw and warm meat*. Saliva rushed to his mouth.

Cheryl squeezed his hand. He squeezed her hand. Cookie clacked its beak. FOOD. FOOD. FOOD.

The sacks of raw and warm meat ran about, screaming.

***

She tried to move but Magnus's look of surprise and horror had her frozen. The stink hit first. Next, the drone of blowflies. Then the crackling and creaking of dried out internal organs flexing inside a dead torso.

Icy fingers grabbed her neck. Helen sprang from the armchair with enough force to launch herself halfway across the room. She spun around.

The zombie wore a two-piece suit and white shirt, no tie, like a businessman relaxing at a bar after work, except the clothes were discoloured and wet. Lips gone; skin rotted away from nose to chin. The teeth orthodontically perfect, bright white and gleaming. Veneers? The tattered face seemed to be smiling. A smile that, quite literally, stretched from ear to ear.

With a limping gait, the zombie stepped around the armchair. Helen took the mallet from her rope belt and dropped it. Groped for the hatchet and couldn't find it. Oh God, this zombie was *fast*. The layers of clothing must have protected its muscles and sinews. One arm slashed through the air, fingers grasping.

Backing up, fumbling with the ball peen hammer, she slammed a hip into the corner of the billiard table and cried out.

Where was Magnus?

She glanced behind.

Just in time to see Magnus take a step on rubber legs and fall to one knee. The air left his lungs in a plaintive moan. The zombie changed direction and went after him. Magnus looked up in defeat and despair.

A switch tripped inside Helen's mind. Terror fell away.

Replaced by seething, furious *anger.*

Fuck you.

The ball peen hammer was pathetic. Little more than a toothpick. She tossed it onto the billiard table and snatched up a cue. Holding it in both hands, she swung it hard and caught the zombie under its chin. The jaw broke on one side and dropped open. Set loose, the tongue flopped and squirmed like a slug. But the zombie's attention remained fixed on Magnus.

She struck again. An ear flew off. Bugs cascaded from the hole left behind. Still the zombie went after Magnus, who was crawling away on hands and knees. Grunting with effort, Helen struck over and over. Finally, the zombie turned to look at her. Its eyeballs were grey and flattened, the irises a pair of pancaked blue discs peppered with dots of petechiae.

The zombie lunged at speed.

Grasped her around the neck with both hands.

The Hollywood teeth leaned in close, gnashing and clattering despite the unhinged mandible. With a shriek, Helen pushed on the forehead. The sodden scalp peeled off in one motion like a shucked bathing cap. The exposed skull shone wetly. Panicked, she pushed again. The cheek sloughed off in a single, greasy swipe. Oh, *Jesus.*

And the teeth kept snapping.

Maggots dropped and pattered over her face.

Short-winded with exertion, Helen shoved the zombie to arm's length and lifted the pool cue. Worked her grip along it. Put the tip against one of the zombie's eyes. The zombie didn't even flinch. She jabbed the stick into the socket. The eyeball gave way with a faint pop. She held on tight. The zombie, in its desperation to bite, drove the cue deeper and deeper into its own eye. The tissue folded up. The cue began to disappear into the skull.

Helen pushed and pushed.

Surely, the cue must be cleaving through brain tissue by now?

And yet, the goddamned zombie kept working its teeth, waggling its blackened tongue.

Dear God, how much further?

Finally, yes, she felt a change of texture through the stick: a dense patch of resistance like a chunk of gristle. With a spasmodic jerk, the zombie stopped moving. The strength left its fingers. Helen stepped back. The hands dropped from her neck. Spurred, she twisted and rammed the cue deeper and deeper into the eye socket until the zombie lost its animation and collapsed. She followed it down to the floor, pushing the cue all the way through until the tip hit the back of the bastard's skull. Only then did she let go.

The zombie lay still. Dead—again—at long fucking *last.*

She touched at her throat. Uninjured. The zombie hadn't had enough strength to choke her. But it had left behind some kind of cold slime… She wiped it off and examined it. Oh, Christ. *Flesh.* Pieces of the zombie's cast-off skin, pieces of rotting fingertips. Repulsed, she slapped at her throat and flapped her hands. The tiny clods flew off. Her body shook and she gulped air. Then she saw Magnus.

Oh no, he was lying on his *face*.

She hurried to his side, dropped to her knees and went to turn him. At her touch, he rolled over and grinned, bleary-eyed and sallow.

"Fucking hell," she said. "Are you having a heart attack?"

"No."

"Are you sure?"

He considered for a moment. "No."

"You mean 'no' you're not having a heart attack, or 'no' you're not sure?"

He shrugged. "Take your pick."

"Can you get up?" she said.

"I'll try."

"Let's take off the tool belt first, okay? You'll be more comfortable."

Nodding, his fingers stuttered on the buckle. Helen's heart quailed. She brushed his shaking hands out of the way, took off the belt for him, and lay it on the floor.

"Thank you," he said.

"Okay, up you get," she said and put the crook of her elbow under his neck.

He grimaced as he struggled into a sitting position. "The zombie. Is it dead?"

"As a doornail."

"Good job." He closed his eyes.

"You're in no shape to go anywhere. I'll do the plan by myself."

"What?"

"Ride your quad bike near the main building to lure zombies. I'll do it myself. You stay here and I'll come back and get you. I don't know when, but there's plenty of food, plenty of beer. You'll be okay for a while."

He opened one eye. "Have you ever ridden a quad bike before?"

"No, but how hard could it be?"

"An attitude like that is what gets people maimed or killed. A quad bike is a very dangerous machine. Rollovers cause head injuries, crush injuries—"

"Look," she said, "calm down. I can ride a postie bike, can't I?"

"It's nothing like a postie bike. No. We stick to our plan. All I need is a bit of rest."

"Don't be stupid. Give me a few pointers on how to ride the damned thing."

"No."

"For Christ's sake, Magnus!"

"My mind is set. You won't change it. Please help me into a chair."

She gritted her teeth, dragged his arm over her shoulders. "You're a stubborn old bastard."

"Yes, I am." He sucked in a harsh breath and pointed. "Look out. There's another one."

Helen let go and stood up. An old woman with waist-length, stringy grey hair was edging unsteadily from the hallway into the games room, smacking her lips and working her gums.

"Oh, fucking *hell*," Helen groaned, stamping her foot. "How much easier would it be if the hallway had a goddamned door we could close? Pass me the shovel."

"Spade."

"Whatever. Just pass it to me, would you?"

Spade in hand, she strode towards the old woman. This was the zombie that Magnus had smacked in the head with his elbow. So, a cracked skull wasn't enough to decommission them. Good to know...To her amazement, Helen didn't feel the slightest bit afraid. Was this her new normal? Inured already? Well, if nothing else, her composure proved you could adapt to any circumstance—no matter how bizarre—given enough time and exposure. Or maybe her adrenal glands were fatigued. Either way, she appreciated the respite from pants-shitting terror.

She smashed the spade down on the old woman's head. The skull broke open like an egg. The zombie crumpled to the floor in a frail, untidy heap of skin, bone and bugs.

Standing near the mouth of the hallway, Helen shouted, "Any more of you pricks hiding down there? Come on out. I want to get this bullshit out of the way, once and for all." She paused, listening. "Hello? Can anybody hear me? Hello?"

Fine, she would check each room.

She went to take a step. But the long hallway was so *dark*. The open doors seemed hushed and expectant. The single closed door rattled in its frame as the one-armed zombie trapped inside struggled against it. The chopped remains of the forearm lay at the threshold. The light was too dim to see the remains clearly. What if those severed fingers were inching across the floor? A ribbon of fear wended through her chest. No. On second thoughts, no, she wouldn't check the rooms. *Couldn't* check the rooms. Besides, there weren't any more zombies. Her calls would have brought them out. Right? Right. How strange there were no zombie pigs. The reason why came to her almost immediately: pigs weren't used to being indoors, so the idea to stroll into a house would never have occurred to them. She put down the spade and rested the handle against the wall.

"Let's go to the kitchen," she said.

"The bunkhouse is clear?"

"As far as I can tell."

She helped Magnus to his feet and put an arm around him to offer support.

"I can manage from here," he said, brushing her aside. "Thank you."

He shuffled, bent over as if nursing a gut ache. Pinpoints of sweat peppered his balding scalp. His face looked pale and yellow. Helen wasn't a doctor, but she suspected a heart attack. Tears prickled hot behind her eyes. The efficacy of CPR outside of a hospital was about ten per cent. What terrible odds... Hold on a second. Maybe she shouldn't rush to assume the absolute worst-case scenario. Maybe his signs flagged some other malady—

Oh, *shit*.

Helen's back stiffened.

He had walked in socks along his zombie-spattered veranda.

Ridiculous. She had inspected his bare feet, hadn't found any cuts from the smashed zombie bones. At least, no visible cuts. The mode of transmission from the dead to the living may be unknown, but transmission was *likely*—what else could explain Professor Boyce's infection besides a bite from a zombie? And perhaps infection didn't require something as dramatic as a bite. Perhaps something as fine as a papercut could transfer the contagion via the skin. If that were the case, then Magnus was quite possibly—

"Why are you looking at me like that?" Magnus said.

"Like what?"

"*Perkele.* I'm telling you I'm not having a heart attack."

"Shit, mate, I don't know what to think." She pulled out a kitchen chair for him, and he sat down. "Tell me your symptoms," she continued. "Any pain down your left arm? Up your neck and into your jaw?"

"How many times do I have to say it? This is not a heart attack."

"Okay. Are you diabetic by any chance?"

"No." He pressed the heels of both hands into his temples. "For what it's worth, I haven't eaten since five-thirty this morning."

Oh, thank God. A plausible explanation. "Meaning low blood sugars. Hypoglycaemia."

He conceded the point with a shrug. "I could be dizzy from hunger, yes."

She had a couple of microwave-ready meals in the freezer. Cooking from scratch was not something you wanted to do at the VITERI bunkhouse. It was a place for frozen pizza and oven-ready quiche. Beer and spirits and mucking about, dancing with your crush while getting tipsy…

Pulling the microwave meals from the freezer, she said, "You like spicy food?"

"There's no time. We have to go help the others."

"Mate, we can't help them if you pass out. I don't know how to ride a quad bike, and you won't tell me. But don't panic: these meals are quick to heat and quick to eat. So, do you like spicy food or not?"

He sighed. "If it's not too strong."

She waved one of the boxes. "A Spanish dish. Chicken and chorizo with rice."

"What's chorizo?"

"A type of sausage with paprika."

"Yes, thank you. I'll call Stella and Rick. To tell them we'll be ten minutes." He dialled, waited, frowned. Hung up. "Voicemail."

"Voicemail?" Helen swallowed against a jag of panic. "What do you think that means?"

"Professor Boyce…?"

"No. Professor Boyce is tied up. Joan Kendall would have made sure of that."

"The zombie in the morgue?"

"A moot point," she said. "Zombies don't have the smarts to open doors."

Magnus didn't look too sure. Helen almost suggested he call back, yet thought better of it. If something terrible had happened in the main building, they would find out soon enough.

Lunch was ready in two minutes. Just in case, Helen sat where she had a clear line of sight straight through all the living area doorways to the hall. The spade was propped against a wall in the games room, its blade covered in congealing muck.

Don't look at it, she reminded herself as her stomach turned over.

16

The sight hit Stella like a punch to the solar plexus. The breath left her in a rush—*ungh*—and didn't come back. At the same time, a firework of adrenaline exploded inside her chest and sent white-hot sparkles surging through her limbs. The sparkles burst into crippling bloom at her hands and feet. *Kapow*. Holy frick, her nervous system had caught fire. And it *hurt*. Hurt like the devil. Stella had never before experienced an adrenaline rush with this degree of brute force. Then again, she had never before experienced a sight quite like this.

Her mind stepped sideways.

Sideways?

No other way to explain it. Instead of sitting square and looking straight out of her two eyes, her mind had noped out, shifting itself from the main arena. That's why she was feeling groggy and fuzzy and calm. Emotional shock. Or psychological break. She had read about this kind of phenomenon. When reality becomes too much, the mind stops trying, throws up its hands, and walks away. What else could account for this weird detachment? She should be screaming right now. Screaming her lungs raw. Oh yes, that's right; she still hadn't drawn a breath. It was as if her body had forgotten how.

I've lost my mind, Stella thought, marvelling at the novelty. Lost it without any effort whatsoever. Like forgetting where you put a set of keys. Would she ever find it again? More to the point—would she have *time* to find it again before dying?

Because she was going to die very soon.

Stuporously, she pondered the events of the previous few moments.

Rick had just hung up the phone from Magnus. Rick had come up with a pretty good plan of escape, actually. If it went as described, they would soon be sitting pretty at a café in Wooriyanda, sipping cappuccinos, waiting for the heavily-armed Special Operations Group to sweep through VITERI and clean up the mess. Yep, the lucky survivors of this cataclysm together, safe and sound, drinking coffee and eating cake: herself, Rick, Joan, Magnus, Helen, Walter... No, wait. *Not Walter*. He would have to stay behind. He was now part of the "mess". A pang of sorrow trembled along her nerves.

And then...and then after Rick had said to Magnus, *Cheers, mate*, and disconnected the call, he had put the mobile back in his pocket. Had turned to Stella with a smile, as if he were about to say something cheeky yet reassuring. And God, how she needed to hear something cheeky yet reassuring...

But movement at the other end of the corridor caught her attention. His too.

White and cream and brown and green.

A blur of white and cream and brown and green.

She had turned her head. Looked down the corridor. The building was an L-shape. The shorter leg of the L was a petite corridor that led to the back patio. She remembered thinking, *who has come in from the patio?* Walter, the only other smoker on staff, was inside his office. Then she realised, in the first split-second before the white-and-cream-and-brown-and-green made sense, that Walter's office door stood ajar. Presentiment prickled the hair on her head.

White and cream and brown and green—

The white of Walter's lab coat.

The cream and brown plumage of the kookaburra sitting on his shoulder.

The green of the scrubs worn by...*Cheryl Zhao* of all people. The deceased Cheryl Zhao...

And in the next split-second, just before she lost her breath and her mind, Stella had absorbed and understood the terrible sight in its terrible individual components.

Firstly—

By rights, Cheryl Zhao should have been dead. *Properly* dead. The not-ever-getting-up-again kind of dead. Rick had said so. *Violet killed Cheryl Zhao. Attacked her like some kind of wild dog. Bit out her throat.*

Well, yes, fair play; the girl's throat was indeed missing.

The torn skin pale, droopy, ragged as a ripped bedsheet. The interior of her neck dark red. She was holding hands with Walter. And, oh my word, her *other* hand... Stella's vision pinned into a narrow tunnel just to look at it. The fingers were doubled up in a tight spasm, the tips locked against the palm, thumb dangling loose. It was a non-functioning hand. That was clear. Not only from the hand's unusual posture. Oh, no. The confirmation was in the *forearm*. The flesh and meat were stripped, the two long bones exposed from wrist to elbow. No muscles or tendons remained to work the hand or fingers. Gone. Chewed away. Eaten. With a bit of tattered meat left about the wrist and elbow joint. It reminded Stella of a gnawed chicken wing. Exactly like a gnawed chicken wing. Yet Cheryl didn't seem to notice. The ruined arm hung at her side, with the hand shrivelled closed like a dead huntsman spider.

Secondly—

Walter looked like the very definition of an animated corpse. If Stella had doubted his transformation before, she doubted it no longer.

Thirdly—

The kookaburra, which Walter had named Cookie, resembled road kill. Busted up a little, as if it had bounced off the bonnet of a speeding car and tumbled into the weeds and gravel of a roadside. The asymmetrical tilt of its body. The dry, dusty, messy feathers. The lopsided hunker of its clawed feet digging into Walter's shoulder. So, this is how Walter had got infected: the zombified Cookie had attacked him and mauled his hand during smoko on the poop deck. And what was that on its head? A tiny hat, Stella realised in surprise. A fricking straw boater... Somehow, the hat made everything worse. Made everything more nightmarish and insane.

The ensemble paused at the mouth of the main corridor as if posing for a portrait. So very still.

Father. Daughter. Pet.

Dead. Deader. Deadest.

A hellish little family.

And that's when the breath had left Stella in a rush. *Ungh*. And her mind had left soon after. I've lost my mind, Stella thought, marvelling at the novelty. Lost it without any effort whatsoever. Like forgetting where you put a set of keys. Would she ever find it again? More to the point—would she have *time* to find it again before dying? Because she was going to die very soon.

White-cream-brown-green.

For those initial couple of seconds, time had spooled out lazily. Now something inside Stella grabbed at her perception of time and reeled it back, hauling in her consciousness which squirmed and fought at the end of the line like a hooked fish.

Snap.

Her cramped lungs expanded with a gasp. Air rushed in. She tightened her abdomen, bent over and screamed.

Joan Kendall's scream was high-pitched and shrill.

Rick Evans's scream sounded more like a bellow.

They were screaming together. Loud enough to concuss Stella's eardrums.

Cookie shook its wings. The straw boater spilled off. Cookie fell from Walter's shoulder, dropping as if lifeless. Thank Christ. Screw *you*, you piece of shit, Stella thought with a vicious flare of joy. One less monster to worry about—

Oh, but no, *no*, the bird didn't hit the floor. Instead, it looped up in a clumsy parabola, wings fluttering. Cookie was attempting to *fly*. And it flew like a moth—bucking, dipping, yawing—feathers rustling as it slewed drunkenly through the air along the main corridor. The beak stretched open. Stella wished for a tennis racquet. Volley!

But she didn't have a tennis racquet.

She had nothing. Except the urge to sit down and rest.

Emotional shock.

Psychological break.

Walter and Cheryl, hand in hand, approached. He shuffled along the corridor, knees locked, feet sliding like an ice skater. She crept along on tiptoe. Rigor mortis. Their leg muscles must be seizing up. Cookie veered into a wall, rebounded, adjusted its flight path.

Kill the bird.

Huh? Stella felt herself frowning. *What did you say?*

"Kill the bird!" Joan shouted again.

Stella took another breath. Looked around. And there was her boss, Professor Joan Kendall, cheeks flushed, eyes staring in hectic terror. There was the visitor, Detective Senior Sergeant Rick Evans, his mouth agape, still holding shut the door to the morgue because—oh, *frick*—there was a zombie, the big one called Butch, on the other side trying to get out. Remember? *Wake up*, Stella told herself in a panic.

Wake up, wake up, wake up!

Their weapons cache sat on her desk. Knives, fire extinguisher, aluminium water bottle tied to a belt. *Useless*. She needed something like a bloody tennis racquet. Something solid that she could wield two-handed. She snatched up her document tray, a solid piece of equipment made from punched metal, and dumped the paperwork. Holding the tray in both hands, she hurried down the corridor towards the pitching bird.

I'm going to knock you right into next week, you fricking bastard.

She'd had just two tennis lessons in her life. Got a stitch on the first one. Tore a rotator cuff on the other. Had given the sport away as too vigorous for her short and stocky build, but by crikey, she could hit the ball! Each time, every time. Not like the other old biddies who had attended the lessons, who would swing and miss, swing and miss, no matter what the coach advised. Stella had good hand-to-eye coordination and, not wanting to waste it, had taken up ping pong. And was a bloody good player! The ping pong table sat under the pergola at home. She was reigning family champion. Had been from the get-go. Con was unable to best her. Nor could Melanie. And Melanie's husband...well, he was a skinny chemistry nerd. Instead of returning serves, he flinched at them.

"Be careful!" Joan screeched.

Stella knew what she was doing and wasn't afraid. Calm your tits, she wanted to say. If I can hit a ping pong ball, I can hit a zombie kookaburra. But there wasn't time to speak. With a supreme effort, Cookie had flapped its tattered wings and lurched into the air. High up towards the ceiling where Stella couldn't reach.

Shit.

Beak stretched wide, it fixed her with one red-rimmed eye and dive-bombed. *An overhead shot.* Stella wasn't too flash at returning overhead shots. The shoulder she had injured during her second tennis lesson had never quite recovered. She lifted both arms anyway and swung.

BAM.

The document tray slammed into the kookaburra. Like a tennis ball perfectly struck, the kookaburra shot across the corridor at speed and smacked against the wall with a brittle crunch. Feathers fluttered as the bird crashed to the linoleum.

"Score!" Stella cried, pumping her fist.

Joan hurried over, lifted her foot and stamped on Cookie, repeatedly, crying out through clenched teeth with every effort as she mashed the bird's head into the floor. Thrilled, Stella wanted to take back every bad thought she'd ever had about her boss.

Walter twitched into life. Feet gliding across the linoleum, legs pumping, mouth twisting into a snarl and arms outstretched, he made a beeline for Joan. Would hitting him with a document tray have any effect? No idea. Stella would soon find out.

Before she could take a step, Rick darted forward with a gun in his hand. He brought down the grip on Walter's head. Once, twice, three times. Each blow rocked Walter's skull and concertinaed his neck. Walter put up no resistance whatsoever. As if he didn't even *realise* that Rick was bashing him.

Yelping, hands flapping, Joan ducked past Stella and headed for the reception desk. Maybe she was planning on getting one of the knives and joining in the fight—

And suddenly, Cheryl was right up in Stella's face.

The girl had crossed four metres in a trice. Jaws wide open, lips peeled back.

In a reflex action, Stella swung the document tray. It smacked against teeth. She swung again. A clattering of incisors fell from the girl's mouth. And again. This time, the tray buckled. Cheryl kept advancing. Her good hand reached out and plucked at Stella's jacket. Oh *frick*, Stella needed a better weapon, something heavier. *The fire extinguisher.*

She stumbled backwards, aiming for the desk.

Rick was still raining blows on Walter's head. The pale, balding pate had a dent in it now, dead-centre on the crown, a crater as deep as a soup bowl. Stella gagged. Belted Cheryl in the jaw with the jagged edge of the tray. Cheryl's chin opened up and peeled away, revealing a glistening nub of white bone.

"Joan!" Stella shouted. "Get her with the fire extinguisher!"

"*Butch!*" Joan squawked.

"Hurry! I said, get her with the—"

Oh SHIT.

The realisation came to her. To combat Walter, Rick had had to let go of the morgue door.

She turned. The terrible sight loosened her bladder first and then her hands. The document tray slipped to the floor.

Butch was tall and heavily built, yes, but it was the bulky gym-tortured muscles that made her quail in horror. This donor was the largest man she had ever seen. It must have taken considerable dedication to transform himself into a figure that would inspire fear on sight. And cripes, did he inspire fear. The shaved head, beard, tattoos (a bandanaed skull inked on his chest, a snake coiled around one bicep and a broadsword on the other, a horned demon grinning from his belly); all of these things sent a clear and purposeful message: *fuck with me at your peril.*

"Rick!" Stella yelled. "Butch is out of the morgue!"

The next half-minute descended into chaos.

Screaming. Dodging. Hitting.

Somehow, Stella had the fire extinguisher by the handle and was spinning in crazed circles, smashing it against teeth and clawing hands. Cheryl slipped to her knees and Stella brought the extinguisher down on her upturned face. *Cra-a-ack.* The breaking of bone like the loud snap of a tree branch.

And Joan, flailing the aluminium bottle by the belt.

Rick with a gun in each hand, punching and pistol-whipping.

Walter refusing to drop.

Butch swinging meaty arms.

Everyone shuffling, jumping, twirling, ducking, weaving; an insane dance.

Sights flashed staccato as if she were staring at a strobe light. Stella couldn't figure it out. She was sure that she wasn't blinking. Sound had disappeared too. This didn't make sense either. She felt as if she were underwater and drowning. Maybe that was how six-year old Melanie had experienced the bottom of the pool so long ago, that summer when she had nearly died in her uncle's backyard; sensory perception no longer in a clear and steady stream of consciousness, just snatches of nonsensical dribs and drabs. Maybe this is what dying felt like. For all Stella knew, one of the zombies had bitten her already. Severed an artery. She could be bleeding out. The thought sent another jag of adrenaline coursing through her. She tried to focus, to see and process and understand what was happening, and couldn't. Lost, she kept swinging the fire extinguisher.

On and on went the ruckus.

Cheryl's forehead gave way and crumpled. Still she reached out to clutch at Stella.

Walter snapped his teeth at Joan while she bashed him frantically with the water bottle.

Rick now trying to hit Butch with a chair... Butch moving fast enough to deflect the chair using both giant hands...

We can't fight them forever, Stella thought in terror. Oh God, she was already winded. Stabbed through with a bad stitch. Rotator cuff burning with pain. The zombies would soon wear them down and overwhelm them.

Acting in concert, as if from telepathy, Walter and Cheryl simultaneously joined Butch's efforts and lunged at Rick. With three of them on the attack, he'd get bitten for sure. Stella would do her best with the fire extinguisher but she could only hit one zombie at a time—

Butch shoved Walter and Cheryl away. Like he didn't want to share the spoils. Walter and Cheryl failed to notice. They simply straightened up and pressed forward, jaws churning. Butch again threw them aside.

Everyone shuffling, jumping, twirling, ducking, weaving—

Someone grabbed Stella's arm.

Dragged her along.

The corridor shimmied and spangled in her vision. A doorway. A room. A bright window with slitted venetian blinds. Desktop, multiple computer monitors, the speckled green leaves of a devil's ivy plant on the windowsill—

Kieran Pocock's office.

Rick, she had said. *On your way past the bunkhouse, did you see anybody? A young bloke?*

I saw the remains of a person eaten down to the bone... The clothing was bloody and torn, but there were these fancy men's lace-ups...

"I'm about to be sick," she gulped. "Out of the way, I need the dunny—"

"Shut up," Rick said, and shook her elbow. "Shut up and listen to me."

"Huh—?"

His red, sweaty face came into focus. So, it was Rick who had frogmarched her out of that melee. Why hadn't retreat occurred to her as an option? He slammed the office door.

"Where's Joan?" she said.

"Over here."

Stella began to shake violently. "What are we gonna do?"

"Shut the hell up and listen."

He let go of her. She staggered, bumped into the desk. Rick was pressing his back against the door. Heavy thumps sounded from the other side.

"Oh shit," she said. "That's Butch, isn't it? He's trying to break in."

"Joan got hurt."

"What?"

Rick compressed his lips. "Joan got hurt."

Bang, bang, bang on the door. Hard. As if from a battering ram. The wood shivered and bucked. Disoriented, Stella crawled her gaze across the room until she found Joan. The director's eyes were wide and startled, her skin ashen. There was blood on the sleeve of her ripped jacket. Stella's heart dropped into her stomach.

"Bugger, did I hit you with the fire extinguisher?" she said, hoping against hope. "Did I?"

Joan took off her jacket. On her wrist was a deep, tattered bite-mark.

***

They ate. The food tasted *good*. Magnus felt better. He had been more ravenous then he realised. This was the first time he'd eaten a microwave meal and it wouldn't be the last.

Unless, of course, he didn't survive VITERI.

There were a few different ways to die. Zombies may ambush him. Or else the heavy pressure inside his ribcage, which felt strangely like an ever-inflating balloon, might be a heart attack. Unless the pressure flagged the start of his transition into a zombie. After all, he had walked barefoot over chopped zombie flesh and bones. Infection was a possibility. However, he wouldn't mention this concern to Helen. No need to scare her more than she already was. Besides, he had his .22 rifle. If it became apparent that he was changing, as Walter had changed, then he would shoot himself before he lost his mental faculties... He thought of Leena, adrift in her maze of dementia, and the comparison stung him.

Interrupting his own thoughts, he said, "Rick knows how this incident started off."

Helen paused the fork halfway to her mouth. "For real?"

"Yes."

"Let's hear it."

Magnus sat back in his chair. "Earlier today, I helped Cheryl Zhao and the detectives put their donor inside a car boot. Then I rode back to my cabin to work on my shopping list. I didn't look out the window. I didn't see it."

Helen put down the fork. "Didn't see what?"

"The cloud. Small and close to the ground. Rick described it as unusual. It looked like..." Magnus paused. "Like dozens of bare female breasts hanging down."

"Is that right?"

"Rick's words, not mine. I hope you don't think I'm—"

"He saw a mammatocumulus."

"Sorry?"

"A mammatus cloud," she said. "Pretty rare. They usually appear before a bad storm. No surprise there. The weather bureau predicts a bad storm later today: a 'rain bomb'. What's a mammatus cloud got to do with zombies?"

"It was the wrong colour. Not white or grey as you would expect. Orange like a sunset."

She frowned. "Orange? That's weird."

"Yes. And there were other strange colours too. Browns and greens."

"I must have been inside the bunkhouse at the time. Making breakfast, I guess." She looked stricken. "I mean *brunch*."

"Some unknown substance like seeds or pollen dropped from this cloud. Very fine and white seeds. They disappeared when they touched anything. After the seeds fell, the donor in the car boot came awake."

"Christ. Really?"

"Yes."

"That's insane. And the cop saw this with his own eyes? You're sure?"

"Positive."

"Incredible." Helen put a hand to her forehead. "Oh wow, that's seriously fucked up."

Magnus nodded. "The detective has an explanation: scientists pumped special chemicals into the cloud to see if the dead at VITERI could be brought back to life."

She blinked. "What scientists?"

"Rick didn't know. Mad ones, probably."

"Mad scientists."

"Yes."

"Huh. Okay, what chemicals did they use?"

Starting to blush, Magnus shifted about in his chair. "Who can say?"

"*I* can say. Oh man, let me tell you something. There's no chemical or bunch of chemicals on earth that can reanimate dead tissue. So, there's *that*, for starters."

"It's just a theory—"

"No, it isn't. Not even in the ballpark. Where's the scientific method? The deduction of how and why from observations, facts, and patterns? The ability to make any measurable predictions? You might as well blame aliens. Or sentient dolphins." She laughed and shook her head. "Jesus, spare me. Mad scientists? That's the dumbest hypothesis I've ever heard."

He felt stupid and didn't like it. "I agree with Rick. This isn't happening anywhere else."

"And your evidence for that claim?"

"What the detective saw. What he told me."

"Okay," she said. "For the sake of argument, let's assume the seeds from this weird cloud are responsible. Now, which scenario sounds more likely? That the apocalypse, by some miracle, is localised precisely to the VITERI site. Or that hundreds or thousands or even *millions* of mammatus clouds are raining down this magical zombie jizz across the whole country—across the whole *planet*, for that matter—and we simply can't see them from here."

"Good point. But what makes your theory better than Rick's?"

"Because I'm not theorising. I'm trying to show you that it's silly to speculate beyond our current experience without sufficient evidence."

"Fine. I understand."

"Until we get more information, we have to keep an open mind. Escape from VITERI might be out of the frying pan and into the fire. We'd be crazy to assume otherwise."

"Yes, fine. No need to go on."

She sighed. "You're not sulking, are you?"

He ate the final mouthful of rice. "We should try calling Rick again."

"Okay."

"Coordinate the plan and ride the quad bike to draw the zombies away."

"Go for it. Do you feel well enough to drive?"

"Yes." Magnus narrowed his eyes at her. "Forget I mentioned any kind of theory."

"Again: *not* a theory."

"You can be very annoying," Magnus said.

"Just call Rick," she said, putting down her fork. "Let's get this show on the road."

***

The door shuddered against his back and shook in the frame. Rick braced his feet against the linoleum. Any minute now, that big bastard would smash through the door and rip out Rick's spine. His kidneys seemed to shrivel in dreadful anticipation. Now what?

Come up with a bloody plan, he berated himself. *Begged* himself.

Figure something out.

But how? They were trapped in an office with no means of escape.

Joan Kendall, leaning against the desk, was staring blankly at her bitten and bleeding wrist, tears coursing down her cheeks. Stella had a comforting arm about the woman's shoulders. Damn, I wouldn't get too close if I were you, Rick thought. How long did it take for a living person to transform into a zombie? Hours? Minutes? It had taken Violet, the donor in the car boot, a matter of seconds—

BANG. The door punched into Rick's back, staggering him.

The bastard must be using his shoulder. Thank God he was dead and didn't have full strength—

BANG. A section of the door splintered.

Rick closed his eyes and bit at his trembling lip.

His mobile rang. Fumbling, he snatched it from his pocket. The caller might be his detective inspector advising that the goddamn salvation of heavily-armed specialist police forces was approaching the gate, ready to kick arse. Hope flared weakly in his breast.

Answering the call, he said, "Rick Evans."

"It's Magnus. Put your phone on speaker."

A letdown. What a palpable letdown. Rick complied anyway. "Okay, go ahead."

BANG.

"We're about to leave the bunkhouse. Are you ready?"

"No, no. We're stuck in one of the offices with zombies trying to get in. Three of them. The one from the morgue is breaking the door down. He's a bloody big bastard, some kind of weightlifter. We're fucked, mate. We're fucked."

The sound through the earpiece became muffled as if Magnus were holding the phone against his body. Rick could hear the murmur of rapid talking. Magnus must be consulting with the student, Helen Macauley. The line cleared.

"We'll do a drive-by as planned," Magnus said. "The noise might distract your zombies and make them stand at the windows. Then you can run out the front door and to your car."

BANG.

"We've got another problem," Rick said. "Joan got bit."

Stunned silence.

A young female voice—Helen—said down the line, "Is she okay?"

"Far from it!" Joan yelled, her chalky-white face streaked with tears.

BANG.

"Hurry," Stella wailed. "Butch is busting up the door."

"Don't panic, zombies are pretty easy to kill," Helen said. "They're slow and dumb as dogshit. Too brain-dead to defend themselves against attack."

BANG.

"Butch can defend himself!" Stella said. "He's not too brain-dead!"

"Hold tight, we'll be right there," Magnus said, and disconnected the call.

Stella's eyes were glazed. "You reckon they'll turn up in time?"

"No idea," Rick said.

But honestly? Probably not.

BANG.

17

"Did you hear that?" Helen said. "About their weightlifter zombie that can defend itself?"

Magnus didn't reply. He was busy fastening the tool belt around his waist, distracted by his numb and clumsy fingers. Heart attack or zombie infection? Without experience of either condition, he had no clue. Nor did he want to "speculate without sufficient evidence"... Then again, perhaps his symptoms were stress-related. Once they got away from VITERI, he might feel better. Sometimes the simplest explanation was the right one. That had been a mantra of Yngvar's: *Don't tie yourself in knots.*

"Hey, are you listening?" Helen said.

"I don't care about a smart zombie. I care only about clearing the zombies away from the door of the main building."

"We'll be riding close to them."

"Yes."

"I should sit in front of you on the quad bike."

He looked up. "Why?"

"To fend off zombies with the spade while you steer. Unless you can run them down?"

"No. The bike would tip over."

"Okay, I'm sitting in front with the spade," she said "And the umbrella. Will you have enough room? Can you reach around me for the controls?"

"Yes."

Helen scraped her hair back from her face with both hands, dug into a pocket of her jeans and brought out a tie. Grimly, face set, she fashioned her gore-spattered hair into a ponytail.

"The problem is," she continued, "the noise we make won't just attract the zombies that are hanging around the main building. It'll attract them from all over VITERI."

"I see. That's true."

"Christ knows how many we've killed, but we started the day with about one-hundred-and-twenty corpses; that's including donors and pigs. If we killed, say, ten of them, there's still a hundred-and-ten left. At a conservative estimate."

Magnus nodded, slapped at his secured belt, took out his keys. "Ready?"

They locked eyes. A loaded, pregnant moment. In another life, he could have become friends with this feisty young woman. But in this life? Well, it was too late and too bad.

"I'm sorry I didn't get to know you before today," he said.

"Same here."

She put out her hand. He clasped it. After they shook, Helen put her arms about his waist. He hugged her in return.

***

"Why is Butch different?" Stella said.

BANG.

"Clearly, he abused anabolic steroids," Joan said. "With those track marks on his arms, probably intravenous methamphetamine or ketamine as well."

"You mean drugs changed his chemistry?" Rick said. "Even after death?"

"In a situation like this, without precedent, literally *anything* could be possible."

BANG.

She was right. Throw logic and common-sense and experience out the window. This situation was a whole new kit-and-kaboodle. *The dinosaurs didn't adapt and so they died*, his eldest daughter liked to singsong, usually as she was rolling her eyes at his reluctance to do something *young* like download a pointless app on his phone. No, he couldn't afford to be a dinosaur right now. Adapt, adapt, adapt. He had to go home to his missus and kids. A stab of sorrow took his breath and stung his eyes with tears.

BANG.

"Listen," Stella demanded.

For a second, he thought she was about to launch into a pep-talk or suggest an alternative plan. But she was pricking her ears. Then he heard it too. The high-pitched thrum of a motor ringing its nuts off. *Magnus and Helen*. On their way, riding the quad bike.

Rick's guts flopped queasily.

It was nearly time. Nearly time to show what he was made of. And what was he made of, exactly? No idea. His everyday life was not dangerous. In fact, he had never been in danger. Not really. Had never been tested by fire. And yet, very soon, he would have to leave the relative safety of this office. Run the gauntlet to his car. Drive it back to the front door. Take a shotgun from the boot and clear the way for Stella and Joan to escape. (Hang on, *not* Joan. She was a zombie now, wasn't she? A zombie in waiting. Damn. What the hell were they going to do about Joan? Don't think about it yet, that's what. Wait until the time comes.)

He took a steadying breath. His heart galloped.

This escape plan had been his own idea. But now, the thought of leaving the office paralysed him. Could he do it? Did he have the stones? Perspiration ran in hot rivulets from his armpits.

BANG.

A section of the door broke away. Stella recoiled and screamed.

Then a mad press of dead faces and hands hit the office window with a loud *crack*.

***

The quad bike made a hell of a racket. Helen tightened her grip on the umbrella, clamped the haft of the spade tighter under her other arm. She had the spade resting on the handlebars, its blade jutting out like an impromptu jousting lance. A zombie lance, if you will. *A zombie lance is the correct parlance.* She tried to smile as if amused by her impromptu line of poetry. Tried and failed. Her toes cramped inside her boots and she flexed them to no avail.

Magnus was pressed at her back, his hands on either side of her, steering the bike. How was he feeling right now? He had seemed to rally after having a bite to eat... *Bite...* The skin on the nape of her neck crawled. She imagined him leaning down, jaws agape—

Bitch, concentrate on what you're doing.

The clear blue sky had gone. In the time they had spent at the bunkhouse, woolly skeins of grey cloud had formed, high overhead, barrelling in from the south. Those clouds would descend and darken into gunmetal blue soon enough. Each one contained tonnes of hailstones the size of golf balls according to the weather bureau. It would be a terrible storm. The kind that triggers flash flooding, dents cars, breaks rooftiles, rips up asphalt, brings down trees. A storm of the century, they were calling it. Well, didn't that just put the icing on this godforsaken dog turd of a cake?

The main building emerged from the bush. Carport, water tanks, generator room. And zombies fucking *galore.* Crowding the steps. Butting against the front door. Milling amongst the parked cars. Humans and pigs, clothed and naked, ranging from intact with marbled skin to blackened, fouled and rotting, with every state of putrefaction in between. The sight cramped her lungs into frightened nubs.

"How many, do you reckon?" she said.

"Too many to count," Magnus said.

But why would zombies make a beeline to the main building? What was drawing them here from every point of the VITERI grounds? It sounded crazy, but perhaps they shared a common "memory" of the place, a recollection of the morgue's cool sanctity. Well, why the hell not? The morgue was the last place they had been clean, comfortable, safe under a roof before getting slung into the dirt, buried in shallow graves, wrapped in tarps, exposed to the elements. Who—living or dead—wouldn't wish to get out of the sun, wind and rain?

Helen tightened her grip on the spade, on the umbrella handle.

Magnus rode closer, closer. Damn, the plan wasn't working. The zombies remained fixated on the door and windows. Hang on...a few of them stopped moving. Cocked their heads. Helen held her breath. The zombies turned to face them. *All at the same time.* As if psychically connected. Goose flesh crept down her legs. The spade dwindled from a lance into a pathetic matchstick. Magnus slowed the bike and came to a stop. The zombies regarded them with empty eyes, waiting.

"Okay, we've got their attention," he said.

"Now what?"

"We do *this.*"

He papped the horn. It worked on them like a starter pistol. Incited, they hobbled and hitched and gimped towards the quad bike. The breeze shifted and the stink reached down Helen's throat to stir the Spanish rice in her stomach.

"Don't sit idling for too long," she said. "They're travelling pretty fast."

"Patience. We want them to latch onto us."

She glanced around. Movement in the trees. Flashes of mottled skin, tattered clothing, pink snouts. She clenched her sweating hands. Christ, the advancing horde was so *quiet*.

"You checking your mirrors?" she said.

"Yes."

"Zombies are closing in from the sides."

"Yes. And they're behind us too."

"Let's get out of here," she said.

"A few more seconds—"

"No, a few more seconds and we'll be surrounded."

"We have to wait until we've gathered as many as we can," he said. "There's no point leaving stragglers. How will Rick get to his car?"

A cracking peal of thunder made her flinch. Out of the horde, a naked female loped towards them, arms loose and dangling as if boneless.

***

The zombies hammered their fists against the window of Kieran's office. The crack in the pane lengthened and grew offshoots of smaller fractures. Any second now, the sheer weight of pressing bodies would break the glass and zombies would spill inside the room. But not, Stella thought, before Butch got inside.

Between a rock and a hard place.

The interior doors were cheap. Hollow-core. Butch's meaty hand punched through the laminate veneer and groped about, his scrabbling fingers as white, wrinkled and puckered as raw tripe. Stella screamed again. She couldn't help herself. It aroused the zombies but she simply couldn't *help* herself.

Rick took a gun from his waistband and brought it down, over and over, clubbing the forearm. That achieved precisely bugger-all. Butch grabbed the gun and wrested it away. Was Rick a trained copper or not? Fricken hell, Stella thought, hurry up and *do* something. But Rick just yelped in alarm. She turned to the window. Agitated at the sight of her, zombies renewed their battering. A spiderweb of fresh cracks spread through the pane. She reached up and closed the venetian blind. The zombies hesitated for a moment as if befuddled.

BANG.

The bottom of the door splintered. Butch must be kicking at it.

BANG.

A chunk of veneer fell away. Butch shoved his face into the fresh hole in the door, baring his teeth and snapping his jaws. Oh look, Stella thought abstractly, he's got STRAYA tattooed above one eyebrow. What a complete and utter bogan. Then she snatched up the fire extinguisher and hit him square on the tattoo like it was a bullseye. That didn't faze him.

BANG.

The door juddered open. Rick flung himself against it, desperate to hold closed what little remained of the door. Joan screeched. Stella lifted the fire extinguisher again and scanned for instructions. *Wood, paper, textiles, rubbish, flammable liquids, live electrical equipment—*

She spun the cylinder, found what she was searching for.

"Pull the pin," she read out loud, gabbling fast at the top of her voice. "Aim at base of fire, squeeze the lever, sweep."

She pulled the pin. Rammed the hose into Butch's mouth.

Let her rip. Squeezed the trigger.

KAPOW.

With a mighty hiss, the extinguisher bucked in her hands as if it had *detonated*. One moment, Butch's face was framed in the door. The next it was gone. Choking clods of white powder filled the air. She peered out through the fog, eyes watering as she coughed and hacked. And there he was, the bastard.

"He's on the floor!" she cried. "I knocked him over!"

"Let me see!" Rick yelled.

Joan shoved them both out of the way. High spots of colour flamed in her cheeks. "I'll lead the three zombies onto the back patio. Stella, trail behind us at a safe distance. Once we're clear, shut the back door and lock us out."

Stella lost her breath. "Jeez Louise, say *what?*"

"Trail behind and lock us out," she said, and pushed through the broken door.

Rick grabbed for her and missed. "Don't do it."

But Joan was already at a trot along the corridor. Walter and Cheryl, bobbling their dented, ruined heads, took off in pursuit. A bizarre sight: Joan lumbering like an elephant rocking from one foot to the other, Walter skating across the linoleum on stiffened legs, Cheryl tiptoeing as if her calf muscles had seized. It would be funny if it wasn't so ghastly.

"Come back here," Stella hissed in falsetto.

"I'm as good as dead anyway," Joan called.

Dear God, was she sacrificing herself for them? Volunteering to undergo a terrible death, *getting eaten alive*, to give Rick and Stella a chance of escape? Yes, Joan had been bitten. Yes, she was infected, the same as Walter. And yes, she would turn into a zombie, the same as Walter, given time. But holy crap, to decide that getting *eaten alive* was the better option? Stella felt faint. Oh my God, she thought breathlessly, stunned. Oh God, God, *God—*

Butch rolled onto his stomach, pushed up on his massive arms.

Shit, he was *getting to his feet.*

Rick flattened himself against the wall out of sight. Stella ducked away. Would Butch go after Joan? Or charge into this office and attack? Stella's heart pounded and stuttered. Her fate would be decided within the next few seconds. The wait was agonising torture. Her legs trembled and her hands went numb. The seconds ticked by, years apart.

Finally, Rick snuck a peek and exhaled. "He's going for Joan."

Stella felt a shudder of relief, then hated herself because of it.

Poor Joan!

Rick stepped into the hallway for a better view. Stella peered around the jamb. The scene was a drunken footrace with Butch taking up the rear, walking in a sideways rolling gait and strenuously swinging his arms as if wading through deep, rushing water.

Shocking. Unbelievable. Who would have suspected Professor Joan Kendall of being *gutsy*? Not Stella. Cripes, the amount of times that Stella had bitched to Con about Joan's strict and irritating nature. Every night, wasn't it? Just about. A running joke between them. "Tell me what the old battle-axe did today," Con would remark as they made dinner. Stella would regale him—exaggerating for comedic effect, naturally—and they would laugh. At Joan's expense. Oh, God. Stella felt sick with remorse. With self-loathing.

I'm sorry, she wanted to yell, I'm so sorry for the nasty things I've ever said about you.

But making a sound would attract a zombie's attention. And unlike Joan, Stella didn't have the balls to take that kind of gamble.

Joan reached the end of the main corridor and turned left towards the back door. The zombies followed. They were gaining. Would she reach the door before they reached her?

Stella listened to the zombies hammering, licking and slobbering at the cracked window pane, slipped off her bangles—the blasted noisy things—and flung them onto the desk. She went to leave the office. Rick gripped her arm.

"Where the bloody hell do you think you're going?" he said through teeth.

"To do what she told me to do: lock them outside."

"Are you crazy?"

"Mate, we're not getting away from here if I don't."

She pulled free and hurried down the corridor, stepping flat on her wedge heels. The breath rasped loudly in and out of her mouth, which couldn't be helped, since her heart was beating fit to burst. She couldn't hear any other footsteps. Perhaps Joan had already led them onto the decking. *Please God, please make sure that Joan's plan worked.* The prospect of rounding the corner and seeing the zombies huddled over Joan and chewing on her corpse—

The corner. Stella had got to the corner. Her nerve faltered, stalled.

She looked back. Rick waved. Useless mongrel, she thought. What kind of a copper—or gentleman, for that matter—would stand aside and allow an older woman to play the hero? She was sixty. Sixty-one in December. Had a senior citizen's card. Was entitled to discount meals at pubs, for goodness sakes, and three-dollar vouchers for the pokies. How spineless was Detective Senior Sergeant Rick Evans of the oh-so-elite Homicide Squad to hide away and let *her* take the risk?

That flare of annoyance was the nudge she needed. She peeked around the corner.

Empty corridor! Open back door!

Joan had done it!

Stella sobbed. On wobbling legs, she staggered towards the door, sliding one hand along the wall to help keep her balance.

And then the scream hit her.

Freezing her in place.

She had never heard anything like it before. Not in all her long life. It flashed a boom of adrenaline through her body, hard enough to hurt, to raise every hair and shrink her vision so that everything went dark for a split-second. Dazed, she stumbled and fell against the wall.

The scream sounded again.

Full-throated and drenched with terror.

In her mind's eye, she saw the attack. Saw them ripping and rending and gnashing at Joan.

The high-pitched, tortured screaming went on and on.

Hauling herself upright, gasping, Stella slid along the wall towards the open door. The open *glass* door. She began to cry in earnest. What if she got to the door and actually *witnessed* the attack? No. Her mind teetered on the very edge of breaking. No, no, she wouldn't be able to stand the sight. Would go mad. Never to recover. Never ever ever—

Joan screamed, and this time, it sounded choked and burbling. *Liquid.*

Dear God...

The door was an arm's length away. A zillion miles away. There was the table setting and ashtray. There were the gum trees beyond. And there, among those trees, marched countless zombies getting closer. Stella leaned on the jamb, heart roaring, pulse jackhammering at her ears. Movement from the patio fluttered in her periphery. She squeezed shut her eyes and flung out her hand, groping for the door knob. Knocking sounds, like *feet drumming on the decking*, brought the bile to her mouth.

Don't look, don't look, don't look—

Where was the door knob?

She couldn't find it. Couldn't find the blasted thing.

Oh, how much longer until Walter, Cheryl or Butch spotted her? Raced over and claimed her? They may have spotted her already. Her time was up. She would be killed and eaten right alongside her boss. Correction: eaten and *then* killed. These zombies weren't like lionesses, weren't kind enough to suffocate you first before chowing down. They ate like great white sharks. One bite at a time until you died.

The screaming stopped abruptly.

Startled, Stella held her breath.

Now just wet and sloppy sounds. Making her remember that time when Con had babysat his sister's Labradors and the noise those dogs had made while scarfing their dinner of canned food. Stella hiccupped on vomit. Then her fingers closed around the smooth steel of the door knob. Thank heavens. She wrenched the door closed. Grappled with and turned the lock. Okay, she thought, heaving and gulping. Okay. She opened her eyes.

On the other side of the glass door stood Walter.

Yelping, she leapt back. Walter sprang against the door, hitting it with his face and both palms. He seemed to gaze at her. Eyes blank. Nose mashed on the glass. Jaws wide and champing. Lips working obscenely. Cheeks and chin covered in shining gouts of blood. *Joan's blood.* Stella, paralysed, couldn't tear herself away. Another zombie—not Butch or Cheryl but a *stranger*—jostled Walter for space and began tapping its putrid palms against the glass as well. More hands reached out. The bastards must be climbing over the patio railings. Joan's dying screams must have sounded like the ringing of a lunch bell.

"Rick?" she called. "The door's locked. Come and get me. I can't move." *Where was he? What was taking him so long?* Her voice took on the shrill edge of hysteria. "Rick! RICK!"

"I'm right here," he said, racing towards her.

Weeping, she pointed weakly at the door.

He reached her side, baulked. She noticed his bugged eyes, the rivulets of perspiration streaming from his hairline, and wondered how her own terrified face must look.

"Do you think they'll break the glass?" she said.

"Probably not. It's tempered, not like window panes." He took her arm. "Come on."

Eyes closed, she leaned against him while they retreated towards the main corridor. At Walter's office, she had a sudden thought and broke away.

"What are you doing?" Rick said.

"Pinching a smoke."

What a bugger there wasn't booze in the kitchen too. She could neck a bottle of Moscato right about now. She found the cigarettes. With shaking hands, she managed to spill a couple onto the desk, put one to her lips. Blessed relief made her sob. *Goodbye withdrawals.* Now, where was the lighter? Not on the desk, not in the drawers... Typical. Just her bloody luck. Close to a full pack of fags and no fricking— On a hunch, she patted her pockets. *There!* When she'd shared a cigarette with Walter, she'd kept the lighter out of habit. The flame crackled the dried tobacco.

She inhaled...

The familiar taste, the warmth of the smoke hitting her lungs, that fuzzy little starburst of bliss in her head; ah, how could she have ever imagined a life without nicotine? She dragged greedily. Felt calmer. More in control of herself. For a moment, she experienced a pang of guilt—she had promised Con and Melanie that *this* time she would quit for good—but pragmatism took over. Why give a shit now? In all likelihood, she was going to die today. Living long enough to die of cancer seemed an unimaginable luxury.

From outside came the sound of gunfire. That would be Magnus with his .22 rifle.

"Let's check the CCTV," she said, pocketing the pack and lighter. "See how Magnus and Helen are getting on out there."

***

The racing zombie covered a lot of ground. She had light brown hair and grey roots. A naked, soft and middle-aged body. Magnus recognised her as the donor belonging to Cheryl Zhao. What had been the donor's name?

Violet.

He shuddered. The memory felt years old, *ages* old, although the event had only happened at lunchtime. Rick Evans swaddling Violet with a beach towel. The four of them—Cheryl, Magnus, Rick, the other detective —carrying Violet and placing her into the car boot. He had held this woman's corpse in his own hands, tenderly, as if holding a newborn baby.

And after he had ridden away, the strange seeds had fallen, and Violet had come awake, climbed out, and slaughtered Cheryl... Now Violet was charging. How was she moving so fast? Why wasn't she as slow as the others? Perhaps because she had been in cold storage until a few hours ago. Muscles, tendons and ligaments preserved against rot. What other explanation could there be?

"Go!" Helen shrieked, jabbing him repeatedly with her elbow. "For fuck's sake, go!"

Helen's panic woke him from his dazed reverie. He opened the throttle. The quad bike leapt forward. Zombies were all around them.

"Lift the umbrella," he said. "I can't see."

Instead, she threw it aside to brandish the spade. What if zombie birds or possums dropped on them from the trees? Hopefully they would bounce off rather than latch on and bite.

Violet changed course, sprinting in a wide arc as if to cut them off. So, she had cunning. The ability to plan ahead. Magnus broke into a sweat. The crushing, suffocating sensation in his chest intensified; what felt like a balloon lodged within his ribcage had expanded just that little bit more. He brushed sweat from his eyes, gripped the handlebars, accelerated.

Had he left their run too late?

Zombies flocked from every direction. The pigs trundled lopsidedly on bent and blackened trotters. The humans staggered and waddled. Arms stiff. Shoulders rolling. Jaws opening and closing. *Perkele*, was he changing into one of these devils? There are worse things than being dead. A fatal heart attack was his preferred scenario. If he were a praying man—

"Look out!" Helen shrilled.

Magnus blinked, gasped. He was riding straight towards Violet. With a fierce wrench of the handlebars, he steered away. The left front tyre dug into the ground. The rear tyres lifted. The engine roared as the bike's back end suspended itself in mid-air.

Time stopped.

Magnus contemplated the inevitable.

Quad bikes were prone to tipping or flipping. Notoriously unstable. It didn't take much. A steep gradient, a hidden obstacle, unreasonable speed, a reckless manoeuvre. Neither he nor Helen wore a helmet. They were going to roll and be injured or even killed. He remembered a snippet of advice from the safety manual. Remembered it clearly, photographically, the black type on white paper floating in front of his eyes: *Do not carry a passenger on the quad bike. A passenger interferes with the rider's ability to maintain balance.*

Balance!

Magnus stood on the pegs and leaned back as far as possible. The bike dropped onto its four tyres with a spine-compressing jolt. Found purchase. Zipped ahead, fishtailing.

Violet loomed.

Too late, he couldn't evade those bared teeth—

Helen swung the spade, almost upsetting the bike again. The spade chocked into Violet's neck and stuck fast. Its blade must have lodged between vertebrae. Helen didn't let go of the handle. Violet was wrenched to her knees and dragged. Now attached to a fulcrum, the bike stuttered sideways on its wheels and began to circle Violet while she gnashed her teeth.

"Drop the spade!" Magnus yelled. "Leave it!"

"No, fuck that!"

Helen wrenched at the handle. It didn't come loose. Violet scowled at them as her body turned, turned, turned in the dirt. The bike was making a rut. Leaf litter sprayed from the tyres. The first wave of zombies was nearly upon them.

"Let go of the spade!" he insisted.

Instead, Helen kicked at Violet. The zombie detached from the blade and tumbled away. The bike straightened up. Magnus cranked the throttle and pushed the bike to almost 20kmph, double his usual speed, the fastest he'd ever dared travel over the park's bumpy terrain. Helen propped the spade on the handlebars. Zombies whizzed by, close enough to touch. The bike blew through a drift of blowflies. Helen recoiled and swatted. Magnus shut his eyes as insects bounced off his face. The frantic buzzing at his nose and mouth made him panic and shake his head. Could the flies smell death on him? Was he dead already?

"Wait, go 'round the building!" Helen yelled. "Go 'round!"

Panting, wheezing, the balloon in his chest crushing his lungs, Magnus looked ahead. Nothing but trees. The main building was in his side mirrors: he had overshot it. *Helvetti.*

Braking, he pivoted with one foot on the ground to facilitate the abrupt change of direction. Enough. He must take control of his emotions. Killer balloon inside his chest or not, he had an obligation to save Helen and as many others in VITERI that remained alive, and so he must *concentrate*. Aim the bike towards the back patio.

Vision blurring, he focused on the decking enclosed by horizontal wooden palings. Checked his mirrors. The zombies had fallen back. *Luojan kiitos!* The bike had outrun them. And would continue to outrun them if only he kept his wits. Now, he must ride the length of the building towards the carport and start making laps. He eased off the throttle, just a little, to reduce the risk of tipping.

"We'll be okay," Magnus said. "It's okay, we're nearly there—"

The sudden, hideous scream made both of them jump.

"What the *fuck*?" Helen cried, and then she pointed at the back patio. "Oh, Jesus. Isn't that Joan Kendall?"

18

Screaming, Professor Joan Kendall ran across the decking with both arms outstretched as if reaching for salvation. Three zombies tackled her. They bit and clawed and wrestled. It took a few seconds for them to drag her down. She fought hard. Then they all sank out of sight together behind the palings. The screams subsided into agonised whimpers. And stopped.

Helen felt as if she were asphyxiating.

A face popped up over the railing. So fast, so unexpectedly, that Helen flinched.

Briefly, hope soared as she imagined it to be Professor Kendall—*she's broken free, she's going to escape*—and every single time that the woman had ever given her the shits washed over Helen in a wave of nostalgia and regret. Professor Kendall wasn't a pedantic cow after all, she reasoned, but a *perfectionist*. The one who made sure that VITERI worked like the proverbial well-oiled machine. When Professor Kendall had tried to ban alcohol from the bunkhouse, instituting a bag-check procedure that lasted a few days before the student union had successfully campaigned against the invasion of privacy, classmates had dubbed her "Bitchy McBuzzkill". Unfairly, as it turned out. Professor Kendall's every authoritarian decree and dressing down had been for the good of VITERI. Helen understood that now.

Helen was about to wave.

But the face over the railing didn't belong to Joan Kendall.

Moustache and goatee. Bald scalp. This must be the donor from the morgue, the weightlifter who could fight back. *Defend* himself. As he got to his feet—revealing a thick neck, huge shoulders, a fat and muscled torso, tattoos, all spattered with fresh and glistening blood—he seemed to spot them. Seemed to visually *track* them as they rode by the patio.

Helen craned to see past Magnus's bulk. The donor collapsed head-first over the railing. Was he fainting? No, he was gripping the palings, swinging his legs over, executing a clumsy manoeuvre to jump down from the patio.

"He's coming after us!" she shrieked. "We have to attack him! Turn back! Turn back!"

Magnus executed a U-turn. The donor struggled towards them, trundling his limbs as if through molasses. Okay, he wasn't agile. That gave Helen a window of killing time. But the spade wouldn't be enough. The thickness of his muscle tissue resembled armour.

"Give me your rifle," she said.

Magnus complied. She jammed the spade handle beneath one thigh. Loaded a round.

Dad had taken her hunting for rabbits a few times during her primary school years. But they're so cute, Helen had argued tearfully on their first hunt. Don't be fooled, Dad had said, these feral animals are bloody pests. They compete with our native mammals and cause Aussie species to go extinct. As Dad had explained it, shooting these interlopers was a community service. But damn, rabbits were *quick*. There one moment and gone the next. Dad had picked them off with ease, but Helen? Missed more often than not. *You're doing a great job, sweetheart. It's tough to draw a bead on a moving target.* How many years had it been? It didn't matter. Dad had taught her how to hunt with a .22. If she could hit a weeny little rabbit dashing about at break-neck speed and camouflaged by long grasses, she could hit this zombie with ease, like taking a shit.

She pressed the rifle's butt into the hollow of her collarbone. Supported the barrel in her left hand. Gazed down the sight. Breathed out, steadied, pulled the trigger.

The donor's head snapped back. Righted itself.

She shot again.

The tissue of the left eye erupted. The donor stopped walking, frowned as if puzzled.

She squeezed the trigger one more time. The donor quivered and dropped.

"Fuck you!" she shouted in delight, and slung the rifle over her shoulder. "Okay, let's go, Magnus. 'Round the building."

He obeyed. Helen propped the spade on the handlebars and kept scouting, checking the side mirrors. Yes, they were attracting plenty of zombies. Drawing them into a pointless circle. Soon, after gathering as many as possible, Magnus would take off in a perpendicular line through the bush, luring them away like a dystopian Pied Piper so that Rick could get to his car, utilise the weapons if necessary, and drive them out of this godforsaken place.

She laughed. Wow, this crazy plan is actually going to work, she thought in amazement. She might live after all. And whether or not this zombie plague was limited to VITERI? Well, she would deal with any new horrors if she got the chance.

The quad bike motored on. Zombies fell into step behind.

"I'm starting to feel pretty confident," she said. "Aren't you?"

No answer.

"Magnus? Did you hear me? Are you feeling confident?"

Again, no answer. In a sick flood of dread, it occurred to her that he hadn't uttered a word. Not one word this whole time.

***

"Oh, what a good girl!" Stella cried. "Helen got the prick. Hah! Did you see? Ooroo, Butch!"

Stella was puffing on the cigarette, drawing breath after breath without pause. Surely, the lack of oxygen must be making her dizzy? Rick, a lifelong non-smoker, envied her this small comfort. What he would give for something, any inconsequential thing, that might help him feel better. As it was, his guts churned with stress, and perspiration drenched his armpits. On the CCTV monitors, he watched the progression of Magnus and Helen on the quad bike. Soon, he would be expected to go outside, try to reach his car…

Stop being a coward, he admonished himself. These middle-aged women had shamed him. First, Joan had committed suicide to protect them. Strictly speaking, to avoid turning into a zombie, sure, but also to protect them. And then Stella had shown herself to be made of sterner stuff than Rick. As soon as Joan had suggested her ludicrous course of action—*I'll lead the three zombies onto the back patio. Stella, trail behind us at a safe distance. Once we're clear, shut the back door and lock us out*—Rick had actually snorted in disbelief. Trail behind at a safe distance? Was the old bird having a lend? Screw that. Rick had no intention of leaving the room. But Stella had gone and done it without hesitation.

Now, she was glued to the CCTV monitors.

He stared at the side of her face, searching for answers. Okay, fine, so he was embarrassed. He should have volunteered to secure the zombies on the patio, not her. When Stella had pushed through the broken door, he should have dragged her back inside and said, *You stay here, I'll take care of it*. Why hadn't he? Stella's wet piss-stain down her trousers didn't make him feel better. It made him feel worse. Petrified, she had found enough courage to go and lock the back door anyway.

No, he was the only coward here.

Violet killing Cheryl Zhao, the kangaroo disembowelling Garcia…was there a pattern? Of people suffering because of Rick's failure to take action? Self-disgust made him groan.

"You okay, mate?"

He opened his eyes. Stella was staring at him, her brow crinkled with concern.

"I'm fine."

She pointed at a monitor. "Look. They've rounded up the zombies."

It was true. *It was true*. As if to confirm Stella's observation, Magnus tooted the horn and began to steer the quad bike away from the building towards the bush. The grisly assortment followed. Magnus worked the horn again—*shave and a haircut, two bits*—which was the signal. Rick's signal. To go outside. Outside. *Outside*. His shoes felt nailed to the floor.

He became aware that Stella was pressing items into his hands. He closed his fingers around the grip of a fire extinguisher, the butt of an empty gun. She was ushering him to the front door. They passed the barricade of furniture shoved against the broken window. The flailing arms gone: no zombies on the porch. Maybe all the zombies *were* following Magnus. Maybe none were waiting for Rick. None waiting to eat him.

"Rick?"

He snapped to attention. "Huh?"

"Jeez, you're not inspiring any faith."

The blood flushed to his face and he pulled his arm from her grasp.

"Listen up," he said. "When I get to my car, I'm chucking the key into the centre console. That way, if I'm…if I don't…if they…well, you or anybody else will be able to drive it."

"Oh God, don't talk like that."

"I'll be back soon."

"The coast is clear. You'll be okay."

"See you in a minute," he said and stood at the door.

"Good luck," she said and waited.

When he didn't move, she darted forward and opened the door.

When you feel scared for your life, Rick thought, the emotion is strong enough to convulse your intestines. To shake them about. He had never known this phenomenon before. This is what some of my homicide victims might have experienced, he thought, at the very moment they realised death was imminent. What Alexandra Wilson may have felt. (I'm sorry I never got to find out who killed you.) Damn. Who would have guessed that intestines could be so mobile? So jumpy? He had to remember to breathe. *In through the nose. Hold. Out through the mouth.*

The breeze fanned his sweat. Rick stumbled outside. Stella closed the door behind him.

Click.

Bushland. Grey clouds hanging heavy and low in the sky. The roar of blood in his ears.

He went to take a step. Lost his footing momentarily. The porch was smeared in dark, greasy slime. Decomposition fluids. Every puddle covered in flitting blowflies. He should be able to smell the putrefaction and hear the flies but he was enclosed inside a bubble, inside a dream, and he began to run, groggy and lax. One footfall after the other.

Run, run, run.

The world joggled in his vision. He couldn't feel the ground beneath his feet. His lungs pushed and pulled air. Run, run, run. There was his car. Both his hands were full. He dropped something—the fire extinguisher—and reached into his trouser pocket. Pressed the button on the fob. The parking lights flashed.

Nearly there, nearly there.

To die now would be an injustice. So close, so close.

He opened the driver's side door, went to climb inside, remembered his promise to Stella and tossed the key into the centre console. Issuing from the cabin, the familiar scent of Lawrence Garcia hit him like a slap across the face: the sandalwood of aftershave, the vanilla of hair product. This morning's drive from the Melbourne City Police Complex rushed back:

When we get there and I introduce you to everybody, Rick had said, *don't call the place a 'body farm'.*

Why not? You do.

Yeah, but not to the people who work there.

The zombie kangaroo had flicked its ears, scratched its stomach. Rick had told Garcia to *get out of the way*, but Garcia hadn't and now he was disembowelled and dead.

Except he wasn't dead.

No, he was walking over.

Suit jacket unbuttoned. Unusual. Garcia made a point of releasing the button whenever he sat down and fastening it again when he stood up. One of his many pseudo-suave quirks that Rick found pretentious and annoying. Now the jacket hung open. Shirt tattered and bloody. The combed-back pompadour marred by a sideways list. Strands of loose hair. Leaves and dirt stuck to the styling product. The young man approached with his arms at his sides and both palms out, the standard body language for coppers that meant, *Relax, I'm not holding a weapon.*

Cold prickles raced along Rick's skin. "I thought the kangaroo killed you," he said.

Garcia smiled.

Rick began to shiver. "I should have checked. I didn't check. You got hurt and then, shit, I don't know. I panicked."

Smirking, Garcia raised his eyebrows in an amused, dismissive gesture that seemed to say *Ah well, what can you do?*

"Stop right there," Rick said. "You're making me nervous."

Behind Garcia were a half-dozen or so zombies. Emerging from the trees. Staring at Rick with that same unblinking fascination.

"Stop!" Rick shouted, lifting his gun, his empty joke of a gun.

A flash of movement in the corner of his eye turned his head.

Violet.

Gambolling towards him, nerveless arms flopping, mouth open.

Oh, he should have figured on this. Should have realised that zombies were like baby ducks, freshly born, ready to imprint their fixation on whomever they first laid eyes on. Of course, Violet had tracked him across the VITERI grounds. Of course! He'd been as good as dead ever since she had clambered out of the car boot and gnashed her teeth at him. Now he could admit this truth to himself. That his death had been preordained from the beginning.

Unless...

He had time to duck inside the BMW? Slam the door?

No. Icy-cold arms enfolded his neck.

In the next moment, he and Violet were cheek against cheek.

The bite on his neck didn't hurt as much as he had imagined. His missus came to mind. His daughters. This would be tough on them. Yes, he was a stick-in-the-mud, and yes, his three women liked to roll their collective eyes at him, but they loved him. He knew this to be true. And they would miss him sitting at the dinner table, would long for his silly arguments, his push-back against their new-age fripperies. And he would miss them too.

God almighty, would he miss them.

He saw the boiling clutch of clouds and tried to find a significance, a depth of meaning. The last thing he would ever see—turned out to be Garcia.

The leaves in Garcia's pompadour were so off-putting.

"Help me," Rick whispered.

Smiling, Garcia ran his fingers through Rick's hair, then fiercely doubled his hands into fists. *Trapped.* Garcia stretched his mouth to reveal the silver fillings in his molars. In every single molar. Didn't the kid brush his teeth? This would be Rick's last coherent thought and it struck him as shallow. Stupid. If only he could think of something more profound.

***

Helen adjusted one of the side mirrors to look at Magnus's reflection. His pale, impassive face shone with sweat.

"Are you feeling all right?" she said.

He glanced into the mirror, locked eyes with her, and nodded. Whether or not he was telling the truth, she didn't have time to investigate.

"I reckon he's reached the car by now, surely to Christ," she said. "Go back. Ride as fast as you can, okay? Leave these zombies eating our dust."

Magnus cut right in a wide swathe. He had been travelling quite slowly, allowing the pursuing zombies to bunch up, so the U-turn left the whole lot of them behind. They stopped in their tracks to gape at the bike in what seemed like surprise and disappointment. Helen laughed and flipped the bird. Magnus opened the throttle.

The sun had disappeared, hidden behind dark cloud. Leeched of colour, the bush whipped by in bleak shades of grey and brown. It seemed ominous. Then again, Helen reminded herself that she wasn't the superstitious kind. Clamping the handle of the spade beneath her armpit, she checked the .22 and found it out of ammo.

"You got any more cartridges for the rifle?" she said.

He didn't reply. She studied him in the mirror. His lips were turning a light shade of blue. Cyanosis from a heart attack? Or a zombie infection? No chance for contemplation as the main building emerged from the trees. Presumably the flashy BMW was Rick's car. How come it was still in the parking area? Hadn't the plan included Rick driving right up to the porch? Her pulse began to race.

"I can't see him," she said. "Slow down."

Magnus did.

"We're gonna do a recce first," she continued, "and check the car before we hop off the bike. We might need to hightail it out of here."

They made a circuit of the carport. Unless he was lying across the seat, Rick wasn't in the BMW. He wasn't anywhere. Had he even left the main building?

She pointed at the car and said, "Get next to it."

The doors were unlocked. She peeked inside. Empty. The key lay in the centre console. A bad sign. There's no way a copper would leave his car unlocked when it contained firearms. Therefore, Rick had made it to the vehicle, tossed the key into the console and, for reasons unknown, had simply walked away, or else—

Magnus tapped her shoulder, making her jump. Looking up, she spotted the group of zombies heading over from the trees. Fuck. There was just *no time* to figure any shit out. Couldn't she have a single, solitary minute to figure shit out, to think it through? *Fuck.*

"Come on, we're taking the car," she said.

They alighted from the bike and Magnus killed the motor. Dropping the spade, Helen got in the car's front seat, dumped her weapons in the passenger-side footwell, and took the wheel. Magnus tore off his tool belt, got in the back and started pulling on seat release mechanisms, presumably to access the firearms in the boot. Did his actions resemble the disorganised behaviours and dumb thought processes of a zombie? Not a chance. The sudden flood of relief made her teeth chatter. *Heart attack*. Or maybe angina. Well and good. She would call for an ambulance as soon as they reached civilisation.

It took her a moment to find and identify the controls. She started the ignition. Put the car into reverse. Released the handbrake. The zombies were hurrying now, taking longer strides. She backed out of the parking space, switched to "drive", and zoomed the car in a plume of dust along the building's face, braking at the porch steps. Stella should not only hear the car but see it; either through the windows or via the CCTV monitors.

If she was still alive, that is.

Idling the engine, Helen stared at the front door as the seconds ticked by. Chewed her lip. Checked the mirrors. Zombies were beating a path from every direction. Stella had better get out now, *immediately*, or she wouldn't make it across the porch.

Come on, Stella. Hurry up. *Come on.*

Grunting, Magnus began to haul the cache out of the boot. Two shotguns, both of them 12-gauge by the looks of it. Boxes of ammo. Tasers. Batons. Cans of mace. Shit, even a couple of cricket bats. Hope surged afresh.

"We're gonna make it out of here," she said, and her chin quivered.

Magnus, loading a shotgun, didn't respond.

"Can you speak?" she continued. "Please say something."

"Something," he replied with a smile, his voice a dry croak.

So, he wasn't mute, but still… She pushed aside her unease and glanced again at the building, then at the approaching zombies. Fuck, if Stella didn't appear soon—

The front door flew open!

Stella raced out, handbag worn crossways over her body, holding an item triumphantly overhead, her face a grimacing mask with huge and frightened eyes. She got in, falling against the front passenger seat, panting, sobbing. She slammed the door hard enough to rock the car and make Helen wince.

"Thank God, thank God," she was gibbering. "Thank God—"

"Where's Rick?" Helen said.

Stella goggled about the cabin with glassy eyes. "He's not here?"

"No! Did he try to reach the car or not?"

"Well, sure. Not five minutes ago. The CCTV cameras don't cover the carport but I watched him leave the porch. He told me he'd put the key in the console in case he… Oh, shit, he might be… Do you think he might be…?"

Helen clenched her jaw. "Yeah, I do."

Hiccupping, Stella bit on a thumbnail. An object was tucked in her fist.

"What have you got there?" Helen said.

"Huh?'

"What are you holding?"

Stella, perplexed, regarded the object and then tearfully broke into smiles. "Oh, the remote control for the gates! I almost forgot. I had to dash back to my desk and find the bugger."

Helen felt chilled, weak and shaky. *The double-gates.* She'd forgotten about them. So had Magnus. Rick too. The locked gates—the only exit from VITERI—hadn't featured in their escape plan. She wanted to kiss Stella.

"All right, let's get the fuck out of here," she said, and swung the steering wheel.

There was a small crowd of advancing zombies. Bony hands reached out for the car, rasping along the paintwork. An elderly woman, her scalp of frizzy white hair slipping off her skull like a lopsided hat, leaned over the car bonnet and waggled her tongue. Helen ran the woman over. BUMP CRUNCH SINK as the desiccated corpse flattened beneath the front tyres. The car must weigh over a tonne, after all. Even a living person would be squashed. BUMP CRUNCH SINK went the back wheels. Stella retched, pressing a hand to her mouth.

"Keep your eyes shut," Helen said. "Don't watch."

"No, I'm good," Stella whispered. "Thanks anyway."

Helen pressed the accelerator. The car cleaved through zombies. They floundered and fell aside. The gates were dead ahead.

Stella jumped in her seat. "The fire extinguisher!"

"What about it?"

"It's lying there on the ground! I gave it to Rick. He must be nearby. We ought to—"

"Wherever he is, he's dead."

Stella regarded her with wounded eyes. "You don't know that for sure."

"Open the gate."

"But we should—"

"For fuck's sake! Do as you're told."

Fumbling, Stella worked the remote. The first gate clattered and rolled back. Helen eased the car into the gap and braked. The gate trundled closed behind them, slowly. So very fucking *slowly* that a handful of zombies had enough time to follow them inside. *Shit.* The zombies tapped and knocked and rubbed at the windows, leaving oily smudges of putrescence. Helen regarded Magnus in the rear-view mirror. Stony faced, he glared out his window, a shotgun held upright.

"Don't open the second gate yet," Helen said. "We have to kill these pricks. But first—Magnus, unlock your phone. Give it to me."

"What for?" Stella said.

"VITERI is one big crime scene. I don't fancy being accused of murder. I'm taking footage before we go. To prove our story. Otherwise, who's gonna believe us?"

Stella nodded, her eyes glittering with unshed tears. "Smart idea."

Magnus gave Helen the mobile, the video camera open. She pressed *record.* Lifted the mobile. Studied the screen…

How surreal: as if she were sitting on her couch at home and watching a movie.

The saturated colours. The two-dimensional images. The grotesque and completely impossible sight of living corpses. Lips and eyelids missing. Skin the hue and consistency of wet newspaper, crawling with bugs. This is what dissociation feels like, Helen mused. A respite from reality. A greatly appreciated solace for the troubled mind. Viewing zombies in this second-hand way seemed almost enough to transform the experience into nothing but a nightmare, a bad fever-dream. Tomorrow morning when she woke, she would wonder if she hadn't hallucinated the entire thing.

She pressed *stop*.

"I've got the footage," she said. "Magnus? Go ahead and kill 'em."

She put the mobile in the console. Retracted the two rear windows a little way. Enough to fit the barrel of a shotgun. Jammed her fingers in her ears. Closed her eyes.

The boom of each discharge was *LOUD*.

They would incur permanent hearing loss. A small price.

The acrid stink of gun smoke filled the cabin.

While Magnus slaughtered zombie after zombie, Helen drifted away and imagined how luxurious it would feel to have a bath. A bubble-bath. With coconut-scented suds. Fluffy towels waiting. Her mind went further. Conjured a retreat overlooking a verdant mountain range crisscrossed with the swoop of bright, raucous parrots. An extensive room-service menu propped next to the mini-bar. King-sized bed with crisp white sheets. Bottle of sauvignon blanc in a chiller bucket. She pushed her fingers deeper inside her ears as the shotgun boomed on and on, and imagined chamomile and honey teabags. Chocolates on the pillow. A tall vase of orchids. Complimentary slippers—

"That's it, I think," Stella said. "That's all of them. Helen?"

She blinked. Looked about. No more standing zombies in this tight space between the two gates. She engaged the transmission. The exterior gate opened. *Ta-dah*. Rolled back to reveal the grand prize, which happened to be a second chance at life.

Momentarily, she choked up.

The end of a long, hard race... Marathon runners often collapse when they cross a finish line. Now she knew why. Her legs shook. Her foot stuttered on the accelerator. Lactic acidosis, she reasoned. No, it was more than that. A mental and emotional reaction to the cessation of fear. To the stunning realisation that she had survived. Escaped a horrible death.

It was a lot to take in.

A lot to process.

The car exited VITERI. Helen braked. The exterior gate closed behind them with a jangle. *Safe*. No one spoke. The invisible fist let go of her heart. Ahead, the dirt track ran in a straight line between gum and tea trees. This track would lead them onto the asphalted road and, ultimately, to the town of Wooriyanda.

Bell birds sounded. Rosellas chittered.

Helen squeezed her hands on the wheel. A coffee, she thought. Goddamn, a steaming hot espresso. And a slice of cake. Preferably carrot, although she would settle for caramel. Shit, even *almond* would do at this point, and she despised marzipan. Supposedly, there was a kick-arse café in town. How the owners and clientele might react to the gore-spattered and dishevelled VITERI trio, Helen couldn't fathom and didn't much care.

"All right, let's go," she said.

"We're not leaving yet," Magnus growled, still holding the shotgun.

19

Magnus looked *terrible*. Eyes sunken, face the colour of cheese, head and neck lathered in perspiration. Was he dying? Christ only knew how he had managed to ride the quad bike. Helen wanted to take the shotgun from him but was afraid, somehow, that any sudden movement would provoke him. Would result in her staring down the barrel. Magnus's eyes were flinty. Remote. Cold. Adrenaline stitched along her spine.

"Why shouldn't we leave?" Helen said.

She could hear Stella's breath: shallow and quick. Spasmodically, Magnus's hands clenched and relaxed around the shotgun.

"Magnus?" she said.

"Yes?"

"Why don't you want us to leave?"

"Because we have to destroy VITERI."

She glanced again, longingly, at the track. Then she said, "It's one-hundred-and-fifty acres, mate. We couldn't destroy VITERI if we tried."

Magnus laid the shotgun next to him, grabbed the back of a head-rest and hauled himself upright. The whites of his eyes were bloodshot. He said, "Zombie birds and possums will get over the fence and spread the infection to other animals, and then to humans. What if VITERI is ground zero?"

"And what if it isn't?" Helen said.

"Either way, we've got nothing to lose," Stella offered. "If it's ground zero, we contain the spread. And if the world is swamped with zombies, well, we did our part to wipe out a few."

"Oh yeah?" Helen said. "Wipe them out how?"

"With fire," Magnus said.

"Fire? Come on. Unless you know how to rub two sticks together, you're out of luck. Car dashboards aren't fitted with cigarette lighters anymore."

Stella made a peeping noise, scrabbled in her pocket and brought out a cheap gas-lighter. She held it up with reverence as if it were a precious jewel, her lips quivering, eyes wet.

"I thought you'd quit?" Helen said.

"Very good," Magnus said, his chuckle a wheezing stricture. "Perfect."

"No. Are you kidding me? No, forget it. We're smack-bang in the middle of state and national forests. In *October*. During a *dry Spring*. One spark, and the lot goes up. Jesus, you want to burn down the whole of Victoria?"

"Hey, wait a minute," Stella yelped, bouncing in her seat. "The storm. Look out the window. See? It's coming. The weather bureau is spot-on. We set the fire, destroy VITERI, and let the rain put the fire out."

A feasible plan, but still…

Helen stared into the side mirror and her skin crawled. A couple of dozen zombies were pressed up against the fence, straining and groping their fingers through the cyclone wire. More were coming. Probably the crowd that she and Magnus had lured away from the main building, now attracted by the sound of the BMW's engine. She thought of Alisha's last terrible moments—face cannibalised, eyes turned into puddles of blood—and riled.

"Let's do it," she said, putting the transmission into "park".

She got out of the car. Stella did the same.

"Stay there," Helen said to Magnus, and he gave a weak wave of acknowledgement.

She approached the fence. Agitated, the zombies reached out. The breeze was at her back; a southerly, bringing over the cool and crisp air from Antarctica, the very bottom of the world. Setting the fire would be easy. Convenient. They could do it right here, in fact. Stoop down. Ignite the grass. Let the wind carry the flames north throughout the VITERI grounds.

There were so many eucalypts.

Truly a plant species built for combustion. Each tree sheds vast amounts of leaves and bark, which rapidly dry out to make a fuel bed at the base of the trunk. Once a tree catches fire, its simmering oils release flammable gases and then WHOMP. Instant fire-ball. The flames leap from one canopy to the next. That's how bushfires move so fast. Not because of flames on the ground but because of crowning. In the tinderbox of the Australian bush, one spark can become an inferno within minutes. Helen was about to create an inferno.

Commit arson.

Was about to engineer a catastrophic amount of destruction.

If she managed to ever sleep again without nightmares, it would be a miracle. The zombies she had killed were already dead, strictly speaking, but you can't hatchet a person's skull into soup and kid yourself it isn't murder. At least, murder on some level. Morally, if not legally. Okay, you could argue manslaughter. Self-defence. But in her heart, she would always know that the donors had been walking—if not respiring—and she had cut them down. Considering she had already crossed the line, why *not* massacre scores of zombies with fire?

Why not indeed? She tried to smile. *In for a penny, in for a pound*: wasn't that something Mum always used to say? So, go ahead. Commit arson too. Burn the whole goddamned lot.

The dark grey clouds were rolling fast, reminding her of waves breaking on a surf beach. Sometimes, a cloudy sky doesn't produce rain. Sometimes, the clouds roll on by. What if the weather bureau was wrong? They were wrong so often that it was a running joke amongst Melbournians. What if the rain bomb didn't happen and Helen's fire ran out of control? Potentially, she would destroy thousands of hectares of bush. Countless animals. Houses. *People*. Bushfires killed people. Bushfires killed people all the time.

She stepped closer to the fence. Stared into the blank, milky eyes of a zombie. Blowflies flitted and buzzed at the zombie's lashes, walked across its corneas. The stink of rot tamped Helen's lungs. Other zombies clustered, reaching for her, desperate and hungry. Relentlessly hungry. And they would never stop feeling hungry. Not ever.

"Give me the lighter," she said.

"Oh, sweet," Stella said, blowing out a held breath. "I figured you wanted *me* to do it. Sorry to be such a wuss."

"A wuss? Nah. You survived, didn't you?"

"No thanks to me." Stella looked ready to start crying again. "If not for you guys, and for Joan…and Rick…"

"Hey, we forgot about the gates. Without you, the three of us would be stuck—" she said, pointing at the zombies, "—on *that* side of the fence. Okay?"

Stella sniffled and handed over the lighter.

A disposable with a transparent case, fluorescent purple.

Helen ran her thumb over the serrated metal spark-wheel. Remembered the few months, as a teenager, when she had smoked a bong and lit the mull with a similar crappy lighter. They don't call it "dope" for nothing. Whenever she had got stoned, she became stupid. Happy to sit and gape at a fucking wall. And after a while of regular use, grass had taken away her edge, her motivation. What a pointless exercise. She had quit and vowed to never smoke again. Now she was about to light another kind of grass. To kill another kind of stupid dope. There seemed to be a connection there, a thematic parallel, but she couldn't join the dots.

"Are you right?" Stella said. "You want me to do it? I will if you want me to."

"No. That's okay."

Her thumb worried at the spark-wheel. Was she doing the right thing? Or would she regret this pivotal moment for the rest of her life? The Universe never pulls back its curtains to show you the hidden wheels and pulleys. Helen braced herself. *Here goes—*

Stella staggered back. "Oh, no!"

"What? What's the matter?"

"*Look.*"

Helen did, in the direction Stella pointed. Felt the blood drain from her face and the strength leave her knees. Behind the fence were Professor Walter Boyce and Cheryl Zhao.

Or what was left of them.

Their humanity had gone. Consciousness, personality, essence. For Christ's sake, their *souls* had gone. She could see it in their faces. Just dead tissue animated by some kind of force. Galvani's "twitching leg" experiment with dismembered frogs and electricity came to mind. Stimulus, response. Stimulus, response. Stimulus, response… *Out, out, brief candle! Told by an idiot, full of sound and fury, Signifying nothing—*

Wait.

Professor Boyce and Cheryl were holding hands.

Side by side, fingers interlocked.

Helen felt shaken. Were they *comforting* each other? Perhaps zombies weren't as mindless as she had assumed. Perhaps they were aware of their plight. As frightened and bewildered as you might imagine to be if, after death, you found yourself wrenched back from the other side and turned into a monstrous abomination.

"I didn't know Cheryl," Helen said. "I only knew her by sight."

"She was a good student," Stella said. "Very conscientious. Excellent grades."

"Something ate her forearm."

"Oh, yes. My word. Something surely did."

Helen gazed along the line of zombies, searching now for Alisha's face. For Alisha's *non*-face. If she was at the fence, mutilated yet animate, Helen would go mad.

"Walter?" Stella said, voice quaking. "Can you hear me?"

"Don't. He's gone. Long gone."

"Coo," Stella said. "*Coo!* Give me the response. Walter? Give me the answer."

"What the hell are you talking about?" Helen said.

"Our little joke. One of us yells 'coo' and the other yells 'wee'. A bit of fun. It drives Joan up the wall. 'Coo-wee'. Get it? Two mates having a bit of fun. We were friends, you see? Workmates but friends. Walter? Can you hear me?"

"Stop."

"Walter? It's me. Walter?"

"I think you should wait in the car. Listen to me. Go wait in the car."

Stella scrubbed at tears with the back of a hand. "Righto. I'm no good to you here, am I?"

"Not in the slightest."

With a weak smile, Stella went to turn away, then startled and shrieked out of nowhere.

Exasperated, Helen gritted her teeth. *For the love of God, what* now?

"There's Rick," Stella cried. "And he's got the young copper with him."

Two men. Both in suits. One of them in his forties or thereabouts, the other perhaps thirty. Freshly deceased. Skin still pink, eyes clear. Wash off the blood, cover the gaping wounds and you'd never guess—apart from the gnashing teeth, the empty gaze, the clutching hands...

Helen dropped to her knees, flicked the lighter, and held the flame against the grass. Nothing happened. *Shit, shit, shit.* Arson was harder than she had anticipated. She flicked the lighter again. No, it was okay, the flames had taken hold. They were hard to see in sunlight, that's all. The curl of blackened grass blades spread gently, slowly, moving between dead and shambling feet. Leaf litter caught and curled. Embers shone red, lifting in the breeze, travelling a few centimetres to kiss the ground again and ignite.

The fence clinked and clanked as the zombies pushed against it.

Fuckers.

"I've got an idea," she said. "A nasty one. You might not want to see. Go wait in the car."

The zombie directly in front of her happened to be female; whether in the bloom of youth or old-aged, the state of decomposition made it hard to tell. She was wearing a dressing gown over a nighty. The dressing gown was quilted, the nighty pink and calf-length, both items made of polyester or similar man-made materials. Stained, damp in patches, but still highly flammable. Helen set fire to the hems. Stood back.

The nighty shrank and melted, fast and bright. The dressing gown smouldered, then caught. Soon, the bobbed hair blazed. Insect larvae popped like corn kernels. Fatty liquids sizzled. The air stank of barbecuing tissue.

Helen moved along the fence. Lit denim jeans. A bathrobe. Pyjamas.

Paused in front of Professor Boyce and Cheryl. Professor Boyce in his lab coat. Cheryl in her scrubs. Both lightweight cotton fabrics made from cellulose. The open weave allowing the free flow of oxygen, a fire accelerant—

"You can't be serious," Stella said. "What the frick are you doing?"

"Laying them to rest."

She lit their clothes. Touched the lighter here and there to the hems. Professor Boyce and Cheryl, excited by her proximity, rattled at the fence and strained to reach her with their fingers and lips. The flames travelled the fabrics in glowing red lines. Intensified. Grew into tongues. Professor Boyce and Cheryl didn't seem to realise, even as the flames lapped around their faces.

Helen stepped back. Surveyed her handiwork.

The zombies were bunched together. The fires began to spread from one to the other.

Interesting. The human body—alive or dead—burns the same way. First, the skin's epidermis fries. Then, the underlying dermis shrivels, browns and splits. The yellow subcutaneous fat erupts and burns low and slow just like, well… like *tallow*. Which was handy. Once these zombies got going, they would blaze for hours. Each one a candle spreading the fire throughout VITERI. A gruesome, get-the-fuck-out-of-here candle. Would the zombies assume the pugilistic posture, common in severely burned corpses? As heated muscle tissue shrinks, the knees and elbows bend, the fists clench, and the corpse looks like a boxer shaping up to an opponent. Perhaps whatever agent had animated these zombies would alter this phenomenon too, but Helen didn't plan on hanging around to find out.

The smell was awful. She began to walk further away along the fence.

"Where are you going?" Stella cried. "Don't leave me."

Helen kept walking. Zombies followed her. The footsteps of the ones on fire kindled the grass and leaf litter in their wake. The breeze fanned the flames back, back, back against the trees. Towards the carport. Her hatchback would be a write-off. Would insurance cover it? Not if Helen confessed to arson. And definitely not if civilisation was on the brink of collapse. Insurance companies didn't cover disasters because they were, apparently, Acts of God. Was *this* an act of God? A vengeful God? A Biblical plague with zombies instead of locusts… *Don't lose your focus*. Concentrate. Had she done enough? Was the fire sufficient to spread? How easily would the VITERI buildings catch fire? Magnus's cabin, at the northern end of the grounds, would burn last.

Magnus…

Helen stopped walking. The zombies stopped as well. She contemplated the BMW. The windows were tinted. She couldn't see inside. Was Magnus dying?

Please hang on, she thought. Hang on and I'll call an ambulance as soon as we reach Wooriyanda. Then again, if he were changing into a zombie, she would have to kill him. Despite what they had been through together, she would kill him without hesitation.

Stella, shoulders hunched, was hugging herself, tears streaming down her cheeks.

"Come on," Helen said. "We're done."

She strode quickly, Stella lagging behind and hiccupping on sobs. They got in the car. Magnus appeared to be asleep. Or unconscious. This entire time, Stella hadn't made any reference to his obvious incapacitation. Was she too distraught to notice? Helen decided not to bring it up. She put the car into "drive" and coasted. The tyres crunched over gravel. Stella twisted in her seat to look out the rear window.

"A few trees are on fire," she said.

"Good."

Stella fussed about, fidgeting. Then she said, "A zombie can't feel pain, can it?"

"Don't torture yourself about Professor Boyce. There's no point."

Stella switched on the radio. An old hit from the eighties: *Alone with you* by Sunnyboys. Helen tried to focus on the melody, yet her eyes kept straying to the mirrors. There was something hypnotic about the burning zombies, the casual manner in which they strolled about, oblivious to the flames consuming them. Black smoke funnelled off their heads, reminding her of distress flares. The sight made her feel sick. And yet…and yet she couldn't stop looking. The zombies wandered, dripping sloughed skin, casting off embers and setting fire to the ground, leaving trails of fire in their wake.

"Can I have the lighter?" Stella said.

Helen handed it over. Stella lit a cigarette.

"Want one?" she said, proffering the pack.

"No thanks."

The track made a turn. Enough bush was between them and VITERI that the zombie-candles were no longer visible. Helen exhaled. Considered Magnus in the rear-view mirror. Still out cold. His mouth open. How had she not noticed his teeth before? Long and jumbled. Pointed. She stared at the track.

Cigarette smoke filled the cabin despite Stella's open window. Helen cracked the others.

"Aw shit, sorry," Stella said, fanning one hand. "Want me to put it out?"

"That's okay."

"I've been trying to quit the ciggies, honest. But why bother quitting now?"

Helen smiled. "Go ahead and enjoy yourself."

"Cheers."

Gum trees, bushes, shrubs. Where was the wildlife? Helen eased her foot off the accelerator and began taking notice of the surroundings. She had been coming to VITERI for a while. Couldn't remember if there were usually animals on show.

"What are you looking for?" Stella said.

"Wildlife."

"You reckon zombie animals are out here too?"

She rubbed her neck. A headache was starting up. "No idea."

Stella dragged on her cigarette, one breath after another. "I made one call to my husband," she said, "and it went to voicemail."

"Uh huh."

"I could have called him again, but I didn't."

Helen scanned the landscape. "There's a café in Wooriyanda that apparently has good coffee. You know the one I mean?"

"I didn't call him again because I was scared."

"Try another radio station. This one's playing ads."

"Did you call your family?"

Despite herself, Helen thought of Mum. *Are you still a dyke?* From long practice, she pushed the thought aside. "No, I didn't call them."

"What if everybody we love has changed into zombies?"

"Then we'll turn into zombies too. Listen, we either make it or we don't. Two mutually-exclusive options. No need to speculate. We'll find out soon enough."

Stella extinguished the cigarette with licked fingers, dropped the butt out the window, glanced around at Magnus, and started to frown. Ah fuck, Helen thought. Here we go—

"Is he ill?" Stella said.

"Worn out."

"He's so *pale.*" Stella bit at her fingernails. "Walter got pale in the beginning too."

"Not every medical issue flags a zombie infection."

The track straightened out. A crack of thunder made them momentarily cower. The clouds, grey as pewter, boiled and foamed. A wind gust rocked the car. Helen snapped off the radio.

"Here comes the storm," Stella said.

Not yet, Helen thought. Please, not yet. VITERI hasn't been razed to the ground.

She spotted them through the trees and braked: joeys, does, boomers. A petite mob of about fifteen kangaroos. They were spread across a section of grass, taking it easy, each one leaned over from the haunches and cropping. She lowered the driver's side window all the way to give them a good view. Then tapped the horn.

"Don't," Stella whispered.

"Relax, we're safe in here no matter what."

The kangaroos, as one, lifted their heads. Simultaneously. It reminded her of the way zombies reacted. For a moment, panic beat in her throat. Then logic took over. The roos were simply responding to the sound of the horn. What they did *next* would be significant. If they raced towards the car, teeth bared... It would be decided, wouldn't it?

The kangaroos worked their jaws sideways, munching the grass.

Helen leaned on the horn.

The roos stood bolt upright. Stopped chewing. Stared at the car. Frozen. Was this text-book behaviour for startled kangaroos? Helen didn't know. The intensity of so many eyes frayed her nerves. She pressed the accelerator. The car sped off, churning gravel, raising dust.

"Were they zombies?" Stella said.

"No."

Stella twisted in her seat. "They're not coming after us."

"Because they're not zombies."

"We should have waited a bit longer. To find out for sure."

Helen indicated the back seat with her thumb. "We don't have time to wait."

"Oh, shit. I forgot. Hey, Magnus, are you okay?"

"Leave him alone. Let him sleep."

"What if he's dying?"

"If he's dying, we can't help him."

The track took one more bend and ran thereafter in a straight line. The eucalyptus trees were set back within paddocks on either side. Where had the birds gone? Out here, the sky should be full of rosellas, cockatoos, galahs...shouldn't it? Most likely, the impending storm had driven the birds to shelter in the trees.

The gravel started to feel more compact beneath the tyres. Up ahead was asphalt. A crossroad. Helen braked at the intersection, looked both ways. No vehicles. She turned towards Wooriyanda. After the bump and shimmy of the track, the road seemed as smooth as glass. Minutes passed. The road stayed deserted. No traffic in either direction. Helen checked the fuel gauge. Nearly full. If required, they could keep going for hours.

"Where *is* everybody?" Stella said.

"At home, probably. Country areas aren't well travelled."

"That's bullshit and you know it."

"All right, how about this: people don't want to drive around in a hailstorm."

Stella considered for a moment. "Fair enough."

The road wound through bush. Old weatherboard houses peeked out every now and then. After a hairpin corner appeared a strip shopping centre. Pub, art gallery, restaurant, toy store, supermarket. Helen eased her foot off the accelerator. The parking bays held cars. An encouraging sign. But there were no pedestrians. The shop windows were too dark to show the interiors. Each shop might be thronging with customers. Or not. Helen glanced at the dashboard clock. Late afternoon: a dead time for shopkeepers. Especially out here in the sticks. How these proprietors made a decent living, Helen couldn't even begin to fathom—

"I don't like this," Stella said.

"Why not? I haven't spotted any zombies yet. Have you? Magnus guessed right. VITERI *was* ground zero."

Stella twisted in her seat. "He's opening his eyes."

Helen braked in the middle of the road. Turned to study Magnus. His eyelids were slitted. Body still, heavy as a sack of grain. Hands relaxed, fingers motionless. Barely breathing. She thought of him sprinting down the bunkhouse hallway, smashing the zombie's face with his elbow to defend her, and tears stung. Her chin trembled. She watched him for a few seconds longer. No, he was unconscious. His eyes must have opened involuntarily.

"I'm okay," he said, surprising them both. "Only tired."

"Give me your phone and I'll call an ambulance," Helen said.

"Find out what's happening first."

So, he was worried too.

Helen pressed the accelerator. "I'll call from the café. We're going to wait there for the cops. Magnus?"

No answer. Shit. He must have passed out again. What if she couldn't get through to emergency services? *Don't think about that yet.*

"Stella, where's the café?" she said.

"About a minute along this main drag on your right."

They drove. Knotted clouds, blue-black and hunkered low to the ground, began to spit but not enough to require windscreen wipers. Surely, VITERI must be an inferno by now. She imagined the donors and pigs ablaze against a backdrop of burning eucalypts, the zombies shuffling mindlessly, bumping into each other, oblivious of the conflagration as it withered them into ash. She glanced into a bakery. Felt a spike of adrenaline. Shadows roved behind the window panes. The shadows of normal people going about their business? *Living* people?

"Slow down," Stella said. "Here's the café."

Helen braked. Pulled into a parking space. Cut the engine. Soft drizzle dotted the windscreen. Trees reached up behind the buildings. Clouds roiled. Lightning zigzagged. Squinting, she fixated on the café window. There were people inside. They were moving. Strolling about. Milling.

"Are they infected or not?" Stella said.

"I don't know. But either way, we have to get out of the car eventually."

Together, they stared at the shadows pacing and criss-crossing. Blood drummed at Helen's solar plexus. Roared in her ears. As if short of oxygen, her lungs kept pulling air, taking great and gasping draughts, again and again. Calm down, she thought. There are firearms in the car. Ammunition. If necessary, they could defend themselves. At least for a while.

"Oh, frick," Stella whispered. "I'm scared."

Helen reached out and took her hand. "Me too."

END

www.ingramcontent.com/pod-product-compliance
Lightning Source LLC
Chambersburg PA
CBHW032007170626
46807CB00006B/2684